The

VIENNA

WRITERS

CIRCLE

D1331687

Windsor and Maidenhead

95800000223017

ABOUT THE AUTHOR

J. C. Maetis is better known as British thriller writer John Matthews whose books have sold over 1.6 million copies and been translated into 14 languages. Maetis is the name of his father's Jewish family, who left Lithuania for London in 1919 in the wake of Jewish pogroms. However, many of his extended family sadly died when Hitler invaded Lithuania in 1941, and so this book is a tribute to them. Maetis now lives in Surrey, England, and is working on his second book, *The Fortune Teller of Berlin*.

The

VIENNA WRITERS CIRCLE

J. C. MAETIS

PENGUIN BOOKS

PENGUIN BOOKS

UK | USA | Canada | Ireland | Australia
India | New Zealand | South Africa

Penguin Books is part of the Penguin Random House group of companies
whose addresses can be found at global.penguinrandomhouse.com.

First published in Canada by Mira 2023
First published in the UK by Penguin Books 2023
001

Copyright © J. C. Maetis, 2023

Printed and bound in Great Britain by Clays Ltd, Elcograf S.p.A.

The authorized representative in the EEA is Penguin Random House Ireland,
Morrison Chambers, 32 Nassau Street, Dublin DO2 YH68

A CIP catalogue record for this book is available from the British Library

ISBN: 978–0–241–99889–2

www.greenpenguin.co.uk

To my father's family, both Holocaust victims and survivors. And to my mother and father, who played an integral part in WWII to save my current family, and that of many others, from a yoke of persecution and prejudice. While not wholly successful in every nation or facet of society, thankfully that spirit lives on today.

The

VIENNA
WRITERS
CIRCLE

PROLOGUE

Lublin, Poland, April 1942

I'd never been so thirsty, my mouth so dry.

My lips were cracked and sore, my tongue swollen and sticking to the roof of my mouth whenever I tried to swallow—which I'd given up on several hours ago. No saliva. So all that now passed through the sandpaper tunnel of my mouth was my own shallow, labored breathing.

Not that I was the only one.

Almost seventy people were now crammed in the cattle truck with me. Though I'd given up counting after fifty, when they'd started to get hemmed in so close it was impossible to view those at the far end of the truck, let alone attempt a head count.

The same dry, cracked lips and distended tongues all around me. And a bleary, lost look in their eyes, as if suffused beneath a faint mist. *Do my own eyes look like that now?*

Pulling out of Neisse station, when I'd had enough saliva

in my mouth to talk, I'd struck up a conversation with a gray-haired, stiff-backed man named Ernst, who a year ago ran a shoe shop on Vienna's Kärntnerstrasse.

I nodded enthusiastically. "Ah, Kärntnerstrasse. I know it well. I used to meet up with a couple of friends regularly at the Café Mozart, just around the corner from there. And of course the main police station is at the end on Kärntnertorpassage. I knew a police inspector there very well, Josef…" I broke off as Ernst's eyes fixed on me keenly.

"Police inspector?" He raised a brow. "Not some sort of informer, are you?"

"No, *no*," I said hastily, my gaze falling to his Star of David armband. A reminder that informers had been behind many, including myself, ending up in this cattle truck. "In any case, he was just with the Vienna police force, not the Gestapo."

"I see." But it was accompanied with a shrug, as if Ernst hardly discerned any difference.

"I used to see him just to get information," I added.

"Information on *what*?" Ernst's eyes were still heavy with suspicion.

"Nothing specific or important." I shrugged. "Just general details about criminals. I was a writer, you see."

"Like a reporter or journalist?"

"In my early days, yes. But later I stuck mainly to writing books."

Ernst nodded slowly, looked around at the dismal cattle carriage, then back at me, his eyes in turn falling to my lack of star armband. "Obviously, you wrote about something you shouldn't have, eh?"

"Yes. Something like that."

That would have been the far simpler explanation. Because explaining to this man consigned to hell simply for being Jewish that in fact I was originally Jewish, but had for the past three years buried my Jewish identity in order to try and survive would have just raised a sly sneer, *Didn't do much good, did it?*

Running that gauntlet had worked for a while, but in the end being sent to a camp had come suddenly, without warning. The only preparation a last-minute, emotional meeting with my agent, Julian Reisner: I'd be transported as a Catholic dissident rather than a Jew. *And don't admit you're Jewish in there. It'll be tough… But ask for Dieter Meisel as soon as you get to the camp, make sure he gets the letter I've given you. He's the vice-commandant there.*

It'll be tough. That became clear from the outset as I was led away by two soldiers and shoved at rifle point into a cattle truck with twenty others. Then the steady descent into hell as the train trundled slowly east…

Ludenburg… Neisse… Oppeln… Kielce… Warsaw… Lublin… Chelm…

The journey seemed never-ending, the truck getting hotter, more cramped and fetid with each stop. Bodies jammed up tight against each other, hardly room to move or breathe. And with no choice but to relieve ourselves where we stood—the stench of two days' urine and feces now had an ammonia bite to it, robbing what little fresh air remained.

Shallow, labored breathing and some heavier, tortured gasps punctuated by occasional groans and wails—which might draw a few stares. Not so much of pity or concern, but surprise that anyone had the strength left to cry out.

The largest groups had been loaded on at Oppeln and Warsaw, and I'd become separated from Ernst by those fresh surges of people. Probably best. My mouth was too dry to continue talking, even if I'd had the strength or will to do so.

And some had already succumbed.

I could see four bodies lying prone on the ground, and no doubt there were others at the far end out of sight. From one body there'd been some movement and barely audible groans for a while, but for the past few hours now any movement had stopped and there'd been silence.

Some eyes lingered on the bodies longer than they should. Somber reminder of the fate awaiting if the train journey continued much longer.

It was cold early morning and at night, and the first people on had shuffled around to keep warm. Now nobody had any room left to move, and the stifling press of fetid bodies had risen the temperature tenfold. An unbearable heat which had also sucked the moisture out of our mouths.

That afternoon some raindrops from a heavy, slanting rain outside sneaked through a chink where the compartment's wood boarding had broken away. Three mouths close by opened up, seeking those few precious drops like newborn chicks for their first feed. One of them then started licking the dampened wood at the hole's edge.

I could hardly move by that stage with the press of bodies around. All I could do was look on with bewildered envy.

As I felt someone brush hard against me, I clutched tight at my woollen coat—the automatic response to pickpockets— before reminding myself I had little worth stealing. *Currency has no value where you're going*, Julian had advised. *The only thing that can be traded is tobacco.* So sewn into the lining of my coat were several pouches of tobacco and a few personal family photos. *All my life had now boiled down to.* My heart clenched with the reminder of the family I'd left in Vienna, my eyes stinging. But there were no tears; not sufficient moisture left in my body even for those.

I must have fallen asleep at some point, that same press of bodies holding me virtually upright—because next thing I recalled was jostling movement and the shouting of German soldiers.

"*Sich beeilen.* Come on…get moving. Out…*out*!!"

I shuffled along with the surge toward the opening: eight huddled bodies on the floor now, though I could see one faintly stirring.

"This way…keep moving. Keep in line."

Eyes stung by the sudden light—even though the sun was cloud-shrouded and weak—my gaze fixed on an SS guard to one side. In particular on his holstered water flask.

"Please…" I implored, holding a hand out. "Some of your water."

The guard frowned, looked at me as if I was dirt.

"I… I'm not Jewish," I pleaded, recalling Julian's advice. "I'm Christian…like you."

The guard glanced at my lack of star armband and raised an eyebrow. "You obviously upset *someone*," he commented.

"Yes, I… I suppose I did." I cast my eyes down. It was clear that I wasn't going to get anywhere. Then I recalled the letter and the name Julian had given me. I fished the letter out of my inside coat pocket and passed it across. "I was told to ask for Dieter Meisel when I arrived, make sure he got this letter."

"Dieter Meisel is the vice-commandant here at Sobibór." His brow furrowed. "Who gave you his name?"

"A friend of mine in Vienna. I believe he knows him." I didn't want to go into the detail of saying it was my literary agent; that seemed irrelevant.

From his insignia, I noticed then that he was a mid-ranked SS-Scharführer. He held a black cane in one hand, almost matching his dark hair slicked back either side beneath his cap.

"I see." The guard looked at the letter thoughtfully, his stern expression easing after a second. He waggled the letter briefly. "I'll make sure he gets it." Then he reached out and patted me on one shoulder. "And look. You're obviously a good fellow— not like the *rest* here." He scowled at the passing throng. "But unless or until there's a direct instruction from the likes of Vice-Commandant Meisel, it would be more than my life's worth if I was seen giving you water. Besides, I'd probably be ripped apart by the rest of this mob for what was left."

"I see…yes."

"But a quick tip to help you out…"

The SS guard's eyes gleamed, as if he was about to share a precious secret. I leaned in closer.

"The first thing they do when you get inside is put you in the showers. Get rid of the dirt and grime of the journey." His eyes shifted again to the passing mob. "And the *louse* from this lot."

I nodded.

"The water's cold, so brace yourself." He grimaced tautly. "But it's also fresh and good for drinking. So lift your mouth to the spray and drink your fill!"

"Thank you…" I nodded eagerly as I started to shuffle away, joining the throng. *"Thank you."*

All I could think of from that moment on was that ice-cold water hitting my parched mouth.

I thought about it as I shed my clothes in a large dormitory with two hundred others.

I thought about it as I stood waiting to go into one of the shower cubicles—the wait seemed interminable.

An increasing trembling in my legs too, to remind me I had little strength left—sudden fear that I might pass out before I reached the showers.

And then finally we were inside—eighty or ninety to each large cubicle. The door clunked shut behind us.

I had to nudge an elderly man aside to get directly under one of the shower nozzles. Then, as I heard a faint rattling surge in the pipes, I tilted my head and opened my mouth for the nirvana of the first water to touch my lips in three days.

1

Poets are masters of us ordinary men, in knowledge of the mind, because they drink at streams which we have not yet made accessible to science.

—Sigmund Freud

Mathias

Vienna, Austria, March 1938

I, Mathias Kraemer, recall vividly the first real warning I took notice of. It was the moment an SS officer walked into the Café Mozart and asked if there were any Jews present, and which Jews they knew of who regularly frequented the café.

I was sitting with Johannes at a table about eight yards from the serving counter where the SS officer was making his inquiry with two waiters. Thankfully, there were two tables between us and the SS officer, otherwise his eyes might have automatically rested on us.

We should have paid more heed to Sigmund Freud at that last "Circle" meeting; he'd warned that with the advent of Anschluss, things might close in fast.

Among Vienna's many splendid cafés, we preferred the Mozart because it was not too pretentious. Arguably, the Sperl or Landtmann were more opulent and had finer decor, but for us the Mozart's overriding feature was its brightness and openness. From practically any seat in the Mozart, you were bathed in light and could watch the passing street activity. We'd in fact viewed the SS officer outside through its grand front windows in the final paces of his approach. But now as he spoke to the waiters, we might have preferred somewhere with more secluded corners.

We met at practically the same time every week, 6 p.m. every Tuesday. Office and shop staff at the end of their day, along with the first of the pre-opera, concert and theater crowd. And on many occasions our literary agent, Julian Reisner, would also join us and we'd talk about the progress with our latest books or the state of the book market and the world in general.

At forty-seven years old and with Johannes only celebrating his thirty-second birthday weeks ago, there was a reasonable age gap between us, but we felt as close as brothers rather than just cousins; that extra bond perhaps because of our shared profession. I'd been writing crime thrillers for sixteen years now and Johannes was in his fifth year of the same. I'd in fact initially introduced Johannes to Julian. It hadn't been just a familial favor; after some initial guidance, I'd felt Johannes's writing was strong. Julian had agreed. At forty-one, Julian not only bridged that age gap between us, but acted as mentor and guide to both of us.

"I wish Julian was with us now," Johannes muttered under his breath. "He'd know just the right thing to say to keep us calm."

"I think that's exactly why he's not with us now. Especially after that last Circle meeting. Anschluss was only three days ago, and he's got a fair few others like us on his books." Though my voice was little more than a hissed whisper, I didn't want to openly say "Jews" with the SS officer only eight paces away. "Then on top he's got a number of political writers and potential subversives. When I spoke to him, he said his phone has been busy trying to explain the current situation to a lot of people, not just myself."

Anschluss, the takeover and annexing of Austria by Germany, had taken place with hardly a single bullet fired.

At the root of that acquiescence had been a shared vision and identity, not just the fact that Hitler was originally Austrian German. Anti-Jewish sentiment had therefore been brewing in Austria for some while; Anschluss, and the appearance of an SS officer in the Café Mozart, was simply the final visible rubber-stamping. It was official now.

The two young waiters looked vague, shrugging, saying they had no idea which of the café's patrons were Jewish or not.

"Come now," the SS officer pressed. "It beggars belief that you have no idea. How long have you both been working here?" He was no more than early thirties, but now he adopted a stern-ness beyond his years, sharp blue eyes scanning them intently. "It could go badly for you if you're not honest with me."

One of the waiters looked uncertain, as if he was about to say something, when another voice came from behind.

"My staff are perfectly correct in saying they would have no idea." Otto Karner, owner of the Café Mozart, boldly approached the SS officer. "Nor do I—and I've been running this establishment now for nine years."

"Isn't that somewhat remiss of you—not knowing who your patrons are?"

"It's not our job to delve into our patrons' background." Karner smiled tightly. "Merely serve them the best coffee, pastries and cakes in town."

The SS officer observed Karner with undisguised disdain, as if Karner himself might be Jewish. Karner had dark hair and incongruously a Chaplin- or Hitler-style moustache—they were very popular right now—but there the resemblance ended. Karner had a snub-nose and was far more portly, built like a butcher or opera singer. His bulk often pressing against silver-gray or white linen suits, as if he was running a café in Morocco or Panama rather than Vienna. A small black or navy blue bow tie was the only contrast in this ensemble.

"The proprietor at the Café Central said he had no problem with identifying his Jewish patrons for us." The SS officer's lips curled mordantly at one corner. "Why would you wish to make things more difficult for yourself by not complying?"

"That might be because the Central is Hitler's favorite Vienna café." Karner shrugged. "They might have simply been keen to assure that no Jews would be present if and when the Führer deigned to pay them another visit. They could have just been humoring you."

I had to resist from smiling at Karner's boldness, masking any trace by taking another sip of my coffee.

"Make no mind." The rising flush in the officer's face quickly covered by bluster, he pushed Karner aside with one hand and stood proudly a step beyond, as if he suddenly was in control at Café Mozart rather than Karner. "I have an announcement to make."

He surveyed the café keenly as he called out, "Pay attention!" He waited a moment for the gentle murmur of conversation and tinkle of cutlery to subside. "My name is Scharführer Heinrich Schnabel of the Austrian SS. All Jews present here now should make themselves known to me—without fail!"

I felt my next swallow of coffee trap in my chest halfway down, fear gripping me as his eyes scoured the café. Could this Schnabel have already seen some Circle photos and so could pick us out?

We'd been members of Freud's Circle—a unique collection of scientists, philosophers, psychiatrists, mathematicians and writers formed by Sigmund Freud, Moritz Schlick and Edgar Zilsel in the late 1920s—for five years now. Our entry to the Circle had been twofold: my uncle Samuel Namal, Johannes's father, as a leading statistician and mathematical theorist, had been part of the original Vienna Circle, and Julian Reisner had also acted as literary agent for some of Freud's books. At that last meeting four days ago, Freud talked about his own family's safety and that of other Circle members—whether there would even be the option of any of them being able to leave Austria after Anschluss. But he'd also raised concerns about old Circle photos, worried that the Nazis might use them to identify and track down members.

I glanced across and saw that Johannes was seeking refuge at that moment in staring at the half-eaten chocolate cake on his plate, his fork toying with the next piece to lift up—perhaps afraid to do so in case he similarly had problems swallowing it.

Of the two of us, I looked more typically Jewish, with dark brown hair and brown eyes. Whereas Johannes had light brown hair and hazel-green eyes. He could easily pass for Austrian Catholic or Lutheran. My uncle Samuel, Johannes's father—who'd sadly died just four years ago—had married a blonde Catholic Austrian girl, and those genes had passed to Johannes. Because of that difference in our looks, few looking on in the café would guess that we were related.

The seconds ticked by, feeling like a lifetime.

A gentle murmur of conversation returned after a moment, but more stilted and unsettled now.

"What, nobody?" Schnabel exclaimed in exasperation. The Jewish population in Vienna was 190,000 now—over 10 percent of the population. It seemed inconceivable that in a café with over forty people, not a single Jew would be there. He took a fresh breath. "Perhaps I should remind that right now there's an amnesty. Any Jews who make themselves known to me will be duly noted and nothing more will come of it. Whereas if they hold back and let things slip beyond the amnesty period, it will become more difficult for them."

I felt my spirits sinking, almost wishing that my body would sink too through the floor and I'd become invisible. Would this Scharführer Schnabel perhaps later recognize me and hold it against me that I'd been obstructive?

"Nobody?" Schnabel's penetrating gaze scoured the café, doubting, disbelieving.

And as the seconds ticked by, I wondered whether to offer myself up, a sort of sacrificial lamb to save the rest of the café from this unbearable tension. After all, he'd said that everything would be okay, *Nothing more will come of it...* But then the moment went.

"Okay. You have all had your chance." Schnabel turned and strode away, turning back briefly as he was by the door. "If any of you have a change of heart, you should present yourselves at Karmelitermarkt before midnight tonight—that is when the amnesty runs out. After that, it will be too late."

A moment after Schnabel had left, Otto Karner ambled over to our table. He grimaced. "I fear he'll return."

I nodded somberly. "I fear so too. Given that, do you think this amnesty he mentions might be a good idea?"

"No, I don't. You can check it out if you want, but I think it's most likely a trick. Look at what happened with Hitler. Only a couple of years ago he makes a speech announcing that Germany has no intentions of interfering with Austria's internal affairs, let alone annexing it. And now this!" Otto held a hand out helplessly.

Johannes commented, "With the likelihood of him returning, are you saying that it might become more awkward for us, and for you? That perhaps we shouldn't return?"

"No, I'm not saying that at all." Otto appeared irked by the suggestion. "You know that if he returns, I'll say the same thing, keep protecting you." He smiled crookedly. "So you're far better off here than how he paints things at the Café Central, where they'll give you up like a shot to keep the Führer happy. So unless it's your intention never to go out for coffee or cake again, you're safer with me than…" Otto's voice trailed off as he became aware of a waiter close by nodding at him.

Otto Karner followed the waiter's gaze and turned to see Scharführer Schnabel, having talked briefly with a couple at a table outside, looking back through the front window toward us.

2

Jews and Gypsies are no longer considered German Reich citizens and do not have the right to vote in either Reichstag elections or the Anschluss.

Johannes

I checked my watch as I ate the last of the dinner Hannah had prepared.

"Is it alright?" she asked.

I suddenly realized that I'd been gulping it down without really concentrating on what I was eating. I paid more attention, savoring the current mouthful: lamb goulash with sweet paprika and potatoes. "Very nice—as it always is." Hannah was a good cook, but her repertoire extended to no more than eight or nine dishes, which she'd regularly rotate.

"Good, Momma," our youngest, Elena, just four years old, agreed with a big smile. Hannah had spent a few minutes dicing her lamb into smaller pieces as we'd sat down while Elena protested, "I'm not a baby anymore—you don't need to."

Our eldest, Stefan, now nine, simply smiled and nodded, not wanting anything to interrupt his racehorse eating—though his was more through enjoyment than eagerness to be somewhere else.

My mind was already half on the plans I'd discussed earlier with Mathias.

It was decided that one of us should check out the "amnesty" that this SS officer, Schnabel, had mentioned. It was decided it should be me because I looked the least Jewish; in fact, strictly speaking, I wasn't Jewish at all. My father had been Jewish, but my mother Catholic, and in Judaism the religion runs through the mother. But the problem was my father had been a very prominent figure in Austria, one of its leading statisticians and also a proud and outspoken member of the Social Democratic Party, the main opposition to the Nazis. So, in many ways my father's son, I'd be seen as a "token" Jew and agitator.

I'd asked my father one day whether marrying outside of his religion had anything to do with his equally outspoken atheism—my father never did anything by half measures—but he'd just gently smiled. "No, your mother just happened to be the prettiest girl I met at college. It was as simple as that."

Well, if I was my father's son in any way, the apple doesn't fall far from the tree and all that, I'd followed exactly the same path when I first met Hannah. So beautiful, hair the color of sun-bleached wheat, eyes a limpid green, I could hardly resist her.

But I wondered if subconsciously there was something else going on—the question I hadn't been brazen enough to ask my father at the time: that his partly burying his lineage to his children was to shake off the Jewish stigma seen increasingly in Austria since the 1920s. And I was doing the same in marrying Hannah, to further shake off that stigma, make my family safer.

I looked across the table at my perfect Austrian family: Elena with her hair almost as blonde as her mother's, Stefan with his light brown hair and hazel eyes taking more after me. It seemed only yesterday that my father was nestling them on his lap or holding them up proudly and gently kissing their foreheads—though it was in fact over four years ago when, at the age of sixty-four, he'd finally succumbed to the cancer eating him away.

This now was the only possible silver lining I could see to his death. This madness with Anschluss and rampant Nazism—it would have killed him to see it. I smiled inwardly at the oxymoron.

We'd even had one of those classic family portraits taken in sepia a year ago to permanently enshrine it in time, which now had pride of place on our sideboard: the perfect Austrian family. Even the staunchest Aryan Nazi viewing it would no doubt remark, "Ah, what a lovely family!"

Halfway through Hannah settling the children down in bed, the phone rang. Mathias.

"You haven't left yet?"

"No. I'm heading out in a moment. I wanted it to be dark, but not too late. Why?"

Slow exhalation from Mathias on the other end. "I wondered whether you should go. Otto might be right—it's all a trick."

"We won't know unless one of us checks it out. And I'll be fine—I'll just hang back in the shadows observing." I eased into a lighter tone. "Besides, I look more Aryan than…than Hitler."

At the other end, Mathias chuckled. That was all that was left to us now: trying to make light of this new dark and threatening storm. "Take care," he said. "Don't take any risks. Hitler and the Nazis aren't worth it."

As I was putting on my jacket and hat in the hallway, Hannah asked, "Everything alright?"

"Yes, fine. That was just Mathias then." I didn't think Hannah had heard any of our conversation, she'd still been busy with the kids. Besides, there was no point in worrying her unnecessarily when it was all probably nothing. "He was reminding me of a new writers group I'd promised to check out. I won't be long—no more than an hour or so." I smiled reassuringly.

"Okay. See you later."

But as Hannah smiled back and leaned in to kiss me just before I went out the door, I sensed an uncertainty beneath. I began to wonder whether she had overheard part of my conversation with Mathias.

The Karmeliter area of Vienna was strongly Jewish, with its market very much a centerpiece. An expansive cobblestone courtyard a hundred square yards, it was open to all traders throughout the week, with the Jewish trading days predominantly Wednesdays and Sundays. A profusion of bright vegetables and fruit from surrounding farms with live poultry in small cages and sometimes a whole tethered lamb. The only difference with the Jewish days was there'd be stronger displays of pickled fish, olives and sweet treats such as baklava and halva.

My father used to live on the edge of the district, but now I lived over a kilometer southwest. As if I'd been moving away from my Jewish background not just with marriage choices, but geographically too.

I'd decided to walk. Best I avoided trams or buses where my identity papers might be asked for. While I wasn't strictly Jewish, Namal was a common Austrian Jewish name, and someone might remember my father, *Ah, the son of Samuel Namal, the outspoken Jewish socialist and anti-Nazi. I have someone who'd like to ask you a few questions. Come with me.*

I became increasingly uneasy as I got closer to the Karmeliter area. At least three shops boarded up so far that I'd passed— which I hadn't noticed when I'd last been here two weeks ago—another two in the street ahead. Had they been Jewish-owned stores? The name MARX on the farthest shop sign with two yellow lines through it leading to a Star of David in the same yellow paint gave me my answer. I swallowed. Things were moving far faster than I thought.

As I turned into the next street, two more shops boarded up, then another one twenty yards opposite with part of its boarding ripped away and the window behind smashed.

More noise from the end of the street, a murmur and rumble of voices—the main market square was only fifty yards away. Sounded like a reasonable gathering. A middle-aged couple walked toward me, shoulders hunched. They kept their eyes stolidly ahead, didn't make eye contact. Not far behind them were two men in their early twenties, who did look at me before passing.

I looked back briefly. Were they following the couple perhaps? Sudden scuffling and movement made me jump, my heart in my throat. Two cats who'd been pulling at a rubbish bag scampered off only a foot ahead of me. I closed my eyes for a second as my pounding heart eased back. I shouldn't have come. Maybe I should just head back before it was too late.

But I found the rumble of voices ahead, with a now stronger light visible, drawing me on. Curiosity killed the cat.

On the wall to my side, an anti-fascist and -Nazi slogan had been hastily painted over, but it looked like they'd used the same yellow paint, now watered down—so that traces of the slogan still showed through. Then on top in bolder black paint were the words: Amnestie Sammeln—Amnesty Gathering…and an arrow pointing toward the square twenty yards away.

As the square opened out before me, I saw the source of the stronger light. Two sets of arc lamps on tripods each end of a long trestle table with the same Amnestie Sammeln banner along its side.

As I'd promised Mathias, I shuffled to one side and hung back in the shadows at the back of the square observing. No market stalls or fruit and vegetables today, no olives, baklava, halva or poultry in cages—just that long well-lit trestle table and some German soldiers one side and a small line of what was probably Jews the other. All looked very orderly.

A couple of German soldiers behind the table appeared to be taking details, nodding at intervals as they made notes, then they would stamp a paper and the next in line would approach. I saw that those who'd had their papers stamped were standing in small huddles at the far end. Some other soldiers were there, but they seemed to be talking amiably with the Jews—no sign of discomfort or the situation being forced, let alone arrest. Maybe Schnabel had been telling the truth after all.

But then I noticed something more disturbing to one side. In a corner of the square a group of people had lit a small bonfire. At first, I thought it was just to keep them warm. But then I spotted a Nazi flag being waved by one of them and saw what they were throwing on the fire: not just firewood, cardboard or papers, but books!

I moved closer to see the books being thrown onto the fire: Bernstein, Freud, Schnitzler, Remarque, Werfel, Zweig... All Jewish or dissident authors!

The closest German soldier shouted toward them, "You shouldn't be doing that here!"

"How else do we let these Jew dogs know they're not welcome in Vienna!" one of the protestors yelled back.

It struck me then what had happened. Word had got around that Jews were being given amnesty in the square, so a Nazi protest group had turned up to intimidate them.

Hauptmann, Einstein... Roth... Salten...

But as the flames of the fire leaped higher around the books, I saw another reason the soldier might not be keen on them having the fire there. Two buses on the far side of the square, previously in shadow and darkness beyond the harsh glare of the arc lamps, were suddenly illuminated. And on one of the buses, an old lady was tapping against the glass and pointing to something in the square, as if she'd left something behind. But the soldier at its side was vehemently shaking his head. As if to say, *You've been let on the bus, but you can't come off.*

Otto had been right. It had been a trap after all!

I staggered back from the flames—not only the heat, but what it represented! Shifted back into part-shadow again. But as I did so, a couple of books thrown on caught my eye. Even if I hadn't already recognized the covers, the name was emblazoned boldly on them: Mathias Kraemer. His trademark silhouette modern-day–Sherlock Holmes flyleaf photo clearly visible as one of the books flipped open.

None of my own books, thank goodness—but then I wasn't nearly as well-known. Probably one of the few times I'd actually felt grateful not to have wider readership. And as I watched the pages curl and the flames rise from my cousin's book, I must have stayed transfixed a moment longer than I realized. Because when I looked up, I saw someone at the far side of the long trestle table that I recognized: Scharführer Heinrich Schnabel! He seemed to spot me in that moment too, recalling where he'd seen me, because he lifted a hand my way.

I backed swiftly away into the shadows again, but at that moment I felt someone grip tight onto my arm from the side—no doubt a fellow guard that Schnabel had signaled—wrenching me hard away deeper into those shadows.

3

We are living in a specially remarkable period. We find to our astonishment that progress has allied itself with barbarism.

—*Sigmund Freud*

Johannes

I was thrown into the back of a car and seconds later it sped away.

"What the hell are you doing here?"

I was still dazed and in shock, so it took me a moment to orientate and recognize the voice: Josef Weber, the local police inspector that Mathias had introduced me to three years ago and had since become—after numerous bar and restaurant meetings for background research on the police and the city's lowlifes—something of a friend.

"I was in the Mozart earlier with Mathias, and we heard there was an amnesty for Jews in the square tonight—so I came to check it out." I went on to explain about Schnabel's standing announcement to the café, Otto's take on it and what I'd finally agreed with Mathias.

Josef appeared suddenly alarmed, his eyes squinting sharper in the rearview mirror. "My God! Don't tell me Mathias came with you into the square?"

"No. It was agreed that I should come alone—because I look less Jewish."

"Well, at least you're not completely stupid." The trace of a smile curled his mouth as he fleetingly half turned to me. "You should have listened to Otto. If he says it was a trap, an SS officer made the announcement and it looked like a trap—then it's probably a trap!"

"At first it looked okay," I tamely defended. "Forms being signed, soldiers looking cordial and helpful. But then I spotted the buses on the far side."

"You know what those buses are for?" Josef's eyes again in the mirror, sharp, disturbed. "They're there to transport everyone to a nearby warehouse to be locked up. They're told that tea, coffee and a hot meal awaits them for being helpful—but once they go beyond the harsh light of those arc lamps, they're lost. The soldiers' attitudes become equally harsh and there's no turning back." He shook his head. "Two nights ago they commandeered the disused Northwestbahnhof station, turned it into a makeshift concentration camp. It's reckoned that already almost twenty thousand Jews and dissidents are being held there."

The news shocked me, but after Schnabel's earlier café visit and the horrors of the night, perhaps less than it should have. Already I was starting to become numbed to such news. "So what's the point in holding a false amnesty like that?"

"It saves the Gestapo and SS the trouble of hunting all the Jews and dissidents out—you're doing their work for them by turning up." Josef shrugged. "Same reason this Schnabel didn't go table to table in the Mozart earlier asking to see everyone's identity cards. Too much work, and in the process he risks upset-ting the 90 percent upstanding Aryan Viennese citizens. Many of them top-drawer in somewhere like the Mozart."

Suddenly struck with the thought, I asked, "Why were you there in the square tonight?"

"We heard at the Kärntnerstrasse station that there was going to be a little demonstration. Myself and a few others showed up just in case there was any conflict, things flared up."

"Is that your attempt at humor, with the book burning?"

"Unintentional...unless it was a Freudian slip." I couldn't see Josef's smile in the mirror, but I could see his eyes crinkle. "It's not just Jews who might have objected to the book burn-ing, but staunch academics and the literary elite. Freedom of speech and all that."

"I suppose." I sighed softly. "But there was nothing, not a word of objection. The people in that line hardly looked to-ward the Nazi flag–wavers and book-burners, looked afraid to meet their eyes for even a second. It was a people who looked already defeated, Josef. No fight left."

"Because they're afraid, Johannes. As I sensed you were in that moment looking at the fire."

"I saw some of Mathias's books there." I said it plainly, matter-of-factly, belying how I'd felt in that moment. As if my insides had been hollowed out.

"Oh, I see." I noticed Josef's hands grip tighter at the steer-ing wheel and his eyes dart uncomfortably for a moment; as if in acknowledgment that that made it somehow different, more personal.

Josef's shifting gray-blue eyes were the first thing I'd noticed about him. As if constantly trying to work out the angles on an investigation. Late thirties with thinning sandy hair, Josef was medium height, about five-nine, but built like a bull. The many stories he'd related of arresting suspects, barging them against a wall and spinning them sharply around to handcuff, I could easily believe. Not a man to fool with.

Josef huffed out tiredly, "Next time you plan on going to 'amnesties' or any other meetings arranged by the SS, let me know first." He swung his car, a fairly new Steyr 220, the smell of its seat-leather still heavy, into the curb and stopped. "Meanwhile, I'll see what I can find out on file about Heinrich Schnabel."

"Thanks." I looked out and saw that he'd pulled up in front of my apartment block.

"Take care," Josef said. "And give my regards to Hannah and your two lovely children."

4

Marriages between Jews and citizens of German or related blood are forbidden. As are marriages between Mischlinge of the first degree and Germans; between Jews and Mischlinge of the second degree; and between two Mischlinge of the second degree.

Mathias

I decided to walk my son, Ivor, to school.

Halfway along the street, I saw Mrs. Haider, our neighbor from three doors away, returning from the bakery with a bag. I nodded and smiled at her.

"Good morning!"

A smile and nod in return, but it was curt, more restrained than normal. As if she was already starting to worry that consorting with a Jew might get her into trouble. Or was I just imagining it?

After Johannes's call late last night, telling me about the amnesty trick in Karmelitermarkt—the boarded shops he'd seen in the area, the Nazi flag–waving and book burning, and what he'd heard from Josef Weber, our mutual police contact and friend, as Josef had whisked him away—I was being more watchful for signs of change: only one shop so far I'd seen boarded up.

Not that I'd needed much reminding of that change. I'd had my marriage for that.

Four years now since Emilia had finally walked out, leaving me as a single father to Ivor. Like Johannes, I'd also married a good Austrian girl, also Catholic, although Emilia hadn't been in the least religious. But, unlike Johannes with Hannah, my marriage to Emilia had ended disastrously.

Later, when I'd had the conversation with Johannes—another area where our lives had followed similar paths, our respective marriages, not just being writers—I'd voiced whether I too had been guilty of trying to sanitize my family, make them appear less Jewish in the face of increasing acrimony, then finally open hostility, toward Jews in Austria. It hadn't even started as the wish to keep our children safe, because initially there'd been no foreseeable danger. Just acrimony. *"We all want the best for our children,"* I'd commented to Johannes. *"So it was simply the fact that I didn't want Ivor seen somehow as a 'lesser-being.' To have to put up with those comments, gibes and sometimes just looks of disdain. Why should he suffer because of my background?"*

But as I'd said it, I realized in that moment that I too, like Emilia, had allowed myself to become far too reactive to the anti-Judaic sentiment that had crept into Austrian society year by year.

There had been no escaping my own Jewish heritage. My father, Isaac Kraemer, and mother Lena, Samuel Namal's eldest sister, had both been Jewish and regularly attended a synagogue—though I'd lapsed somewhat. But despite the ethnic-marriage step away, Ivor had ended up looking more like me—the same dark brown hair and warm brown eyes—than Emilia.

When I'd first met Emilia, she'd been a struggling actress and dancer with an easy smile, fiery red-tinged hair and a twinkle in her eye. Always glad of a glass of champagne after a performance, whether it had gone well or badly. Maybe a little too "flighty" for some, but to me that had been part of the attraction—I loved her easygoing, carefree spirit and charm. And for Emilia, six years younger than me, perhaps the attraction had been that as a Jewish writer she saw me as different, something of a rebel, unconventional, exciting. Half of her acting friends were Socialist dissidents in any case, so it wasn't such a leap. Always easier to be attracted to rebels when you're young, I thought, before the conventions of society take grip. Emilia and I were married within a year.

Ivor was born four years later. But already those societal conventions, along with the more staid and humdrum rigors of marriage, had started to wear Emilia down. With Hitler's steady rise in Germany in the late 1920s, culminating in him being made chancellor in 1933, the sea change of attitude toward Jews in Austria became more evident day by day. Another factor had been Emilia meanwhile finding more success with her acting career and so moving in more rigid, higher-society circles, drifting away from her old Socialist and rebel-loving dissident friends. As she found the pressures of those two sides harder to mesh in her mind—her society friends and their comments one side, our marriage the other—she tried to bridge that increasing gulf with drink. More champagne and wine after performances, then finally drinking openly at home too.

One day when I commented that perhaps she was drinking too much, she'd glared and snapped back, "And why do you think that is, Mathias? It's not easy being married to a Jew in today's world, you know."

Perhaps another contributory factor had been that my early

writing career hadn't been that successful—my biggest hits hadn't come until Ivor had been six, by which time our marriage was already on the rocks. One night after returning from a champagne-swilled après-performance celebration with her friends, she'd sneered in the middle of an argument, "My friends think your writing is a joke. I mean, it's hardly Goethe or Kafka, is it?" The unspoken and evident truth that literary elitists often looked down on more basic, populist crime and thriller writers. But now that truth hung over my marriage, along with being a second-class Jew.

The final straw came when Emilia met Gerhard, a wealthy German industrialist, who'd taken a shine to her after seeing her performance in *Pygmalion* at Vienna's Ronacher Theater. They had an affair, which Emilia had originally denied, but after six months of Gerhard wining and dining Emilia more openly, she asked for a divorce. I readily agreed. I'd had enough too.

She married Gerhard within six weeks of the decree absolute coming through. During the period Emilia had been at home, between the drink and pursuing her acting career, she hadn't been a particularly good mother to Ivor—perhaps too seeing him as part of the pressure on her, part of me. So she didn't argue for custody, in fact quite the opposite. Knowing that she'd be hopeless at taking care of him constantly, she readily agreed to seeing Ivor just once a week.

The one benefit of Gerhard coming into Emilia's life had been that she'd cut down on her drinking. Perhaps he'd spoken to her or perhaps simply because she felt the pressure of living a double life had gone. Gerhard's business was in automotive components, with a main factory in Stuttgart and a West-Vienna subsidiary plant in Brigittenau. But twenty months after they'd married, he had to be more at the Stuttgart factory, so Emilia moved there with him. Her visits then to see Ivor were at first once a month, then finally every other month.

But with the increasing absences, Emilia would pile it on like a doting mother like she never had before. Turning up in a new Mercedes and sweeping in with a sable or mink coat redolent with Lenthéric, as beautiful as ever, her arms full of presents for Ivor, showering him with kisses and "Oh, my goodness, I've missed you so" hugs.

Then they'd wave goodbye to me as Emilia took Ivor to the park, local fair, circus or cinema, with Ivor beaming when they returned two or three hours later. After one of those visits, while Ivor had been playing with an almost two-foot-long model of the convertible Mercedes Emilia had turned up in, he asked wistfully, "Why can't I see Mum more?"

"Unfortunately, I don't think it would work out," I'd answered after a moment's contemplation. Difficult to explain to Ivor that it was mainly the long absences which made his mother's visits more special.

"Why not? She's a good mother now."

Almost an unwitting admittance that she'd been a bad mother before.

That was even more difficult to explain, so I'd just smiled indulgently and playfully ruffled Ivor's hair. "We'll see."

My answer to so much these days.

When Ivor had asked me whether I'd be walking him back and forth to school every day from now on—normally I'd alternate with my sister, Erica, who was four years younger and also doted on Ivor—"We'll see." With Anschluss, I didn't want Erica possibly being confronted by SS soldiers. Hopefully, I'd be able to answer—or deflect—their questions more adroitly.

Then when I'd picked Ivor up from school yesterday, he'd commented that his class teacher said that from now on a number of the school's children might have to be registered differently. "Something about Jews and Mischlinge. Is that true?" Another "We'll see."

But now as I approached the school gates with Ivor, I could

see the headmaster, Mr. Leitner, looking my way, hoping to get my attention.

I made out I hadn't seen him. Simply gave Ivor a quick parting hug, said, "Have a good day," and turned and walked away.

I had a meeting later with Julian Reisner to go to. Besides, that was the last thing I wanted to discuss with Mr. Leitner right now: whether from now on my son would be a first-, second- or third-class Austrian citizen.

5

What progress we are making. In the Middle Ages they would have burned me. Now they are content with burning my books.

—*Sigmund Freud*

Mathias

Fortunately, I didn't see too many SS or soldiers on the way to and from Ivor's school—at least none that paid me much attention or looked inclined to demand to see my identity card or ask me any questions.

But a block from Julian's office, I saw a group of SS who looked keener and more alert, eyes scouring in each direction. Only a few streets from Heldenplatz, one of Vienna's main squares and parks, it was a busy area, and I'd only seen the soldiers stop one person so far—so I took my chances.

One of the soldiers' eyes drifted my way as I approached on

the opposite side of the street, but they didn't linger on me—then I was lost behind a small group of people heading toward me as I passed the soldiers, and I didn't, daren't, look back. But hardly had my breath eased before I saw another group of soldiers on the next corner ahead. Something was happening!

This group wouldn't be so easy to pass unnoticed, because Julian's office was halfway down that next side street.

I toyed with the idea of crossing over at the last minute, as if I'd forgotten that was the turning I wanted, so was then on the opposite side from them—but that might appear too obvious. And if I crossed over directly toward them, I'd stand out and they'd be more conscious of my approach—so I decided in the end to cross over ten yards short of them, try and merge with some other people walking up that side: a teenage girl with an elderly couple, the man with a cane.

I let fall and stubbed out beneath my shoe the cigarette I'd lit halfway there, my third since dropping off Ivor—already Anschluss appeared to have increased my habit. I paused at the curb to look each way for passing traffic, feeling a twinge grip my left leg—something that returned now and then when I felt tense—timing it so that I was tucked in just a few yards behind them, hopefully partly shielded from the guards ahead. But as we got closer to them, I noticed one guard peer past the couple and the teenage girl, his eyes fixing on me.

And I knew then my luck had probably run out. I'd have to present my identity card and answer some awkward questions. I might be late seeing Julian, if I got to see him at all.

"You look like you've seen a ghost," Julian said. "Here. Get this down you. This kirsch would wake the dead."

I nodded numbly and smiled as Julian poured a generous third-tumblerful of Fürfteneck and set it down by the coffee his secretary, Krisztina, had just brought me.

"It's certainly been a rough couple of days," I said. And as

I sipped at the kirsch and felt it burn stronger in my throat as I swilled it down with my coffee, I brought Julian up to date with Schnabel's Café Mozart visit and Johannes checking out the false Karmelitermarkt amnesty meeting with its sideshow of Nazi book-burning protestors. "Johannes whisked away at the last moment by no less than Josef Weber, just after having seen some of my books thrown onto the fire."

"Fame at last," Julian said, smiling wryly as he raised his coffee cup in a "cheers" motion. He wasn't having any kirsch, said he had a long day of work ahead of him. His expression became more serious. "But it's a measure of how quickly things have moved. I doubt Freud would have made the same flippant remark about Nazi book burning now that they're on his doorstep."

"Already I feel I've seen enough Gestapo and SS for a lifetime," I said, gesturing. "Then discover you've got a few camped out right here on your corner." Thankfully, the guard's attention had been distracted at the last moment by the elderly couple asking about a nearby Nazi rally. But as they'd moved on, I could sense his eyes on me again as I'd walked down the road and stopped halfway, pressing the bell for Julian's office.

I'd closed my eyes as I rode the open-cage elevator up the three floors, swallowing back my hammering nerves.

"As aired at that last Circle meeting, I fear it will get worse," Julian said, his face clouding. "Far worse. Have you read the Nuremberg Laws?"

"Yes." I nodded solemnly. A series of laws introduced by the Nazis in Germany in 1935 which stripped all Jews and Romani of most citizen and civil rights, effectively made them second- and third-class citizens.

"Well, those took place in Germany over a three-year period, some had already started having teeth after Hitler took power in 1933. But a number of those have taken place here in just the last few days, and the rest will surely follow."

As Julian spoke, at points he waved a pink Sobranie in a silver cigarette holder to one side. The Sobranie wasn't lit, nor had a cigarette been lit for some time now. Julian had given up smoking two years ago, and this was his way of not starting again. *Keeping that temptation close, but still resisting it.* I resisted lighting up. Despite my hands still trembling faintly, it would have been unfair to blow smoke in Julian's face and possibly tempt him. A silver cravat matched his cigarette holder and a pink shirt all but matched his Sobranie. Always stylishly dressed, with a shock of swept-back blond hair, warm blue eyes and a boyish face, Julian could easily pass for ten years younger than his forty-one years.

With his sometimes effeminate dress, theatrical mannerisms and the fact that he'd not yet married, rumors had sparked that Julian was homosexual. It wouldn't have troubled me in the slightest if he was. To me he was simply a tremendously warm and generous spirit, and over the years had become a good friend. But from what I'd observed, Julian was very much a ladies' man. The women too loved that boyish charm, and Julian was too busy deciding which latest showgirl, dancer or waitress he liked sufficiently to settle down with. Outside of his impressive roster of clients, he simply didn't show the same commitment with his love life.

Julian shook his head. "The point I'm trying to make, Mathias, is what was suffered in Germany over years will likely be felt here in just weeks or months."

"I know." I sighed forlornly. "Already they appear to be putting the screws on at Ivor's school, defining who is a Jew or a Mischling. His headmaster tried to get my attention to have that conversation—but I avoided him. Feared I might be tempted to reach across and punch him halfway through such a discussion."

"Well, that would certainly have got you a quick trip to a concentration camp." Julian smiled crookedly before his expression sank again. "But as hard as it might be to do so, Mathias, you might have to start considering other options—such as leaving. Zweig saw the writing on the wall years ago and left, and as we know from that last meeting, Freud is now considering leaving too."

I shook my head. "My mother's too old, and she's not well right now. She'd never make it." Now in her late seventies, my mother, Lena, still hadn't got over the death of my father, Isaac, seven years ago. She'd had a minor stroke ten months later, following which mild dementia was diagnosed; then last year when she'd fallen and cracked her hip, Erica and I suggested she move from the three-story Leopoldstadt family home she'd lived in for much of her life—and Erica and I had been brought up in—to a nearby nursing home. The three flights of steps were too much for her to negotiate. But she'd insisted on staying, surrounded by much of the fine furniture Isaac had made as a cabinetmaker for forty years and the fine frills, tablecloths and curtains she'd made as a seamstress. Too many memories. Erica and I saw her regularly to take care of her, well, Erica more than me; and every week I'd take Ivor to see her too. And, despite any dementia, her face would light up when she saw Ivor and she'd talk volumes about old times and past memories. I grimaced after another slug of kirsch. "And her never seeing Ivor again. I couldn't do that to her."

"You think it would be any easier on her knowing that her son and favorite grandson have been sent to a Nazi concentration camp?" But seeing my pained expression, my impossible dilemma, Julian hastily shook his head. "I'm sorry, I shouldn't have said that. Hopefully, that wouldn't happen."

But now I sensed he was just humoring me, trying to soften that portent, which was almost as bad.

Julian pushed an unsettled smile. "It's not an easy decision to make, especially if there's family involved. I have a lot of clients on my books facing the same right now. So I fully understand your desire to look at other options first. Just what I'm saying is, well…if those other options don't look good—you shouldn't discard the option of leaving out of hand."

I nodded somberly. Maybe Julian was right. I should start to consider leaving. "I understand that between taxes, low valuation buyouts and currency exchange, the Nazis take 80 to 90 percent of everything you own just to allow passage?"

"Yes. Which makes the decision even harder. And also a number of people they don't allow to leave." Julian held his hands out. "But for those who are allowed—what price on your freedom, or indeed your life itself?"

"Yes, I know."

And, perhaps, sensing my resigned despondency, Julian's tone immediately brightened. "But there might be other options too—so give me a couple of days to look at those. And we also have Freud's case example. If he does now decide to leave, how he gets on negotiating with the authorities? We can use that as a guide."

I nodded. That's exactly why I'd met Julian now to have this conversation. A finger in every pie, those that Julian didn't know in Vienna weren't worth knowing. If anyone could find a solution, it was Julian.

As I took another swig of kirsch, I clasped my left thigh, massaging. The twinges had eased now. A problem resolved decades ago, it came back now and then when I was tense. I'd been born with my left leg a fraction of an inch shorter. I got increasing back and thigh pain as I got older, but the problem wasn't identified until my teens. From then, my left shoes were specially made with slight uplifts. The pain went and I could walk perfectly normally. But sometimes in extremely cold weather or when tense, some pain spasms would return to my left thigh and back.

"Ah, it appears to have started already," Julian commented as a booming voice from a nearby PA system reached us, followed by loud cheering.

"What's that?"

"Haven't you heard?" Julian was looking at me curiously. "There's a big rally and speech today from Hitler in Heldenplatz. His first public address since Anschluss—there have been posters about it all over the city. That's why the guards at the end of the street."

"Oh, I see. Yes." I had in fact noticed the posters, but the date and time hadn't registered. I'd been too numbed with my own problems.

Julian got up and stood looking out of the window. "We should go and check it out. 'Know thy enemy' as Sun Tzu said."

"I… I couldn't," I stuttered, pointing vaguely. "The guards on the corner."

"They won't pay much attention to you with the people flooding past now." He smiled tightly. "Besides, you've got more chance of losing them in a big crowd than if you're passing them on your lonesome."

Minutes later, we joined the crowd heading down the street and, sure enough, the guards on the corner, or indeed the next one, didn't pay us any attention—probably didn't even spot us with the press of people around.

As we spilled out into one side of Heldenplatz, Hitler's voice boomed out, "…First and foremost to make Austria flourish and expand to become a fortress of national willpower…"

Hitler stood on the balcony of the Hofburg Palace, the new Austrian chancellor, Seyss-Inquart, Vienna mayor Neubacher, and Goebbels at his side. I'd never seen such a crowd in Heldenplatz, filling the square and the park behind, some even having clambered onto the statue of Prince Eugen at its center to get a better view. Long swastika banners were draped behind Hitler on the balcony and hung from practically every other lamppost around the square.

"There must be over two hundred thousand people here," Julian remarked. His incredulous leer became more lopsided after a moment. "Outgoing Chancellor von Schuschnigg claimed there was a lot of opposition to Anschluss and the Nazis taking over—but you'd never guess it from this crowd here."

"Maybe that's because everyone who might protest or stand against it fears getting arrested," I muttered, my voice low for fear of being overheard.

"There is that," Julian conceded with a tight grimace. "I hear Schuschnigg and many of his inner circle have already been arrested."

"…The splendid order and discipline of this tremendous event is proof of the power of the idea inspiring the people. Not just the two million people in this fair city, but sixty-five million of our Volk in an empire!"

The crowd cheered raucously, chanting *Heil Hitler… Heil Hitler!* I felt the press of them all around me. Suddenly it wasn't just the SS soldiers I'd passed to and from Ivor's school or on the way here and now interspersed around the edges of this throbbing, surging throng—it was as if every other eye in the crowd was now singling me out… *Jew! Jew!*

"…I am Austria's son. I am coming home to the place of my birth. Do not doubt for a moment that I do not hold Vienna in the highest esteem. Vienna is a pearl…and I will place it in a setting worthy of a pearl!"

The cheers grew stronger, welcoming Hitler as if he was the rightful returning emperor he proclaimed to be rather than any sort of invader. *Heil Hitler… Heil Hitler!* The sound of it started to spin and throb in my head. I had to get away.

"Are you okay?" Julian asked with concern, close on my heels as I started to push back through the crowd.

"Yes, fine…fine. Just think I've seen and heard enough, that's all." But the crowd seemed tighter around us now as more people had flooded into its edges. More eyes on me as now I tried pushing my way through, the pain spasms in my thigh biting more intensely. *Jew. Jew!*

"...As Führer and chancellor of the German nation and Reich, I now report to history that my homeland has joined the German Reich!"

The roar of the crowd reached a crescendo. My legs felt weak, my throat dry. The feeling that I might collapse at any moment with the heat, press and noise. Edging, squeezing through the tight-packed throng. "Please...let me through."

But something else, too, in that moment. The sudden realization of why more eyes were on me keenly. I was practically the only one at that moment moving away, unlike the rest of the crowd—their eyes fixed with fervor on Hitler ahead, enrapt by his speech, arms thrusting out again in straight-armed salutes. *Heil Hitler. Heil Hitler!*

Here was Julian suggesting I escape Austria, but at this moment I wasn't even sure I could escape this crowd.

6

Soldiers and all proud members of the Reich are encouraged to picket and hold placards in front of Jewish-owned shops and stores, urging fellow Aryans not to shop or trade there.

Johannes

"Jew, Jew... Jew!"

Stefan Namal, Johannes's nine-year-old son, stood with three classmates chanting at him in the playground. Or, more accurately, their ringleader, Horst Braun, was chanting loudly, while the other two, Erich and Franz, just tamely chimed in.

"I'm not a Jew!" Stefan defended. "My mother's Catholic, like yours. And my father's mother was Catholic as well."

"But your father's father was Jewish," Horst said. "And a very prominent one too. We've seen his photos in books in the library." Horst looked around for support. Erich and Franz nodded eagerly. They'd obviously seen the photos and entries too. Samuel Namal, the prominent statistician and political agitator.

"So what." Stefan shrugged. "If it wasn't for my grandfather, half the Luftwaffe and Austrian air force wouldn't have got off the ground." Simply a repeat of the bold claim his father had shared with him. What he didn't go into detail about was how his grandfather had prepared vital wing-airflow and lift statistics; already this little group appeared to have been hit with enough to leave them slightly baffled, uncertain.

"So you admit he was a Jew?" Horst latched on to the only bit he could.

Another shrug, but this time Stefan added, "Yes. And I'm proud of him."

Horst looked horrified, and for a moment Stefan wasn't sure if that was because it was unexpected, so he didn't know how to respond, or its implications? To Horst's side, Erich pulled a face.

"Uuugh. That's disgusting," he said, as if he had a mouthful of dirt. "How can you say you're proud of a Jew?"

Stefan felt his blood boiling. Images flooded back of sitting on his grandfather Samuel's lap and hooking one finger around the pipe dangling from his mouth—it was never lit when he held Stefan—then pulling it and throwing it away. Only small at the time, it would go no more than five or six feet. His grandfather would just gently smile, get up and put the pipe back in Stefan's hand. *Let's see if you can throw it further this time. Let's have a pipe-throwing contest!*

"My grandfather was a good man," he said.

But perhaps with his voice more uncertain, defensive—or because Horst was still stuck on the last comment—Horst sneered back.

"Yeah. And now you're left with his filthy, disgusting Jewish name—Namal. Namal the Jew... Namal the Jew!"

It became another chant, with Erich and Franz quickly joining in: *Namal the Jew... Namal the Jew...*ringing in Stefan's ears as his anger rose. Their faces moved closer as they chanted, Horst pushing at him to prod the message home... *Namal the Jew!*

On the third prod, Stefan pushed back hard, and they quickly went into a tussle.

The punch that came through that grappling caught Stefan by surprise on the side of his head, bringing an extra ringing to his ears, a red haze suddenly gripping him. Stefan punched hard through that haze, felt it connect—the haze becoming a bolder, brighter red as he saw Horst fall away from him, clutching at his burst nose, blood running down his face and chin.

Horst screamed in agony as he fell to the floor, lapsing into a wail, "You've broken it...you've broken my nose!"

Erich had scampered off the second he saw Horst falling, but Franz seemed rooted to the spot in horror, holding his hands up in front of him. A "Please don't hit me as well" gesture.

That red haze lifting, Stefan was suddenly gripped with panic that he'd gone too far. Horst's nose was still streaming blood, some of it now dripping on his shirt. But as Stefan tentatively reached one hand out to lift Horst up, the voice of their class teacher, Mr. Pichler, came sharply from across the playground.

"Namal... Namal—get away from him! What have you done?"

And Stefan thought: *God, I am in so much trouble.*

I knew we had a fight on our hands as soon as I viewed the countenance of the panel of four sitting across the table from us.

St. Joseph's was the best local Catholic school we could find, only a third of a mile from where we lived, so an easy walk for either of us to take Stefan, even when Hannah had little Elena in a pram. Though from the age of eight onwards, Stefan had generally gone on his own, meeting up with other school friends not far up the road to make the walk together.

I should have questioned a couple of days ago when I saw out the window those friends appear to walk faster ahead of Stefan, as if keen to keep separate from him. Only six days since Anschluss and already the effects were being felt. And now we had the culmination of that with Stefan involved in this fight at school.

I'd insisted that Hannah be with me for the meeting. Not only to put on a stronger Catholic, less Jewish front at the school, but also her father was good friends with one of the school's Catholic governors, Mr. Mayr. We knew that Mayr was not a fan of National Socialism, fearing they might sideline the Catholic Church in Austria—but he was careful not to voice that too openly. No doubt fearing that might threaten his position as a school governor. The panel was being chaired by the headmaster, Mr. Stadler, and the other two were Stefan's class teacher, Mr. Pichler, and another governor, Mr. Rosch. We suspected Rosch's presence was to counterbalance Mayr.

Headmaster Stadler started proceedings by reading aloud the details of the fight from a file before him, concluding with a huffed sigh as he looked above his pince-nez glasses, "I'm sure you can appreciate, Mr. and Mrs. Namal, why such an attack on a pupil is totally unacceptable here at St. Joseph's."

"But I understand that this other boy threw the first punch," I ventured.

"That hasn't at all been established," class-teacher Pichler commented. "The other boy concerned said they were just grappling with each other when your son hit him."

"You've talked to the other boy first?" Hannah clarified.

"Yes," Pichler said.

We'd seen young Horst Braun sitting with his father, Dieter, in the waiting room when we'd gone into the meeting. We hadn't been sure if they'd already been in or were yet to be seen. Perhaps they'd been advised to wait to hear the outcome after we'd finished or might be asked in again.

I held a hand out. "What about the other two boys there? They'd have witnessed that first punch thrown by their friend."

Pichler glanced down more uncertainly at his notes. "They said they couldn't see a first punch thrown—or at least couldn't be sure with the tussling."

"Not sure?" I shook my head. "They were close enough to see the punch thrown. It's obvious they're just protecting their friend."

Headmaster Stadler eased another sigh. "I'm afraid that can't at all be ascertained here, Mr. Namal. So I'd prefer you refrain from such remarks."

"Yes. I think it's patently clear already what's happening here," Governor Rosch asserted. "This was obviously an unprovoked assault, and Mr. Namal is clumsily attempting to clear his son's name by laying blame on these other boys."

"Unprovoked assault?" My voice rose an octave. "Whether these two other boys saw the first punch or not, they were part of that provocation against our son. Chanting and calling him a filthy, disgusting Jew."

Stone silence. The ugly side of Anschluss was becoming increasingly apparent, particularly these past few days, but now it sat uncomfortably on this schoolroom table. As if this small, primary school clique had hoped to insulate themselves from all of that. Now I'd slapped it down before them like a rotting fish.

First to break the silence, Rosch smiled gently. "Come now. I'm sure it's not as bad as your son makes out. Besides, national sentiments are riding high right now…but we can hardly blame our children for that. Boys will be boys."

"So, out of the mouths of babes?" I held my stare steady on Rosch. "But how would you feel if the situation was reversed, and my son had called these boys filthy, disgusting Nazis?"

I felt Hannah's hand reach across and grip my thigh at that moment. A clear signal that I'd gone too far. Following in my son's footsteps.

Rosch glared back for a moment, then his ingratiating smile resurfaced. "That's hardly the same."

"Isn't it? What? The ideals of National Socialism must be protected at all costs?" That grip on my thigh tightened.

Rosch's smile became strained. "I think you're intentionally trying to deflect from the violence demonstrated by your son in this incident."

"Yes. We can hardly have violence shown from Jews toward Nazis—that really would be going against the grain."

"Gentlemen, please!" Stadler interjected, eager to bring back some calm and moderation. "The possible political leanings of these boys shouldn't come into it. This is purely the matter of an assault and what action would be appropriate."

The grip on my thigh had remained the same, but I'd noticed Hannah wince faintly as I'd made the comment. I too mentally pinched myself. Before the meeting, I'd found out from Josef Weber that Dieter Braun and Governor Rosch were not only ardent Nazi supporters but also close friends, in fact belonged to the same local NSDAP chapter. But it was important I didn't let on I knew that information; now I might have overstepped that line.

Silence for a second, then Hannah commented, "All I can say is that I've brought Stefan up as a good Catholic. And instilled upon him the importance of always telling the truth, of not lying. So if he says that this other boy punched him first, then I'm inclined to believe him."

"That's very commendable of you," Stadler said. "And the panel accepts your comment in good grace and faith."

But it was clear from the looks exchanged each side, that it could be given only limited credence. No doubt Dieter Braun had said much the same about his own son, albeit basing his belief more on National Socialism and *Mein Kampf* than on the Holy Trinity.

Governor Mayr had stayed silent throughout, calmly observing proceedings—although I was sure I'd seen the trace of a smile cross his face as I'd made my comment about violence from Jews to Nazis. But now, putting his pen down after some brief notes, he commented.

"I'd like to vouch for Hannah Namal, if I may. I've known her parents and her for many years now. And I've always found them a forthright and honest family. If Mrs. Namal says that she trusts and believes her son's account of events, I have no reason to doubt her."

The meeting had been like a microcosm of Anschluss—Jews, Nazis and Catholics convened around a table arguing the toss. Except that this time it was purely our son's fate at stake rather than an entire nation.

Headmaster Stadler informed us summarily that Stefan would be suspended from school for three days, at the end of which we would be informed of the panel's final decision: whether Stefan would be permanently excluded from St. Joseph's or reinstated.

There was nothing more we could do. But as we left the meeting, I noticed Governor Rosch's eyes linger on me as he made a final note on his pad.

7

He that has eyes to see and ears to hear may convince himself that no mortal can keep a secret. If his lips are silent, he chatters with his fingertips; betrayal oozes out of him at every pore.

—*Sigmund Freud*

Mathias

My mother's voice sounded tremulous and uncertain on the other end of the telephone line.

"I heard some knocking downstairs…someone was trying to get in."

"Was it just at the front door?"

"Yes…but I heard them moving around outside too."

I thought for a moment. "Might be just someone trying to get your attention at the front door."

"I don't think so. Hardly anyone calls, except Erica. Besides…

Mrs. Steiner from two doors away had someone break in her home just the other day."

I was suddenly more alarmed. "You didn't tell me this before."

"I... I didn't want to worry you."

I sighed. "Have you called Erica? She's a lot closer to get to you."

"Yes. I... I phoned her before trying you. There was no answer."

A more labored sigh. "Okay. I'll be with you quickly. Just give me a minute to..."

But my mother's voice burst in, a sharp, hushed-breath inhalation. "There's...there's another noise downstairs now. Some... some rustling and scratching."

Then the line went dead.

"Yes, there's been a number of break-ins and some looting in the Leopoldstadt area," Josef Weber confirmed as we sped in his Steyr 220 toward my mother's home.

Leopoldstadt was a strongly Jewish area in north Vienna, with 35 percent of its residents Jewish, far beyond the 10 percent in the rest of the city.

"I didn't know it had got that bad," I said. "I read of a couple of incidents in the newspapers—but nothing too worrying."

Josef grimaced. "Yes. They don't like to paint too dark a picture in the press, alarm people. But we get the sharp end of it at the police precincts, hear the worst."

"I suppose," I agreed lamentably. "In fact, I recall just a couple of days ago passing by Schiffman's department store on Taborstrasse, and there was a group of SS guards and Nazi supporters outside holding placards telling people not to go inside and buy from Jews. Support the downfall they've brought on the nation!" I shook my head. "But I read nothing about it in the newspapers the next day."

Josef looked across at me keenly. "You know why that is,

Mathias? Because the press now is either subject to or controlled by the Reich—or at least feels afraid to report anything painting them in a bad light." Josef shrugged. "Same, too, now with the police force. Most of the hierarchy at Kärntnerstrasse have been replaced by SS. And five days back, straight after Anschluss, I and other officers had to swear and sign an oath of allegiance to the Reich and the Führer. So those of us in the force who were past Schuschnigg supporters—which might indeed be a good 30 percent—or have Jewish friends or contacts, keep quiet about it." A pained smile broke through Josef's taut expression. "In fact, I could probably get shot as a collaborator just by being with you now. So, if we get stopped and anyone asks, I've arrested you for being a stinking Jew, okay?"

Josef's smile broadened and I joined him in a light chuckle. But then as it subsided, I thought about the risk that Josef was trying to make light of. "I'm sorry. I shouldn't have asked you to come along."

"That's alright. I understand your worries." He reached across and patted my shoulder. "And the last thing I'd let Hitler and his trumped-up followers get in the way of is a good friendship."

I'd asked Josef to accompany me because I was afraid who I might run into in the area. Hobson's choice: if I ran into Nazi-sympathizing looters, I might be robbed or handed over to the SS. If I ran into the SS, I might be questioned and detained.

As we turned the corner a couple of blocks from my mother's house, SS guards and uniformed police were visible on the street.

"Ah, right," Josef commented. "A fair few quite evident, I see."

My brow knitted. "Don't tell me they've been the ones involved in the looting?"

"No. We got news at the precincts of some Jewish areas being robbed and looted, so instructions came down the line that the problem should be dealt with."

Initially this confused me, went against everything else I'd so far seen and heard, but I nodded enthusiastically all the same. "One good sign, at least. Them protecting Jewish property like this."

Josef smiled ingratiatingly. "Oh, don't kid yourself for a moment it's for the benefit of Jews. Right now the Nazi Reich is keen to strike a deal with Jews for them to leave the country—in the process leaving most of their assets and wealth behind." Josef lifted one hand from the wheel after turning the last corner into my mother's street. "But there's little point if those assets and wealth have already been plundered. So they're doing it for the protection of what they see as future Reich wealth, not Jewish."

On my mother's street, it was darker than usual. Then I noticed the streetlamps smashed at intervals—probably so that looters could hide easier among the shadows. I could see two SS guards on the street, but they were farther along.

"Looks like they've been checking as they go," Josef said. "Let's go in before they return—see if your mother's okay."

The front of my mother's house had a twenty-foot-square garden. Josef said he'd stay at its end looking along the street while I went in.

I had my own key and didn't even trouble with my normal two light taps before starting to open my mother's door. But with the shadows heavier than I was used to, I fumbled getting the key into the lock.

"Hurry up!" Josef hissed urgently. "One of them is coming back this way."

I finally got the key in, turned it and opened the door. I waited until Josef had hustled in behind me and closed the door again before I called out.

"Momma, it's me—Mathias."

Silence. Fear gripped me that something had happened. I looked up the stairs with concern—since her hip injury, my mother spent most of her time on the first floor, only came downstairs or ventured to the second floor when assisted by Erica or myself.

I tentatively started my way up the stairs, calling out again, "Momma—it's Mathias." But then halfway up, a sudden noise made my heart leap—repeated banging, like gunshots, coming from the kitchen at the back of the house.

I rushed back down with Josef to investigate. Josef drew his gun from his jacket as we approached the kitchen, signaling that he should go first.

We froze as the kitchen door opened, Josef raising his gun—only to be confronted by my sister, Erica, blinking at us in surprise.

"Oh, Mathias… Josef. I didn't hear you come in." She held out one hand with three mezuzahs and some nails. "I was just putting these up. Momma asked me to—said she was frightened."

Josef grimaced as he put his gun away. "Sorry. We thought it might have been an intruder. There's been some looting in the area."

"I know." Erica nodded forlornly. "That's why Mom asked me to put up the mezuzahs. I was starting at the back then working my way through."

Mezuzahs were ancient Jewish symbols used to ward off evil spirits, particularly in protecting a house. Four years younger than me, Erica was vibrant and looked well for her age, with large warm eyes and dark brown hair. She'd gone through a more matronly period six years ago after she'd been jilted at the altar by a long-term lover, taking solace in endless boxes of chocolates and slabs of halva.

Our mother worried that Erica would forever be left a spinster—but the last few years she'd trimmed back. Perhaps due to the new boyfriend she apparently had, or could equally be her hectic schedule: between walking Ivor to school, rushing over to babysit him or up and down the three flights of stairs to take care of our mum, what time did Erica have left for a love life? I sometimes felt guilty about that, wondering whether—despite Erica being such a willing soul and always eager to help out— too many family demands were being put on her.

As Erica led us upstairs, she explained that our mother, Lena, had asked her to put up some mezuzahs the day before when she heard about break-ins and looting in the area—but had obviously forgotten.

"That's what I was out getting when she heard some banging downstairs and phoned you. Then when I came in downstairs, she said she wasn't sure who it was at first—so put the phone down on you and hid in the back room. But only remembered to tell me ten minutes after." Erica smiled at us, as if in apology for our mother's behavior. "When I phoned you back, you'd obviously already left to come over."

"So where's Mom now?" I asked as we came onto the first-floor landing.

As if in answer, Erica called out, "It's okay, Momma. You can come out now!" Then in a low mumble to me and Josef: "I told her to stay in the back room and keep the door shut and locked until I came back up."

"Are you sure it's safe?" My mother's tremulous voice drifted from behind the door.

"Yes, Mom," Erica replied. "It's just Mathias and Josef."

A moment as that information was deliberated, then the latch turned and the door opened.

"Mathias... Mathias! You came over—you needn't have." We hugged, and I found myself enveloped in that familiar cloud of lemon and lavender. If anyone washed more times in a day and splashed on more fresh scent than my mother, I'd yet to meet them. She held my face gently in both hands—which I've always hated—as she pulled back and studied my face. "You look a bit worn and worried."

Inwardly, I smiled. *I was fine before I had to rush over in the dead of night worried sick about you.* "Difficult times," I said. But even that

felt like a minefield. The last thing my mother needed reminding of was the nightmare of Anschluss with looters practically
at her door. I sighed as I took a seat and my mother retreated
to her favorite armchair. "The important thing is you're okay."

"Yes." My mother's expression was lost for a moment, as if
questioning why she shouldn't be. "Erica came over and she was
just putting up some mezuzahs. How's Ivor?"

That was the other thing with my mother. Despite the sup-
posed dementia, she'd make sudden leaps to new subjects—so
that sometimes it was difficult to keep up with her. Her hair
now light gray with only a few strands of her original brown,
her eyes were an indefinable fusion of green and gray, but with
still a sharp inner light. And I sometimes wondered whether
my mother simply played up being forgetful when it suited her.

"I'll make a pot of coffee for us all," Erica said from the doorway.

"I'll help," Josef chimed in, and I was left alone with my
mother.

"Ivor's good—he's well," I said. But that felt like another
minefield. My mother probably picking up with her sharp eyes
that I usually said he was "very well." But I didn't want to openly
lie and overstate anything. Nor did I want to get into the difficult area that Ivor would now be categorized as a Mischling,
so might have to join a different class, or even leave for another
school. So I sought refuge with rambling on about a current science project Ivor was doing particularly well with.

But it was a difficult and lonely canyon, talking about something so mundane while the pressures and horrors of Anschluss
loomed each side of that canyon—trying hard not to even acknowledge them. And I saw my mother's sharp eyes shift down
after a moment, as if guessing that I was rambling—or perhaps
I'd lost her halfway—fixing on my hands unconsciously clench-
ing in my lap. Despite all my efforts, she knew the truth.

"That's okay," she said softly. "You don't need to explain. I know that things aren't easy for you either now."

And I felt in that moment like bursting into tears and giving her another big hug. Why did she always have to be so understanding?

But then shamefully my next thought was that if my mother had been so spooked by these neighborhood looters, maybe she could be convinced to leave Vienna, if in the end Julian thought that was the best and safest thing.

"And Johannes and his family?" she inquired.

"They're coping okay, under the circumstances." I pushed an uneasy smile. "Saw him just the other day."

Lena nodded, her thoughtful expression broken as Erica's voice came from behind us.

"There we are." Erica set a silver tray down with a pot of coffee and some pastries. Josef brought the cups and plates on a separate tray.

Erica was only halfway through pouring when a heavy, insistent banging came from downstairs.

"That's the sound I heard before," Lena said with a hushed breath, her eyes filled with anxiety.

"Someone at the front door," Josef said. He held a hand toward us. "Look. You all stay here and keep this door shut. I'll go and see to it."

The sound of Josef trundling down the stairs. Another heavy door-knock as he reached the bottom.

We stayed, breath held, frozen behind the upstairs door. But I wanted to see what was happening—have some warning if someone was heading up toward us. I signaled for Erica to switch off the light, then peered through a two-inch gap as Josef opened the front door. With our room in total darkness, nobody would see us.

An SS soldier in full uniform stood on the porch. "Is this your home?"

Josef glanced around quizzically for a second, held out a palm. "Do you see anyone else here?"

Despite my galloping nerves and dry mouth, I couldn't resist a smile. Josef had spent too much time in my company: he'd learned the art of answering a question with a question to avoid telling a direct lie.

The SS soldier simply gave a perfunctory nod. "And is this a Jewish household?"

"Do I look Jewish?"

"No, I…" And as the soldier stammered slightly, Josef took out and showed his police badge. Slightly red-faced, the soldier promptly tipped his cap. "I… I see. Apologies, Inspector. Good night."

"Good night."

Josef closed the front door, but waited a moment in the hallway to make sure the soldier had gone before walking back up the stairs toward us.

"I think that calls for a celebration!" Erica said, getting a bottle of plum brandy my mother kept for special occasions from a side cabinet.

First Julian, now my sister. What was it with everyone thinking I needed hard liquor to get through Anschluss?

And as we smiled, raised our glasses and thanked Josef for his help, the storm clouds threatening our community seemed a million miles away in that moment. When we'd finished our coffees and plum brandies, Erica said she should get on and finish putting up the mezuzahs.

But halfway back down the stairs, Josef paused, struck with a thought. "Wait! That's the last thing you should be putting up—particularly over the front door. It will simply announce that this is a Jewish household." Josef instructed us to stay in the upstairs back room again and not answer the door to anyone until he got back. He held out a hand. "And let me have your keys, Mathias, so that it looks like my house if anyone's still watching when I walk back in. I won't be long."

We waited another tense seventeen minutes in that upstairs back room—though it felt like a lifetime—for Josef to return.

I nodded with grim approval when Josef showed me what he'd got. Then I stood below holding the wooden chair that I'd brought from the kitchen and watched as Josef climbed up and nailed the cross above my mother's front door.

8

As the Gestapo officer, Heinz Piehler, looked around his home drawing room, Sigmund Freud observed him as calmly and neutrally as he was able to muster. Freud didn't want to risk any outward signs of disdain or hostility, which might endanger himself or his family.

Piehler wore a dark gray suit and was accompanied by two other men, one also in plain clothes, his Gestapo assistant, and an SS officer in full uniform. These other two stayed strangely static as Piehler walked around the room. Piehler stopped and traced one finger across a small brass Buddha on a bookshelf.

"If you are allowed passage out of Austria, a Kommissar will be appointed to appraise your various works of art and your private papers." Piehler looked back at Freud, smiling thinly. "While I might have appreciation of such objects, I don't have in-depth knowledge of them. This man, Kommissar Sauerwald, will have."

"I see."

"Sauerwald is a party member, but like you he's also very much an academic, so hopefully someone you can trust."

Freud nodded. "Seems quite a reasonable and admirable arrangement."

Piehler held his gaze keenly on Freud for a moment, trying to gauge whether he was being sarcastic. "We wish to be fair with you. At the end of Kommissar Sauerwald's evaluation, you will be asked to sign an acceptance of it—in part as a reflection of that fairness."

A slower nod this time. It was becoming clearer now. He would be asked to sign an acceptance of that valuation and whatever large part of it the Nazis would take to allow his passage out of Austria, so that it appeared he was fully in accord with it. "As you say, appears a perfectly fair arrangement."

Again a steadier stare from Piehler for a moment. "You will also need to share with Sauerwald any bank accounts you hold, and show him any and all statements. It's important to hold nothing back—in order to ensure that a final valuation is fair."

"I perfectly understand." Freud felt his jaw tightening—a common symptom in any case with his increasing mouth cancer—as he fought to keep his expression calm and neutral, not betray his pent-up frustration and anger.

Piehler continued pacing after a second, eyes darting keenly around the room. "I see you have a number of photos of immediate family, but none it seems of friends and associates."

"My wife has put those in various folders and separate albums." Freud smiled tamely. "Only so many photos a room can take without appearing cluttered."

"Yes, of course." Piehler returned the smile equally tamely. "Hopefully Kommissar Sauerwald will also be able to appraise those to see if they are of any value."

Josef

After nailing the cross above Lena's door, Josef didn't feel like just going home for the night. So after a snack at a Würstelstand, a leisurely bath, changing into an evening suit and splashing on some fresh cologne at home, he headed to his favorite nightclub, Der Blaue Engel.

Smoke was heavy as he walked in, swirls of it rising through the spotlights aimed at the central stage. In the glow of that spotlight was the most beautiful woman he'd ever seen. But then he'd become something of an expert on how she looked: he'd been coming to see her one or two nights every week for the past four years.

Now twenty-eight years old, Deya Reynes was as fresh and beautiful as the first day he'd met her; but then maybe, too, he was biased: love is blind.

Josef could see that the audience was equally captivated. She was wearing a full flamenco outfit today, long wavy black hair and large amber eyes completing her exotic Spanish senorita look. Deya Reynes wasn't just her stage name, but her name in real life; or, at least, had been for the past six years. Josef, along with club owner Max Adler, was one of the few people who knew that Deya was originally a Romani gypsy. Her past and identity buried so long ago that Josef couldn't even recall her original name; or in fact if Deya had ever told him. Deya loved mysteries.

The identity change had not only been because of the anti-Romani stance with the rise of the Nazi party, but also hiding away from her violent and abusive ex-husband, who she left a year after their daughter was born.

That identity change had in fact been made by a cousin of Deya's, Lorenzo, which he later developed into a useful sideline business with the increasing number of Romani and Jews in the city keen to bury their own identities.

As Deya stamped her heels more dramatically, flouncing her skirt higher at points, Josef smiled as he noticed some men close to the stage trying to see if she was wearing any underwear. She blew a kiss Josef's way as she spotted him three tables back.

Then, following a more pronounced castanet clicking and heel stamping—almost like a drumroll—Deya swept her flamenco skirt away and threw it to one side, answering that front-row curiosity. Underneath, she wore frilly black lace panties and matching stockings held up by garters.

Raucous cheering and laughter rose from the far side of the room, but as Josef looked over he saw it was equally because another bottle of champagne had been opened as a club girl draped herself in the lap of an SS officer, another girl raising her glass and giggling among the group of nine: four uniformed SS, two of whom Josef hadn't seen in the club before, two brownshirts and three police SD, one of them Kurt Landmann from his own station. Josef lifted a hand in acknowledgment and Landmann smiled and waved back.

Five or six showgirls worked the audience, wearing only bolero tops, lace corsets and underwear, trying to entice customers into buying as much overpriced champagne as possible. And for an extra "fee," sometimes they'd disappear into one of the curtained booths at the back of the club.

"You saving yourself just for Deya, as usual?"

"As usual." Josef smiled tightly as club owner Max Adler approached. Josef held a hand out and Max joined him at the table. "Being unpredictable is not a trait to be admired, you know."

Max chuckled. "Don't worry. We've got only one new girl working tonight. I'll warn her not to pester you—that you've only got eyes for Deya."

Always the same routine. Josef would turn up toward the end of the night when Deya was on her last couple of dances and the other girls knew meanwhile to leave him be. He'd order a bottle of champagne which Max let him have cut-price due to his regularity, plus in part he paid his way with backup security. Der Blaue Engel attracted a fair few of Vienna's lowlifes and Josef would often advise Max which ones might be troublesome. And a few nights when customers had got too heavy-handed with the girls or a drunken brawl had broken out which the bouncer had trouble handling, Josef had helped eject them.

Deya would never spend any time with other customers or go to the curtained booths while Josef was there, and while no doubt she did on the five or six nights he wasn't there, or even before he arrived, he never asked. That part of Deya's life he now accepted—the chance of changing that went five years ago—but they both studiously sidestepped the details. Too painful. It was far from the ideal arrangement; but dating a club girl like Deya, probably as good as it got.

As more cheering and raucous laughter came from the SS and SD police tables at the end, Josef commented, "Looks like a good crowd tonight."

Max glanced toward them, smiled tightly. "I don't know about good. We're busy, at least."

Josef nodded. As a Jewish club owner, he knew that Max had been walking a thin line these past few years, and now even more precarious with Anschluss. Though Max had partly himself to blame; he'd purposely aimed to attract the military and police at his club, in fact was originally going to call it Der Blaue Max, after the military medal. Before someone suggested that naming a salacious club after a military honor might be seen as disrespectful—so he'd opted in the end for Der Blaue Engel, after the Marlene Dietrich film, which had hit screens two years before he opened the club.

Max was assured that name would equally attract military men, which it did. But now with the advent of Anschluss, it no doubt felt they were too close for comfort. Max's only saving grace, and probably why he'd so far been left alone, was that he was a veritable giant of a man, approaching six foot four, and hale and hearty in manner. Not a timid Jew they could shove around. Despite themselves, the Führer-ass-lickers warmed to his personality, and the club girls loved him too, looked upon him as a big, protective teddy bear.

Max lit up a cigar, adding to the smoke swirls drifting up through the spotlights. "Things haven't changed in here at least," he commented wistfully, as if by omission acknowledging the changes outside. He was silent, thoughtful for a moment, perhaps contemplating those changes, but deciding in the end this wasn't the right time or place to talk about them as he glanced again toward the SS and brownshirts at the end of the room. Then, as Deya approached the table having finished her dance, he got up with a smile. "I'll leave you two to it."

"I wasn't expecting you here tonight," she commented as Max drifted away and she took her first sip of champagne.

"No. I came on impulse in the end." Josef pushed a smile. "Tough night."

Josef hadn't intended to say anything originally, but as Deya looked across sympathetically, tracing one azure fingernail around the edge of her champagne glass, he felt sucked into those warm amber eyes like he had been for seemingly half a lifetime, and he found himself opening up about the events of the night: his Jewish writer friend's aged mother afraid for her life, and nailing a cross above her door to hopefully ward off future looters or the SS.

Deya was thoughtful for a moment. "Is that why you came to see me now? You thought this family might need Lorenzo's help?"

"No. I came to see you," Josef said flatly. "Felt I needed the company." Then, realizing that might sound dismissive and offhand, he shook his head. "They're not anywhere near that stage. He can't even get his mother to contemplate leaving, even if she was well enough to travel." What had started purely with identity masking for Deya and her cousin, Josef knew, had increasingly verged into helping people leave the country the last two years; the identity changes simply a prelude to that. And no doubt now there was even heavier demand.

Josef took out a packet of Sports, offered one to Deya and lit up for both of them with a silver lighter.

"Well, let me know if and when they're ready," Deya said, blowing out the first smoke. "Because Lorenzo's not long ago taken on a new Jewish partner in that business, Alois, known and trusted by that community. Lorenzo changed Alois's identity to Lutheran shortly after the rest of his family were sent to Mauthausen." She looked to one side briefly, as if concerned she might be overheard. "Word has it, it will just get worse."

"I hear that too." Josef shrugged. "But, as I say, right now this friend is far from ready—if he ever gets to that stage."

For the remaining twenty minutes until Deya's next dance, their conversation was lighter, more general—though it seemed strange, and perhaps carried with it a shade of guilt, talking about how their respective weeks had been, recent shopping trips and a "lovely watercolor" Deya's daughter, Luciana, had painted at school and brought home—when around them the city was in chaos.

Although they inadvertently touched on the subject again when Deya commented that she'd noticed her favorite cosmetics and perfumes shop, Krucie's, which Josef knew was Jewish-owned, was closed and boarded up. And all the time avoiding the unspoken question between them: With this increased focus, was Deya concerned that her own buried gypsy background might be uncovered?

It wasn't until halfway through Deya's next dance—a Salome-style routine with different colored veils discarded at set intervals—that Josef finally started to feel more relaxed, more mellow.

"Someone I'd like to introduce you to," Kurt Landmann's voice crashed in from the side as he approached with one of the SS officers Josef hadn't seen in the club before. "Heinrich Schnabel, newly arrived just last week."

"Pleased to meet you," Schnabel said, reaching a hand out. They shook. "My responsibility is the first and eighth districts, which I understand also partly overlaps your own patch. So I daresay we'll be bumping into each other again, cooperating where necessary."

It wasn't until Schnabel mentioned the area he was covering that it clicked: the SS officer that Johannes had mentioned walking into the Café Mozart!

"I look forward to it," Josef said with as much enthusiasm as he could muster. "Where were you stationed before?"

"In Linz. Where our beloved Führer spent much of his childhood."

"Very commendable."

An awkward silence settled. Something else was clearly on Schnabel's mind. He glanced back at Max Adler, who was now standing at the bar. "I see that you appear to have no problem fraternizing with Jews."

"He's the owner of the club." Josef shrugged. "So somewhat difficult to avoid."

"I see."

"Max is okay," Landmann offered, keen to break the second tense silence to fall in as many minutes. "He takes care of us well."

"I daresay he does," Schnabel said, as if that was by the way. Irrelevant. "But I'm sure it can't be easy for you."

Josef met Schnabel's steady gaze. That easy confidence and arrogance which assumed that everyone detested Jews, Mischlinge and gypsies as much as he. Josef had seen it countless times before, even with his own father—the cause of many arguments between them. While he'd been dead now almost three years, that reminder often felt uncomfortably close.

"We all have our crosses to bear," Josef said with a wry smile, recalling the cross he'd nailed above Lena's door just hours before.

"I'm sure we do." Schnabel returned the smile curtly. "Look forward to meeting you again, Inspector Weber—very possibly on our shared patch."

It took several minutes after the exchange for Josef to get his equilibrium back, feel mellow again. But then as Deya finished her routine ten minutes later, once more he found himself on edge.

As Deya left the stage, she had to pass within a couple of yards of Schnabel's group, and he seemed to go out of his way to intercept her and guide her by one arm toward his table. Some words were exchanged, then Deya appeared to protest and point toward Josef. But Schnabel leaned in closer at that moment and said something that made her face cloud. And it wasn't until one of the other showgirls at the table said something and also pointed Josef's way that Schnabel finally relented and let go of Deya's arm.

As Deya walked toward Josef, he saw Schnabel raise his glass and smile at him. And Josef wasn't sure if it was by way of apology for stepping in when he shouldn't have, or some sort of challenge: *The girl might be with you tonight. But there will be other nights.*

9

Unexpressed emotions will never die. They are buried alive and will come forth later in uglier ways.

—*Sigmund Freud*

Johannes

Over the next few weeks we observed Vienna and the nation as a whole sink into an anti-Semitic abyss the likes of which I have never known before.

More Jewish shops were boarded up, some through forced closure, others the owners fearing smashed windows and looting. A number were also daubed with the Star of David or JUD, often in yellow paint. Incidents of incitement and open violence against Jews were rife, with the number of Jewish suicides in Vienna increasing tenfold.

At the end of the three-day suspension, we received news from St. Joseph's that our son, Stefan, was to be excluded permanently from the school, ausgewiesen. Summoned in front of the same four-man panel, Headmaster Stadler appeared to show genuine remorse as he handed us the formal written notice. "Because your son has been a good student." Which he needn't have added.

Then we started the tedious task of finding a new school for Stefan. Out of seven we wrote to, two refused outright, three didn't even give the courtesy of a reply and the two remaining interviews weren't encouraging.

"I note that your son is a quarter Jewish," the first headmaster we sat in front of commented. "Only a grade down from a Mischling, but sufficient for him to legally be considered a Reich citizen and so allowed entry to our school. But I'm afraid we view attacks on fellow pupils very seriously. We'll let you know."

Stefan's fistfight being recorded as the main reason for his expulsion at St. Joseph's caused a similar problem at the next school interview. Although this time when the headmaster asked pointedly why Stefan had hit this other boy, I answered equally pointedly: "Because this boy and two others were pushing and taunting our son and calling him a filthy, stinking Jew."

The headmaster just stared back blankly, as if he hardly saw anything wrong in that, or perhaps he was thinking: *That's to be expected in today's Austria. If your son can't weather that, then he's not going to last long in this society.*

I'd gone with Hannah each time to put on a more Catholic front, but it had made little difference. Seeing my despondent face that night after yet another school rejection, a nearly-in-tears Stefan commented that he was sorry he'd punched Horst, "And caused you and Momma all this trouble."

It broke my heart. I ruffled Stefan's hair and gave him a reassuring grimace. "It's okay. You did the right thing, standing up for yourself. But right now some people might not appreciate that." I realized I was getting dangerously close to a "bad time for Jews" speech, which Stefan might understand in four or five years' time, but not now. How do you explain to a nine-year-old they've been born the wrong race or religion for a certain moment in history?

I called Mathias the next day and commented that with the events currently unfolding, "Perhaps a meeting with Julian would be helpful."

Mathias agreed. "Same place?"

"Same place."

Throughout the call, we didn't discuss the dire nature of those events, any hint that we were Jewish or where we were meeting. Already we feared telephone calls might be listened in to.

But on my way to the Mozart Café, a middle-aged woman half knocked me over as she flew against me, sprawling to the ground a yard past, contents of her shopping bag spilling out. I looked back and saw that she'd been pushed by one of four SD guards in front of Gerngross department store waving placards—JEW OWNED STORE—DON'T SHOP HERE! Another measure of how quickly things had descended into hell: I'd got so used to seeing these placard-wavers that I hardly paid them attention anymore.

The guard stood over her menacingly. "Why do you continue to shop here and ignore our notices?"

"Be-because I was measured for this dress a few weeks ago before you were here with your placards," the woman stammered. "And they called just now to say it was ready."

"You shop here regularly?"

"Yes."

"So you're a Jew yourself?"

It was more a statement than a question, as if the guard knew that very few Reich-honoring Aryans would ignore their placards. The woman just nodded numbly.

A thoughtful nod in return, then the SD guard raised a boot. The woman put one hand over her face, fearing that she was going to be kicked or stomped on—but he stepped onto the dress spilled by her side, grinding and smearing it into the dirt of the pavement.

"There! Now you have a dress more fitting to be worn by a Jew."

Eyes welling, the woman simply nodded again. Perhaps partly thanks and relief that she hadn't been harmed, or fearful that if she did protest she might be. She stuffed her soiled dress back into her shopping bag.

But as I reached a hand out to help her up, I saw the SD guard glaring at me. I'd felt inconspicuous until that moment because a small group had gathered around to watch the spectacle. But I noticed now that while some were poker-faced, emotionless, many were smiling, with a few actually breaking into clapping and cheering.

I quickly retracted the hand and walked away. I felt abject shame in that moment: shame to be Viennese, shame that I'd now joined them by turning my back. But I had my own family and survival to think about—no doubt what many in Vienna, including those poker-faces, were now thinking.

I felt the SD guard's eyes still on me as I headed away. Only as I took the next turn into Haidmannsgasse did I notice that he'd turned his attention away, one of the cheerers now patting him on the back.

I was still shaken by the incident when I got to the Café Mozart, explaining what had happened to Mathias and Julian as we ordered our coffees.

Julian shook his head lamentably. "They had Jews scrub all the walls clear of anti-Nazi slogans before Hitler's visit. And I hear just last week the SD and brownshirts forced Jewish actresses from Der Josefstadt Theater to clean public toilets."

Mathias was thoughtful for a second, his expression grave, before he started on the more personal account of looting close by in his mother's street and how fearful my aunt Lena had been.

"In the end, Josef nailed a cross up above her door." He forced a tragicomic smile. "Hopefully, that will throw them off the scent, keep them at bay."

But I could read the unsaid thoughts in the worry on my cousin's face: *For how long?* And what would happen if the SS called again and Josef wasn't there?

As much as my father, Samuel, had been a family figurehead, since his death my aunt Lena, despite her age and frailty, had taken over that role. The last surviving member of that generation on the Namal side of our family.

We'd decided on meeting at the Mozart because we weren't sure how safe we'd be at any other Vienna café. Schnabel had apparently only shown up again once since, but as an extra precaution, just in case early evening was his favorite time for calling, we'd decided to meet midafternoon.

We also sat toward the back of the café and had an arrangement with Otto that he'd signal if he saw Schnabel approaching, in which case we'd dive into the kitchen and hide there until he was gone. The warmth and ambience of the café—mellow blended aromas of coffee, strong tobacco, chocolate and cinnamon—at least carried the sense of a safe cocoon, even if only on the surface. Familiar ground.

Julian took a fresh breath. "The issue was raised at that last Circle meeting, and I've mentioned it again since to Mathias—but I think it's something you should both now consider more seriously." Julian's gaze shifted directly to me. "The option of leaving the country. In the end, there might be little other choice."

Mathias appeared lost in thought again for a moment, then shook his head. "With the looting so close to my mother's house, it might be possible to convince her—but I'd feel guilty using the Nazi's own tactics to try and persuade her." He smiled awkwardly. "And she's terribly stubborn—she'd probably say no.

Apart from the worry that such a journey would kill her anyway at her age."

I nodded sympathetically. "I could say the same right now." I explained about Stefan being expelled from school for hitting another boy who'd called him a "filthy Jew," and how finding a new school for him was proving difficult. "Now I could use that to urge Hannah that the 'time is right' to leave. But I don't think she'd be willing to be cut off from the rest of her family—her parents, sisters and her brother."

After a moment contemplating our respective impasses and sipping at our coffees, Mathias asked Julian, "Any more news with Freud?"

"Yes. It looks like he's made the decision to leave, but it remains unclear what members of his family, if any, will also be allowed out. They've appointed a Gestapo district chief and a Kommissar to look into his case." Julian's jaw stiffened. "But Freud might not in the end prove a useful guide."

"Why's that?" I asked.

"Freud is a particularly high-profile figure, as was Zweig. A lot of other artists and politicians speaking out on their behalf—Dalí, Einstein, H. G. Wells, British and American ambassadors. For other writers, it might be different."

Mathias's brow knitted. "Are you saying we might not be let out, even if we do decide to leave?"

"No. I'm not saying that at all. A lot of writers and artists are being allowed out—I just don't know where the dividing line falls." Julian took another sip of coffee, grimaced. The right words were obviously proving difficult to find. "Look, Mathias. Without putting too fine a point on it—your sales have been very good these past few years, you've started to find more readers. But you're still a long shot from the likes of Freud and Zweig, and Johannes here is—"

Julian broke off as he noticed Otto looking our way with concern and holding a hand up. Otto shifted back to a hawklike stare through the front window of the café. Someone was obviously outside that concerned him—perhaps Schnabel or another SS officer. A frozen moment, my heart in my throat as we feared we might have to bolt for the kitchen door at any second—that moment stretching out, feeling like a lifetime, before finally Otto relaxed, waved the all clear.

I eased out my breath, didn't even realize I'd been holding it. Julian, too, took a moment to regather his thoughts.

"As I was saying, Johannes, you're a step down again from that level of fame." Julian held out a palm. "You're just starting out, so to be expected. But your sales are certainly respectable, and growing." He sighed. "It's just, well… I simply don't know how either of you will be dealt with. It would be potluck. And the most worrying thing, what I'm uncomfortable about most of all, once you've put your names down as wanting to leave, the Nazis will have every last detail about you, right down to your last tie-pin. Your heads will be in the noose. If they decide not to let you leave, they'll be able to do what they like with you."

A heavy silence fell at our table, the murmur and clatter of the café around superimposing for a moment. It was one thing to be facing difficult decisions; it was quite another to know they might be futile, whatever we decided. As if sensing our concern with that fresh hurdle, Julian's tone brightened.

"One advantage at least of not being as famous as Freud or Zweig—hardly anyone knows what either of you looks like."

"Your ability to always look for that silver lining is admirable," Mathias said with a lopsided grin. "Do you think that might actually help?"

"Yes, I do." Julian glanced briefly toward his cigarette holder in the ashtray, which today had an unlit turquoise Sobranie to match his silk shirt. "Your own dust-jacket photo, Mathias, is little more than a shadowy profile, and Johannes's is halfway towards that. Nobody could possibly recognize either of you from those."

Julian looked at us keenly. "The advantage here is that if either of you had been as well-known or recognizable as Freud or Zweig, an SS officer would have already been at your doors asking for all your details and a full list of your assets." Julian watched the realization dawn on us.

"I hadn't thought of it like that," Mathias said, his gaze lost for a moment.

Something else, too, that struck me poignantly in that moment: every now and then, as with any café or public place, I'd notice some individuals looking our way casually or distractedly for a moment. If we'd been famous or even halfway recognizable, by now someone would have been racing along the road to alert the nearest SD or SS guard: *the Jews Kraemer and Namal are in the Mozart!* In this case, lack of fame was our fortune.

"On which same subject, being recognized—have you both destroyed any photos of yourselves together with Freud or his inner circle?" Julian asked.

I nodded as Mathias answered that he had. "The only photos we had were those taken two years ago with yourself and Freud after his University of Vienna lecture."

"Good. I got rid of those, too, along with many others." Julian took another sip of coffee. "Because it appears Freud's initial suspicions were right—the Gestapo have started inquiring about photos of his friends and associates."

At the end of the last Circle meeting, Freud had commented that, as difficult as it might be, members should destroy any photos they had of themselves with himself or any other inner Circle members. "Because even if I do leave, it will no doubt not end there. The Nazis will use those photos to track down my friends, associates and other Circle members. And that responsibility is something I'd rather not have on my shoulders."

But Freud had gone on to comment that for those deciding not to leave, or unable to, "There might be other possible solutions." And I'd noticed him glance toward Julian in that moment. With the detailed information now being shared, I wondered if Julian was more involved in aiding Freud than he was letting on.

Julian took a fresh breath. "But while you have the advantage of anonymity now, it might not be there for long. Once the Nazis are onto you or take your details, it will already be too late. And the option of leaving might also soon go. Could be only a month or so." Julian shrugged. "But with the way everything has closed in so fast, equally it might only be days or a week. So don't take too long deciding."

10

All Jews and Mischlinge are henceforth disallowed employment in all government-regulated professions such as doctors, teachers, lawyers and judges. Non-government employers shall include in their regulations an Aryan paragraph excluding both Jews and Mischlinge from employment.

Mathias

Ivor had been too young to see *King Kong* when it first came out, so when he discovered that a rerun was showing at the nearby Elysium cinema, he asked whether we could go?

I paused for a moment. Apart from taking Ivor back and forth to school, I'd hardly been out with him anywhere since Anschluss. Too afraid of getting stopped by the SD or SS on the streets and questioned.

It suddenly struck me how unfair that was on Ivor, living like hermits, our lives frozen. And perhaps that's what the Nazis wanted in any case; that we simply wouldn't be visible anymore, we'd become nonpersons. The thought that we might be partly playing into the Nazis' hands tipped the final balance for me.

"Yes, let's go," I said. "It'll be good to get out, and we haven't been to the cinema for a while." Besides, I thought, in a dark cinema for a couple of hours, we'd probably be safer there than anywhere.

"That's great…great!" Ivor's eyes lit up. "I saw a poster in the streets for *King Kong*, and there was a preview clip when we went to see *Zircus Saran* a few years back. It looks really exciting."

We checked and saw there was an early-afternoon screening and on the way there I nipped into our local confectioners to get a packet of mints for myself and a Milka chocolate bar for Ivor, his favorite. Make it a real treat of a day for him. As I paid, Mr. Seidl behind the counter, now in his sixties, commented, "By the way, Mr. Kraemer, I just finished reading your last book. Very good."

"Thank you." I smiled and took my change. "I'm glad you enjoyed it."

"I particularly like the part where Marie gets away from the main villain…er, what's his name now…?"

"Gerner," I prompted. Despite Mr. Seidl professing to like the intricacies of plots in crime thrillers, he didn't have the best memory these days.

"Yes…yes. Gerner. That's it!"

But at that moment, I froze. The shop bell behind had rung and a middle-aged woman walked in followed not far behind by a young SD officer.

"Would you mind signing my copy for me?" Mr. Seidl asked.

"Maybe another ti—" I started, thinking of nothing else but rushing away at that moment—but then I saw that Mr. Seidl had already started rummaging below the counter. He brought my book up proudly with a smile and slapped it on the counter.

"There we are."

And it would have seemed strange and somewhat rude if I'd refused, possibly drawn the SD guard's attention all the more to us. "Yes, of course," I said.

As I signed, I prayed that the SD guard wasn't paying us too much notice, that he wouldn't suddenly blurt out: *Isn't that one of the books on the banned list from the Jew Kraemer?*

But at that moment his view of us was half-blocked by the woman who'd come in just before him, and in any case he seemed busy scanning the rows of sweet jars behind the counter.

"There you go," I said with a warm smile, sliding the book back across, but with my hand mostly shielding my name.

— "Why, thank you…"

"Got to go," I said quickly. "*King Kong* awaits at the local cinema—we don't want to be late for him." My smile shifting to Ivor, I swiftly shepherded him out before Mr. Seidl might be tempted to announce to the shop: *Mr. Kraemer here is a local author—he wrote this book!*

It wasn't until some way through the film, Ivor already half-way through his chocolate bar, that my nerves settled down. Perhaps because I found it hard to get drawn into this giant monster on-screen with the very real monsters outside plaguing my mind. The core concept of escapism, to get away, even briefly, from the harsh realities of life—why, I reminded myself, the Busby Berkeley spectaculars had been such hits at the height of the US and German Depressions—wasn't working this time. Though the action and dramatic images on-screen did have a numbing, soporific effect after a while.

As King Kong started climbing the Empire State Building, Ivor exclaimed, "It's exciting, isn't it? Are you enjoying it, Papa?"

"Yes, I am," I lied. I'd obviously appeared distracted with my own thoughts, so perhaps Ivor's question was the reminder I needed. I was here for Ivor's enjoyment more than my own. I should make more of an effort—cast my troubled thoughts aside and try and enjoy it more, or, at least, appear as if I was doing so.

And I thought I was doing reasonably well with that until eight minutes later those harsh realities from outside crashed in: flickering flashlights at the back of the cinema! At first, I thought it might be the usher, but as I glanced round, I saw two SD guards making their way down the aisle, checking the identities of people on each side.

I fixed my gaze straight ahead again, my heart pounding hard.

On-screen, the fighter planes were circling, moving in—but all I could think of in that moment was the two guards moving in. They were already about a third of the way down, eight or nine rows behind us.

I noticed then that they were checking no more than three or four seats in from the aisles each side. We were two seats from the end.

"Let's move along here." I nudged Ivor and started to move.

"Why's that?" Ivor asked halfway along our shift to six seats farther along, past a middle-aged couple in between.

"Because you'll get a clearer view here—nobody in between." I'd noticed a woman directly in front of Ivor partially impeding his view at moments when she adjusted position. Where we were now, there was nobody in front.

I prayed that the two guards behind hadn't noticed us move seats, had been too busy with their flashlights inspecting identity cards. But that would be my excuse if they had; though I knew once they'd asked that question, they'd ask for my identity card too.

Machine guns were hammering on-screen, almost in time with my pounding pulse—King Kong starting to totter. I closed my eyes for a second, tried to steady my breathing and racing nerves. Would this be my downfall now? If they took me and threw me in the back of a truck consigned to a concentration camp, they'd take Ivor too. I shouldn't have risked coming out with him.

The flashlights moved closer, and I fixed my gaze straight

ahead again, trying to appear enrapt in the images on-screen as King Kong stumbled and fell.

The light hit our row.

"Karten, bitte? Cards, please?" A young SD guard, no more than twenty-five, shone his flashlight on the identity card of the man at the end of the row. The woman next to him was already offering her card, which he took with a curt, "Thank you."

As he finished checking her card and handed it back, his flashlight shone along the row toward us. It seemed to dwell on us awhile—my heart in my throat in that moment that he had seen us move. But it could be that he was contemplating whether to ask for the papers of the middle-aged couple the other side of the two seats we'd left.

After a moment—seeming to me another tense, breath-held lifetime—he appeared to think better of it and moved on to the row in front.

Though it wasn't until the two guards had finished checking all the rows and left the cinema that I felt I could finally ease out my breath.

And at the end of the film, I held back with Ivor until practically everyone else had left, in case the two guards had lingered for a while. If they were still in the foyer, then they'd hopefully be kept busy checking the papers of others passing through. They weren't there.

As we got outside of the cinema, a vendor had a copper cauldron fired up, coating peanuts in hot sticky toffee.

"Can I have some, please, Papa?"

I recalled that on past visits, I'd treat Ivor to a small bag. But then I noticed another group of three SD guards ten yards away along the pavement, and by that time my nerves were completely shot.

"No, you can't," I snapped. "We've got to get home."

As we hustled along, I could feel Ivor's eyes on me, hurt and confused by my sharp tone. I closed my eyes again for a moment in silent penance to a God I hardly prayed to anymore. Julian was right. It was time to leave. I could hardly bear another minute of this, let alone weeks or months. The question remaining was whether I could convince Erica and my mother to leave.

11

Civilization began the first time an angry person cast a word instead of a rock.

—Sigmund Freud

"How are you getting along with searching out all the Jews in your district?" Kriminaldirektor Piehler inquired.

Heinrich Schnabel was standing by a large picture window looking out over the Wien River as Piehler approached him. They had gathered at the Hotel Metropole, which was midway through being converted to Nazi HQ in Vienna, this cocktail party now the first official group event to mark that takeover. Schnabel was wary. After all, there were many higher-ranking officers in the room whom Piehler could have taken the trouble to talk to; so Schnabel surmised that Piehler saw the issue of some importance.

"Well, we had quite a successful night with the amnesty ruse at Karmelitermarkt. And many others of course discovered individually through random searches and questioning."

"Yes, of course." Piehler sipped at a dry white wine. "But I daresay it must become tiresome at times hunting them down like that one by one. So much left to chance."

Schnabel raised a brow in faint reproach. "I'm not one to shy away from diligence and hard work."

"I'm not suggesting you are. But if something could short-circuit that—deliver a number of high-profile Jews and dissidents in one stroke?"

Now Piehler had his attention. He smiled wryly. "I'm quite a fan of efficiency too. Tell me more."

Piehler looked to one side, as if checking that nobody else was listening in. "It involves Sigmund Freud. We're making arrangements by which he can leave—so at least one less prominent Jew on your district to worry about. But it was his circle of friends and associates I was more interested in—most of them Jews or subversives. The most prominent ones we know about because they, too, have been in the newspapers. But there's a larger, broader circle which I was hoping we could home in on from Freud's photo collection. But when I visited him a few days ago, none were visible."

"Very strange."

Piehler held out a palm. "Freud said his wife had put them in various folders and albums. But Kommissar Sauerwald, appointed to sort through and value Freud's possessions, says that he's not come across any photos either outside of immediate family."

"Stranger still." Schnabel sipped at his vodka martini. "So the main assumption is they've either been destroyed or hidden away."

"Yes. Which means those photos are of far more significance than even I initially considered."

Johannes

"I've had enough, Johannes. I think it's time to take up Julian's suggestion."

"What happened?"

"I don't want to go into too much detail—but it was when I went the other day with Ivor to the cinema. I shouldn't have taken him out. Anyway, I've phoned Julian and asked for another meeting. I can give you all the details then."

Despite Mathias hopscotching around the details—paranoid to say too much in case our calls were being listened in to and would bring the Gestapo to our door—I found myself doing the same.

I sighed. "I'm not sure Hannah would be ready for that. Whether I could convince her." The terrible wrench for her—cut off from her two sisters, a brother and her parents who were both still alive—Mathias was well aware of from our last meeting.

"That's what we can discuss with Julian at this next meeting. See what other options there might be—if any."

"I suppose." I eased a resigned breath. "When's it arranged for?"

"Later this week. Same day, time and place as last time."

"Okay." More hopscotching, so that even if someone was listening in, they wouldn't know where and when we were meeting. "I'll be there."

The call was still on my mind when an hour later I put on my jacket and hat and shouted out that I was going to office stationers Ebner's. "I won't be long."

I didn't think Hannah had overheard me talking about "convincing" her—but it was a conversation I was going to have to have with her at some time. Like Mathias, I, too, had become something of a hermit, avoiding going out if I could—but I needed a new typewriter ribbon, so a call of necessity, and Ebner's was only a third-of-a-mile walk from our apartment.

"Ah, Mr. Namal. Haven't seen you in a while," Clara Ebner greeted me as I walked in.

"I seem to turn up for the same thing each time." I smiled meekly. "New typewriter ribbons."

"Olympia-8, if I recall correctly?"

"Your memory serves you well."

Clara Ebner was in her late thirties with mid-brown hair, a comely smile, and always seemed to wear bright floral dresses. Clara or her younger brother, Felix, usually served me, and their elderly mother only twice. I'd never seen their father.

"Five months to be precise," Clara said as she took the ribbon box down from the shelf and checked it against a register to her side.

"What's that?"

"Five months since you were last here. Your last order. And the one before that was only four months." She smiled. "So that's good—they're lasting longer."

"Maybe not so good." Feigned downturn to my return smile. "It means I've been writing slower." I didn't want to go into detail about how Anschluss and trying to find a new school for Stefan had impeded my work.

But it was a subject that Clara broached as I was about to leave; though not at all how I'd expected.

As Clara handed me my change, her expression clouded. "I'm afraid this might be the last time I'm able to serve you, Mr. Namal. In future, you'll have to get your ribbons elsewhere."

For a moment, I thought Clara was going to say that she knew I was half-Jewish and had received a directive not to serve Jews or Mischlinge anymore—but she went on to explain that the shop would soon be closing.

"Why's that?" Then it immediately hit me. "I didn't know you were…" Suddenly I was hopscotching again, as if even that word was now risky or offensive to repeat.

"I'm not," Clara said. "I was born and raised Catholic, as was my brother. And my parents, too, were Catholic, as far as we knew—until just last week."

I stood there transfixed as Clara related her account—breaking off at one point to serve another customer before continuing. Both her father and mother had been born Jewish, but had converted to Catholicism two years after their marriage in the late 1890s, not long before she was born. She and her brother, Felix, had no idea their parents were Jewish and didn't know the reason for their conversion until they asked their parents last week after they were hauled in for questioning by the Gestapo. "Apparently, it was due to the anti-Semitic edicts and actions of Karl Lueger, mayor of Vienna at the time."

I nodded. I'd heard about Lueger banning Jews from municipal positions, including many teachers and doctors, from my father. Anti-Semitism in Vienna had some history to it.

"Although, of course, my parents didn't declare that as the reason to the Catholic clergy handling their conversion. And they embraced Catholicism without reserve—with both Felix and I completing our Holy Communions and Confirmations, and us regularly attending church as a family." Clara shook her head, her eyes starting to well with tears. "And the saddest thing is, they never trusted Felix or me with the truth about their background. Feared we might spill the beans, I suppose." She bit back the tears with an ironic grimace.

I held a hand out. "But surely with them both converting so long ago, it will be okay?"

"Apparently not." Her grimace became more strained. "We spoke to an adviser who also works for the church, and he says that the new Reich is going as hard on those who have converted, sometimes harder. Sees them as betrayers, trying to infiltrate unseen among 'good upstanding Aryans.'"

I realized in that moment she was quoting Hitler directly, and I'd in fact heard a recent rally speech where he admonished, "be wary of the hidden Jews." But as Clara added, "It looks like even those who've married Jews won't be safe anymore—might be seen as some sort of traitors," my blood ran cold. Would Hannah even be safe, married to a half-Jew, a Mischling, like me?

"How do you think they found out?"

"Perhaps through church records. But could have been other ways too. A lot of eyes and ears out there right now."

Another chill ran through me as I recalled Governor Rosch's smug expression at that last school meeting. "And what happens now?"

"There's an SD and Gestapo meeting at Morzinplatz next week to decide whether my parents' conversion should be revoked—after which time, if it is, Felix and I will be considered Jews."

"I'm so sorry." Then immediately bit my tongue after saying it—again, slipping too easily into the Nazi ethos that being considered a Jew was something to be sorry about. "If it's any consolation, I'm facing a similar problem now. My father was Jewish."

Clara nodded numbly, and I suspected she already knew; perhaps from my name, Namal, or she'd read or heard about my father.

Clara said her parents feared the worst from the hearing. "That's why I said I thought the shop here would have to close soon."

But seeing Clara so fearful and distraught, I felt I couldn't leave things on that note, I had to offer some hope, however tenuous. So I mentioned that I was meeting some friends in a couple of days to find solutions to my own problem, "And if anything useful comes out of that, I'll let you know."

Outside, it was a sunny spring day, the sun warm on my back as I walked along. But inside my head, the clouds were dark and heavy. My main worry all along had been that being half-Jewish and with my father such an outspoken anti-Nazi agitator, I'd be at risk. Yet I'd always thought that with Hannah being fully Catholic and our children only a quarter-Jewish, they'd be safe. Though now if Hannah might be seen as some sort of traitor for marrying me, it changed everything. My whole family could be condemned!

I was so immersed in the dark thoughts spinning in my head that I didn't notice the three SS guards on the opposite corner until they were about two hundred yards away. One appeared to be directing the other two, giving them instructions.

No matter, I'd take the next left, head around the block and avoid them.

But as I got only twelve yards from the turnoff, something seemed familiar about the SS guard giving instructions; and in that moment, as if he felt my gaze on him or a spark of recognition had also hit him then, he turned more directly to look at me. Schnabel!

I kept up a steady pace the remaining five yards toward the turn, shifting my gaze to straight-ahead nonchalance, as if nothing was amiss.

Though just before I took the turn, I saw Schnabel hastening at a rapid pace toward me, one of the other guards following close at his heel.

As soon as I was fully into the turn and out of sight, I also started walking at a rapid pace, almost at a run.

A busier street, but not enough people around to get lost among. Schnabel would easily see me. And it was mostly residential—no shops or hotels I could suddenly dive into.

As I was halfway along, I saw Schnabel and the guard turn the corner running at full pelt, now only a hundred or so yards behind me. All pretense lost, I started running flat out, too, the shout of "Hey du, halt!" coming from Schnabel as I was just thirty yards from the end of the street.

The few people around were slow in paying attention—the shout was distant, and they weren't sure at first it related to me.

I turned right at the end. A busier street, Argentinierstrasse. Any shouts from behind would hopefully be lost among the bustle of people and traffic. I looked frantically around for shops, bars or hotels to dive into before Schnabel turned the corner. Nothing! But then I noticed the tram at a stop forty yards ahead, three or four people getting on.

I put on an extra spurt towards it—at least seeing people running for a tram wasn't an unusual sight in the city—and I'd just tucked in behind the last person getting on when Schnabel and the guard appeared around the corner forty yards away.

Another shout of *"Hey du, halt!"*—but it was half-lost among the bustle and traffic noise on the street.

My heart was in my mouth, though, as I got on and paid, fearing that as they got closer, Schnabel's shouts would be heard and the tram driver would hold up. A more insistent shout of "halt!" did come a moment later—but it was lost among the grind and trundle of the tram moving away.

I went only a few rows down, keeping well away from the back where through the rear window I caught a glimpse of Schnabel and the guard receding, their run faltering and finally stopping as they gave up the ghost.

My trapped breath eased out. I decided not to get off at the next stop or the one after, in case Schnabel or the guard got a second wind and decided to start running again after the tram.

But then as the tram pulled away from the second stop, I noticed an SD guard get on, initially shielded among a group of people. I quickly moved down the tram, as if I, too, had just got on and was finding my seat, finally choosing one near the back.

For a moment, I feared that Schnabel might have radioed ahead—but the SD guard didn't appear to be looking for anyone in particular, just studiously checking identity cards as he went down the aisle. This was exactly why Mathias and I had avoided public transport the past few weeks—but then what other choice had there been with Schnabel on my tail?

I looked desperately out of the window, timing the distance to the next stop. I needed to get off before he reached me!

The tram was only half-full, so he was making quick work of it—already just past the exit door. I'd have to pass him to get out.

"Ihre Karten bitte. Cards please?"

Four seats ahead. The tram finally started to slow in its approach to the next stop.

I got up when he was just two seats ahead. But I'd mistimed it. He made quick work of checking the cards of the couple at his side—turned to me expectantly, as if there was still time to check my card before the tram stopped.

I fumbled, reached into my jacket, praying the blood-rush to my face wasn't too evident—but at the last second the woman whose card he'd just viewed and handed back distracted him, asking the directions to Ressel Park.

The tram screeched to a stop, the doors opening. I held a hand half-up in apology as I rushed out, eager not to miss my stop.

I paced quickly away, as if I was focused solely on where I was headed—a set appointment or perhaps late for work—and didn't pause or look back until I heard the tram trundle into the distance and knew I was out of sight. I closed my eyes for a moment, catching at my breath. I'd made it!

But I was now over half a mile from home and still had to run the gauntlet of possible SD or SS guards in between.

I ducked into a phone kiosk halfway along Mittersteigstrasse and called Mathias. "I think I, too, am ready now to take Julian's advice."

"Why? Have you spoken to Hannah already?"

"No, I haven't." Clara Ebner's heartbreaking account still burned through my mind. "But I heard a story earlier that might help her decide."

12

All Jews, Romani and Mischlinge are hereby forbidden from attending movie theaters, the opera and concert halls.

Mathias

When we met at Café Mozart that Tuesday at 3 p.m., Julian looked more worn and ragged than I could recall seeing him before. He also had two or three days' growth, which was unlike him; usually he was clean-shaven. Even his unlit burgundy Sobranie in his silver holder didn't match his shirt or jacket today, which were light and olive green, respectively.

And as Johannes related Clara Ebner's agonizing account, Julian seemed to sink down farther. He shook his head. "So many stories I'm hearing like this now."

With his harrowed look, staring blankly into space for a moment, as if in search of a solution that wasn't quite there, I asked, "Are you okay, Julian?"

"Yes, yes." He snapped to, smiling tautly. "Just that I've heard most of those stories in just the past week or so. Between phone calls and personal visits, hardly chance to breathe."

"What do you think happened in Clara's case?" Johannes asked after a pause in respect of Julian's recent burden of Anschluss stories.

"I think she could be right," Julian said, taking a sip of coffee. "I think it could be through church records. As you know, the Nazis have always had an uneasy relationship with the Church. Yet they know that most Austrians are Catholic or Lutheran and take their beliefs seriously—they can't afford to upset them. So I think that attitude—halfway between laissez-faire and sufferance—has been on the understanding that many church records should be opened to them. Almost as if to say, *If you let us flush out the hidden Jews in our midst, we'll leave the rest of you alone.*"

"Incredible that the Church would agree to that," Johannes said, half closing his eyes for a second; the burden clear on his face. How safe might his own family be?

"It's by no means an open arrangement," Julian said. "So how easily records are offered up will differ from parish to parish, one priest to another. Indeed, some priests are actively shielding records, others even assisting Jews and helping them escape."

Johannes shrugged, as if that roulette-wheel situation was scant assurance. "Clara conceded that it could have come about through other ways. Lot of eyes and ears out there now, she said."

I looked briefly around in the café. I was getting to the point of hardly feeling comfortable anywhere anymore. But our table was toward the back again and a clear two yards from the next table. With our voices kept low, we couldn't be overheard. Still, though, even the occasional glance our way would make me feel anxious.

And I felt an extra pang of concern now with Johannes's plight—suddenly realizing that his own family, despite being half-Catholic, might not be safe. I recalled the words of his father, my uncle Samuel, to me practically on his deathbed. *Take care of Johannes. Keep an eye out for him. My death will hit him hard, and he's not as strong as you.* Partly due to my being fifteen years older than Johannes, partly my experience, but I understood the plea: Samuel was asking me to be a sort of replacement father figure and mentor to Johannes after he'd gone.

Julian suddenly looked up and held one hand up toward the entrance. I looked over to see Josef Weber walking toward us.

"Sorry, I was about to tell you that I'd asked Josef to join us here today—to discuss another possible option I had in mind." Julian checked his watch. "But he's turned up six or seven minutes earlier than planned..." Julian's voice trailed off as Josef approached. Greetings, hearty handshakes and backslaps all around, another coffee ordered for Josef from the nearby waiter.

"I met him just the other week," Josef commented with a jaded exhalation as things settled back down. "This Schnabel fellow." Josef took out a packet of Sports and offered me one, which I accepted. He knew that neither Julian nor Johannes smoked, and I'd in fact cut back to only five a day a few years back; but now with Anschluss I was up to twelve a day or more.

After blowing out his first plume of smoke, Josef told us about being introduced to Schnabel in Der Blaue Engel by a fellow officer from his own station. "That's why I didn't find much on him on file. He's newly arrived from Linz. 'Where our beloved Führer spent much of his childhood,' in his own words."

I nodded thoughtfully. "And your overall impression of him?"

"Very curt, very exact." Josef held a hand out. "On the face of it, a die-hard Nazi. What you see is what you get."

But I noticed an uncertainty behind Josef's eyes. I knew that look. "But what?"

Josef nodded thanks as the waiter set his coffee down, took a sip. "Just that, well, nobody's that gung ho a Nazi, totally committed, are they? There's always some bit reserved for themselves, their own thoughts." He eased a reluctant smile. "Maybe not as much as I reserve—but always something. Some little corner."

I grimaced. "Except right now everyone might be afraid to admit or show that reserve. They have to appear totally committed."

"True. There is much of that now." Josef tapped his cigarette in the ashtray. "Except that if it's partly an act—you wouldn't find out how much personal reserve they had until they were pushed hard."

We fell silent for a moment.

Johannes took a sip of coffee, then asked Julian, "You mentioned 'another possible option'?"

Josef looked at Julian keenly. "I think we need to determine whether Mathias and Johannes are committed to leaving before looking at other options and involving my contacts."

I sank into thought for a moment. How to explain rationally the nightmare past few weeks—the upending of every precept I'd ever held dear? "I can't speak for Johannes, but initially leaving was the last thing I wanted to consider. I still have heavy concerns that my mother wouldn't even survive a journey of any length." I held a hand out. "But with how things have been these past weeks, I don't see any other choice anymore."

Julian looked at Johannes. "And do you feel the same way now?"

Johannes admitted that he did. His initial worry had just been for himself, but he always thought his family would be safe. "But now with Clara Ebner's story, I'm far from sure anymore." He closed his eyes again briefly in penance. "And yet I feel almost guilty using that to convince Hannah—see her cut off from her whole family."

"There is another option," Julian said after a weighted pause; a last moment of consideration before sharing it. "In name and spirit—as you both now have professed being committed to— you would leave the country, along with your families. But in essence you would remain here—though not at all as the people you are now." He held a palm toward us. "Although to make clearer how that would happen, I would need to share the story of one of my other clients, Luis Brennel."

If there was one thing Julian loved, it was telling a story, a yarn. But having simmered us to the desired level of confusion and piqued our curiosity, he dived into the story of Luis Brennel in grand style.

Brennel had been a ghostwriter for many years, usually for political or dissident figures, many of whom no longer lived in Austria. The books often caused outrage with the political figures and parties that were the main subjects, but the named authors on the covers—various dissidents and rival politicians— were safe from reproach or attack because they lived abroad. "And nobody bothered Luis Brennel, because they had no idea he was actually the author of those books." Julian waved his silver cigarette holder briefly to one side, as if it was a conductor's baton. "Besides, Luis shouldn't have been held to blame, because he was merely conveying the ideas and thoughts of those various politicians and dissidents, who for the most part couldn't write for toffee—thus Luis's intervention, usually recommended by me. Which was why I felt responsible when one day his life was threatened."

Four years ago Brennel had written a book on behalf of Helmut Konig, an early defector from the National Socialist Party in Germany. Konig had in fact been one of the founding members of the party, but had fallen out with Hitler over various policy issues. "Worse still, he saw the danger of those policies and Hitler's overall agenda and ambitions. After breaking away, Konig wanted to write a book about his experiences, in part as a form of warning to the German people." Julian sighed. "Problem being, while his thoughts and feelings were strong and fiery, his writing style was clumsy and rambling, so I introduced him to Luis Brennel to ghostwrite the book. The arrangement was that Brennel's name would not appear anywhere on the cover or there be any reference to him inside—as the case with other books Luis had written on behalf of political dissidents." Julian took a hasty sip of coffee, looked at his cigarette holder with its unlit Sobranie in the ashtray, commenting wistfully, "God, if ever I was in need of a cigarette, it's now." Josef offered him one of his, but Julian declined. "No, no. I must be good."

"The book came out and was a bestseller in Austria. Particularly among Dollfuss and Schuschnigg supporters. It even sold well for the first eighteen months in Germany, too, until the stage that Hitler had risen fully to power and had the book banned. Hitler supporters and the Nazis were of course furious and there were calls for Konig's blood, with numerous death threats against him—but he was at that point safely ensconced in Stockholm, Sweden, with his wife and family."

Julian paused for a second, his expression pained. This next part was obviously difficult. "But at some point, it came out that Luis Brennel had written the book for Konig." Julian held out a palm. "We don't even know how it came out. But suddenly much of that anger was directed toward Luis—even though he'd been little more than a conduit for Konig's thoughts and views. Luis started to receive death threats too. But unlike Konig, Luis was very much here and visible in Vienna. Something needed to be done."

We'd become so wrapped up in Julian's story about Luis Brennel that we hadn't at first noticed Otto holding a hand up toward us, looking eagle-eyed through the front entrance. And when we did, we thought it might be just a false alarm like last time. But as Otto started frantically waving toward us, we realized that this time it was real. Someone was heading our way!

I stubbed out my cigarette, and Johannes, Julian and I rushed quickly for the back door to the kitchen, praying that we might make it in time.

Josef watched Heinrich Schnabel talk for a moment with Otto by the café entrance before Schnabel lifted his gaze and noticed Josef at his table toward the back. With one hand half-lifted briefly in acknowledgment, a subdued Heil Hitler, Schnabel approached.

"Ah, Inspector Weber, no less. I said our paths would cross again." He smiled ingratiatingly. "I see you are indeed preceding me in police matters—including finding out which Jews might be regular customers here."

"Among my many other duties on my patch," Josef answered obliquely. "First and foremost, obviously, pursuing serious crime and the people responsible."

"Yes, of course." Schnabel looked back towards Otto Karner, beckoning him with one hand, as if he was a waiter. As Otto came up to the table: "Perhaps you could impress upon Mr. Karner here the good sense in informing us about the Jewish customers he has. Not just for his own sake, but those of his other customers. Not forcing me to return with a couple of SD guards to go table to table demanding to see their identity cards."

"Yes, I'll do my best," Josef said primly. While such identity checks were regular occurrences on public transport and at general gatherings, they were almost unheard of at high-class cafés like the Mozart, Sperl or Central, or indeed the opera or society concerts and balls. Almost as if the cream of Austrian society must remain unsullied by all this unsavory "Jew hunting." Josef smiled tightly. "I'll appeal to his better nature. If indeed he has one."

"Indeed," Schnabel agreed with a barely concealed gloat, as if to say: *At last you're seeing reason, becoming more one of us*. As he turned and surveyed the crowd in the café, Josef raised a brow at Otto, making it clear he was just playing to the gallery. "Because it's simply not conceivable that in a café of this size, there would not be regular Jewish clients. And I'm not talking about the prominent ones—the Freuds, Bondys, Herzogs and Schiffmans—we know about those. I'm talking about all those 'hidden Jews' our Führer has recently talked about. I'm sure Mr. Karner knows all too well who those are among his customers." Schnabel spoke as if Karner wasn't there, yet stared at him keenly as if he was very much there.

But then Schnabel's gaze suddenly shifted as he became more aware of Josef's table: three spare coffee cups, two of them still a third-full, and a cigarette stubbed out halfway.

"Some company recently left have they, Inspector Weber?"

Josef nodded. "Yes. Two sergeants and a constable I was briefing. Once I've made it clear what I want from them, I want them to get on with their duties—not sit here smiling at me as they finish their coffees."

"I see."

Josef's nerves were racing, but his hands were steady, the only outward sign a small nerve pulsing in his neck as he observed Schnabel's reaction.

Schnabel appeared to accept his account, or at least not openly doubt it. But then as Schnabel surveyed the café again, his eyes seemed to fix on something toward the kitchen door at the back. His eyes narrowing as they focused on the object, Schnabel started his way toward it.

Cold storage. It seemed fitting that that's where we'd hear the final part of Julian's account about Luis Brennel and how it might relate to us—because that's how it had felt the last few weeks: our lives on hold, partly frozen.

Having gone first of all into the bustling kitchen, we'd feared that if anyone peered through the glass porthole in its door, they'd see us. So we'd been pointed by one of the pastry chefs toward the cold-storage larder to one side.

We sat in there silently for the first minute, breath held, eyes anxiously on the larder door in case it burst open any second and we were discovered. But then it seemed strange sitting there saying nothing; and, realizing we couldn't be heard beyond the thick door and the clatter of the kitchen beyond, Julian started speaking again. Though sotto voce, just in case.

"So, this problem with Luis's life threatened—how best to solve it?" He looked at us and gestured. "And Luis was in a similar, if not worse, situation than the two of you—four children, his mother and father both elderly, and his wife with a rare blood condition and in need of regular transfusions. Leaving was not an option, or certainly not a good one." Julian eased out a resigned breath. "So that's when I introduced Luis to some contacts Josef had told me about the year before."

I was reminded that Julian's association with Josef went back longer than my own; in fact, it had been Julian who had first recommended Josef to me for crime-procedural research for my books. Julian went on to describe a chain of forgers, notaries and document clerks in hospitals, morgues, and birth and land registry offices that had helped Luis Brennel bury his old identity and establish a new name and life.

Julian sighed. "But it's far from an easy exercise, and costly too. You'd be looking at losing 30 to 40 percent of everything you have. And 15 to 20 percent reduction to ensure a quick sale of your properties, then the rest paying this chain of people—some of them indeed who have previously gone through the process themselves." Julian shrugged. "But then what price on your life and welfare?"

Johannes's sullen contemplation lifted after a second. "I suppose at least better than the 80 or 90 percent I hear gets lost trying to leave the country."

"Yes. And we see that in particular now with Freud's case," Julian said. "He'll have to forfeit most of his assets in order to leave. And while his wife and daughter might be allowed out too—it might be several months before they can do so. Almost as if they're being held here as a ransom against Freud saying anything bad about the Reich." Julian shook his head. "They're even asking him to sign a paper declaring that he's been treated well and fairly by the Nazis before he goes."

I joined Julian in shaking my head lamentably. "Incredible."

Julian looked at me keenly. "But there's something else with the Freud case. It appears his four elderly sisters won't be allowed out, and there are even fears they might later be sent to camps." Julian sighed. "Which bodes badly for your mother, and partly why I'm mentioning this other option now."

I felt my stomach dip. Even if I and Johannes were allowed to leave, it appeared unlikely we'd get Lena out. "Are the people organizing all of this Jewish?"

"Some of them are now," Julian said. "And a few, too, that are also strong anti-Nazi, past Schuschnigg supporters. But this network started with Romani gypsies." Some latent recognition crossed Julian's face. "In fact, I think you previously met the cousin of their leader. A woman that Josef was with one day when he told me he bumped into you in Neumann's Department Store."

Quick flashback to a woman ten years Josef's junior with long dark hair and soulful eyes. "Originally from Valencia, if I recall." The main thing to stick in my mind from when I next saw Josef and teased him about what a rare beauty like that was doing with a lug like him.

"Yes. That was the cover story for her. That she came here as a young child with her father from Valencia twenty years ago when he took a valet's job at the Imperial hotel. But she's a Romani gypsy, and her cousin has since arranged new identities for a number of other Romani too." Julian took a fresh breath. "Plus a number of Jews and dissidents, particularly with the advent of Anschluss."

"And what are the risks involved?" I inquired.

"The risks attached are high. If your false identity was uncovered—deceiving the Nazis like this, you would face almost certain execution or consignment to a camp." Julian met my gaze steadily, morosely. "But so far nobody arranged by this network has been exposed."

Almost certain death or consignment? I felt myself begin to

shiver, a light cramp gripping my left leg; though perhaps that was the chill of the larder getting to me. But then everything else faced so far—the Hitler rally in Heldenplatz, having to discuss my son's Mischling-Reich-citizen status with his headmaster, the cross nailed above my mother's door to deter looters, on edge with the sight of every SS guard, or sometimes even with the looks from some Austrian citizens—all of that felt like a slow death in any case. And running that gauntlet, maybe we were kidding ourselves anyway: consignment to a camp and death were all that awaited.

"These people with new identities are obviously moving from their homes," Johannes commented. "If they're not going out of the country, then where? To other small towns in Austria?"

"No, they're generally avoided," Julian said. "Newcomers are too easily noticed in a small town or village. So, it's often Vienna, but a completely different district to previously. Or sometimes other large towns—Graz, Linz, Salzburg. Someplace where it's easy to get lost among the general population." Julian was struck with an afterthought. "Though sometimes their new identities will originate from smaller towns. Because record keeping in those often wasn't too diligent and so—"

Julian broke off as we heard shuffling outside the larder door, the handle starting to turn.

My heart was in my throat, thinking that whoever Otto had frantically signaled us about had discovered our hiding place.

But as the door opened, Josef stood there with a strained smile. "It was Schnabel. He left a couple of minutes ago—it's safe and clear now." Josef held up a burgundy Sobranie, and Julian glanced down and noticed it was missing from his silver holder. "We'll have to be more careful in future. Thankfully, Schnabel thought that another of the Mozart's illustrious customers must have dropped it."

13

What is bad is whatever causes one to be threatened with loss of love. For fear of that loss, one must avoid it. This, too, is the reason why it makes little difference whether one has already done the bad thing or only intends to do it.

—*Sigmund Freud*

"Another one for your friends at the university to look at?" SS Junker Lange inquired as Kommissar Sauerwald was heading out the door with a cardboard box.

"Yes. Hopefully one of the last. My expertise covers a fair few areas, but some of this unfortunately steps outside of that." Sauerwald smiled tautly. "I want to make sure to get the valuations right."

Lange held his eyes on him as he made his way down the stairs with the box. "Do you want a hand with any of those?"

"No, it's okay. Some of these artifacts are quite valuable, and I wouldn't want you to be responsible if any of them are found damaged."

Just before he went from sight, Lange appeared to lose interest and turned from the doorway.

Hopefully, nothing untoward noticed by Lange.

For the first few days, Sauerwald had done nothing but read through Freud's voluminous papers and notes. It was only then that he decided to change tack from the strict instructions he'd been given. The boxes he took ended up in private storerooms in the bowels of the University of Vienna Library, privy only to himself and a select few others. The boxes he returned with were somewhat different; but he doubted this junior SS officer left to oversee him would know the difference between specialist Freud papers and general academic theses of scant value. The problem with appointing a lowly Junker because the exercise was seen as too tedious for anyone more senior.

Valuable artifacts were also often hidden under papers in the boxes, and where necessary, cheap replicas returned. In any case, from what he'd gleaned from Gestapo Heinz Piehler's instructions, various "Freud Circle" photos either in files or albums were their primary interest—so that was obviously what Junker Lange's main eye had been out for. But Sauerwald had been able to answer honestly: he'd seen none of those. No hiding or subterfuge had been necessary.

Johannes

As I put my key in our apartment door, I heard voices on the other side of it. I paused, listening closer, fearing we might have an unexpected visitor. A female voice answering Hannah, which relaxed me more—it wasn't an SD guard or anyone official, men exclusively controlled those roles—easing the last of my anxiety and my held breath as I fully opened the door, chiding myself that I was being ridiculous. A reminder of how quickly things had descended to this stage: I was afraid now to even walk into my own home.

My braving out any residual concerns was affirmed when I

heard Mrs. Fischer's voice. Magda Fischer was head of the Catholic women's league at our local church and lived only a couple of streets away. She came over every so often for tea and a chat with Hannah.

I'd just returned from visiting the local library. Only a few hundred yards away—partly why we'd chosen an apartment in the area—so little chance of passing any SD guards. I was still only going out rarely, Hannah did nearly all the shopping now: her ID card showed her as a hundred percent Catholic, a full-blown Reich citizen.

But I'd been putting off doing research on my latest book, and it hit me that I'd never seen any SS or SD intruding upon the quiet of the library. Similarly, I'd never seen them disturb a church congregation. Despite the Nazis' pig-trough brusqueness and brutality, some things appeared sacrosanct.

I was slow hanging up my hat and jacket in the hallway, didn't want to intrude too abruptly—but then Hannah's voice sailed out.

"Is that you, Johannes? Mrs. Fischer was just asking how your mother is?"

"She's fine." I walked in and greeted Magda Fischer with a smile. Ten years older than Hannah, she sat perched on the edge of the sofa, her dark corn hair as usual tied in a tight bun, the same light blue hat she wore to church at her side. "Thank you for asking."

"Because I was just telling Mrs. Fischer, Magda, that was why you weren't at the church last Sunday—because your mom wasn't well."

"Yes, yes. Of course." I caught Hannah's faint glare as she spoke. Obviously, that was the story she'd spun to Mrs. Fischer rather than admit that, despite the SS never disturbing church congregations, I'd been desperately afraid of the three-quarter-mile gauntlet to get there, with two checkpoint corners in between. So I'd sat alone at home for a couple of hours, a chance to get on with some work; except that, like so often recently, most of that was staring at a blank page, hoping for inspiration beyond the turmoil of my thoughts. "Just a little scare—nothing to worry about in the end."

"Good to hear." Mrs. Fischer nodded, took a sip of her tea. "I'm so glad those prayers we said for your mother appear to have helped."

"It seems so." I smiled gently. A year after my father's death, my mother had a heart attack and appeared near death's door at one point. Hannah and Magda Fischer had led prayers for her the following Sunday, and whether miraculous or purely coincidental, my mother had pulled through in grand style. So much so that shortly after she'd embarked on a strict fitness regime, walked everywhere she could, including the two miles from her home to city center. And just last year she'd gone on a hiking holiday near Innsbruck. My mother, Franciska, was probably one of the fittest sixty-three-year-olds in Vienna. The next on my list after talking to Hannah. Another reason I'd gone to the library: getting the right words in my mind for both of them. "She's recovered well."

Magda Fischer returned my smile sympathetically, and in the silence following it struck me that probably wasn't the main reason she'd visited. "I… I haven't finished them yet," I said, the realization sparking. "Although the poster should be finished by tomorrow."

When I'd returned from seeing Mathias and Julian at the Mozart, Hannah informed me that Mrs. Fischer had left a brief sermon and a poster for me to prepare. A skill I'd developed as a young calligrapher, ink-pen etching various elaborate type styles. Once Hannah had let slip about it at church, it was something I got roped into helping out with every now and then. The sermon had to be in Old Latin Italics, the poster in Gothic Luthersche.

"We don't need them until the Sunday after next," Mrs. Fischer reassured. "So I certainly wasn't chasing you up, Mr. Namal. We're very glad of the help as it is."

"Magda actually came about something else," Hannah offered. Then, as a brief silence fell again, she added, "Some tea might still be hot in the pot, if you want it."

"Yes. Thank you." Evident that they wanted to be left alone again, I went into the kitchen.

I couldn't see or hear Stefan around, so no doubt Hannah had asked him to remain in his room and keep quiet, so that there wasn't the awkwardness of having to explain to Mrs. Fischer why he wasn't at school. All of us tiptoeing around Anschluss, trying to pretend it wasn't happening.

Something else. As I poured a tea for myself, suddenly it struck me what that might be. I hadn't wanted to hit Hannah with the whole thing all at once: following Clara Ebner's harrowing story with immediately telling Hannah that the only options were to leave the country and her family behind, or we assume fresh identities. So I'd shared Clara's account two nights ago, then would let that settle in Hannah's mind for a day or so. I was in fact going to broach the rest last night, but again I'd put it off. Then in the silence of the library I'd worked the right words over again in my mind, resolving to tell Hannah as soon as I got back home. But then Magda Fischer had been here as I walked in.

I think much of my reluctance and procrastination was that even that first part on its own had been difficult for Hannah to accept, shaking her head halfway through, shadows heavy in her eyes. "Surely the Church wouldn't do that?"

Had Hannah got Magda Fischer over now to ask the same: *You know the church probably better than me. Would they do such a thing?* I went over to the kitchen door, listening for a moment. But from what I could hear, it just appeared to be inconsequential gossip: a slight limp from Pastor Venell as he'd approached the lectern that Magda hadn't noticed the week before. Is he alright? A totally inappropriate hat with bright flowers that Mrs. Hoegler had been wearing at the last service.

I sat back down at the kitchen table, glancing toward the

wooden plaque on the wall: Home Sweet Home, Trautes Heim, Glück allein, intertwined with roses, daisies and bluebells. But for how long? I contemplated wistfully. Although we'd been here half our married life and it felt like home, we didn't actually own the apartment. While that would make moving easier, it also meant that half the savings we'd put aside to buy our own place in a year or two would go to pay this chain of people to help us establish new lives and identities. Hannah's parents also said they'd help out financially when we were ready to buy— her father was a partner in an established bakery—but I could hardly urge Hannah to ask them to contribute to this: *Could you let us have that money so that we can leave or change our identities and hardly ever see you again?*

The options that Julian had laid out were stark: if we left the country, they might never see Hannah or their grandchildren again. If we changed identities, visits would be sparse and would have to be carefully arranged.

I wondered if that was why I was delaying telling Hannah. The choices were simply too horrendous. With always that final doom-laden line to try and make it more palatable: "But far better than risking ours or the children's lives." Shamefully, using the ultimate Nazi threat to make it easier to convince Hannah.

Which gave me mixed feelings about Magda Fischer's visit now. On one hand it was a reminder of a life we might soon be leaving behind—one more person to forget or we'd have to avoid. But while she was blathering away to my wife about mundane, petty church issues—which seemed even pettier and more inconsequential contrasted against the horrors outside—it was delaying me having to tell Hannah.

And so I was happy for the moment to sit in the kitchen and sip at my tea, looking thoughtfully at the flowery Home Sweet Home sign—putting off as long as possible the moment I'd have to throw a rock at it.

14

Extramarital relations between Jews or Gypsies with Reich citizens are forbidden. A Reich citizen is a subject who is of German or related blood, and proves by his conduct that he is willing and fit to faithfully serve the German people and Reich.

"I see you don't have any photos of your friends and associates in the Circle evident," Schnabel commented, admiring a couple of photos of Edgar Zilsel's family displayed on a sideboard.

"After Moritz Schlick's death and the dissolution of the Circle, there didn't seem much point in hanging on to them. The memories too painful."

"But I understand some meetings took place after that?"

Zilsel answered cautiously, unsure how much Schnabel might have learned. "We only had a couple of meetings after that, but they were of little importance. As you are no doubt aware, a number of Circle members left Vienna shortly after Schlick's death."

"Yes, I'm quite aware of that." Schnabel looked at Zilsel sharply. "You didn't hang on to any Circle photos for nostalgic reasons? Perhaps put them in folders or albums as Freud initially claimed his wife had done?"

"No. I don't have any of the old Circle group photos anymore. I threw them out over a year ago, along with a lot of old papers." The last thing Zilsel wanted to do was to give this Schnabel cause to search his home.

"I see." Schnabel held his stare on Zilsel for a moment. The last of the four visited on his checklist, the others had all answered in a similar vein or had claimed they hadn't had any photos taken with Circle members to start with. "It seems remarkable that among every other Circle member I've visited, not a trace of any old Circle photos remains. What are the odds on that, do you think?"

"I wouldn't know." Zilsel met Schnabel's stare firmly, despite his stomach doing somersaults. "I'm not a gambling man."

"Of course not. You're just a master mathematician." Schnabel smiled primly. "Very precise."

Josef

"What do you think your two friends will decide in the end?" Deya asked, tracing one finger absently on Josef's chest.

"I don't know. They might not both decide the same thing." Josef blew a plume of smoke toward the ceiling. "They're both weighing up perhaps not seeing some of their family ever again. But I don't think they've considered not seeing each other again. Which will be the case if they decide differently."

They were in Josef's second-floor apartment on Krugerstrasse, dappled orange light from the street playing across the bedroom ceiling. They'd left Der Blaue Engel just over an hour ago and were only halfway through their coffees before they started kissing, rapidly becoming more fervent as they removed each other's clothes on the way to the bedroom. Josef noticed their lovemaking had been more urgent and desperate of late, as if with Anschluss and the threat of war looming, they feared there might not be much more time left to enjoy it.

Deya was pensive. "Do you think either of them might decide to stay here in Vienna and simply keep their identities as they are?"

"I doubt it." Josef shrugged. "Certainly not Mathias. In fact, whenever he sees his mother, I have to run him there. She's six kilometers away, too far to walk, and he avoids public transport for fear of getting stopped by the SD or SS. He can't keep on like that."

Deya nodded. They both knew that once stopped and details taken, the option of changing identities became more difficult, if not impossible. And in some cases Jews were just summarily thrown in the back of a truck and sent to a concentration camp.

After another draw on his cigarette, Josef commented, "I was wondering whether we might go out to Danube Island this Sunday? Maybe take a picnic." The same routine every other Sunday. Deya would take Luciana to church in the morning, then Josef would pick them up straight after and they'd go out for half the day. Luciana would sit beaming in the back of Josef's car, knowing that Josef would later spoil her rotten with ice creams and treats. Practically the only time they all went out together as a family.

"Yes, I think that would be great. Luciana would look forward to it…me too." Deya fell silent, darker shadows drifting into her eyes after a moment. She took a fresh breath. "Something perhaps I should have mentioned before…that SS officer, Schnabel, he came back to the club four days after you first saw him there."

Josef looked across, trying to read into those shadows. "I could see you were bothered by him that first time. What did he say to you?"

"He said he didn't know why I was wasting my time with you. That with the new way of things now, you'd soon be a relic in the police force."

Josef smiled dryly. "Not only a nasty prick, but deluded too. Carried away with his own grandeur."

"That's why I didn't tell you initially. I knew it would upset you." Deya looked down for a second, her expression clouding. "But it's what he said when he came back to the club that bothered me more. He started getting friendly, buying me champagne—then got around to where I got my exotic looks from? When I told him it was my Spanish background, he raised a sharp brow, challenging, *Are you sure you're not a gypsy or a Jew?*" An edgier silence for a second. Deya gently took Josef's cigarette from his hand and drew on it before handing it back. "I shrugged it off with a disarming smile—*Of course not. Why on earth would you think that?* Initially, he'd been half-smiling, teasing—but then as he answered, *No particular reason*, his eyes seemed to be searching mine, as if he suspected I might be lying."

Josef shook his head. "All this madness. Maybe I should do what I should have done years ago. Make a decent woman of you so that you don't have to spend any more time with assholes like Schnabel. Not only playing games with you and testing you with comments like that, but…" His voice trailed off, realizing he might be getting into an area they'd agreed long ago to avoid. The thought of other men pawing at her.

"How would that help, Josef? If we were married and my background came out, your career would be ruined and you'd no doubt be joining me in a concentration camp. Your father's concerns would be proven right—become some sort of strange prophecy."

Josef sighed heavily. "You know my father changed his tune later on. His views softened, particularly about the Nazis."

"Yes, I know." Deya looked at Josef understandingly, tracing her finger again on his chest, though softer now, as if she was trying to soothe him.

Josef could almost hear the unspoken: *But we both know it was too late by then.* He looked up at the dappled street light playing across his bedroom ceiling.

The shadow of his father still hung over him.

His father had also been in the police force, part of the old school at Kärntnerstrasse station, which had no doubt helped Josef's early transition there. But there the advantage of being his father's son ended.

His father had been a Nazi supporter, the cause of many words between them. Yet in their heated debates, his father would describe himself as a "lukewarm" Nazi, didn't see himself as ardently racist against Jews and gypsies.

But when Josef fell in love with Deya, that was put strongly to the test. His father along with one other officer—by then long retired and dead—were the only ones at Kärntnerstrasse to know about Deya's buried gypsy background, having handled the past abuse case with her ex-husband. His father put his foot down. As if to say, *It's one thing being tolerant of gypsies and Jews, it's quite another to bring them into the family and marry them.*

Yet his father would never put that spotlight on his own racism, would always shift and deflect to others, other possible reasons: "If her gypsy background came out, just think what it would do to your career in the police? Or if you had children, how they might suffer in today's society, especially with Nazism on the rise?"

So Josef would always defer, put off his decision to confirm his love for Deya, marry her. And then when finally his father was ill and fading, it had been Josef putting it off: "I can't do that to him. Knowing how he feels about our marrying, it would kill him…"

Understandably, Deya got fed up with waiting and started seeing someone else. And when eight months later that relationship didn't work out, Deya started to work at Der Blaue Engel. She'd had enough of waiting in hopes of a serious relationship or marriage—she might as well use her beauty as best she could to carve out her independence and bring up her daughter.

Then, perversely, in his fading years, Josef's father's views about Nazism had changed. Or perhaps the increasingly hard-line shift in Nazism had widened that gulf from his own views.

But by then it was too late for Josef with Deya.

"I'm sorry," he muttered.

"Don't be," Deya placated. "Now wouldn't be the right time in any case."

Josef nodded forlornly. And now there'd be other excuses: Anschluss, more uncertainty, war possibly looming, busy with referrals to Lorenzo for new identities, comfortable now with her independence.

Would there ever be a right time for them?

15

Everyone has wishes which he would not like to tell to others, which he does not want to admit even to himself.

—*Sigmund Freud*

Mathias

We had it all planned. I sat in the front of Josef's car, Ivor in the back. Josef would swing around to pick up my sister, Erica, then we'd all head to my mother's house in Leopoldstadt for me to try and explain everything.

"Momma. Ivor and I have to leave Vienna, leave the country. For the sake of our well-being and possibly our lives. It's not safe for us here anymore." Then with my mother aghast and in shock, I'd offer, "But there is another possible option…"

I'd explain that we'd find a place almost identical in the south of Vienna and we'd move everything so that she'd have all her favorite things still around her. All the furniture my father had made. It would hardly seem any different. "Or we could find a large place all on one floor, if you felt it might be easier to get around such a place now…"

All planned. Until halfway there when we saw the roadblock ahead.

Josef slowed to a halt behind a tail of seven cars. Early evening, two soldiers were behind a small barrier with bright lamps, two other soldiers checking the IDs of two young men and a girl stood by the front car. One of the men was then turned around and a soldier started to pat him down, searching.

"What are we going to do?" I asked anxiously.

"I don't know." Josef stared ahead blankly. "Something's happened. They appear to be checking everyone."

We watched helplessly—the sense of being trapped, no possible escape—as they finished with the first car.

As flashlights flickered toward the next two cars in line, the punch from Josef came to the side of my face without warning. Then another quick jab, making my nose bleed.

"What the hell…"

"No time to explain. Bear with me," Josef said with a hissed breath. "There's a bottle of schnapps in my glove compartment. Take a few quick slugs and splash some on your jacket too." The flashlights started to drift back to the third and fourth cars in the line. "And quick!"

My ears still ringing and my cheek throbbing from the punches, I felt the schnapps burn down my throat, then did as Josef asked and splashed some on my jacket. I'd just tucked the bottle back into the glove compartment a second before one of the flashlight beams hit us.

"Now appear as bleary-eyed and woozy as possible," Josef said, hitting his horn and pulling out to pass the cars in front. As we approached the guards, one of them raised his machine gun and pointed it directly at us, the flashlight from a third guard also now fixing on our car. Josef flashed his headlamps in return, rolling down his window and holding his badge out.

"Inspector Weber, Kärntnerstrasse," he announced as he pulled alongside the first SD soldier with a flashlight. "Just picked this fellow up from a drunken brawl, got to get him to the station."

The soldier's flashlight shifted to the back seat. "And the boy?"

"His son. He was with him when the fight broke out between two fathers at a birthday party." Josef shrugged despairingly. "Some parents."

The soldier nodded. "Shouldn't you be headed the other way for Kärntnerstrasse?"

"Yes. But I was on my way to a robbery scene in Praterstern when this fight spilled out onto the pavement practically in front of me." Another shrug. "Busy night. My sergeant is already at the robbery scene. He'll keep an eye on these two while I investigate."

I felt the flashlight on me more directly then, half blinding me, so it wasn't too difficult to appear bleary-eyed as Josef had suggested. For a moment I feared the soldier was going to ask me out of the car anyway to check my ID. But after a final quick appraisal, he straightened up and waved us on.

"Local police inspector with two suspects," he called out to his fellow guards. "Let him through."

I kept my gaze fixed stolidly ahead as we went past the remaining guards, didn't dare look at them, and Josef sped up quickly the other side, as a police inspector heading to a crime scene would. I noticed Josef's eyes drift briefly to the rearview mirror.

"They're busy with the next cars in line, aren't paying us any attention." Then with a taut grimace my way. "Sorry about that."

"Needs must," I said, tentatively touching my bruised cheek. I smiled back wryly at Ivor, who had been silent throughout it all. "Josef doesn't usually hit me."

"I understand." A hesitant, uncertain return smile, as if with the events of the past few weeks he wasn't certain of anything anymore. Bit by bit shutting down his emotions as a protective shield.

As we pulled up in front of my mother's house after picking up Erica, there was the shadow of an SD guard farther along the road—but he was too distant to make us out clearly.

Nevertheless, Josef lifted up one hand toward him, as if to say: *I'm just going into my house.* An acknowledging wave came in return. I handed Josef my keys and we went in.

On the way over, seeing the bruise on my face, Erica had asked how I got it. "Don't ask," I mumbled grouchily.

But calling out in greeting to my mother as I went up the stairs to her room, I worried that my appearance would make things more difficult to explain, that I'd have to change the preamble I'd prepared in my mind. But in a strange, perverse way it helped.

"My goodness, Mathias, what's happened to you?" she exclaimed as she saw my face. She scowled and sniffed the air. "And have you been drinking?"

I explained about the roadblock and Josef having to hit me and invent a story to get through it. A strange expression on her face as she struggled to comprehend, but not far different from the aghast look I'd envisaged when I got around to telling her we might have to leave the country for our safety.

"Obviously, I can't go through things like that every time I have to come and see you," I said with a resigned sigh. "We need to start thinking about making some other plans."

"Yes, I think we do," my mother said gently after a moment's contemplation. She called out for Erica to make some tea, then sat back in her armchair and looked at me expectantly, as if this was a conversation she'd known had been coming for some while.

"Well, it appears we've explored every avenue," Piehler commented, sighing dejectedly. "I'm not sure what other options remain."

"Yes, I daresay." Schnabel felt a sense of defeat too, however much it went against the grain. Even more frustrating given the fact that with each visit to Freud Circle members it became increasingly evident that some conspiracy was afoot over old Circle member photos. Piehler had been right: those photos were seen as particularly damning and so had to be concealed or destroyed at any cost. "Would it perhaps help if you went back and questioned Freud's wife further, or I did the same with these remaining four Circle members?"

"No. I don't think that would be wise. Freud's case had to be handled with kid gloves, which didn't sit that comfortably with me." Piehler shrugged. "We even had him sign a declaration of how fair and well he'd been treated. It wouldn't be seen in a good light if we went against that by putting the thumbscrews on his wife or close associates."

"I understand."

Piehler grimaced. "That's partly why I involved you. Not only the extra legwork involved—which I have limited time for right now—but the fact that even my questioning of Freud's close associates might be seen as overstepping the mark. Whereas you, since they're in your district, could get away with that quite innocently."

Schnabel nodded. Probably also the reason why they were meeting now in this nondescript café on the edge of his first district rather than in Piehler's office.

"My own experience with these conspiracies is that they have a limited life. Inevitably there's some weakness or fracture that will make them fail." Schnabel knocked back the last of his coffee. "No doubt, we'll prevail in the end."

"No doubt."

Though from Piehler's tame smile in accord, Schnabel could see that Piehler took the comment in the spirit it had been offered: two senior Reich officers reassuring each other of future success to salve the wounds of this recent failure.

16

Reich party, trade and women's organizations are urged to in-form and "educate" their members not to shop at Jewish-owned stores or relate in business or socially with Jews.

Johannes-Andreas

November 1938

The first thing to alert me was the tinkling of glass close by. We no longer lived in a strongly Jewish neighborhood. With our new identities, we'd moved to the southwest of Vienna to the Neubau area, about a mile north of the Westbahnhof station.

At most, there might have been twenty Jewish-owned shops in the area, so when I heard the tinkling of glass in the next street, followed not long after by a loud bang and shattering only doors away, I knew something was wrong.

As I looked out the window of our third-floor apartment, I

saw that it was Stein's, a Jewish-owned delicatessen five doors along on the opposite side, with its window smashed. Two brownshirts and three other young men in plain clothes stood in front of it, having thrown bricks and finally a handcart through the shop window. Opening our window, I could hear the faint tinkling of other windows being smashed farther away and see some fires burning in the distance toward the city center.

"I should go and see what's happening," I said to Hannah, a yard behind me and also looking worriedly through the window.

"No, don't go," she said. "You should stay here with me and the children."

"I suppose you're right," I said after a moment, though still not entirely happy with that decision. It was almost as if Hannah was saying, and I was agreeing: *It's not our fight anymore.* And in many ways it wasn't. We were different people now, or at least had to cling to those new identities. Conform to type. And the last thing a fully-fledged Austrian Catholic family would be doing is showing concern because a few Jewish-owned shops were having their windows smashed.

We looked different now, particularly me, and we all had different names: I was now Andreas Siebert, Hannah was now Stefanie, and our children were Dominik and Nadia rather than Stefan and Elena.

I'd had the most facial surgery, but even that had been minimal—only a slight thinning and shortening of my nose and tightening of my jawline, the rest dealt with by hair coloring—and Hannah-Stefanie even less so. Her jawline had been trimmed slightly and her hair tinted light brown with a red tinge, whereas I'd gone fully blond. It was one of the few times I'd been blonder than my wife.

The children hadn't undergone any facial surgery at all— Lorenzo, heading the identity-change team, had argued that children changed facially in any case through the younger years, so that was dealt with purely through hair coloring: Elena-Nadia going slightly darker, Stefan-Dominik slightly lighter; though because his new appearance was closest to the original Stefan, he was asked to wear glasses as well—clear glass, so that it didn't affect his eyesight.

The result was that we certainly all looked different; and, most importantly, we had fresh papers to support our new identities. I could finally breathe easy walking the city.

It had been tough getting used to at first, and I'd stood in front of the mirror looking at my new face, saying repeatedly Andreas Siebert, Andreas Siebert…Andreas Siebert, so that I wouldn't forget it. And I had the children do the same because they might be prone to let slip more than I or Hannah-Stefanie.

It was even tougher on the children, my heart breaking at one point as Elena-Nadia had asked why she couldn't see any of her old friends anymore. I explained as best I could, but children can be particularly open and blunt without realizing it.

"But you're only half-Jewish," she protested, still not fully understanding. "And I'm mostly Catholic. So why should that affect us?"

"I know. It's unfair, and I'm sorry." I reached out and gently touched her cheek, my eyes closing for a moment, as if in penance. "But you wouldn't wish anything bad to happen to Papa, would you?"

"No, I wouldn't." A hurt pout, fighting back the tears, as she nestled against my shoulder.

The next morning on the radio, we heard that many Jewish-owned shops had their windows smashed, Jewish homes looted and synagogues burned down. Kristallnacht, the Night of Broken Glass, it was termed, with apparently similar attacks throughout much of the rest of Austria.

My curiosity got the better of me. I couldn't wait to see first-hand what had happened. Besides, there was one particular place I wanted to check on.

Once Stefanie—I needed to stop thinking of her anymore as

Hannah, and the children the same—had left to take Dominik and Nadia to school, I, too, left the apartment. Another advantage of our new identities, there'd been no problem finding a new school for Dominik-Stefan. His history from our new family originally from Salzburg showed no record of fighting in school, and, probably most importantly, no Jewish blood.

I caught a tram part of the way, then walked the rest. I was no longer nervous about my new identity card being checked. The first time I had been, but it had passed muster then and also twice more in the six months since it was issued.

I'd noticed several shop windows smashed looking from the tram, some with glass being swept up—presumably by the owners or concerned neighbors. But I'd wanted to walk the last part to see close-up how many shops in our old neighborhood had been affected.

Rosen's, one of Stefanie's favorite milliners, I saw had its window smashed, a man and teen boy busily boarding it up. Similarly, furniture store Isaacson's in the next street, although that was already fully boarded up. Daubed over the shop signs or fronts—as with many others I'd so far passed—were star symbols and JUD.

Turning the next corner, I found myself in front of Ebner's. It was boarded up, but nothing daubed on it. I'd passed Clara Ebner's name along with her story on to Lorenzo, but had no idea since what had happened to her and her family. Whether they'd decided to change their identities or leave the country.

"Mr. Namal—is that you?"

The voice from my side startled me. I'd been told not to respond to my old name, so even though I recognized the voice, I turned slowly.

I squinted at the woman, not totally sure it was who I thought it was, and I saw her return the same uncertain look. Clara Ebner certainly looked different—her hair now wavy and, like mine, far blonder, her face a shade gaunter. If it wasn't for the fact that she was standing in front of her old shop, I probably wouldn't have put two and two together.

Still, I was tentative when I asked, "Is that you, Clara?"

She just nodded numbly. Then with a faint smile. "If you're after a new typewriter ribbon, I'm afraid you're out of luck. We closed five months ago." Her expression was still slightly doubtful, quizzical. "I wasn't at all sure at first it was you."

"Me too—with you." I smiled tightly back; my question about her identity-change choice answered too. "Some things at least appear to be working."

"I only came by this morning because of the riots last night. I wondered whether they might have ripped away the boarding and tried to break in."

I nodded. "Still appears intact. They also don't seem to have daubed it with JUD or symbols like many other shops."

"That might be because the shop was never officially listed as Jewish-owned on…"

Clara's voice trailed off as she noticed two SDs and a brown-shirt on the corner. We decided to walk along the road away from them, and I got the rest of her story: on property registers, the shop had been listed as Austrian Catholic–owned. She and her brother had opted for identity changes, but her parents felt they were too deeply into Gestapo questioning for that.

"They told the Gestapo that Felix and I had left the country, but we'd already in fact gone to Lorenzo for our identity changes. My parents applied to leave shortly after, but they were refused. Two months later they were shipped to Dachau." Clara looked down, chewed at her bottom lip. "I'm not sure if they're even still alive."

"I'm so sorry." I sighed before lifting to a more hopeful tone. "Is there any way you can find out?"

Clara shook her head. "Felix and I aren't meant to exist—not at least as we were. So we can't risk trying to make contact."

I nodded morosely. One of the downsides of identity changes.

In some sense we'd already ceased to exist: a sort of halfway house to what the Nazis had planned for us. I brought Clara quickly up to date with my own plight with my family, then paused as we got to the end of the street and it looked like we might be going in different directions.

"I don't even know your new first name," I said. I watched her brow knit, as if she might be breaking some unspoken rule. I quickly offered: "Mine's Andreas…we don't need to know last names. It's just so I get your new name right if I happen to see you and greet you again."

Her expression lifted. She smiled; the first fully open smile since we'd met. "It's Jessica."

"Jessica… Jessica. That's a nice name." I smiled and gave her a hug as we parted. "Well, it's good to see you, Jessica. Hope to see you again." Knowing as I said it, and she answered the same in return, that it was unlikely. We'd probably never see each other again.

I got into trouble with Lorenzo over my meeting with Clara-Jessica when I next saw him.

"I told you very clearly at our initial meeting—new identities are not to be shared with anyone from your past."

I defended that I hadn't. That Clara had confirmed that it was indeed her before I did the same. "Otherwise, I wouldn't have said anything."

"Yes, but just imagine for a moment that you hadn't been who you made out—that would have put Clara in an exposed situation. And if she'd been playing a similar dupe, you'd have been exposed."

It took me a moment to grasp what Lorenzo was getting at. I nodded contritely. "I'm sorry. It won't happen again."

"Make certain it doesn't."

Lorenzo's eyes seemed to bore right through me. He was four years older than Deya. Mathias, whose new name was now

Daniel, and I were among the few who knew that they were even related due to Josef making the initial recommendation. A stocky five foot ten, he was surprisingly agile for his size, with a long moustache—which had already changed color twice, along with his hair and name, since we'd first met him—and brooding eyes that would as quickly lift into an easy smile. As a result, he came across as menacing and unpredictable—but I suppose it couldn't be easy running an underground network like this, and he needed those darker, warning looks to keep everyone in line.

"As I said when we first met." Lorenzo blew out smoke from a cheroot he'd just lit. "The most important thing is not being seen by people you might know from before—particular as a family. Because while one of you on your own shouldn't be recognized, together you might strike a chord. So avoid old haunts with your family." Lorenzo stared the message home a second longer before he eased into a warmer smile. "Now, let us join the others."

Lorenzo had at least granted the courtesy of keeping this little reprimand private, beckoning me into a side room as he heard I'd met with Clara Ebner. As we walked back into the main floor of the warehouse, the fourteen there, including Mathias, were halfway through a fresh game of bar billiards. Three had been at our initial induction, one was Lorenzo's new Jewish partner in the network, Alois Mayell, and the other nine I'd never met before.

The bar billiards was part of Lorenzo's cover for these meetings. He'd choose different vacated or derelict buildings around the city and set up the bar billiards table, mainly because it was more portable than a standard billiards table. If they were disturbed by the SD inquiring what a dozen men were doing having a secret meeting, the bar billiards with side bets was the cover story. Such gambling games weren't strictly legal, but the SS and

SD generally turned a blind eye or smiled it off. Far better than them suspecting a clandestine activist meeting.

"Okay, let me return to why I've called you all here today," Lorenzo announced, holding a hand up to stop the game. He cleared the mushroom skittles and nodded to Mayell, who came over with a black carryall and put it on the table.

"Just a few weeks ago, the identity of someone in our network was uncovered." Lorenzo held up a hand as an unsettled murmur rose. "The first one in over ninety people successfully set up with new identities—so perhaps not too much to worry about. But the thing is, when he saw the SS truck in front of his building and heard them coming up the stairs, he cut his wrists." Lorenzo grimaced. "Problem being, he wasn't that successful at it. They bandaged him and hauled him away, and we heard that two days later he died."

Heavy silence fell. At length, a man along from me ventured: "Do you think he was questioned, perhaps even tortured?"

"We simply don't know." Lorenzo shrugged. "Hopefully not—or, at least, if he was, he didn't say anything. Otherwise others would have no doubt received visits by now." As an unsettled murmur resurfaced, Lorenzo held a hand up again. "Thing is, he might simply have been in a hospital awaiting shipment to a camp and died from blood loss or infection. We don't know. But with the possibility that he might have been tortured and could have talked—I need to remind you all of what I stressed at our first meeting: it's vital that you never at any time disclose information about this group."

"We need to safeguard against that," Alois supported.

I exchanged a look with Mathias-Daniel, wondering if he was thinking the same: we hardly knew anything of value about this shadowy network to impart in any case. Our new identities had all been prepared by various notaries, forgers, clerks and morgue workers who we'd never met or knew the names of, and our new papers simply passed to us. Even for our brief surgery we'd been blindfolded and didn't know where we'd been or who had operated on us. And, along with Lorenzo's and Alois's appearances and identities changing each time and having no fixed abode that we knew of, little more than shadows, we also had no idea of the names of the others in this gathering now.

"What happened to his wife and family, if he had one?" I asked. With a family of four to worry about, perhaps it was more on my mind than others.

"His wife and daughter were out at the time," Lorenzo said, his expression taut. "Thankfully, we managed to get them away to safety and arrange new identities."

Lorenzo's eyes shifted from me to run across the group momentarily for any other questions, then he nodded somberly at Alois. "As part of that safeguard mentioned, it's time for you to choose your poison, gentlemen."

Alois tipped up the carryall and an assortment of handguns spilled out onto the green baize of the bar–billiard table.

"We're not like some spy network where we have cyanide pills if you're captured," Alois said. "So if you hear the Gestapo coming up the stairs for you, I suggest you take out as many as you can before turning the gun on yourself."

Lorenzo smiled wryly at our dazed reactions. "But if you're not comfortable with a gun in the home for whatever reason, I hear that drinking drain cleaner or rat poison is quite effective."

The message was clear. We were to kill ourselves rather than run the risk of giving away information. I stared stonily at the array of guns. I was indeed nervous about having one at home with a ten-year-old and five-year-old around, but already I was starting to think of which high cupboard shelves it could be stashed on. I looked toward Mathias-Daniel to see what he might do.

17

The only culture now appears to be one of mass delusion.

—Sigmund Freud

Mathias–Daniel

I put off as long as possible Emilia's next visit to see Ivor, whose new name was now Alex. With her only seeing him every other month, it wasn't too difficult. I only had to make a good excuse for one visit not taking place and I'd already bought four months.

Then, just the day before Emilia was preparing to drive from Stuttgart, I called her from a phone box and suggested we meet and she pick up Ivor at the café in Tiergarten zoo, southwest of the city. I could sense the questions building on her end in the following silence.

I quickly added, "With everything now, there have been some changes with myself and Ivor." All I dared comment with lines possibly being listened in to.

"I tried your home number last week. It rang unobtainable," Emilia said.

I sighed. "Everything will become clear when we meet."

I saw Emilia looking around as she walked into the café, not seeing us, which in a way was a good thing: she hadn't immediately recognized us. I had to raise one hand to draw her attention, and her delayed recognition quickly turned to shock. I swiveled my hand to a stop signal, casting a glance each side fleetingly, so that she didn't blurt out anything awkward.

Thankfully, Emilia stayed tight-lipped, eyes shifting uncomfortably as I explained. Anschluss. Dire situation. My own life under threat, possibly Ivor's too. "In the end, the only choices were to leave the country—in which case you might never have seen him again—or this, an identity change." The nearest people were two tables away, the general clatter and hubbub of the café also heavily masking, but I kept my voice low just in case. Emilia still looked troubled, taking it all in, as she took her first sips of coffee.

"I'm so sorry it's all come to this," she said, her eyes drifting into the mid-distance.

It was a lost look full of regret, and I'd seen similar looks from Emilia over the past year or so, particularly since Anschluss. She'd become more mellow. Perhaps part of that regret was reflecting on how harsh she'd been on me during our marriage, or perhaps with the rest of Austria now being so harsh against Jews, she needed to provide some counterbalance.

With the final sting in the tail that with Ivor now getting older, she feared that he, too, even as a Mischling, might be subject to that racism; something which, against her own son, she found impossible to come to terms with. An internal dilemma making her reflect on, and feel guilty about, her own past racism. Almost a tailor-made Karma, I thought wistfully; but I'd seen it happen with others.

"I suppose there is that advantage," Emilia said after a moment. "Being able to see Ivor regularly." Picking out the one ray of light she saw in all this mess.

"Yes, there is that." I held back from saying more; I wanted her to get there on her own. I'd noticed Emilia's eyes go more to Ivor than me, getting used to his new look: we'd both gone blond, but Ivor a shade more than me, with a faint red tinge.

"In a way, it suits him," she said with a crooked smile as she studied Ivor more intently.

I nodded. Whichever route she chose, and hopefully it wasn't a Freudian slip: *He looks less Jewish now.* It could be simply that Ivor's hair color was now closer to her own, easier to see as her son.

"What are your new names?" Emilia asked.

"I'm now Daniel, and Ivor is Alex."

"Daniel and Alex... Daniel and Alex," Emilia repeated thoughtfully. "I suppose I could get used to it."

Emilia still looked radiant and beautiful, and I had a sudden pang at the lost years. How we used to be. Even her flippant nature, which I'd often associated with her acting and used to annoy me, now had its plus side: she'd become so used to playing different parts every week that now slipping into a new role-play for her son wasn't so difficult.

Then, as if snapping herself back to what she'd come for, she said, "Oh, I almost forgot." Emilia delved into her bag and passed Ivor a silver-paper-wrapped ten-by-seven-inch package. Looked like a book, probably Jules Verne or H. G. Wells, his favorites right now.

"Thank you," Ivor-Alex said with a smile.

"And I've got another bigger present waiting in the car."

No doubt another large model car, I thought whimsically. Or perhaps a tank or fighter plane. "Don't forget, if anyone asks, tell them Ivor—Alex is the son of a family friend."

Emilia looked perturbed by that for a moment, but nodded

her understanding. It was her son's safety at stake as well, not just mine.

"And your cousin Johannes and his family?" Emilia asked.

"They've made a similar arrangement." Pained grimace. "Though for obvious reasons, I shouldn't go into detail." Emilia looked at me questioningly, as if stung that I might not trust her, and I added, "As much for your safety as theirs."

She nodded after a second. "I understand." Accepting that she had enough burden on her shoulders with the secret of Ivor-Alex and me.

We finished our coffees and Emilia gave me a polite hug as we stood to part.

"I'm sure everything's going to work out fine," she said. Though I could see the uncertainty in her eyes as to whether it could. Not just what was happening with me and our son, but Hitler had just moved troops into the Sudetenland and had his eyes now set on invading Czechoslovakia and Poland. War was looming. "What? Shall we meet up again here in three hours?"

"Make it four," I said. "You haven't seen Alex in a while."

I did in fact take one of the guns offered by Lorenzo and Alois at that meeting months later—though I could sense that Johannes-Andreas was more hesitant about it than me—and Alois showed me briefly how it worked: a Browning Hi-Power 640 with a simple sliding mechanism and thirteen-bullet magazine loaded through its handle base.

"Very popular now with the German military," Alois added, smiling dryly. "So somewhat ironic that some of their own might end up shot by it."

Early forties and slim and wiry, Alois in fact seemed to have a permanent faint smile, as if he was mocking the world or had seen so much that he couldn't take it seriously anymore. With his family being both Jewish and dissident Schuschnigg supporters, they were doomed on both fronts. His two brothers had been rounded up and killed within days of Anschluss, and his sister and parents shipped to Mauthausen, where his parents because of their age had been killed practically on arrival. Only his sister he thought had survived, but even that he wasn't totally sure of. Alois, whose original name had in fact been Israel, immediately went to ground and, after his own identity change, offered to help Lorenzo build his network.

"It was either laugh or cry," Lorenzo explained to me and Andreas when he shared Alois's background. "He chose to laugh at the world. He also used to be a crack shot in the Bundesheer, the Austrian army—so he knows his weapons."

The main thing guiding our decision to change identities had been to avoid being split up from our families, but another factor had been author earnings. My books were now banned in Germany and Austria, which amounted to half my sales, and Johannes's books looked likely to follow that route. Whereas Julian felt confident he'd find publishers in Austria, Germany and abroad with our new names, "And you'd also have continuing sales in foreign territories under your old names."

I'd finished my first book under my new name six weeks ago, and Julian had already made good on that promise by securing a German publisher. Andreas was due to finish his in two months.

I looked out the window, dusk light, and checked my watch: 5:46 p.m. It was time. I took the chisel from my top desk drawer, got up and walked into the dining room. The same ritual every three months, I knew the position off by heart now: lift one side of the rug, five floorboards in from the far wall. Prize up with the chisel on a specific part of the floorboard—the other end wouldn't lift—and then I could see the soiled burlap bag, which just looked like rubbish, through the five-inch gap. Reach in and rustle around for two or three diamonds that felt the right size.

That had been the only drawback with the financial arrangements—my cousin Andreas hadn't had the same problem because he'd been renting. But to those who'd sold their properties, much of that windfall had to be hidden and couldn't just show up in bank accounts without raising eyebrows. Everything else had been carefully worked out, sales and notary registrations backdated to before Anschluss—so it looked like we'd left the country—but in reality, after paying off this chain of facilitators, we'd receive some cash and the rest in diamonds.

Diamonds were ideal, because they were so portable and held their value—certainly more than many currencies these days. I now rented—a similar three-bedroomed apartment to our last place, with one bedroom used for my office—so if there were any problems we could move easily. Our wealth went with us.

I put three diamonds deep into my pocket, put the floorboard down, pulled the rug back in place, and placed the chisel back in my desk drawer and locked it.

I could hear Alex still in his bedroom. I peeked my head in on the way out and told him I was going to see someone. "Shouldn't be more than an hour or so."

"Okay." He looked up from the stamp collection he was leafing through. He'd started collecting last year. A sort of escapism, I suppose: bright colors and exotic palms from places he'd like to visit one day; but, since Anschluss, probably felt farther out of reach. "See you later."

"I'm actually seeing the man who gave me some stamps last time." Carl Brunnerman, the jeweler who'd cash my diamonds every three months, had a brother in the merchant navy. When it came out two visits back that my son collected stamps, he offered me some from his brother's last few letters. "I'll bring you back more if he has them."

Alex beamed back. "That would be marvelous. Thank you."

I nodded and made my way down the single flight of stairs and out into the street. Brunnerman's was four miles north near Karlsplatz. A tram took me most of the way, leaving only a quarter-mile walk to his shop.

I looked anxiously around as the tram trundled along. I was

always nervous going to Brunnerman's, because I was also cashing in three months' rent, living and groceries for my mother and Erica. Both now had new names, Lilla and Anna, but my mother had the same cash-windfall problem selling her house and I couldn't expect her to make this trip. The only saving grace was we'd finally convinced her to move to a large bungalow in Penzing, which she shared with Erica-Anna.

I was no longer concerned about ID card searches—four so far without any problems—but I was always worried about getting robbed with diamonds in my pocket. Or how I might explain them away if an SD guard decided to search me.

That was why I went at regular intervals, only carrying small quantities that I could claim I was taking to be set into a ring or bracelet. Any larger quantities and that explanation wouldn't wash, plus the loss risked from theft would be greater.

As I got off the tram, there were still a few people on the street, which made me feel more settled. Thieves normally preferred quieter, darker stretches; there was still some faint light, the streetlamps just going on.

But then among the people on the street, three men just coming out of a café sixty yards ahead—two SS and a man in a brown suit—caught my breath in my throat. One of the SS officers I instantly recognized: Heinrich Schnabel! Perhaps it was partly surprise because I hadn't seen him in almost a year, so he was like a ghost from the past—the meetings since with Julian and Andreas had been at the University of Vienna café. But I suddenly realized I was now on the edge of Schnabel's district one.

My first instinct was to just turn sharply around and head away. But I had the feeling that he'd already spotted me and a sudden action like that would simply raise his suspicions. Besides, I looked different now, I reminded myself, and he'd only seen me that one time.

I decided to brave it out. I kept my pace steady, trying not to pay him too much attention, nor markedly avert my eyes. Just act as if he was the same as any other person on this street. But it was difficult to maintain with my heart in my throat, pounding an increasingly heavy tattoo as we got closer.

Schnabel fired me a polite smile as he approached, but it was little more than you might give any passerby. I returned the same polite smile. Then we were past each other.

I heard his step falter then, a faint shuffle as he glanced back. But if any recognition had hit him in that instant, it didn't last long. A moment later I heard his step carry on.

18

September 1939

Sigmund Freud didn't at first feel his wife's hand clasping his until Martha pressed more insistently, waking him. He blinked at her and stirred, sitting more upright. Some weak sunlight flickered through the trees, and he'd fallen asleep in his chair on the terrace, partially covered in a blanket.

It seemed that all he did these days was sleep, but then he'd been warned by his attending physician, Dr. Stross, that this would be the effect of the increasing morphine doses. At least the searing pain in his jaw was subsiding.

"Are you sure?" Martha asked, pressing his hand again, and he saw the import in his wife's eyes. This might be the last moment she saw him. Her eyes glassy, the tears close.

"Yes, I am certain, my love." He pressed her hand back with what little strength he had left, reassuring. "I've achieved what I set out to this past year, seen you and Anna safe here in London. There's nothing left for me now but…but this unbearable pain."

Martha nodded, holding the tears back. Not wanting in this last moment for him to see her so distraught. She wondered whether war being declared three weeks ago had been a final factor in his decision. One pain and anguish too many for him.

Sigmund glanced at his pocket watch. The final morphine dose had been scheduled for 4 p.m., and he noticed it was already 4:16 p.m.

"I'm sure you, Marie and Ernest will do your level best to get my sisters out of Vienna without my help." He forced a pained smile. "I've been of little assistance in that regard these past months. I'm sure in the end you'll be successful."

The past eighteen months, she and close family friends, Marie Bonaparte and Ernest Jones, had pushed hard with the Austrian Reich authorities to get the release of Sigmund's four elderly sisters still in Vienna. With each passing week, hopes were diminishing. But she knew that however much her husband had lectured about the human tendency to shy away from unacceptable realities, it was important to him to now end on a hopeful note.

"Yes, I'm sure we will," she said, giving one last reassuring hand clasp before leaning over to kiss his forehead and turning away. Not trusting herself to say more.

Martha Freud gave a solemn nod to Dr. Josephine Stross waiting in the drawing room, and managed to hold back the sobs that racked her body until she'd reached the upstairs bathroom.

Johannes–Andreas

August 1940

Walking through Prater Park with my family, it was hard to believe there was a war on. Though the war had officially started almost a year ago, there hadn't been a single bombing of the city, nor any enemy aircraft flying overhead. So life in Vienna went on more or less as normal.

It was a warm, sunny day, and it seemed like half the city was out enjoying the park, with the heaviest crowds around the fair—the main attraction we'd taken the children out for today. They'd been tugging our arms about it the past couple of weeks, and we'd promised to take them the first bright weekend day.

A giant Ferris wheel dominated the fair, and that was the first thing we went on. It had suspended glass cabins, similar to those I'd seen running on the mountain cables at Innsbruck. We were lucky enough to get one with only four other people in along with us—so we had good, clear views on all sides.

As we got near the top of the wheel's arc, the cabin rocking slightly as it adjusted, I felt Nadia's little hand grip mine.

"We're up high now, Papa."

Whether through pure excitement or part fear, I wasn't sure, so I gave her hand a reassuring clasp back.

"Yes, we are." I took a fresh breath. "It's beautiful, isn't it?"

Nadia smiled excitedly and clenched tighter with her hand. The view was breathtaking. We could see across the whole city, even the Schönbrunn Palace in the distance could be made out clearly.

No signs of war at all. Not a single building bombed or burned out. Except all those Jewish-owned shops and syna-gogues, I reminded myself. A portly man shuffled partly in front of us.

I asked Nadia, "Would you like me to lift you up for a bet-ter view?"

"Yes…yes." She beamed.

And as I held her up and felt her small body trembling slightly, I still wasn't sure if it was fear or excitement. Then I felt my own arms start to tremble. "Okay, that's it—can't hold you any longer. You're getting a big girl now."

Nadia beamed wider, as if that was the best compliment I could have paid her.

After some hot dogs and bratwurst, we drifted over to a pellet-rifle game. Five shots, two within the bull's-eye won you a prize. Nadia had her eye on a big fluffy bunny, and Dominik thought he could win it for her.

"Let him at least try," Stefanie urged with a gentle smile after my initial reluctance.

"Okay." I paid and watched as Dominik put only one in the bull's-eye on the third shot, the next halfway over the rim and the final shot wide again.

"Sorry." Dominik looked as disappointed as Nadia as he put the rifle back on the counter. She had a hurt pout, her eyes cast down.

"Let me have a go," I said. I had a plan, but wasn't sure if it would work until I gauged where the first shot went: two inches to the left of the bull's-eye, even though I'd had the crosshairs dead center. I moved the sights off-center two inches to the right. It was a tip Alois had shared when I'd taken my new gun. "The sights on these are set correctly. But if you ever find shots going off at target practice, adjust them back or compensate by that same amount on the target." My next two shots went in the bull's-eye, the fourth on its rim and the final shot through the bull's-eye again.

Nadia clapped her hands and jumped up and down excitedly. "Papa…well done!"

Dominik and Stefanie also beamed and gave a couple of claps as the stall holder handed Nadia the fluffy bunny with a re-signed grimace.

We were so caught up in the excitement of the moment that we didn't immediately register the other light applause just behind us. I turned to see an SS soldier with his colleague smiling at me appreciatively.

"Very good shooting," he said. "What regiment are you with, by the way?"

"I… I'm not with a regiment." It suddenly struck me why he'd picked me out. Most men in the park were in uniform, even if they were off duty. Now in wartime, they wore them as a badge of honor. *Look. I'm a proud defender of the Reich and our nation.* He was no doubt wondering why I wasn't off at the front fighting, or perhaps he was checking for deserters. "I applied to join the 4th Totenkopf regiment, but I'm afraid they turned me down. Color blindness."

"Oh, I see. I'm sorry to hear that."

I fished my ID card out, along with the medical certificate Lorenzo had advised me to always carry to back up that story. *Changing your identity is one thing, but it won't help if you suddenly find yourself fighting for the very people trying to send your people to the death camps. Yet it might be questioned why an able-bodied man hasn't been conscripted.* So far, nobody had asked.

The soldier studied my card and medical certificate and looked me up and down intently before handing them back with a tight smile.

"That's a shame," he said. "Because I'm sure a good shot like you would have served well and been of value."

He saluted, I returned the salute, and after a click of heels he headed off with his colleague.

"Do you want us to leave?" Stefanie asked soon after, when she could see I was still troubled by the incident.

"No. Let's stay," I said after a moment's contemplation. In the end, the incident had been nothing, a storm in a teacup, and, on the bright side, it had at least proven that my medical certificate stood up to scrutiny. Also it would be a shame to cut the day short when the kids were enjoying themselves. "How often do we get days like this all out together?"

We started to relax again, buying some candy floss for the

kids at a nearby stand, playing with a ball and hoop and a ring-toss bottle game—though no prizes won this time.

Stefanie smiled at seeing the children enjoying themselves, but at times I could see the strain beneath. It hadn't been easy for her. While my mother had also changed identity—too risky with her having been married to a prominent Jewish dissident—Stefanie's parents, Austrian Catholic going back generations, had kept their identities and remained in the same area. That meant she could see them only rarely, and had to be very careful. She'd also had to avoid all her old friends and contacts.

Ironically, a thought that spun back sharply fifty minutes later as we left a side gaming-arcade and started to make plans to leave; a face from Stefanie's past over the far side of the fair: Magda Fischer with her young teen daughter. I perhaps wouldn't have noticed her if she hadn't been looking our way, her brow creasing as she looked from one to the other of us, trying to put the pieces together...*while one of you on your own shouldn't be recognized, together you might strike a chord.*

"Don't look now," I hissed to Stefanie as I hustled her and the children away. "But I think I've just seen Magda Fischer." We'd studiously avoided our old neighborhood—but of course this was a park and fair visited by people from all over Vienna.

I caught glimpses of Mrs. Fischer in my side vision between the gaps of a whirling octopus ride in the middle of the fair. She'd started moving our way to get a closer look. We should have left after I'd been questioned by the SS soldier. That had been a sign, an omen.

My breath eased as for a moment she looked lost, as if she wasn't totally sure which way we'd gone. Then as she went completely from view behind the next ride, I rushed us all into a Hall of Mirrors tent attraction to one side. I paid and we made our way along.

Nine mirrors down I noticed a chink in the canvas awning which gave a partial view of outside. I peered out. Nothing for a while, just people passing generally—then I saw Magda Fischer and her daughter approach. It was pitch-black on my side, so I knew I couldn't be seen.

Mrs. Fischer glanced toward the entrance and the sign above, then to the attractions each side—obviously wondering if we'd gone in one of them or simply walked on. Then she and her daughter moved out of my line of vision, so I couldn't see where they'd gone.

"Hopefully, she's not coming our way," I whispered.

"This is madness," Stefanie hissed quietly back.

"I know. I'm sorry." I clasped her hand. A poor reassurance. Sorry you can only infrequently see your parents. Sorry you can't see your old friends anymore. Sorry you've had to go through all of this because of being married to me. The one time I'd said that openly to Stefanie in a moment of utter dejection, she'd slapped my shoulder hard and looked about to slap my face. *Don't ever say that. You've given me two beautiful children.*

So we waited behind the canvas awning with our two beautiful children, breath held, our reflections warped and distorted by numerous fun-house mirrors, as we wondered whether our old life might finally catch up with our new lives.

19

*In addition to Jews and Mischlinge, henceforth Gypsies, negroes
or their bastards shall be forbidden to marry or have sexual re-
lationships with German citizens. This is to further protect the
purity of German blood.*

Heinrich Schnabel sat back in a leather armchair as he read the
transcript. He'd read it several times before, plus also listened to
the original tape recording, but he wanted to refresh his memory on anything he might have missed before.

Schnabel was in a small makeshift office in the basement of
the Hotel Metropole. The conversion to Vienna's Nazi HQ was
now complete: on the floors above, SS and Gestapo officers were
being served coffee, tea and smoked salmon sandwiches on silver trays by liveried waiters—not too different to how it had
been as a functioning hotel, except that now practically everyone was in uniform.

But here in the basement, it was a very different scene. Apart from a few windowless small offices, the rest were holding areas and cells, interrogation or execution rooms. Two doors along was a guillotine room, the heads and bodies loaded on a truck at the end of the day and dumped in a pit. Another room where prisoners were machine-gunned was heavily sandbagged, the foot of sand on its floor only changed when it became too marshy from blood and body fluids.

Schnabel wished now he'd personally conducted that previous interview; he might have got more out of the prisoner before he'd bled to death. The transcript hadn't even come to his attention until recently, when he'd been browsing through old interrogation files for anything that might help with his own cases and the name Max Adler, owner of Der Blaue Engel, had leaped out.

Schnabel walked into the adjacent room. In an old laundry drying area next to the boiler room, Max Adler stood on a small stool at its center, stripped to his undershorts with his arms above his head tied to an iron ceiling beam. His face and body were streaked with blood and heavily bruised, one eye almost closed from swelling. He peered at Schnabel wearily through his remaining good eye.

"So, let us try again, shall we," Schnabel said with a tired breath. "You claim not to know a certain Leon Weinel?"

"Never heard of him," Adler rasped with a faint headshake.

"But I think the person organizing this you certainly know?"

"No."

Schnabel smiled thinly. Adler was obviously keen to keep some answers economical. They'd made sure to keep a radio playing all night while he was chained to a camp bed to deprive him of sleep. He'd be at a low ebb now, his resistance low.

"Let us see what Mr. Weinel had to say on that matter, shall we?" Schnabel held up three fingers to his next-in-command at the side of the room, Kurt Lindner. He'd earlier set up the tape with Lindner to play at set intervals. Lindner pressed Play and the reel turned.

"I... I never knew his real name. He was introduced only as Mauricio, no second name. But by the time I met him the next time, he was being referred to as Fabian, and his hair color and appearance had changed too." Labored breathing, as if even that short speech had taken all of Weinel's strength. "But...but I know that Adler knew him because I saw them in a side of-fice together..."

Schnabel signaled for Lindner to stop the tape and looked sharply at Adler. "So we see from this that you do in fact know him."

Adler smiled crookedly through blood-soaked lips. "He gave his name as Aldo when I met him."

"You told me Tobias last time." One advantage of the sleep deprivation and repeated questioning. They started to make mistakes.

"Even if I ha–have met him twice, he's given me different names each time," Adler spluttered, blood specks spraying on his chest. "So how would that help you? You still wouldn't be able to find him."

Schnabel moved in close. Then without warning he kicked the stool away. "It might help you actually live."

Adler groaned as his full weight was taken on the ropes around his wrists. Schnabel signaled to the far end of the room. Gus-tav, a keen amateur heavyweight boxer before he joined the SS, moved in again. He'd draped his army jacket over his vest so that the sweat didn't chill from his last pummeling of Adler, and now cast it aside again.

It was a measured attack: stomach, ribs, kidneys—but never enough to rupture organs—then another face jab and a final punch to Adler's groin as Schnabel held a hand up and indicated for Adler to be yanked up onto the stool again.

Schnabel didn't want to go too far, encounter the same problem the last interrogation team had with Weinel: although his slit wrists had been bandaged and they'd also taken the precaution of attaching the ropes higher up his forearms—one of his wrist veins had still opened up, and they hadn't noticed until too late with all the other blood on his body.

As Adler was getting his breath back on the stool, Schnabel lifted four fingers to Lindner. The tape played again.

"It…it was when I was on the way back from the toilet that I saw them. Ad… Adler sounded desperate…saying, surely there's some way you can help me…"

Schnabel nodded to Lindner and the tape stopped. "So what was it you wanted help so desperately with?"

Adler took a moment to focus. "It certainly wasn't for…for an identity change. Because here I am still as Max Adler." He coughed and spluttered out another small gout of blood. "Which is what I told the Gestapo whe…when they came to my club and questioned me."

Schnabel took stock for a moment. Weinel had only recognized Adler because he'd seen him before in Der Blaue Engel. But Adler hadn't been part of their group, so therefore no name change. Two Gestapo men had gone to Adler's club to question him, but halfway through Josef Weber had walked in, asking what was going on and that he could "vouch for Mr. Adler." The matter went no further.

That was why this time they'd made sure to pick up Adler after his club was closed and on a night they knew Josef Weber wasn't there.

"You've answered with what you didn't go there for," Schnabel said, his tone jaded. "But not with what you did. So what was that?"

"It was nothing. Jus…just a favor for a friend."

"What? An identity change for them?" Schnabel considered deeper for a second. "One of the girls at the club, perhaps?"

"No…no. Nothing like that."

But with the mention of the club girls, Schnabel noticed a faint flicker in Adler's eye. "So what was it?"

Adler just shook his head, fell silent, and Schnabel's patience snapped. He signaled Gustav to move in again for another brief pummeling, then asked him to get the cattle prod from the side wall.

With still nothing forthcoming from Adler after four heavy jolts, Schnabel sighed resignedly. "I would recommend you don't completely exhaust my patience. I'll just send you through to the guillotine room or to a death camp." Schnabel gestured. "Of the two, I prefer the latter, because you'd have a little more time to contemplate your death…and you might meanwhile be jolted into remembering something. Either way, all your property will go immediately to the Reich."

"Tha…that's where you're wrong." Adler glared back. "You'll end up with nothing."

"What do you mean?"

And as Adler explained between blood-splattered gasps that both his home and his club had been sold and transferred a while back, "A partnership of high-ranking Lutheran-Austrian civ… civilians and a Swiss bank," Schnabel suddenly realized what Adler had been so desperate about. As a prominent and recognizable Vienna figure, identity change hadn't been an option; but his property had been another matter.

Schnabel shrugged indifferently, didn't want to let on that he felt put out by Adler's revelation; at least he'd finally unearthed the truth. "Since you're worth nothing now, that will make you easier to dispense with."

"Perhaps. But I have a prop…proposition for you."

Schnabel raised a brow. "If you hadn't noticed, you're not exactly in a position to negotiate."

Adler nodded somberly, attempted a wry bloodstained smile.

Schnabel listened to Adler's proposition. And while he reluctantly admired Adler's gall, he hated being drawn into negotiat-

ing with this fat lug of a Jew. It went against all of his principles.
But still, he reminded himself, he had the power over Adler's life
or death. Whether he gave an emperor's thumbs-down, or let
Adler live in exchange for half his wealth going into the Reich's
coffers. The ultimate dilemma: satisfying his own moral con-
victions or that of the greater good?

"Could be just a coincidence," Lindner commented.

"Could be." Schnabel's mouth curled.

They sat on a corner in Karlsplatz in a Steyr 50, ideal for surveillance because they were so popular in Austria. Even its beige
color seemed to merge into the stonework of the surrounding
buildings, its strange armadillo shape now also accepted without raising an eye because they were seen on every other street
in Vienna.

Lindner had driven them there. Schnabel hadn't actually
learned to drive, but he never admitted that because it might
be viewed as somehow "less manly." He therefore made out he
was simply taking advantage of the privilege of senior SS officers to be driven everywhere, and took public transport the rest
of the time—which was ample and efficient in both Vienna and
his hometown of Linz.

Eight years younger than Schnabel, Lindner had been chosen
as his assistant because for a twenty-six-year-old he was com-
petent and intuitive and followed instructions swiftly and effectively.

Schnabel had decided upon their surveillance in Karlsplatz
due to one final element Weinel had revealed under interrogation. Weinel said that another of the group returning months
later—Weinel didn't know his name, they were under strict instructions not to share names—said he used to go periodically
to cash in diamonds at a jeweler in Karlsplatz... "I... I didn't
have to, because I was renting—but he said that it was som...

something those who'd sold properties had to do to shield all that extra cash."

"Did he tell you the name of this jeweler?"

"No, he didn't. I su…suppose that also came under the 'no names' rule. All he told me was that it was in the Karlsplatz area."

Schnabel had replayed the segment again the night before in his Hegelgasse apartment while listening to some Brahms. The only composer, along with Bach, that he found relaxed him, allowed his thoughts to run freely; Mahler or Wagner were too rousing and heavy, crowded out any constructive thought.

Karlsplatz? The only problem was that there were four possible jewelers in the area. So they'd positioned themselves at a vantage point with views between clear and minimal of all but one of them. But after a while the surveillance became tiresome, pure drudgery. The only thing to narrow it down had been Weinel commenting that the man said he visited at closing time or soon after—but that still left countless hours to check, especially if the visits were infrequent. Schnabel therefore left it mostly to Lindner, joining him only sporadically.

And it was on one of those occasions, only twenty minutes after he'd joined Lindner, that Schnabel recognized a man going into Brunnerman's Jewelers eighty yards to their right. "I saw him on this very street when I was coming out of the café over there."

And Lindner had responded that it could be just a coincidence.

"Could be."

20

It is a predisposition of human nature to consider an unpleasant idea untrue, and then it is easy to find arguments against it.

—*Sigmund Freud*

The first people to arrive at Der Blaue Engel every day were the cleaner, Emma Stolz, and bar and cellar manager, Lukas Hager. Business hours were between 9 p.m. and 3 a.m., and there seemed little point cleaning straight after closing with so many hours before the club opened again—so that always took place between seven and nine every morning while Lukas took deliveries of fresh beer barrels, wine, champagne and spirits from their local liquor supplier.

The first deliveries usually didn't arrive for half an hour, so Emma would be first into the backyard to sweep and clear up any rubbish that might be there from overnight or leaves blown in. Late November, the early morning light was still weak, and when Emma first saw the object on the ground close to the back-yard gate, she thought perhaps one of the deliveries had come early and they'd merely covered it with a tarpaulin.

It wasn't until she got closer that she realized it was a body, the blood dried and caked over most of it; beyond that dull brown veneer, it took her a moment more to recognize it was Max Adler, the club's owner. Lifeless, no movement. But then a sudden rustling noise made her nerves leap. She looked down and saw a rat sniffing and scurrying around one of his legs.

The leg spasmed a second later and jerked to shift the rat, followed by a groan and cough.

Inside the club, Lukas almost dropped the vodka bottle he was putting into a fresh optic bracket when Emma's scream reached him. He ran out to see what had happened.

Josef

Deya sipped at her coffee, shook her head.

"They beat him to within an inch of his life, Josef. Max was lucky to survive."

"Do you think he said anything?"

"No, I don't think so. He says not."

Josef nodded thoughtfully after a second, sipped at his own coffee. "Then I'm inclined to believe him." From his association with Max Adler over the years, he'd never known him to be a liar. Sometimes stubborn, an offbeat sense of humor, cynical, and becoming increasingly evasive and secretive—as you might expect from many Jews in the city these days—but never outright lying.

It was almost a rerun of their conversation the first night after Max Adler had been taken into hospital. Except that then Deya's hands had been shaking uncontrollably on her coffee cup, her makeup running from tears, and neither of them speculating on whether Max might have talked when at that point he was barely clinging to life.

After nine days in hospital, Max was finally out of danger and came into the club to explain to Deya and Lukas what had happened: in exchange for his life and passage to Switzerland, he'd had no choice but to sign the club over to the Reich. "The gentleman who has introduced himself to you as the 'interim manager' is in fact the new owner. I hope you get on with him and everything's fine." A tight smile as Max had said it; a mixture of doubtful hope and nostalgia. Three days later Max had caught a flight to Geneva. That had been over a week ago, so now they'd had almost three weeks with this new owner.

"What's he like?" Josef inquired. He'd only been back to the club twice in that period and hadn't spoken to new owner Martin Ehrlich for any length of time; at least, not to be able to get the measure of him.

"Okay, I suppose…for a die-hard Nazi." Deya drew on her cigarette, blew out a slow plume of smoke. "Which we expected with someone taking over on behalf of the Reich. He doesn't play that up too much at least. It's just…"

"What?" Josef prompted as he noticed Deya's gaze drift off, as if she was having trouble pinpointing what was troubling her.

"It's just that since Martin has come in, a few of the girls seem to be playing up to him. Karen in particular, as if to say, *I'll show you what a good Nazi-supporting girl I am*. And at the same time all this shit about Max comes out that I never heard before. 'I never really liked him, thought he was a bit creepy if you ask me.'" Deya's voice went higher to mimic one of the other girls. "Stuff like that. Particularly if Martin's around and they know he can hear them, or sometimes direct to his face too. As if they think that's what he wants to hear. Will buy extra favor with him."

"'You're the better owner' sort of thing?"

"Sort of."

They fell silent for a moment. Josef took a sip of his sambuca.

"If things are feeling uncomfortable for you there, maybe you should cut back another night?"

"Maybe." Deya smiled at him. "Would at least give us more time together."

"I'd like that." Josef lit up a cigarette, clasped her hand gently across the table.

Deya had already cut back one night from Der Blaue Engel, and they usually used that night to see each other, which was why Josef hadn't been back to the club much since. Tonight they'd gone to a small local restaurant, Kitzbühel, with quaint Tyrolean decor. Lots of wood and painted flowers, romantic in a twee way—but they served the best schnitzels, goulash and pepper steaks in the area. They were finishing off after dinner with coffees and sambucas.

Josef asked if she thought Max had covered the paperwork trail sufficiently. "Could they trace anything back through that?"

"The main transfer documents are all with lawyers in Switzerland. And you know how secretive they are." Deya tapped ash from her cigarette. "But as an extra precaution, Lorenzo and Alois are staying in Switzerland for a while. They'll come back infrequently from now on. Only for new cases or emergencies."

Josef nodded. "Probably good sense. Everyone who wanted to leave or have an ID change has probably done so by now." The doors were now closed. Any Jews or gypsies left in Austria were pretty well at the mercy of the Nazis. "But while Lorenzo and Alois have gone to ground, what about you? Are you sure you feel safe?"

"Yes, I do, Josef. And you know why." She contemplated him steadily through smoke trails. "We spoke about this last time."

At the height of Lorenzo's operations, when Josef's anxiety had been equally high about connections to her, Deya had been firm in her assurance that, apart from her initial ID change, she'd had no involvement with Lorenzo's operation, and nobody apart from Josef and a couple of others close and trusted even knew they were related. *Even if they did suspect some connection, do you know how many second and third cousins there are in the average Romani family?* Josef had laughed at that, a light-noted finish to their tense exchange.

Josef forced a smile now; reluctant acceptance. "I suppose if Max had said anything, or they'd found a crack in the paperwork trail, we'd have known by now. They'd have started moving in on others."

Deya nodded slowly; her own reluctant acceptance.

But Josef sensed something beneath troubling her. "What is it?"

"Schnabel came in the club again just a few nights back." She blew out smoke on the back of a sigh. "I think he was embarrassed to come by the first couple of weeks with what had happened to Max. But then there he was the other night. Bold as brass. Talked with Martin for a while, then with a couple of the girls."

"Did he approach you or talk to you?"

"No. He stayed clear. But at one point he was staring at me challengingly. And that Karen I mentioned was draped across his lap, giving me the same look, as if to say, *Look who I've landed.* As if Schnabel was some sort of prize she'd beat me to."

Josef shook his head. "I don't like it. Maybe it's time you took me up on my last offer to make a decent woman of you and you leave the club once and for all."

"Thank you, Josef." She looked across soulfully and clasped his hand. "I love you dearly too. But I think we have to make that decision when the time is right for us—not because the Nazis are forcing us into it."

21

Government institutions shall not employ Jews or Mischlinge
and any currently employed shall forthwith be dismissed.

Johannes-Andreas

My fingers hovered over the keyboard for almost a full two minutes before I finally started typing. It still felt a long wait, fearful that I hadn't got the flow of words fully clear in my mind.
But it was better than the six- or seven-minute delay of a few
months ago, or sometimes I'd finally give up and start pacing
again, glancing back at the typewriter as if it was some kind of
enemy that was partially the cause of my block, wondering if I
would ever get the flow clear.

Sometimes those blocks would last a day or two or more, di-
verting with mundane chores or escaping to the library for more
research, along with endless pacing and making coffee and tea
or trying to make notes or start some scenes in handwriting on

a pad before committing to the typewriter. And often those scenes might get written fully in handwriting with countless spider-crawl inserts, changes and notes in the margins, before I'd finally feel comfortable typing it up.

Aside from the desire to tell a story, writing was escapism. And with Austria fully in the grip of the Nazis and in the midst of war, there was probably more need now than ever for that escapism. But, paradoxically, sometimes those problems and horrors were so stifling that you found yourself totally gripped by them, unable to escape.

The first few weeks of Anschluss had without doubt been my worst period of writing; I'd hardly written anything in that period. And while it had eased considerably since, particularly as we'd settled more into our new identities, I could practically measure every drama and problem in our lives by how my writing flow had been affected.

After seeing Magda Fischer at Prater Park Fair, I'd hardly written anything the next day. We'd waited almost twenty minutes before finally emerging from the Hall of Mirrors, and even then still anxious we might bump into her on the way out. Every time Dominik or Nadia became sulky and mentioned missing their old friends: half a day lost. When one of our new neighbors—who by then we knew was a strong Nazi supporter—commented the second time he met me on the street that he thought he'd seen me somewhere before: another half day lost. After two more quizzical looks fired my way when he saw me passing, we decided to move again: four more days lost making the move. Our new life forged was by no means easy, but we consoled ourselves with the fact that our family had been kept together and we were still alive.

Then there was the minefield of what could be written about. People didn't want war stories because it was too much of a reminder of what was going on outside their doors—no possible escapism there. And it was perilous territory in any case because any Nazis had to be painted in a positive or sympathetic light. There were endless Nazi propaganda pamphlets, books and films for that—so no point in going into that territory. Same, too, for the perceived enemies of the Reich: the Jews, gypsies, Communists, Bolsheviks and dissidents; they had to be painted in a negative light. In the end, there was little safe ground in between—so better to avoid the era altogether.

As a result, both Mathias-Daniel and I had set our books under new names in other eras: he'd set his in 1920s Vienna, a sort of Viennese take on the popular Berlin-set Krimi novels. I'd set mine in 1930–31 Frankfurt with the first about a serial killer at the height of the German Depression before the Nazis came to power. Inspired by the true-life account of a serial killer who, Sweeney Todd–style, used the flesh of his victims for pie fillings, I knew the Nazis could look upon that positively: *Ah, look what horrors we saved Germany from.*

It had paid off: Julian had sold rights in Italy before finding a German and Austrian publisher, and I was now on my fourth translation right, with the first book in the series out in five months. Daniel was on his seventh translation, including England, with his first book out in two months.

The wheels of publishing moved slowly, and slower still with all the holdups on my end, real or imaginary. I'd meanwhile avoided any calligraphy work, even if it could provide valuable sideline income, in case it was recognized by anyone at Stefanie's old church: *Isn't that the work of Johannes Namal?*

"We should leave soon!" Stefanie's voice came from the next room.

I checked my watch: 11:42 a.m. One of those mornings when the writing had actually flowed. I'd lost track of time. We were due to leave soon for Stefanie to see her parents.

"Okay. Won't be long!" I called back.

Stefanie only saw her parents every four or five months. Jakob and Edith Müllner were as bewildered and horrified as her that things had come to this now in Austria and their good Catholic family split apart—but like all good Catholic Austrians they stayed quiet and didn't say anything.

Stefanie would meet them at a café three miles from their home, so that any of the neighbors might not spot her. I'd sit meanwhile in another backstreet café with the kids to avoid the whole family being seen together—then we'd all switch around to fresh cafés for another hour while Dominik and Nadia spent time with their grandparents.

As a result, I'd only seen Stefanie's parents for brief seconds during pickups and drop-offs. Small waves and tight smiles my way, as if to say: *You're the reason for all this subterfuge and why we hardly ever see our daughter and grandchildren, but we understand.*

An almost military-style operation with all the running around: another half a day or more lost. Cars were scarce in Austria, but I'd invested in an old Tatra 97 for the purpose.

I was just fishing out my car keys and preparing to leave when the phone rang. Mathias-Daniel.

"There's been a problem. Mikel thinks we should meet up."

"Mikel" I knew meant Josef. We didn't even use real names for other people anymore in case of snoopers on the line. We spoke in code or with nondescript references most of the time. "Same place as before?"

"Same place."

22

The pent-up individual chafing at the bit because civilization has called upon him to repress or deflect his most powerful drives leads to another: that of the internal or "vertical barbarian" who, given the chance, will tear down civilization from the inside.

—*Sigmund Freud*

Helmut Siegl, a young SS Junker in the 11th Standarte, parked the unit's Steyr 50 as far as possible under the shade of a leafy tree opposite the University of Vienna entrance so that hopefully he wouldn't be noticed.

Parked fifty yards ahead was the more ostentatious Steyr 220 he'd been instructed to follow, a top-of-the-range saloon car. To blend in further and not appear "official," Siegl had put on a tweed jacket, his SS tunic laid on the back seat. He could be any Viennese citizen or young university tutor.

Siegl hadn't seen anyone going in with the man he'd followed, and with the steady stream of people both preceding and follow-ing, it could have been any one of those the man was meeting.

But his patience was rewarded when just over an hour later the man came out with three other men in their thirties and forties, one of them dressed quite garishly with an aquamarine shirt and maroon cravat to match his jacket.

Siegl picked up the Leica II on his passenger seat and started snapping away. A few words, handshakes and back-pats between them, then the first man headed back to his car. Siegl had no idea the identities of any of them, even the first man he'd fol-lowed, but hopefully it all might mean something to Schar-führer Schnabel.

Mathias-Daniel

January 1942

"And who should I sign it to?" I asked the woman in front of me, late-twenties brunette in a khaki uniform; probably a Wehr-macht auxiliary clerk or nurse.

"To Ernst Kruber...with all best wishes. It's my father. He likes this sort of book."

I smiled, turned to the title page fifth in, wrote the dedi-cation and signed with a flourish. My eleventh copy signed at Hasbach Bücher's on Riemergasse today, I still had to remind myself to sign as Daniel Lendt rather than Mathias Kraemer. I handed her back the book.

"You should try reading it too—you might enjoy it."

"Yes, I might." A hesitant smile in return. "I'll try and read it when my father is finished with it."

And then the next customer was in front of me.

"Who should I dedicate this to..."

The line of customers became repetitive, seemed to merge into one another after a while, and so I didn't pay much attention to the man in the SS uniform until he was fourth back in the line. I'd dedicated books for other SS at the last couple of signings, and seen one or two browsing both then and now—men in uniform in Vienna shops and stores these days was a common occurrence.

I'd also had my head down for much of the time signing, so didn't really register much above chest level, didn't look up directly at faces until they were next in line and I had to ask the dedication they wanted.

But perhaps something about Schnabel had cut through all of that, led to me spotting him when he was four back rather than right in front of me. Which meant I still had to concentrate on the next three signings without any glimmer of recognition.

"And who was this for again…?"

It wasn't easy. My hand started shaking halfway through the second one. I became worried that my signature would appear unnatural and jerky—especially as I was signing in another name!

At our last meeting at the University of Vienna café, Josef's expression had been grave as he'd laid out what had happened: a man in the network had been uncovered and killed, possibly tortured as well, with club owner Max Adler barely escaping with his life after being questioned by Heinrich Schnabel. "Both unfortunately might have talked. So we all need to be careful. Vigilant." But that meeting had been over eight months ago, and with no other problems or emergencies, we'd become complacent.

Now Schnabel was here…only two customers away!

"How do you spell that last name again—Kannenberg?"

A dapper gray-haired man in his fifties, trilby in one hand, spelled it out, then repeated it, "Kannenberg… Horst Kannenberg."

I wrote the name down on my side pad—bracing my hand hard against it to quell the trembling… *Signing in another name!*

You look different now...you're not Mathias Kraemer anymore—before writing it along with the message on the fifth page and signing. "There you are—hope you enjoy it!"

And then Schnabel was in front of me.

"Who should I sign this for...any message?" I smiled pleasantly, kept my expression bland. Hopefully no signs of recognition. *I wouldn't ask your name if I already knew it, would I?*

"To Scharführer Heinrich Schnabel and the men of the 11th SS-Standarte." He held a hand out. "I'll read it first, then leave it in the mess room for my other men to read if it's any good."

"Sounds like a reasonable ploy." I fought to steady my hand as I wrote the dedication, dark thoughts at the back of my mind that it might be the last thing I wrote—Schnabel nodding curtly, *Thank you for that. Now come with me. I know who you are!* I signed and passed the book back. "Hopefully, you'll enjoy it, so your men will get to read it too."

"Hopefully." Schnabel paused for a moment as he took the book back, peering at me. "Must admit, when I saw you here today, I had the strong feeling I'd seen you somewhere before."

I contemplated him briefly. "I'm afraid I can't say the same. I can't recall seeing you before." I held my best vague look, but inside my heart was racing. *Not Mathias Kraemer anymore...not Mathias Kraemer anymore!* "Though I do meet a lot of people at bookshops and signings like this."

"Yes, yes...of course." Schnabel stepped aside for a moment to allow a woman behind who'd just joined the queue to get her book signed.

As I asked her name and message and signed, I realized that Schnabel had purposely joined the end of the line before so that he could spend a moment talking to me. When she left, he stepped back in again, brow lifting.

"I've just recalled where I saw you before. It was on Mahlerstrasse near Karlsplatz. I was just coming out of a café there when I saw you."

I could hardly forget. I tried to swallow, but my mouth was sandpaper dry. What would be the right degree of recognition for someone I'd passed over three years ago and should mean little to me?

"Yes, I—I seem to remember something now."

I could feel Schnabel's eyes boring through me, assessing. "And even when I saw you then, I had the strange feeling I'd seen you somewhere before…but just couldn't place where."

I felt as if I was falling down a well. My stomach sinking, heart pounding, I smiled back contritely, as if I couldn't help him much with that. I felt my left leg spasming, threatening to cramp. Finally: "Perhaps a relation or long-lost brother."

"Perhaps." Schnabel looked briefly behind to check that nobody else had joined the queue, absently leafing through the first few pages of my new book. "I see that it's set here in Vienna in the 1920s?"

"Yes," I confirmed, glad of the detour to more general territory that didn't involve me. "It's along the line of the Berlin Krimi novels, but set here."

"So quite dark and decadent?"

"I daresay," I conceded. "But hopefully without overdoing it."

Schnabel smiled thinly. "Don't worry about upsetting my sensitivities in that regard." He leafed through absently a moment longer. "Another strange thing. I read through some passages before deciding to buy and have you sign—as one often does." He gestured. "And the style, too, reminded me of another writer, though I can't immediately recall who."

I hit the bottom of the well. Schnabel knew something or had recognized me, and was just playing games with me! My temples throbbed. I felt suddenly queasy, the room starting to sway, the cramp in my left leg biting deeper. I smiled weakly. "Let's hope in following that trend in Berlin Krimis, I haven't been influenced too much by it."

"Hopefully not." Schnabel looked at me intently a second

longer, then patted the book summarily. "I'm sure I'll enjoy it nevertheless. If for no other reason than it's set here in Vienna."

Minutes after Schnabel left, my stomach was still in knots, the queasiness rising stronger. With an excuse to the bookshop manager that I needed to freshen up for a minute, part hobbling with the pain in my leg, I dived into the washroom at the back and was sick.

23

All bank accounts of Jews and Mischlinge shall be frozen and clearly marked as such in accordance with Reich Citizenship Laws.

Attention: Scharführer Heinrich Schnabel, SS 11th Standarte.

Your recent actions have unfortunately caused our department some difficulties. We had another internal team tracking the leaders of this identity-change network from another direction, but with your heavy-handed interrogation of the suspect, Max Adler, our latest received intelligence information is that they have now gone to ground, possibly in Switzerland. This will now make them far more difficult, if not impossible, to track down and apprehend. You should refrain from any further possible clumsy interrogations in this matter without first consulting my department.

Heinz Piehler
Kriminaldirektor,
Geheime Staatspolizei,
Vienna Office

Schnabel spread out the photos on top of the Gestapo memo to not only overlay with what he considered more important and relevant in his mind, but physically too.

He enjoyed most aspects of being an SS officer, but the internal politics at times annoyed him intensely. State-policing and security matters were shared between the local Austrian SS, of which he was one, and the SD, many of whom had arrived from Germany after Anschluss. Then to complicate matters there was the Gestapo, who generally dealt with more sensitive and secret state matters and often operated undercover and in plain clothes. Finally, of course the general criminal police, like Josef Weber, who dealt with non-state-related criminal matters such as robbery, vice and murder. Sometimes those areas of responsibility overlapped, and when they did it could cause problems.

This identity-change network was one such case. The falsifying of documents that might allow Jews, gypsies and dissidents to hide away most definitely fell under Schnabel's remit. But for whatever reason—possibly the forging of state documents on any large scale—the Gestapo felt the investigation might have higher state-security significance. Part of it, particularly at a basic fraud and forging level, could also be seen to fall under the responsibility of the general police.

Schnabel shook his head. While so high-and-mighty reprimanding others over "clumsy" interrogations, the Gestapo should have also considered their own clumsy interrogation with Leon Weinel bleeding to death. In fact, if it hadn't been for him picking up Max Adler's name on that old interrogation transcript, taking matters to the next level would have been missed; indeed, if Adler had talked and given him names rather than negotiate to try and save his own neck, they'd have uncovered the leaders of this network straightaway.

If he'd had his own way, he'd have killed Max Adler there and then, but he'd thought it more prudent that a valuable central Vienna club end up in the Reich's coffers. And what thanks did he get? A snotty memo from the local Gestapo. Although from his past association with Piehler over the Freud Circle photos, he suspected the memo was written mainly for the benefit of the hierarchy looking over Piehler's shoulder; those who had insisted he deal with the Freud case with kid gloves, which Piehler hadn't been particularly happy about.

Still, Schnabel decided he should proceed cautiously, with "clumsy interrogations" the main phrase he should pay heed to. He knew that the Gestapo couldn't order him to cease the investigation entirely—since the shielding and hiding away of Jews, gypsies and dissidents fell very much in his camp—that would have been overstepping the mark. So that internal wrist slap had been restricted simply to "clumsy interrogations."

Schnabel studied the photos he'd spread out on his desktop.

Mindful of the fact that others in his unit might be aware of the memo—Lindner was certainly of sufficient rank to have access to it—he'd instructed a young SS Junker, Siegl, with little or no contact with the Gestapo, to follow Josef Weber and take some photos. He also thought it prudent to keep the threads of this separate as much as possible, so that only he could pull the whole picture together.

The first thing to tease at the back of his mind was that the man he'd passed near Karlsplatz—who later with Lindner he watched go into Brunnerman's—he'd seen somewhere before. But where? He'd been stumped at first, but then he recalled one final thing Weinel had commented before expiring: "Facially, I wasn't changed drastically, and apparently it was the same with the rest of the group. Just mi…minor facial alterations, the rest superficial through hair-color changes and suchlike. But if you studied closely enough, you might see the resemblance to that past self."

That was where he'd been going wrong. He'd been scanning in his mind for an exact match, whereas he should have been looking for a close match. Although it had taken him another three days to finally recall the man he'd seen in the Café Mozart that day soon after Anschluss when he'd walked in and made his announcement. It could be—as this Daniel Lendt had commented when he visited him at the book signing the other day—*Perhaps a relation or long-lost brother.* But now other things were starting to slot into place.

Not long after that first visit to Café Mozart, he'd seen Josef Weber there with three spare cups half-full that looked like they'd been hastily left, and now he had the photos from Siegl of Weber leaving the University of Vienna with three men. One was Daniel Lendt, and the second—if you looked beyond the wheat-blond hair—had a passing resemblance to the other man he'd seen that first day in the Mozart, who'd later run from him to catch a tram. The coincidences were mounting.

In fact, he wouldn't have put a tail on Weber if it hadn't been for him hardly showing up at Der Blaue Engel after Max Adler had left, and Deya Reynes was there less nights as well. His suspicions were verified: a succession of photos of them hugging or kissing as they left a restaurant or getting into Weber's car. They were seeing each other on those nights off.

Schnabel grimaced as he pulled back some of the furthest photos, edging against the photo of his wife and seven-year-old daughter at the end of his desk. Only three years they'd been married—he'd perhaps been too controlling or she too independent-spirited—either way, it hadn't worked out. They were separated and she'd stayed back in Linz. No divorce. He hadn't wanted one in case his failed marriage reflected badly on his career, and she'd gone along with that because her parents were strict Catholic and would have disapproved. So they both kept up the pretense.

All he had left were a few golden memories and that picture of his perfect golden-blond family frozen in time. The last thing he wanted was to sully that image with pictures of Weber with his Spanish or gypsy whore. With the snippet of club gossip he'd heard from Karen last week, gypsy was starting to look more likely.

The Daniel Lendt part of the puzzle had fallen into his lap by chance. Lindner hadn't been getting anywhere watching outside Brunnerman's for Lendt's return, and they'd started to think they might be mistaken—until Schnabel had suggested he wait two more hours each night; finally, three weeks later, Lindner saw Lendt approach Brunnerman's from the other direction. Perhaps being seen that one time earlier had spooked Lendt, so he'd changed the time and way he approached so that he didn't pass the same café.

Then ten days ago Schnabel had seen a snippet in a local newspaper about author Daniel Lendt attending a book signing at Hasbach's on Riemergasse. A small photo of Lendt along with his agent, Julian Reisner—the third man in those university-front photos from Siegl. That final half-empty coffee cup?

Lendt had put on a reasonable performance at the book signing. But Schnabel had sensed some anxiety when he'd mentioned Lendt's writing style reminding him of somebody else. That had been a real claim, not just a bluff to try and draw Lendt out. But again, as initially with the facial recognition, he couldn't for the life of him remember who or where.

The sound of Bach gently drifting in the background, Schnabel started tracing a hand along the bookshelves to one side. He wondered whether discovering that other author would provide the final link?

Hours later, the knocking on Schnabel's door woke him abruptly. He glanced over at the bedside clock: 3:38 a.m. "What on earth…?"

Usually it was he disturbing people at such an ungodly hour, arriving with a rifle-wielding squad in the dead of night to yank a heavily dazed Jew or dissident from their beds for interrogation or to load straight on a truck for the death camps.

As he slipped on a dressing gown and went to answer it, he wondered for an unsettled moment whether the Gestapo had been spying on him, and this was some sort of warning or reprimand about continuing the investigation. But as he opened the door, Karen from Der Blaue Engel stood there. He squinted sharply.

"What in heaven's name are you doing here at this hour?"

"The club has just closed," she said. Then from his stern look realizing that wasn't anywhere near an adequate answer, she smiled provocatively. "And I thought you might like the company. I'm still wearing the outfit I had on for my last routine. I know it's one of your favorites."

Karen opened the front of her camel-haired coat to briefly reveal a purple basque and matching stockings before wrapping the coat around her again. Blonde ringlets touching her shoulders, pale green eyes, lips heavily glossed, for a moment Schnabel was tempted. He found Karen pretty enough and actually enjoyed her company—in small doses. But he wasn't in the mood for her company tonight. He shook his head.

"I'm sorry. Heavy day tomorrow…so perhaps another time when I next see you at the club." With a tight smile, he went to shut the door.

"You know you mentioned about letting you know if I found out anything more about Deya? Well, I think I have."

Schnabel opened the door back a shade wider. "What was that?"

"An elderly man came by the club earlier who hadn't been for a while. He said he knew Deya from years ago—back when she had another name. A gypsy name." Karen smiled tentatively. "I thought you'd want to know straightaway—that's why I came by."

"Yes, of course. You did the right thing." As he opened the door fully, her smile broadened, but he couldn't help noticing the fleeting disappointment on Karen's face that her feminine attributes on their own hadn't been enough to gain entry—it had taken the sharing of information. She knew the way to his heart. "You'd better come in."

24

We are never so defenseless against suffering as when we love, never so helplessly unhappy as when we have lost our loved object or its love.

—*Sigmund Freud, Civilization and Its Discontents*

Deya noticed the man looking at her while she was trying to choose a silk scarf at Tendorf's, a dress shop and milliners on Landskrongasse.

"We do have this one arrived not long ago from Berlin in light blue."

Deya picked up the silk scarf so that it caught the light more. "I was thinking more of something in royal blue with a more subtle pattern. Perhaps ikat or flowery brocade."

"I'm sorry." The shop manager, a woman in her late forties, pursed her lips. "The only one with a pattern like that is this one here."

Deya considered the purple scarf held up for a moment. The

pattern was fine, but she'd have to choose a different jacket; it would clash with the powder blue jacket she planned to wear, whereas she knew that royal blue would blend well.

Josef had phoned and said he planned to take her to dinner at Pfarrwirt. "I have something important to tell you." She'd pushed for what it might be, but he remained secretive, assuring, "Don't worry. Hopefully, you'll like what I have to say—but I thought we should at least make a special night of it."

Special night? Deya would have guessed that alone from the planned venue: Pfarrwirt, one of Vienna's top restaurants. She had a jacket that she felt would look good, but was keen to get a complementing silk scarf for the occasion. She'd already been to the milliner's department at Neumann's and Schiffman's with no luck.

And she was just saying her thanks and goodbye to the shop assistant at Tendorf's when she noticed the man on the far side of the shop floor looking at her. As she felt his eyes on her and looked back his way, he swiftly averted his eyes.

Over the years, Deya had become something of an expert in the way men looked at her. Her first alerts had been Nazi supporters who might question her gypsy background. But years ago, there had been no danger in that, simply acrimony. Then later when she'd had her identity changed to Spanish and after her ID card had been asked for a number of times without raising suspicion, her anxiety eased. Besides, a number of leading SS and Kriminalpolizei knew her well from their visits to Der Blaue Engel. Finally, the men who simply looked at her because they found her an attractive woman. So she'd become used to differentiating between those looks.

This man was elderly, but it was the way he looked quickly away, as if afraid he'd been caught looking, that she found strange. She also had the feeling that she'd seen him somewhere before, but she couldn't place where. Only fifty yards from Tendorf's, she'd already shed off her concerns: perhaps because of his age he'd been simply embarrassed caught ogling at her, or he'd also been struck by some past recognition.

Her thoughts in any case were more on where she planned to go next: Ornstein's on Vorlaufstrasse. Indeed, that would have been her first choice to look for a scarf, since they always had such a wide range, many of them imported from Paris—but she hadn't been back out of respect for Lillian Ornstein since the day she'd heard the SS had piled her into a truck to take to a death camp.

Over the years of visiting her shop, Deya had developed a strong affection for Lillian Ornstein, by then in her early sixties. But what had particularly broken her heart when she'd heard about Mrs. Ornstein was that her two young grandchildren, a boy of five and a girl of seven, had been taken along with her. Mrs. Ornstein's daughter and husband had tragically died in a road accident three years beforehand, and Lillian Ornstein had since been taking care of their children and raising them.

With their ages, Deya had heard they'd all been put to death within days of arriving at Dachau. She hadn't been able to stomach going into the new "Reich-approved" shop since— but needs must. She took a fresh breath as she stepped over the threshold—the first time in almost two years.

The assistant behind the counter was in her late twenties, probably not the owner. Deya tried to dissociate her as much as possible from what had happened to Lillian Ornstein and her grandchildren.

But as she leafed through the selection of scarves, it wasn't easy. She got images of standing in that same spot with Mrs. Ornstein smiling softly as she made a recommendation: *This one would hopefully go well with the dress you mention.* Or often sweetening it with a compliment: *Your skin tone is beautiful, like milky coffee—so you need something to bring that out.*

And something else she noticed as she looked through. "You

don't have the wide selection you used to. When Mrs. Ornstein ran the shop, there were…"

Deya broke off as she caught the crestfallen look on the young woman's face, realizing what she was on the verge of saying. Criticizing Reich-controlled enterprises was dangerous ground, especially if the past owners were Jewish.

The shop assistant looked each side for a moment, as if she, too, was anxious who might have been listening in. "It isn't so much the changeover from Mrs. Ornstein. It's that with the war now on, we don't get the supplies we used to from Paris and elsewhere."

"I see. Yes… I'm sorry."

"A lot of what you see now from Paris is in fact the old stock from when Mrs. Ornstein was here."

Deya simply nodded numbly, her eyes glassy as she perused the selection. The tears close.

The woman appeared to soften more then. "Did you know Mrs. Ornstein?"

Deya froze for a second. Would even admitting that be somehow incriminating? But she knew that with her emotional state at that moment, the lie would show. She eased a sigh: reluctant admittance. "Yes, I did. I used to shop here now and then." One little secret held back. She used to be here every other week.

The young woman looked each side again for a second, then reached out and patted Deya's hand across the counter. "If it's any consolation, some of us here are sad, too, about what happened to Mrs. Ornstein." She smiled tightly, regretfully. "But we do our best."

"Thank you." Deya felt the tears welling stronger then, but she bit them back, dabbing at a couple of stray tears with the back of one hand. And, perhaps, partly in gratitude, she did end up making a purchase. Not the full royal blue she wanted, more of an azure blue—but perhaps it would work.

Paying and thanking the woman again, she managed to hold

the tears back—but halfway along the street from the shop, they started flowing freely. Crying for all the souls lost these past three years. All the ones Lorenzo hadn't been able to save. When you heard the stories, "Ninety thousand have now left Vienna, and as many again have probably perished…perhaps over a million now in the Reich overall," it became just a cold statistic. Didn't mean much. But when you personally knew the people involved, it was different. The pain of their memory—still able to clearly see their faces and hear their voices—gripped your heart. Then multiply that a million times. The pain was too much.

Her eyes were still so bleary with tears when she got on the tram that she didn't notice the elderly man from Tendorf's sat toward the back.

It wasn't until she stopped for coffee at Café Ritter and had composed herself more that she became aware of him again, no-ticing also now a young man in a tweed jacket sat next to him. Perhaps his son, she thought. The old man didn't seem to be looking at her anymore, so probably it was just a coincidence that he was here again now.

She went back to sipping at her coffee, skim-reading a couple of articles in the *Neues Wiener Tagblatt* newspaper on her table before pushing it aside.

"What?" She looked up, startled. The young man had walked across and was holding out one hand.

"Can I?"

Deya realized that he was referring to the newspaper. It was one of the café's with a wood-handled holder that the previous reader had forgotten to put back in the rack. "Yes…of course."

He held the paper over her table for a second, tapping at its front. "Only if you're finished with it, that is?"

"Yes, fine, thanks. I'm finished."

She went back to sipping her coffee, then broke off to check her silk scarf purchase from Ornstein's—trying to picture it again

with the powder blue jacket she planned to wear—before finishing her coffee. But on the last mouthful, the café around her
seemed to blur, and she felt unsteady as she stood up.

She'd hardly taken one step before the table and floor surged
up toward her. The last thing she recalled was the young man
rushing toward her through the haze of people around. "It's
okay, I'm a doctor. I'll take care of her."

Then he was lifting her and holding her up by one shoulder,
her feet dragging slowly beneath her into darkness.

Josef was also at that moment shopping in the center of Vienna.
And if he'd looked in more detail at the people in the tram passing on Mariahilferstrasse—or Deya in turn had been looking
out and not so teary-eyed—they might have seen each other.

They were both thinking the same thing, but in different
ways: she was thinking of a past that she could no longer alter or
make good; he was thinking of a past that he could still hopefully make good—and perhaps should have done years ago—
his eyes fixed across the road until the tram had passed and he
could see the jeweler's front window again.

25

*Jews, Mischlinge and Gypsies are henceforth banned from all
Reich public areas such as parks, restaurants and swimming
pools.*

Deya shuddered as she felt Schnabel's hand trail slowly down
her side.

She'd been stripped down to her petticoat, her hands up high
above her and tied to a beam, her feet supported on a small stool.
Her petticoat was wet from a hosing down, and she noticed
that its force had pulled loose a strap on her petticoat, exposing
part of one breast on that side. She started to shiver as the water
cooled on her body.

"So I ask you again," Schnabel said. "The name of your cousin
and his accomplice who organize this identity-change network?"

"I told you. I don't know what you're talking about."

The questioning had been going on twenty-five minutes before Schnabel lost patience and asked for the hose to be put on

her. The young man she'd seen in Café Ritter, now in full SS uniform, was the one operating the fire hose, its pressure so strong it took her breath away and almost knocked her off the stool. Another more muscly man sat to one side stripped down to his vest.

She had no idea how long she'd been unconscious from what they'd put in her coffee—realizing now the young SS man had slipped it in under the newspaper he'd picked up. There was no window light in the basement to indicate what time of day it was. *I have to meet Josef later*, was the first thought to strike her.

Schnabel paced slowly, deliberately; a cat circling its prey. "As you know, the information I have says otherwise." He picked up a two-page form on a side table with an official stamp and held it in front of her. "As you can see."

She squinted at it, shaking her head after a moment. "It…it's not clear." Her eyes were still watering from cold and fear and the aftereffect of her drugged coffee.

"Then let me read it to you," Schnabel said curtly. "I, Nils Durmann, do hereby declare that I first met Deya Reynes some four or five years ago at Der Blaue Engel, at which time she was known by a gypsy name, Chara or Charani, if I recall correctly. Then when I went back to the club a year later, she'd changed her name to Deya, and I heard from one of the other girls that a cousin of hers had helped with the identity change." Schnabel tapped the declaration. "Then follows a statement from Herr Durmann that he positively identified you as the same person in Café Ritter while accompanied by SS Junker Helmut Siegl. Then I've added my own brief statement that I'm satisfied the information herein is true and accurate before signing myself and stamping."

The elderly man? That was why she thought she'd seen him somewhere. And the girl had probably been Mira. Deya had confided in her purely because she'd been the only other Romani girl at the club and had shown an interest in having her own identity changed, which she finally did a year later before leaving the club.

Deya glanced toward the muscled-man to one side. "Is this the part where you have me beaten to a pulp, like you did with Max?"

Schnabel smiled thinly. "Hopefully, that won't be necessary. I like to be more subtle with women, not so brutal." That wasn't exactly true. Only a month ago a Jewess who he thought was smirking at him, he'd smashed so hard in the jaw with his pistol butt that he'd knocked out two teeth cleanly and loosened another three. He'd then spent the next forty minutes pulling out those loose teeth with pliers while she screamed in agony and finally told him what he wanted. But he couldn't afford another perceived "clumsy" investigation, and while Deya seemed to shiver at his very touch, as if repulsed by it, that seemed threat enough. He ran one hand slowly down her flank. "Just tell me what I need to know, then we can both get out of here."

"I told you. I don't know anything." She shook her head, looked away.

"Tell me…" His hand went down her thigh, feeling her tremble like a frightened rabbit beneath his touch.

Deya closed her eyes and bit at her bottom lip as his hand slid under her slip.

"We both know you're holding back, that you know far more than you're letting on…" He could feel her warmth as he moved up her inner thigh, her trembling biting deeper. "So just tell me…"

She shook her head silently above him, her jaw clenched tight.

But something else in that moment broke the spell. Muscleman Gustav was looking at them indifferently, as if he'd seen this sort of thing before, but young SS Junker Siegl was partly open-mouthed. And Schnabel couldn't tell if it was because he was enjoying the eroticism, or shock—Schnabel reminding himself sharply that sexual consorting between Reich citizens and gypsies was strictly forbidden.

He slid his hand away and signaled for Siegl to put the hose back on her. Cool off both her heat and obstinacy.

Deya gasped as the cold blast of water hit her, spluttering to get her breath back afterward. "All…all you have is hearsay, rumors. You have no proof."

"Proof…proof." Schnabel shook his head in wonderment. "We're living in a time now where simple grudges are being played out between friends, or brother against brother—with little more required than the claim that they're dissidents or activists, and they disappear." Schnabel snapped his fingers. "Never to be heard of again. Here, I have a full and detailed denouncement, countersigned by two SS. You and I both know that this is more than enough to seal your fate. So stop wasting my time."

Schnabel's voice had risen with his last words. She looked at him for a moment, her mind desperately searching for options. But she knew what he said was true. There was no way out. "I don't know," she muttered.

Schnabel's tone tempered. "In a way, I'm doing you a favor here. Offering you an opportunity. I have no particular interest in you—you're small-fry. It's the head of this network, your cousin, I'm interested in. So while I have in my hand here the absolute power to consign you to a death camp." Schnabel gestured toward the denouncement. "If you tell me what I want now, I'll ignore this and set you free. You'll be able to go back to your nice cozy life as if none of this had happened."

For a moment, Deya was tempted. But even if she could trust Schnabel and put her own life before that of Lorenzo's, she knew it wouldn't end there. Schnabel would also want to track down all the people Lorenzo had helped over the years. All those families, too, would be sent to the death camps. All the Mrs. Ornsteins and her grandchildren. She couldn't do that. She closed her eyes for a second, shaking her head. "I'm sorry." Sorry for not acquiescing, was obviously how Schnabel read it from his downcast expression, but it was aimed more at those she'd be leaving behind. Josef. Luciana.

"So be it. You appear to have made your decision." Schnabel exhaled tiredly. "But don't say I didn't give you a fair chance to save yourself."

Josef. Cozy life. One last desperate chance. She blurted out that she was planning to meet Josef later that night. "If I don't show up, he'll know something's wrong. He'll come looking for me. This could all backfire on you."

Schnabel smiled ingratiatingly. "You know how it works. With a denouncement of this nature, I'm simply doing my duty. If he tried to interfere, he could become implicated as well. A police officer helping someone with fraudulent documentation and a known gypsy past—it could end his career." Schnabel shrugged. "He could even end up in a camp with you."

Deya shook her head. "He wouldn't just desert me like that."

"You think not? He certainly wouldn't bother to pursue much, knowing the potential risks." Schnabel smiled slyly as he was struck with the thought. "Ah, the ultimate test of his love for you—that he'd put his career and own welfare first."

Deya glared back. Another painful truth. The deck had been stacked against people like her and Josef from the start, an anti-Nazi policeman and a gypsy—what hope had they ever had? She'd played her last trump card and failed.

But Schnabel was still busy laying down the last of his royal flush. "Or indeed as much a test of your love for him. Would you really be willing to let him risk his career and his life purely to save your own neck—knowing his efforts would probably be futile in any case?"

A light buzzing in Deya's head masked much of what Schnabel said next, repeating his regret at her decision and making the final arrangements—but the mention of her daughter cut through it all, made her jolt.

"What?"

"I said, meanwhile I'll get some of my men to pick up your daughter."

Deya felt the bottom drop out of her stomach. She'd already resigned herself to a death camp, but hadn't realized till that moment they'd take Luciana as well. Obviously, one of the girls at the club, probably Karen, had told them she had a daughter.

"As I mentioned, I'm seeing Josef tonight—so she's with someone else right now." The same woman close by she paid to take care of Luciana on club nights also babysat her when she went out.

"Who is that?"

Deya stared back stonily.

Schnabel met her stare for a moment before easing a sigh, taking stock. She obviously wasn't going to tell him, and while he could dig around and no doubt find the girl, it might take a day or so. Also, while he didn't think Josef Weber would get anywhere pursuing the matter, he could do without the aggravation of fending off his sniffing around and trying to push for her release. But there might be a way of combining the two to advantage.

"Okay," Schnabel said with a resigned huff. "I won't trouble myself looking for your daughter—make your own arrangement with how she's taken care of when you're gone. As long as you write a certain letter beforehand."

"Would you like another aperitif, sir?"

"No, it's okay, thank you." Josef swirled the last inch of Campari and lemon in his glass. "I'll wait for my dinner guest to arrive. I'm sure she won't be long now."

Josef checked his watch as the waiter left his table: 8:57 p.m., almost half an hour past their agreed meeting time, when previously he couldn't recall Deya being any more than five minutes late for anything. Ten minutes ago, he'd gone to use the phone in the restaurant foyer, in case she'd been unexpectedly held up or had got the time or date mixed up. She hadn't answered.

Josef fished the ring box out of his jacket pocket and opened it: a good-sized diamond at its center with small emeralds surrounding.

He'd decided in the end to stop being nebulous, *I should make a decent woman of you…or one day I should…or isn't it about time?* All of those attempts lacked full-hearted commitment. As if his father were still hanging over his shoulder holding him back with some residual doubt. Still worried about his career and what the Nazis would do if they discovered he'd married a gypsy. And Deya was also right in saying that the last thing they wanted to do was get married simply because of the Nazis, because of that threat.

He needed to say outright, "I love you, and I want you to be my wife." And to hell with the Nazis and all the other nonsense going on around them at the moment. Offer her the ring, if necessary get down on one knee and make a fool of himself in front of everyone in the restaurant, and pray she said yes.

"Would you like to perhaps order some wine, sir?" The waiter was back at his side.

Josef considered for a second; he certainly felt like he needed a drink. "Yes, okay." He ordered a bottle of burgundy Richebourg.

But he'd seriously misjudged it. She'd probably sensed what he had planned for tonight, and she'd got cold feet. Knew from his increasing concern about the changes and edgy atmosphere at the club after Max Adler had left that a strong motive had still been that portent of the Nazis hanging over her; the very thing she'd warned was not a good reason for them to marry. And she hadn't had the heart to face him and tell him no.

He still clung, though, to a last vestige of hope that she'd turn up and there'd be a simple explanation—some unexpected emergency cropped up with herself or Luciana—and he found himself looking toward the entrance and checking his watch every few minutes between sips of wine.

By the time it reached Deya being over an hour late, he was halfway through the bottle of wine and ready to give up the ghost. She wasn't coming. Realizing then too what a sad and lonely figure he cut sitting alone at the table drinking. He probably wouldn't order any food now, he'd just grab a quick frankfurter and bratwurst at a Würstelstand on the way home. And he was just about to lift his hand for the waiter to offer his apologies and get the bill for the wine and Campari, when the door usher walked toward him with an envelope.

"This was just handed to me for you, sir."

26

The original nature of man harbors an inclination to aggression that in most people is only barely constrained by the dictates of society.

—*Sigmund Freud*

Deya was kept overnight in a cell in the basement of the Hotel Metropole, only doors away from where she'd been questioned and wrote her final letter to Josef.

Then at first light she was transported along with thirty others to a large building in Herminengasse, where over a hundred were being held, mostly Jews, awaiting transport to Dachau.

Her "Deya Reynes" identity papers had been declared false and been destroyed; she was being transferred to Dachau simply as "Charani the gypsy and dissident." Schnabel wanted to ensure that Josef Weber didn't start searching through records to try and trace her.

Soon after arriving at Herminengasse, "Charani" approached

one of the guards to make the call agreed with Schnabel to set arrangements for her daughter, Luciana. After checking a register and some notes to see that had been approved, the guard accompanied her to the one public phone in the building and stood by while she made her call.

An hour later a woman who introduced herself as "a relative of Charani's" arrived at the building, and Charani explained to the guard, "She's the woman I phoned earlier. I need a few minutes alone with her to make the final arrangements for my daughter."

The guard perused the woman for a moment: in traditional Romani wear, with a bright flowery-brocade jacket and flowery headscarf, he could see the strong resemblance between the two. Clearly a relative. "Okay. Be quick, though."

He showed them to a small room used as a makeshift cell along the corridor, and was about to rap on the door four minutes later when the two women emerged again, giving each other a parting hug.

The woman in her flowery Romani dress gave a quick wave as she left the building, and a pensive, disconsolate Charani, aka Deya, returned to join the others in the crowded holding rooms.

Two hours later they were all loaded on a train at Aspang station to take to Dachau.

Late the next day, Schnabel received a call from Camp Commandant Walter Keppler that "Charani the gypsy" had arrived at Dachau.

"She was in the latest consignment arrived just an hour ago. Pretty woman," Keppler commented absently.

"Yes, she is. But a gypsy, nevertheless."

"Yes, of course."

Schnabel had called Keppler the day before and asked to be notified. A fellow Austrian like himself, they'd reached a swift accord. One thing Schnabel had often pondered: why 70 percent of camp commandants were Austrian Germans, like Hitler. Did they feel some added allegiance because of that shared birthplace, or was it that the Führer felt this particularly tough and sensitive task could be trusted more to fellow Austrians than Germans?

"Is she a very active dissident?" Keppler asked. "Might she cause some trouble within the camp?"

Schnabel read what Keppler was asking: Should she be put to death straightaway?

"No, not particularly." Schnabel sighed. "But she has withheld information of some value to the Reich." Schnabel's parting words to Deya had been that hopefully some time in Dachau would bring her to her senses. Schnabel shared the bones of his inquiry with Keppler. "It might be that now she's actually in the camp, she'll relent and decide to talk. But it's unlikely…and I daresay after a few weeks that hope would fade entirely. So do with her what you wish."

The message clear: dispose of her straightaway or hold on for a few weeks in the hope of gaining information to aid the Reich. It was up to Keppler. Schnabel wouldn't be so presumptuous as to tell an experienced camp commandant what to do with his prisoners.

"I understand," Keppler said. "I'll inform you immediately if she says anything."

Schnabel couldn't resist a faint smile as he hung up. Even if Deya did survive those few weeks, it looked like her interrogation would in part continue.

Schnabel turned his attention back to the two books to his side. He'd finally recalled where he'd seen a similar style to this new writer, Daniel Lendt. Six years since he'd read the novel by Mathias Kraemer, *Stadt der Schatten* (*City of Shadows*), he'd picked it out from his top bookshelf, and started comparing the two, making notes as he went.

By the time he'd reached the eightieth page, he was already

convinced that the styles were not only similar, but practically identical.

He picked up from his bookmarked position on page 114, going back and forth between the two books as he continued with his notes.

27

No Jews, Mischlinge or Gypsies shall be on the streets after six o'clock at night. They should also at all times allow clear passage on pavements to Reich citizens, particularly officers and soldiers of the Wehrmacht or SS, if necessary walking in the gutter or road.

Daniel

Dear Josef,
I'm sorry to leave so suddenly like this. Especially when you had a special night planned for us.

But you know I've felt more and more uneasy at the club recently, and in the end it all became too much for me. I had to leave with Luciana.

I'll be in touch again when I know we're safe and settled. Once more, I'm so sorry.

Love,
Deya

I lifted my eyes from reading the letter and looked across the table at Josef.

"Have you looked for her?"

"Of course. She's not been at her place for five days now, none of her friends have seen her, nobody at the club either—none of the girls there have any idea where she's gone." Josef ran one hand unevenly through his hair, looked ragged from lack of sleep, worry and the drink he'd no doubt consumed the past few days.

Even now he had a half bottle of peach schnapps at his elbow that my mother had dug out of a kitchen cupboard.

When Josef had told me he wanted to talk about something, I'd already planned to see my mum and Erica-Anna.

I'll come and see you there, if that's okay, Josef had said. *I haven't seen your mum in a while, and it would be good for me to get out of the city, get some fresh air.*

The new bungalow my mother shared with Erica-Anna was still officially in Vienna, though on its outskirts. But with the increased patchwork green of farm fields and riding stables, it had more of a rural feel. Because of the added distance, I'd bought a secondhand Stopel 100 for the regular journeys two months ago.

"Have you come to nail another cross above my front door?" my mother greeted Josef, smiling crookedly. "That's at least something you could do honestly this time—with me now officially a Catholic."

Though as Josef had gibed back, "I think it's more a question of whether someone should nail a cross to my chest," I knew Josef had something serious to discuss, if I hadn't already guessed from his harrowed look.

So when after the greetings and a few pleasantries exchanged with my mum and Anna, Josef asked if I had a drink, I knew he wasn't thinking of just tea or coffee.

My mum quickly offered some peach schnapps from her friend up the road. "Tomas makes it in his bathtub, but it's really good."

On my last few visits, I'd heard about my mum's new friend, Tomas, a retired dairy-farm manager who came around to play cards and dominoes with her and Anna. And now an illegal home-distiller as well. I smiled. Did everyone have a secret side game from the Nazis?

My mum and Anna rejoined Alex in the lounge, where he had been halfway through showing them the latest stamps in his collection, leaving Josef and I alone in the dining room to talk.

Josef shook his head. "I've lost her, Mathias." When we were alone, not in public, he used my original name rather than Daniel. "And all because I left it too long…"

As Josef went on to talk about his father's "lukewarm" Nazism and the bad decisions Josef felt he'd made as a result, I could see from the shadows in his eyes that this was something that had haunted him for some while. I tried to bolster him as much as I could, make him feel better.

"But, as you say, your father's views softened with time…and when he was ill and in his last years, I can see why you wouldn't have wanted to upset him then."

"Yes, thinking about my father. But I never troubled to look at it from Deya's view, did I?" Josef took another slug of schnapps. "To her, it might have seemed as if I was partly siding with my father. Waving a flag for his prejudices and fears…even after his death."

I contemplated for a moment. "The two are separate, but sometimes they merge." Josef squinted at me uncertainly. "After all, look at me. I ended up marrying a nice Catholic girl. I used to tell myself that it was simply because I found her attractive and liked her carefree spirit—but we were never really suited. So maybe something else was going on." I shrugged. "Obviously, nobody would claim I was prejudiced against my own people, and back then general prejudice against Jews wasn't nearly strong enough to engender any fear. But maybe subconsciously I knew that things would fester and get worse, become threatening. Not safe anymore for me or my future family, and that led me to make a prejudicial marriage choice based on that fear." I held a hand out. "And perhaps your father saw the same."

I watched Josef slotting the pieces into place in his mind. "You know what he said to me once? He said that if I had children with Deya and her background came out—just think how they might suffer in today's world with Nazism on the rise?"

"Did Deya know how your father felt?"

"Pretty much." Josef took another slug, his expression strained. "But strange thing was, sometimes she almost sided with him—particularly when we touched on the subject not long ago. Seemed more concerned about my career and welfare. As if to say—if she did end up going down in flames, she didn't want me going down with her." Josef closed his eyes for a second in pained penance. "There just never seemed a right time for us."

I reached across and touched Josef's arm, consoling. "You can't blame yourself, Josef. Seems to me your father and Deya were as much servants to that prejudice, that fear, if not more." Josef appeared to struggle accepting that. I held out one arm. "And look at me now. My whole family moved and with new names. I've been servant to it too. We've all made decisions we perhaps wouldn't have because of the Nazis."

"I suppose."

But as I watched Josef stare emptily into the air, searching for reasons still beyond his grasp, I realized it was scant consolation. And probably unfair: my decision and Johannes-Andreas's had kept our families together, whereas Josef was now split from the woman he loved, fearing he might have lost her forever.

And as Josef fished the ring out of his pocket and laid it on the table between us, explaining how he'd planned finally to do the right thing, but was already too late, my heart broke completely. Josef stared at the ring morosely. "I think she guessed what I was about to do, and it frightened her. She ran off." He took another slug, grimacing. "Damned when I don't do the right thing, damned when I do."

"I'm so sorry, Josef." I patted his arm again, gripped stronger. My own eyes welling in that moment along with his, I suddenly felt I needed a drink too. Until that moment, I'd been drinking water. I reached across and poured a heavy shot of schnapps into the same glass, bringing it from a quarter to half-full.

And it struck me then how strange it was that Josef was sharing all of this with me now, that he didn't have anyone at the police station or others he could share it with. How alone he was, especially now Deya had gone.

But I suppose with now the police and half of Austria full of Nazi sympathizers, this was the last thing he could share with them—his lost love for a gypsy girl who'd buried her identity. It was only people like me who knew that secret that he could share this with.

In that respect, we'd become banded together, closer, due to our rejection from the rest of society. Or fear of it.

We finished the bottle of schnapps between us, and afterward I didn't think Josef was in any fit state to drive, nor a good idea that he was alone in such a maudlin mood—so I offered he stay the night at my mum's. He was reluctant at first, but I was insistent.

"Alex and I are staying too, and Erica... Anna is preparing roast chicken for us all. I'm sure it will stretch." I smiled. "And chicken liver to start, prepared like you've never had before."

Josef nodded and smiled his acceptance; his first easy smile since he'd arrived.

Fifteen minutes later we started settling down for the evening, Josef sat on the sofa as Alex proudly showed him his stamp collection, with Josef teasing, "So this Baden 9 Kreuzer stamp you'd love to find. Surely a detective like me should be able to find it for you..." And I thought how good Josef would be with children, how sad it would be if he never had his own. An added poignancy to his fear that Deya had gone and he might never see her again.

As I drew the curtains on my mother's front window, I paid little attention to the beige Steyr 50 parked sixty yards down on the opposite side of the road.

28

We are threatened with suffering…from the external world, which may rage against us with overwhelming and merciless forces of destruction; and finally from our relations to other men. The suffering which comes from this last source is perhaps more painful to us than any other.

—*Sigmund Freud*

"Did you forget something, Krisztina?" Julian Reisner looked toward the door to the adjoining reception room as he heard movement on the other side; his secretary had left only a minute ago and perhaps she'd forgotten her hat or gloves.

His heart dropped as Heinrich Schnabel walked in, but he quickly composed his face. After all, he wasn't meant to know him or see him as a threat; if it hadn't been for the internal file photo Josef Weber had shown him one day, he wouldn't even know what Schnabel looked like. He raised a brow. "Can I help you?"

"That would depend." Schnabel took a seat on the other side of his desk. Julian saw that he was carrying a large black leather bag. Schnabel reached into the bag and took out a copy of Daniel Lendt's *Als Nachtpässe* (*As Night Passes*), placing it on the desktop as he took a fresh breath. "I had the pleasure of meeting one of your authors a short while ago, a Mr. Lendt, and he kindly signed his book for me—which I've since read. Very entertaining."

"I'm glad you enjoyed it." Mathias-Daniel had mentioned Schnabel coming to a signing two months ago. But it wasn't something Julian felt would be mentioned under normal circumstances between them, so he said nothing now. Kept his expression neutral.

"Not highbrow literature by any means." Schnabel's lips curled. "But entertaining enough in a superficial, not-too-demanding way."

Silence fell, and Julian felt butterfly contortions in his stomach as Schnabel stared across at him. Hopefully, he was meeting that gaze placidly, wasn't giving away his nervousness.

"But as you've probably guessed, I haven't come just for a pleasant chat about how I enjoyed one of your author's books," Schnabel said. He looked aslant for a second. "You know, it's strange. The writing struck me as familiar—but I couldn't at first place from where. Then I finally recalled a book by a certain Mathias Kraemer I'd read some years ago."

As Schnabel took *Stadt der Schatten* from his black bag and placed it on the desktop next to Daniel Lendt's *Als Nachtpässe*, the contortions in Julian's stomach wormed deeper. He kept his expression deadpan, only a faintly quizzical rise to his brow, as if to say, *So?*

"But let us go through and look at the similarities, shall we…?" Schnabel went through the two books methodically, a painstaking stripping down of every likeness in sentence structure, verb and adverb use. "See how often he uses the term 'forcefully,' *gewaltsam*, rather than the far simpler 'strongly,' *stark*.

We have numerous examples of that between the two books on the following pages…"

Julian felt his jaw clench tight as Schnabel went through each example. Wouldn't that be read as the normal impatience with such a tedious exercise: Where is this heading?

"The sentence structure we also see is almost identical in these passages…" Schnabel knew what he was doing. Like a malicious child with a spider pinned down by its thorax while he pulls off its legs one by one, he looked up at Julian at intervals, nodding with a gentle gloat. Seeking his silent approval, or perhaps to say: *Look how thorough I've been.* "Finally, we have the way that both Kraemer and Lendt often end scenes with a question. Or will sometimes break off halfway through and re-join the same scene later."

Julian shook his head, waving his silver cigarette holder to one side. "It's just a coincidence. A lot of thriller writers use devices like that. Ending scenes with a vital question or cliff-hanger."

"But it's beyond mere coincidence, isn't it?" Schnabel let out a tired breath; the first sign he was losing patience. "We're not talking about the way that Thomas Mann was influenced by Goethe, Tolstoy by Victor Hugo or Carl Schmitt by Ernst Jünger—in which case we might see some similarities between their work. We're talking about a practically identical writing style, with fifty or sixty examples which I've painstakingly been through chapter and verse." Schnabel smiled fleetingly at the inference, his countenance dropping as sharply again. "Or am I wasting my time with you?"

"It's not that, it's just…" As Julian's voice drifted off, Schnabel appeared to notice then his silver holder with its unlit cigarette dangling in the air along with his thoughts.

"Don't you want to light that?" Schnabel reached into his side pocket, held out and flicked a gold lighter.

And for a moment, seemingly transfixed by the flame, his stomach in knots, Julian was tempted. He felt like just saying "thank you," lighting up and drawing down the first smoke in years, feeling it suffuse through him and ease his wire-taut nerves.

"No, thanks," he said finally, snapping back to. "I've given up. As long as I can leave the cigarette unlit, it means I've won. I've resisted the temptation."

Schnabel looked at him curiously for a second as he sat back. "Let me cut to the chase, Mr. Reisner. It's my strong belief that Mathias Kraemer and Daniel Lendt are one and the same person."

"That's ridiculous!" Julian exhaled with a nervous half laugh.

"Is it?" Schnabel reached again into his black bag and took out a collection of photos, laying them out one by one facing Julian. "And I believe Mathias Kraemer... Daniel Lendt as he is now, has had his identity changed by a network which you fully know of and has likely helped other authors on your books."

Julian felt as if a trapdoor had opened beneath him. Various photos of himself, Daniel, Andreas and Josef. Most of them by the entrance of the University of Vienna, but also a few of Daniel greeting Josef at his mother's house. Schnabel's final cards now on the table. Julian shrugged, clinging to the only remaining life raft.

"Nothing unusual. They're my authors—so of course I'd be meeting them regularly."

"And Josef Weber?"

"He's a policeman attached to the Kärntnerstrasse station I've recommended to a number of authors for research on investigative matters."

Schnabel nodded pensively. "I might have accepted that if it wasn't for the fact that one of our informants on this network said that facial alterations were slight. And then I recalled two men I'd seen in Café Mozart a few years ago..."

As Schnabel expanded his theory that the two men he'd seen that day were the new authors in the photos, Julian realized this wasn't a two-way conversation. This was a lecture, a homily. Schnabel had something specific in mind.

Schnabel prodded at one of the photos with Andreas, commenting that he was sure he was the same man who had run from him to catch a tram. "Although his hair then was brown rather than blond." Schnabel lapsed into thought. "Now I could ask you about the men heading this network. But all you'd likely be able to tell me, as with the others, is a couple of first names, now changed a dozen times since." Schnabel shrugged. "Besides, we hear they're now very likely in Switzerland. But you could certainly give me Kraemer...or should I say Lendt."

As Schnabel's eyes fixed sharply on Julian, he started shaking his head. "I—I couldn't do that."

"Or to bring this into sharper focus for you, if I called a squad in now to search your office, no doubt they'd find other authors you've shielded with identity changes. And we'd unearth the link between Lendt and Kraemer in any case—so your obstruction would have served no purpose."

There it was: give up Kraemer, or risk all the other author identity changes that might be found in his files. The Jews, dissidents and ghostwriters for Nazi-opponents now living in exile. But all that kept spinning back was his long and trusted friendship with Mathias-Daniel. His mother and sister were also fully Jewish, so no doubt they'd be joining him in a death camp.

"I—I can't." Little more than a tremulous murmur.

Schnabel looked at Julian disdainfully. "You also have yourself to consider. Aside from your possible role in this cover-up, there are rumors that you're homosexual. You'd last no more than five minutes in a camp."

"Tho-those rumors are untrue," Julian stuttered. "I've had a number of girlfriends."

Schnabel contemplated Julian coldly, taking in his bright maroon shirt and cream cravat. "Looking at you now, who would believe that? If I made an official denouncement, you know what would happen." Schnabel hissed in his breath. "But still, if you've made your decision."

Schnabel reached for the phone on Julian's desk.

"No—no," Julian stammered. "But I can't give you Kraemer, don't you see? I… I've known him for so long."

Schnabel's hand hovered over the phone. "If you don't want me to call in a squad right now, this instant—then think of someone else, someone of real value. I can't go back to the unit empty-handed, you understand."

Julian nodded vacantly, like a condemned man choosing between hanging and the guillotine. He started to turn other possibilities over in his mind—it felt less personal, less painful, if he termed them possibilities rather than people—but all those seemed equally horrific and unthinkable. He found himself shaking his head again, his body trembling uncontrollably.

Schnabel smiled at him. "If you're having trouble deciding, then perhaps I could help you by tossing a coin."

"No, it's okay…it's okay." Though Julian knew that it wasn't, and probably never would be.

29

Daniel

The knock came on my door not long after I'd returned from Brunnerman's, and at first I thought someone might have followed me back from there or been waiting outside my apartment building, watching for my return.

I was still nervous each time going to Brunnerman's, worried that I might get stopped by the SD or robbed while carrying the diamonds—but at least it was only every three months, and now that I'd changed my route and time I went, I hadn't bumped into Schnabel again in the area. If he went to that same café at a set time periodically, then I was now almost two hours past that time.

But at that later hour, the shadows were heavier in the streets, more chance of robbers lurking. So my nerves were still on edge each time I visited Brunnerman's, with also the uneasy feeling a couple of times that I was being watched.

My nervousness didn't in fact completely recede until I was back in the apartment, my part-held breath easing out as I shut the door behind me. I took the bundle of cash from my inside pocket and went into my bedroom, lifting out a bottom drawer there and hiding it underneath. That, too, was always a worry returning from Brunnerman's, that amount of money on me also making me a target for robbers or awkward questions from the SD or SS.

"Ivor! Mr. Brunnerman gave me some stamps again for you," I called out toward the kitchen. As with Josef and me, I also still used his original name rather than Alex when we were alone. He was preparing some toast and jam to go with his hot chocolate as I walked in. Now fourteen, Ivor-Alex had grown the last year, and seemed to have developed a horse's appetite on the way. "Some really colorful and exciting ones this time."

As I spread out the selection of stamps on the desktop from Kenya, Mauritius and Mozambique, zebras and ocean views with swaying palms, Ivor beamed.

"Thanks, Papa, they're great. I don't think I've got anything like these."

I patted his shoulder and we smiled at each other. He was getting too old and big now for the little-boy hugs I gave him a year or so ago.

The knock came at the front door then, and all the nervousness I felt going to Brunnerman's suddenly resurged.

I moved toward the door with trepidation.

Andreas

The knock came on our door not long after dinner.

Stefanie went to answer it. Another heavy knock came just as she was reaching to open the door, and I should have realized then something was wrong.

I held one hand up to halt her, but it was already too late.

Two SS guards burst through as Stefanie barely had the door a few inches open, knocking her backward.

All the gun training I went through with Alois hardly helped. A squad of five men wielding rifles, two of them peeled off and caught up with me halfway through my run to the bedroom to grab the gun on its high wardrobe shelf, tumbling me over and pinning me to the ground.

Stefanie was quickly at the back of one of them, clawing and pounding at him—but he swung round sharply and hit her in the chest with his rifle butt, knocking her to the floor.

"We only want Johannes Namal, the Mischling half Jew," announced a third man, who appeared to be leading the squad. "We have no interest in the rest of you."

With the use of my original name, it dawned on me what had happened: they'd uncovered my identity change. The children had shrieked with alarm and Nadia was now sobbing and shaking with fear, Dominik appearing braver and holding back his tears as he glared at the guards.

Mathias-Daniel! It struck me in that moment that a similar squad was probably on their way to him. The promise I'd made to Aunt Lena. I must try and warn him! But the grip on my shoulders was like a vise.

As Stefanie got back on her feet and the same guard warned her off by raising his rifle butt again, Dominik lunged toward him, fearing the soldier was going to hit his mother again. And as the other guard fended Dominik off with one arm, I saw my opportunity. For a brief second, the soldier's grip on me relaxed. I burst free toward our half-open apartment door, pushing brusquely aside their leader caught by surprise by the sudden affray—then I was through and out, leaping down the stairs breathlessly, taking the steps two and three at a time.

A shot rang out, some plaster bursting from the wall a foot to my side. Then I was quickly taking the turn on the second landing to the next flight down, out of sight. I bounded down like a man possessed, ragged breath rasping in my throat. Another shot came just as I was swinging open the main door to the apartment block, hitting its frame—then, turning to my right, I sprinted frantically along the pavement. If I could just make it to the next street turn before the soldiers came out, I might get away clear. Fifty yards ahead, thirty. Enough at least to make a quick warning call to Daniel from the kiosk halfway down. My heart pounded hard, my breath falling short. Ten yards.

But then just before the turn, a shout from behind froze my heart and breath.

"Stop! Or I will shoot your son!"

My step faltered. I turned.

The lead soldier of the group had one arm clasped around Dominik's neck, a gun held to his head.

I held one hand out in plea. "No…no. Don't harm him!" I started walking back hurriedly, still with my hand held up. "I won't cause any more trouble. I'll go quietly."

The soldier remained stone-faced, only easing into a smug smile as I came within a few yards and he trained his gun on me and released Dominik. "So, all is good." His smile as quickly dropped and he nodded curtly to two of the other soldiers who had joined him.

I was bundled brusquely into a truck to one side, attempting a meek reassuring "I'll be okay" grimace toward Dominik before glancing up to see Stefanie looking on helplessly, longingly, from our apartment window. Both of us probably thinking the same thing in that moment: it might be the last time we saw each other.

30

Jews, Mischlinge and Gypsies are required to register all prop-
erty and assets. They are forbidden to own any public or strate-
gic buildings, or properties "of interest or importance," and these
may be appropriated by the Reich at will.

Spring had arrived, but in name only on this cold and desolate
early morning at Vienna's Aspang station. And probably felt
even more so to the men, women and children huddled on its
platform awaiting transport to Sobibór concentration camp in
Poland—a number of them snatched in the middle of the night,
so not wearing coats or warm clothing.

Johannes-Andreas was among those, still wearing the light
pullover and shirt he'd been wearing at dinner when the soldiers
stormed in to grab him. So a warm coat was one of the main
things—along with a small suitcase with essentials and change of
clothes—that Julian Reisner made sure to bring Andreas when
he met him on the platform that morning.

As Andreas put on the heavy black wool coat, Julian leaned in closer. "Along with some personal family photos, some tobacco is sewn into the lining—one of the best things to trade inside the camps. That's why the coat feels so heavy. But the most important thing to remember is the letter in the coat's pocket. Make sure to give that letter to Vice-Commandant Dieter Meisel the moment you arrive."

Andreas nodded numbly. "Do you know what happened?"

"No, I don't." Julian looked to one side briefly so that Andreas hopefully wouldn't read the guilt eating him away. Facing Stefanie and seeing her and the children so tearful and distraught last night as he'd picked up these few things to bring Andreas had been particularly difficult. "Some sort of breach in the network, I think. Probably from that chap they questioned a short while back."

Andreas nodded. "And have they arrested Mathias as well?"

"No. I don't think so."

Silence for a second, broken by a shrill whistle and the shouting of guards along the platform.

"And I'm being transported as 'Andreas Siebert, a dissident'?"

"Yes. Hopefully, will make things easier for you than if you were a Jew—so don't admit that in there." Julian glanced over his shoulder at Schnabel observing them from fifty yards back. Along with this last-minute meeting now, one of the few concessions he'd forged with Schnabel for this Faust-style arrangement; but he suspected the main reason Schnabel had agreed to it was because Andreas's original papers had been destroyed and new copies would take time. Schnabel didn't want the delay.

Two soldiers hovered close by, one of them looking sharply at Andreas as he barked, "Beeile dich! It's time!"

Julian pulled Andreas into an embrace. "It'll be tough—but I'm sure you'll survive." Tears welled in his eyes from the cold and his emotions.

"Your confidence is reassuring," Andreas muttered, his eyes distant, finally closing in resignation as he patted Julian's back. "I'll do my best."

"Don't forget that letter…" Julian called out as Andreas was pulled brusquely back and led at rifle point by two soldiers toward the waiting cattle truck.

And as Julian watched the compartment door slam shut on Andreas, despite his hopeful assurance of a moment ago, he had the same uneasy sensation Stefanie told him she'd had when she'd watched Andreas being taken away by the SS: this might be the last time he saw Andreas.

"Very touching," Schnabel commented as Julian walked back toward him. "I daresay you didn't tell him about our little arrangement."

Julian didn't answer, simply glared back before looking toward the last people being herded onto the train.

"You shouldn't harbor such resentment and anger. It's not good for you." Schnabel smiled thinly. "After all, it could have ended up much worse for you. You could have been joining your friend right now."

Julian closed his eyes for a second, a shudder running through him. With how he felt right now, he might have welcomed that: some punishment for what he'd done.

"We all have our crosses to bear," Schnabel commented thoughtfully, observing Julian's reaction.

There had been compromises on both sides: Schnabel would have preferred a full-blown Jew like Kraemer, but his ears had pricked up when he'd heard that Johannes-Andreas's father was no less than the prominent Jewish dissident Samuel Namal. A worthy substitute and feather in his cap.

The threat of raiding Julian Reisner's office had in part been a bluff. He doubted Reisner would have left evidence of name-identity changes obvious or easy to find; it could have taken days, if anything was found at all. Also, Reisner was well-connected, had represented books, too, by some high-ranking Reich officers. He'd worked both sides of the fence. A call from Reisner to one of his Reich contacts halfway through such a raid might

have simply gained Schnabel another wrist slap from the Gestapo for "clumsy" handling.

No, a short–sharp agreement under pressure had been the best
way to proceed. None of Reisner's conditions, such as meeting
Namal-Siebert at the last moment and bringing him some personal
belongings, had been untoward. Indeed, one condition had seemed
somewhat excessive the other way. Schnabel shook his head.

"I daresay you also didn't let on to your friend that it was your
insistence rather than mine that he be sent to Sobibór. Not only
one of the Reich's furthest-flung camps, but also not one of its
kindliest." Schnabel's mouth arched sardonically. "One might
almost get the impression you don't like him."

Julian looked at Schnabel icily. "Or maybe the fact that I'm
ashamed of what I've done—so the further away, the better. Out
of sight, out of mind."

"Alles beendet… All done!" the shout came from a soldier as
the last cattle-truck door was slammed shut. Shrill burst from a
whistle, then seconds later the train started moving out.

They watched it silently for a moment, then Julian turned to
Schnabel. "Are you and I all done now too?"

"Yes." Schnabel eased out a weighted sigh. The final part of
his arrangement with Reisner. "And I'm a man of my word. I
won't be contacting you anymore regarding pursuit of Kraemer
or any other clients on your books."

"Fine." Julian grimaced tautly. "Then to paraphrase a popular
parting—I hope I won't be seeing you again." He turned and
walked away from Schnabel, and twenty yards from the station
lit his first cigarette in six years.

Andreas

The doors shut on the cattle truck. Darkness. Until after six or
seven minutes when my eyes had adjusted and could make out
the shapes and features of some of the twenty or so people in

the same compartment with me. Then started the three-day descent into hell.

Ludenburg... Neisse... Oppeln... Kielce... Warsaw... Lublin... Chelm...

My brief conversation with Ernst, the Kärntnerstrasse shoe-shop owner. The numbers increasing with each stop—forty, sixty, eighty. The press of bodies so tight that there was hardly room to breathe; no choice but for everyone to relieve themselves where they stood—an increasing ammonia bite to the stench of urine and feces, robbing what little fresh air remained.

Clinging to the hope that I'd last the journey—a few already collapsed on the floor, some groaning, some now ominously quiet and still—clinging to my coat with its letter, tobacco and photos of my family.

And in the midst of the darkness of that journey, my aunt Lena's face was there before me. The promise I'd made to her about Mathias.

I'd gone to see her shortly after she'd recovered from her stroke. She'd thanked me for my care and attention, then commented wistfully, "But I worry more about Mathias. How he'd cope if anything happened to me. With him now split from Emilia, he might be lonely. He doesn't have the same support you have with Hannah."

"He's still got me. I'd be there to support him. You know how close we are."

"I know." Aunt Lena had looked at me soulfully before a faint smile creased her lips. "Strange. Mathias said much the same to your father, Samuel, before he died."

"I... I didn't know."

Lena as quickly snapped to, suddenly realizing she'd said something she shouldn't have; vestiges of her stroke still clouding her mind. "I'm sorry. I shouldn't have said anything."

But I was still grappling for an explanation. "Why didn't Mathias tell me?"

Lena shrugged. "Perhaps he thought it might embarrass you. So he kept it quiet." She smiled gently, held one hand out. "As I hope you, too, will say nothing about our little conversation now. It's enough that I know you'll keep an eye out for Mathias, without embarrassing him over it."

Though perhaps as much to save Lena the embarrassment of letting the cat out of the bag over Mathias's promise to my father, Samuel.

The result was that neither I nor Mathias had initially known about the promises made to watch out for each other; and now with the passage of events, Mathias might never get to know.

I don't think so, Julian had said as to whether Mathias had been arrested as well, but there had been a shade of discomfort and uncertainty, as if he knew more than he was letting on. Was Julian also holding back secrets, trying to protect me from knowing the worst?

So many buried secrets.

I swallowed hard, the dryness in my mouth hardly leaving enough saliva even for that. Getting progressively worse with each hour, so that all I could think of in the end was water. If I could just get some water, I might survive. That deliberation began to rise above all else—thoughts of Stefanie and my children overriding those of Mathias and Lena with the passing miles, but even those beginning to fade after a while, their images starting to blur and drift in my mind with my increasing delirium.

So much so that when I did finally see the SS guard with his water flask, I almost forgot to give him the letter to hand to Vice-Commandant Dieter Meisel.

"Please…some of your water?"

My sinking dismay that he couldn't offer me any lifted by the fact that the showers with fresh water were close. Only minutes away!

Though that shuffling into a dormitory to shed my clothes,

then finally being led into a large shower cubicle with ninety other men, seemed to take forever.

The sound of a motor starting up and a faint rattling surge in the pipes. I tilted my head and opened my mouth for the nirvana of the first water to touch my lips in three days.

31

Out of your vulnerabilities will come your strength.

—*Sigmund Freud*

Obersharführer Dieter Meisel, vice-commandant at Sobibór camp, had just come out of a meeting with Commandant Walter Toepfer when Rottenführer Hofer, a private, approached with an envelope.

"I was asked to give this to you, sir?"

Meisel studied the envelope. It had his name typed on the front, but aside from that its outside told him little. He started opening it. "Who gave this to you?"

"One of the new prisoners arriving handed it to Scharführer Vogt. He asked me to bring it to you."

"I see." Scharführer Helmut Vogt was a sergeant under his command who usually oversaw new camp arrivals.

Meisel opened the letter fully and started reading. Mild interest rapidly became more intense, then finally alarm. He looked sharply at Hofer.

"Why wasn't I given this letter straightaway?"

"Uh…you were in a meeting with Commandant Toepfer, sir." Hofer was suddenly uncertain under Meisel's harsh gaze. "And also Scharführer Vogt thought it was probably just from a local synagogue or IKG office."

Meisel nodded curtly. New prisoners arriving sometimes carried letters of plea from synagogues, community leaders or the local IKG, but these were invariably ignored. "Regardless, that would be my decision to make, not Scharführer Vogt's. Where is this prisoner now?"

"They arrived fifteen or twenty minutes ago." His uncertainty wormed deeper under Meisel's expectant stare. "So he…he's probably already in the showers now."

Showers! Meisel's brow arched sharply.

"Come with me now!" he snapped. "And pray we're not too late."

A gangly forty-two-year-old, Dieter Meisel looked reasonably fit, but Hofer had hardly ever seen him running before. Usually, his gait was leisurely, his decisions too often made at a sedate pace between puffs on a clay pipe. Now Meisel was running like a man possessed, Hofer, fifteen years his junior, having trouble keeping up.

The officers and guard buildings were separate from the three prisoner-compound areas, in turn separated by a wire-fenced asphalt path leading to the gas chambers, which had become nicknamed "the tunnel."

Halfway along the tunnel, already breathless, they could hear the heavy reverberations of the tank motor pumping carbon monoxide into the adjoining chamber "shower" rooms.

It sounded as if they might already be too late.

Daniel

However much Josef tried to reassure me, I couldn't escape the sense of feeling trapped, of things closing in on us.

I stroked my forehead after taking a slug of beer. "Deya gone, now Andreas. You don't think the two are somehow connected?"

"No. I don't think so. Deya's letter was very clear that she's gone away with Luciana—possibly out of the country."

"But you don't know where?"

"No." Josef took a sip of his own beer, thoughtful for a moment. "I called the only contact number I have for Lorenzo—some bank lawyer's office in Geneva. I got his call back just this morning." The procedure the same each time: *Leave a telephone number, preferably a phone booth so that it doesn't trace back to you, and a specific time to call at least eight hours from now, and by that time I'll have spoken to our mutual friend and will phone back at that time with news.* "He agrees with me that Deya might have left the country, but apparently has no idea where she is. If she's in Switzerland, she certainly hasn't made contact with Lorenzo yet."

"Strange that she wouldn't even tell Lorenzo where she's gone."

"Not particularly." Josef held a palm out. "If she fears his network has somehow been breached, she might want to keep clear of him for a while until she's sure. Certainly, Schnabel sniffing around her more at the club might have been enough to make her panic and head off."

We sank into our beers for a moment as we contemplated the various options.

We'd stopped off at a bar less than a mile from Andreas and Stefanie's apartment. I felt I needed something stronger than coffee, and Josef had quickly nodded his accord—still on something of a binge since Deya had left.

Although I'd phoned Stefanie as soon as I heard, we'd waited two days for her to get over the shock before actually visiting her. Whether my imagination or not, there seemed to be more family photos evident on sideboards and tables, or sometimes just single portrait-photos of Johannes-Andreas. As if, with him now gone, she needed extra reminders. So that in one way at least he still felt close.

The scene Stefanie had related when they came to pick up Andreas had been heartrending. I knew only too well the feeling; when I'd answered my own door the other night after returning from Brunnerman's, my heart had been in my mouth. But it had just been Mrs. Schmid from along the hallway, complaining about the water being cut off in the building for a while earlier. Had I experienced the same problem?

I'd offered to help Stefanie out with some money, but with a gentle, tremulous smile in thanks at the offer, she shook her head. "It's okay. We've got some savings put aside, and my parents have offered to help too. Also, Julian has been really helpful." She bit at her lip, the tears close again. "He said he'd forego his future commission on all Andreas's books…plus he'd also try and get a ghostwriter to finish the one he's halfway through, so that we can get income on that too."

I wished Stefanie had accepted my offer. It would have salved some of the guilt I felt over my deathbed promise to Uncle Samuel. In the end, I'd let him down. I hadn't been able to help save his son, and seeing Stefanie and the children so distraught had torn my heart out. Telling myself that there was little I could have done hardly helped.

Straight after picking up a few things for Andreas that night from Stefanie, Julian had contacted Josef to tell him what had happened: *Schnabel already had Andreas's full name and knew his identity was false, so obviously a breach somewhere in the network. If I didn't give Schnabel his address immediately, he'd search through all of my files. I feared that might uncover many others…so I had little choice.*

I looked at Josef levelly. "Do you think Schnabel might already have other names, including myself, but he's just picking us off one by one?"

"Don't think so. Julian says not." A trace of uncertainty in Josef's eyes, then he eased a pained smile. "Besides, if that was the case, they'd already have been at your door, dragging you off."

Only after the third gulp of water, coughing and retching up much of the first two, did Andreas appear to recover, focus more on his surroundings.

"And you are Andreas Siebert?" Vice-Commandant Meisel confirmed, concerned for a moment that Hofer had pulled the wrong man from the shower chamber.

A slow nod in response, as if he didn't immediately recognize his own name.

Hofer had found, too, that the prisoner had been slow to raise one hand in recognition as he'd gone along the three chambers, opening the door of each and shouting "Andreas Siebert!"

Four other guards had to be summoned to prod the other prisoners back in at rifle point as Hofer had pulled Andreas from the chamber, a barely audible groan escaping his lips, "Water… water."

Meisel had gone to the adjoining engine room shouting "Stop!… Abschalten!" to Haas, the operating Scharführer— but it was by then too loud, its throbbing roar filling the small room as the rev-counter rose, and Meisel had to reach over and switch off the ignition key.

"What's wrong?" Haas inquired.

"Someone in one of the chambers who shouldn't be there."

Haas grimaced tautly. "Took a little to get going today—so you might be lucky."

Meisel returned an equally taut affirmation. The engine was old, so some days it took two or three tries to fully fire up and run.

But when they'd finally pulled this Andreas Siebert from the chamber, Meisel wasn't sure they'd indeed been "lucky." Siebert looked delirious, half dead.

After the spluttering third gulp, Meisel instructed Hofer to give him the full water flask. "He can hold it and carry it with him."

Meisel directed a nearby guard to grab a blanket to wrap around him from the nearby barracks room. Then after a few more sips from the water flask, Andreas was brought to his feet and they hobbled back along the wire-frame "tunnel." Halfway along, he was finally able to walk without being propped up by Hofer.

Andreas paused a couple of steps after, looking back questioningly towards the groans and screams coming from the chambers behind them. Still trying to make sense of where he was? ...Or pondering the fate he'd just escaped?

"The letter your agent wrote to me," Meisel said, as if in explanation. "I'd better show it to you."

32

Obersharführer Dieter Meisel,
Vice-Commandant, Sobibór Camp,
Sobibór, Poland

April 28, 1942

Dear Obersharführer Meisel,
You might recall a manuscript you sent me some months
ago titled Eine Flackernde Kerze (A Flickering Candle). I
wrote back to you saying I thought the manuscript showed
much promise, but needed a fair amount of work before I
felt confident showing it to editors.

You answered that you might need some help with that,
was there anyone I could recommend? At the time, there
was nobody I could immediately think of, but I am now in
a position to be able to recommend such a person to you,
who I have asked bring this letter with him for your atten-

tion. Misfortune obviously for him that he should end up in a camp, but could transpire to be good fortune for you.

His name is Andreas Siebert and he's an excellent young writer who I have worked with for many years. Aside from being able to help you with your manuscript, he's also an excellent and fast typist and a highly skilled hand-calligrapher. So there are many office duties he could hopefully assist with, aside from his aforementioned writing and editorial skills.

With kind regards,
Julian Reisner
Literary Agent

Andreas

Stone silence as I finished reading. My eyes were still watering slightly, my vision bleary, so it took me a moment to read, let alone absorb its portent.

My life hinged on a single piece of paper.

Before settling down to read the letter, Meisel had got Hofer to usher me toward the showers in the guards' compound and meanwhile find my small suitcase with its change of clothes.

The water was warm and welcoming, and I closed my eyes as I felt it wash over me, wash away three days' dirt and grime from the cattle-truck journey; but it couldn't wash away the horrors, my mind drifting to the wails and groans of the "shower" I'd just come from.

Ernst, the shoe-shop owner I'd struck up a brief conversation with, I saw was herded into the next cubicle along. But it was the children who clenched at your heart. A man not much older than me with his son of five or six, holding the boy tight and putting his hands over the boy's eyes; as if, even in that final moment, it was important he shield the boy from the horrors around him.

"Are you alright in there?" Hofer rapped sharply on the shower door.

"Yes…yes."

Then when I was sitting in Meisel's private office, a frail girl called Elsa, only sixteen or seventeen, with dark hair and a forced smile which never quite reached her gaunt eyes, brought me a coffee. Meisel explained that Elsa and another girl cooked and cleaned for himself and a few other officers.

The coffee tasted like mud with chicory in it, probably coffee essence from a bottle, but as my first hot drink in three days, I savored it.

Meisel observed me keenly as I read the letter, puffing on a clay pipe he'd just lit.

"So, do you think you might be able to help?" he inquired as I finished.

And now my life hinged on a single decision.

"I think so. Of course, I'd need to read it first…" A faint shadow crept into Meisel's eyes, a mixture of uncertainty and disappointment. I hastily reassured. "But, yes, I'm sure I'll be able to."

"Good…good," Meisel said after a moment's deliberation. He got up and went over to a side cabinet, started looking through some cardboard boxes at its bottom.

I noticed that Meisel was slim and tall, six foot two or more, with a slight stoop possibly from greeting and talking to people smaller than him. Eight years or so older than me, with a mop of chestnut hair shaved severely around the back and sides, and gray-green eyes.

Meisel finally pulled a box out, lifted some files and loose papers from its top, then dug down and lifted out a five-inch-thick block of white paper tied with a navy blue ribbon.

"Ah, here it is. Eine Flackernde Kerze. All five hundred and twenty-six pages of it." He came over and passed it to me with due reverence, as if it was his most prized possession, which, as I knew from my own writing, in many ways it was.

It felt heavy. With still feeling so frail, I wasn't sure I'd even be able to lift it and carry it around.

"I hope you enjoy it," Meisel said.

"I'm sure I will." I smiled hesitantly. I'd read many books in my time with the hope and expectation of enjoying them, but never one where my life depended on it.

Both life and death had a certain rhythm to it at Sobibór, one often contingent on the other. The trains arriving with new prisoners. The engine starting up to pour in carbon monoxide. The Sonderkommandos rattling through the tunnel with their carts to load up the dead from the showers and dump them in trench-pits dug beyond the death chambers.

The Sonderkommandos only managed to live because of the dead. If there were not fresh bodies to dispose of regularly, they'd be put to death as well. I was outside of that cycle because my survival had nothing to do with death.

Much of the background to Sobibór I learned on my fourth day here from one of the Sonderkommandos, Jan Renner. Jan was in his midtwenties, touching six foot and built like a bull with hair so blond it was almost white. I shared a dormitory with Jan and eighteen other Sonderkommandos where our food and conditions were better than the other prisoners; but of course our main privilege was that we were still alive.

Most of them kept to themselves with only a few words exchanged here and there, but Jan had taken a particular interest in me because he'd been only thirty yards beyond the chambers digging a fresh body trench and had seen me dragged from the showers at the last moment.

"So, what made them suddenly decide at the last minute to save you?" We sat in front of the dormitory on two upended crates. Jan lit the cigarette he'd just rolled up and pointed toward the death chambers. "What makes you so special?"

"A letter I brought with me. Vice-Commandant Meisel decided I'd suddenly be useful to—" I broke off, reminding myself what Meisel had said about secrecy "—to help with some typing and secretarial duties. I used to be a journalist, you see."

Jan drew on his cigarette, looked wistfully into the distance. "If I ever run out of bodies to dump, I must improve my typing skills."

I could see the wheels turning in Jan's mind: Would typing on its own be enough? "I also do some fine-ink calligraphy by hand. You know, fancy writing for posters for the camp." I held out two hands to indicate a large poster. "Achtung! You must meet your quota of fifty bodies dumped a day!"

Jan's laugh was delayed, as if he wasn't used to hearing jokes in a place like this. He slapped my shoulder as he beamed. "You're okay, Andreas. You're okay."

We were firm passing-friends after that, spoke to each other each day when we had the chance, and three days later I heard Jan's account of why he'd been saved from the death chambers. He pointed toward them.

"There's three of them along with the small adjoining room for the engine, and Commandant Toepfer says we might end up with five or six. I helped build them only months ago." Jan waved one arm out. "Along with everything else you see here."

I took in the spread of the camp, a handful of concrete buildings surrounded by thirty or so smaller barrack-style huts. "What? All this—with only twenty of you?"

"There were originally a hundred of us, with the guards, half of them Ukrainian here, directing us at rifle point. As soon as we were finished, they selected the twenty strongest, then the rest were killed." Jan's gaze was lost for a moment, as if in memory of those eighty dead. An uneasy smile creased his mouth.

"How ironic is that? Being put to death in the very gas chamber you helped build."

Jan looked up as he noticed Scharführer Vogt, the sergeant who'd initially directed me toward the showers, looking toward us from the far side of the compound.

"Watch out for him as well. Vogt's a snaky shit at the best of times. But I hear he got some sharp words from Meisel for not getting your letter to him straightaway. So Vogt's nose is out of joint and he's got an eagle eye out for you."

"I'll watch out."

"Make sure you do. Because the second Meisel's back is turned, Vogt will have you in that gas chamber he originally steered you toward." Jan stood up, anxious that Vogt might start heading towards us. "Catch you later."

Something else for me to worry about along with the tight-rope I was walking with Meisel's manuscript. I headed toward his office to put in two hours more work on it before dinner. One safe sanctuary at least away from Vogt.

I'd finally turned the last page on Eine Flackernde Kerze just the other day, but would have finished it earlier if it hadn't been for Meisel's insistence on secrecy.

"You can only work on the manuscript here, in my office. It should never be taken out, and under no circumstances mention either that you're working on my manuscript, or indeed that I've written one. It's just between the two of us."

I wasn't sure if that secrecy was for my benefit or Meisel's, but I quickly nodded my accord. "I understand."

"Your presence here will be explained by various office duties and some calligraphy for camp notices and posters—which I'll go into more detail about later."

Following that meeting, I'd put my head down and read Eine Flackernde Kerze four or five hours each day in Meisel's office, making notes as I went, and finished six days later.

In parts it was clunky and didn't flow well, in others dis-

jointed and didn't make sense, and many passages were over-
written with endless, flowery descriptions which got in the way
of the main story. But if I just said it was a "mess" and I didn't
know what I could do with it, I would immediately outlive my
usefulness to Meisel.

So I started to look keenly at the other side. Yes, I could see
the promise that Julian had obviously seen in Eine Flackernde
Kerze, set mostly in Vienna in the last decade of the Hapsburg
Empire between 1908–1918. There was the essence of a great
story at its heart, particularly the relationship between Tobias
and Karina. And Meisel's writing was also strong at points. Yet
all of that needed bringing out far more. It would need work;
a lot of work.

But it was going to be a hellish tightrope to walk: if I was
too tough on Meisel trying to knock his book into shape, he
might become defensive and dismissive and quickly curtail our
working relationship. Yet if I was too light on him and didn't
do what I thought was necessary to make the book work—if it
went back to Julian and he still thought it was unpublishable,
or editors he shared it with thought the same—we'd be back to
square one in any case. Worse still, Meisel might partly blame
me for that failure, feel my work on it simply hadn't been good
enough. That, too, could end my usefulness to him, see me
quickly back in a gas chamber.

I cradled my head in one hand, recalling Julian's disparag-
ing comment about a prominent author with another agent: *He
can't write to save his life*. Yet here I was doing exactly that: writing to save my life.

33

*Jews and Mischlinge are henceforth banned from taking part in
public contracts or founding private enterprises and businesses.*

"I'm a man of my word."

Heinrich Schnabel also considered himself to be a man who
was very precise in the vocabulary he used, and he recalled
clearly the promise he'd made to Julian Reisner: *I won't be contacting you anymore regarding pursuit of Kraemer or any other clients
on your books.*

Knowing even as he'd said it that he had no intention of
ceasing his pursuit of Mathias Kraemer–Daniel Lendt directly.
That's why he'd only promised that he wouldn't be contacting
Reisner anymore about the matter.

Besides, their observations of Kraemer with his regular visits
to Brunnerman's were too far advanced—along with his own
curiosity as to what was going on between the two—for them
to stop now. Having started that process with Lindner, he'd kept

Lindner to that assignment. His use of Junker Siegl for aid with other stalking and interrogations had been mainly to keep the threads of the investigation separate, so that at all times he was the Meister pulling everything together; he needed to maintain ultimate control. Plus he'd avoid any possible tattling to the Gestapo about "clumsy" pursuits or interrogations.

But he'd kept Lindner on a tight rein with those observations. He'd instructed Lindner not to go into Brunnerman's after Kraemer-Lendt's last visit and officially inquire what he'd been doing there. No doubt in any case Brunnerman would have a good cover story that he'd simply been buying some jewelry or getting a watch fixed, and Kraemer would then be forewarned and change jewelers or the time he visited.

Schnabel had, though, approved Lindner going into the shop in civilian clothes a few days later and simply browse as if he was any customer. Lindner had reported that there was a very limited jewelry display, but a wide selection of watches and clocks. *Practically every type of clock imaginable on his back wall—ormolu, carriage, grandfather and numerous types of cuckoo clock.*

Lindner had also ascertained over that period that Kraemer-Lendt's visits to Brunnerman's were every three months give or take a couple of days, and generally between 8 to 9 p.m.

Schnabel checked his watch: 8:48 p.m. "Looks like we might be sitting here tomorrow night as well." Two nights already they'd been sitting in this same position in the unit's Steyr 50, fifty yards on the opposite side from Brunnerman's, a large plane tree offering heavy cover.

Schnabel had determined that the only way was to catch Kraemer-Lendt red-handed, which required two of them. One to stay in the car on lookout, the other meanwhile to go up the side passage and look through a narrow high window. If anything suspect was seen during that discreet viewing—the front window was too open for that, they'd be seen—one would signal the other and they'd move in.

"There he is!" Lindner exclaimed as he saw Kraemer-Lendt approach.

Schnabel checked his watch again: four minutes to nine, just as they were thinking of giving up the ghost.

They watched Kraemer-Lendt go into Brunnerman's, but Schnabel kept one eye on his watch, timing two minutes before he went up that side passage.

"This one's a good color and quite clear. Probably a VS1," Carl Brunnerman said, looking up for a moment from examining the diamond through his eyepiece. He put it on the small scales to his side. "And weight is 1.54 carats."

"Bigger than I thought it was when I picked it up," Daniel said.

"Yes. Good size…though the others were smaller. Let's add up. A 1.26 carat, a VS2. One of 1.31, but only SI1…" Brunnerman spoke out loud as he made some notes on a side pad. He looked up after a moment. "That would give you 3,460 Reichsmarks…slightly more than last time."

Daniel nodded his accord. He practically knew the diamondgrade terms off by heart now from his past visits. "Large notes again, if you can. Less to carry," he said as Brunnerman turned toward the array of clocks behind him.

Now touching fifty, with a shock of heavily graying brown hair, Carl Brunnerman was one of the few people in Lorenzo's network who was full-blown Catholic Austrian on his papers, so no ID change had been needed. Daniel had learned his background on the last few visits: Brunnerman's grandfather had in fact been Jewish, but because it was on his own father's side, it hadn't descended. "My grandfather was one of the leading Jewish diamond merchants in Vienna," he'd told Daniel on his second visit. "Which I used to boast about ten years ago, how I was carrying on that tradition—but something I daren't mention now."

Recommended to Lorenzo by a Jewish customer, Brunnerman had readily accepted. "I kept thinking to myself, what if my grandfather had been on my mother's side? And what about all those Jewish clients who want help now? If I simply turn my back on them, I can't hand-on-heart still claim I'm carrying on my grandfather's tradition."

But to avert suspicion, he'd reduced the size of his diamond and jewelry displays and instead put out an impressive array of watches and clocks.

Brunnerman looked briefly behind to ensure nobody was watching through the front shop window—then went to a specific clock, one of four ornate ormolus, set its dials to 11:27 and pulled down the arm of the gold cherub on its left side. A click sounded behind, and with another quick look back, Brunnerman pushed the wall behind. A three-foot section of panel opened. Daniel stepped through the gap, and Brunnerman closed the panel behind them.

They were now in a small eight-by-three-foot room with a safe at one end and a bench table on the other.

Brunnerman opened the safe, put the diamonds inside, took out a bundle of cash and started counting it on the bench table. "...four-hundred and sixty," he announced as he laid down the last notes, putting the remainder back in the safe.

But having pulled down the inside lever and opened the panel again, Brunnerman suddenly froze as it was only a few inches ajar. A shuffling noise from outside the shop. He hastily closed it most of the way back, peering through a one-inch gap.

Daniel's nerves were on a knife edge too, that uneasy feeling of being watched on previous visits resurging. Could someone have followed him to Brunnerman's tonight?

But after a moment, Brunnerman appeared to relax. "Only a woman passing. Stopped for a second to put up her umbrella. She's gone now."

They came out of the rear cubbyhole section and Brunnerman swiftly shut the panel behind them, turning the ormolu clock dials back to the right time: 9:17 p.m.

"Oh, before you go," Brunnerman said after Daniel thanked him and was about to leave. Brunnerman fished into a drawer and pulled out an envelope and three postcards. "Some more stamps from my brother for your son. One from Java, another from Sarawak…"

Schnabel was also alarmed for a moment as it looked like Kraemer was heading out straight after the wall panel had shut again behind them.

He wouldn't have time to make it back to the car before Kraemer came out!

But then Brunnerman said something else and Kraemer was drawn back into conversation again.

Schnabel used the delay to head swiftly back to the car, instructing Lindner, "Drive!" the moment he was inside.

"Anything interesting?" Lindner inquired as they reached the end of the road.

A light rain had begun to fall, the wiper blades the only sound for a moment as Schnabel got his thoughts clear on what he'd just seen.

"Nothing interesting, I'm afraid," he said with an exasperated sigh. "Just appears he was picking up a couple of watches from being fixed."

34

Words have a magical power. They can bring either the greatest happiness or deepest despair; they can transfer knowledge from teacher to student; words enable the orator to sway his audience and dictate its decisions. Words are capable of arousing the strongest emotions and prompting all men's actions.

—*Sigmund Freud*

Andreas

Over the following weeks, I settled into some sort of routine at Sobibór, which helped distract from the death and deprivation surrounding me.

Every morning, I'd put in three hours with Meisel's manuscript and typing camp correspondence before lunch with Jan and the Sonderkommandos in hut five—I was never allowed to stay and eat with Meisel in the officers' quarters—then another hour or two after lunch back in Meisel's office.

Meisel was there most of that time, either us working together on his manuscript, reading incoming correspondence,
mainly from Reich HQ in Berlin, or handwriting his replies
for me to type later.

"My handwriting's worse than a doctor's," he explained in
my first week there. "Barely legible. So your typing skills will
come in very useful. I had a fast and efficient typist when I first
arrived, but she fell ill, and her replacement was so slow it was
painful." He waved a discarding hand to one side. "She's now
helping out in the laundry."

As Meisel spoke, a rare trace of a half smile had broken
through, as if he was afraid to show any chink in his more re-
mote, harder shell; but what did constantly break through, show
his more vulnerable side, was an underlying sadness and regret.
And I saw it evident, too, as I worked on his manuscript. Pain
and suffering literally dripped from several passages. Had that
been from his experiences in here and other camps—Jan told me
he'd previously served at Chelmno—or from somewhere else?

While we worked together, Elsa would bring us tea or coffee
with trembling hands. Not from nervousness, but simply that
her arms were so frail she'd struggle with the weight. In turn,
half smiles from her as she set the cups down—though her pain
and regret were far easier to fathom. She'd lost both her parents in the camp.

And while I was left alone in Meisel's study, I'd peruse its
contents more freely. Two side cabinets and a bookshelf in dark
walnut to match the two desks; Meisel's with green leather inlay,
where I'd pull a chair to one side when we worked together
on his manuscript, then a smaller desk in the corner with an
Olympia typewriter for when I worked alone. An assortment
of framed diplomas and family photos on the cabinet tops and
one side shelf: a studio portrait of Meisel in full uniform with
his family—a boy of perhaps eleven, a far younger girl, and his
wife holding a newborn baby. Then a later photo with the eldest

boy then in his late teens, the girl early teens and the baby now a boy of six or seven. Farm fields stretched behind them with mountains in the distance. Looked like Innsbruck or nearby.

I've made it as cozy and welcoming as I could, Meisel had commented on one of the first days when he'd noticed my eyes drifting briefly around. The contrast to outside in the camp was absolute.

I'd never inquired about Meisel's family, felt it might be intruding too personally, and he'd never offered any information.

I had to look away from the photos after a moment, my eyes misting as I thought about my own family. They'd have no idea if I was even still alive. I'd asked Meisel at the end of the first week whether I might be able to write to my wife, let her know I was okay, and he'd informed me that the only letters allowed out of the camp from prisoners were through the Red Cross. "But their visit is not due for another two months. Check with me then."

Two months? Stefanie would be beyond despair by then.

With the mix-up over the showers, I didn't get a medical check for infectious diseases such as smallpox or typhus until the second day. Helmut Vogt stood to one side presiding, having removed my wedding ring just beforehand. Perhaps something missed when I'd stripped for the initial "shower," or perhaps those were removed afterward along with gold teeth from prisoners.

"No jewelry and adornment allowed in the camp." A faint smug smile as Vogt slipped it into his pocket, as if to say: *I couldn't take your life, but your wedding ring will do as consolation. For now.*

After the first week, I'd end each day with two hours laboring helping Jan Renner. Meisel had made the suggestion, concerned that questions might be asked if I spent all my time in his office.

During those work stints, I'd found out more about Jan. He wasn't a Jew, gypsy or dissident, so how had he ended up at Sobibór?

He explained that he was from the German-speaking part

of Silesia near the Oder River, originally part of the Austrian-Hungarian Empire. "Then Hitler invaded." Jan shrugged. "We've become used to being controlled by someone else."

His father was a miner, as was he. But his father was also a mining trade-union representative, and when the Nazis took over they saw him as a Communist agitator. "They shot my father in the town square along with a group of other Communist trade-union members as a warning to others. My mother, two sisters and a brother fled the next day to Warsaw.

"Then as Germany's grip tightened on Poland, I fled over the border and joined the Red Army." Jan clenched a fist. "All I could think of was fighting the Nazis who'd killed my father." Captured by the Nazis during the battle of Moscow, he ended up in a Minsk labor camp. "Then finally I was transported here, to Sobibór."

Jan's latest work duty was building the fourth and fifth gas chambers ordered by Commandant Toepfer. My job was to supply the mortar, stirring it to stop it hardening, while Jan undertook the more skilled task of laying the cement blocks.

Fifteen of the fittest and strongest men had been picked from the last consignment arrived to assist us and half a dozen other Sonderkommandos.

On our third day, one chamber already a quarter-built, the sun was quite strong on our backs. And it was easy for a moment to forget our surroundings, escape into the warmth of that sun, my mind drifting back to summer picnics with my family. Or that first day I'd taught Stefan-Dominik to swim at Lake Achensee, its waters so clear and pristine blue we seemed to be able to see through it to infinity…or with Nadia only months ago, high on that Ferris wheel at Prater Park, the whole of Vienna spread before us…

"How much sand to cement again?" One of the new arrivals asked me.

"Four to one should be okay." Only a week ago Jan had told me, and already I was talking like an expert.

I struck up a conversation with him and his friend afterward, who had only met each other two months beforehand in the Chelm Ghetto before being shipped to Sobibór. But as we spoke, I noticed Jan looking over at intervals. Although I didn't get to hear Jan's concerns until I went to help him with the next line of blocks.

"After a while, you learn not to get too friendly and close with some people." Jan went on to explain that most of that fifteen would be killed as soon as the task of building the two chambers was completed. "The same as that hundred with me when we first built the camp. I got friendly with some of them, and it tore my heart out when they'd gone. I wished I'd never got to know them in the first place."

But then an hour later, just as we were packing up, Jan appeared to break his own golden rule as he waved and smiled to a girl passing thirty yards away.

"That's Rina—she's pretty, isn't she?"

"Yes, she is," I agreed. Slim and gaunt, like many in here, but that seemed to make her brown eyes even larger, more soulful.

"Elsa, the girl that brings you coffee each day in Meisel's office—Rina's her elder sister." Jan's expression dropped. "I mentioned before that Elsa's parents were killed as soon as they arrived. But what I didn't tell you is that their young brother, only seven, was killed at the same time." Jan shook his head. "Rina begged for Joshua's life, said that they should take her instead, but Vogt was having none of it. Said that she was useful, whereas her young brother wasn't. But if she argued anymore, he'd decide that she wasn't useful either and they'd both perish. So the two girls only have each other now."

I closed my eyes for a second, a shudder running through me. I felt it pressing on me, guilt that I should survive when so many others had perished; I felt it particularly when I heard stories about young children being killed, or watched them being herded into the gas chambers with each set of new arrivals, or witnessing them actually in a chamber as I had that first day. Did that feeling lessen with time with the numbers killed? Or would that then make you as inhuman and unfeeling as the guards?

"It's good then that Rina's got you, too, now for a friend," I said. The only silver lining I could think of.

Jan nodded solemnly. But then he appeared to pick up on my unspoken question—answering both her usefulness and why he'd broken his golden rule.

"She's a skilled seamstress—so assists the tailor. Always officers who need new tunics or buttons and insignia sewn on. So hopefully she'll be around for a while."

I was quickly learning the rules at Sobibór. It was okay to be friendly with people, if you knew they might be around for a while.

The trick then was working out who would live and who would die.

But only days later, I began to wonder how much longer I might survive at Sobibór.

The argument with Meisel came out of the blue, without warning.

We'd been discussing a key scene with Tobias and Karina when they first heard about the death of their son, Jakob, killed in action in the first year of World War I on the Serbian front.

"I think we need to look at this scene closer," I commented. "It's simply not working as it is."

"Oh, in what way?" Meisel's brow knitted.

"The emotions need to come through far stronger. After all, this is the first time that Tobias and Karina are together after their son has died…to be able to share their thoughts, their feelings."

Meisel just stared at the page blankly, still seemingly perplexed. "But I thought I handled the emotions very well here. In fact, I thought it was one of my best scenes in the book."

I'd had defensiveness from Meisel on some past scenes, too, and I'd always backed off. Reminded myself that this was his baby, something he'd spent months or a year or more writing. I couldn't just pull at its arms and legs or tug them off without it causing some pain and righteous defense on his part. But this was such a crucial scene that if it wasn't handled right then it weakened everything leading up to it, and much of what followed made less sense too. I needed to stick to my guns.

"Yes, parts of it are handled strongly." I sweetened the pill as much as I could. "But they're nearly all from Tobias's perspective. We get little or nothing from Karina, what she's thinking or feeling. And that makes her come across as uncaring, as if the death of her own son means little to her."

But Meisel just continued to stare at the page blankly, his jaw working tightly as he struggled to grasp what I was getting at.

"I'm sure that wasn't your intention," I said. "But right now we are left with an imbalance."

"An imbalance?" Meisel's tone sharp, questioning.

"Yes. But if Karina's emotions are brought out more, then we'll start to…"

The sound was like a pistol shot as Meisel slapped one hand sharply on the desktop. "This isn't going to work!" he snapped. He stood up, his expression thunderous, and went over to the side cabinet where a stack of papers lay by a register. He'd earlier broken off from that register to start work on the manuscript, some sort of inventory control, but now returned to it.

"May I make a suggestion," I commented after a moment.

Meisel didn't respond at first, kept his back resolutely to me as he worked silently making notes in the register. Finally: "I have no interest in hearing further suggestions from you. We are finished for today."

I left with a subdued "Goodbye…and sorry." Not sure immediately what I was saying sorry for. Sorry for foolishly over-stepping the mark, or sorry that it has caused you such upset?

First thing the next morning, Elsa came over to the Sonderkommandos' dormitory with a note that I should not come to Vice-Commandant Meisel's office until he summoned me again. I spent the following days helping out Jan with labor-ing or tilling soil and planting in the farm patch—90 percent of which went to feed officers and guards.

Then at the end of the fourth day, while I was helping Jan lay blocks in the final stages of finishing off the first new chamber, I saw Helmut Vogt walking across the compound toward us, his eyes fixed keenly on me.

And I knew that Meisel had probably reached a decision about me. I'd outlived my usefulness.

35

"Leaving so early," Schnabel said, putting a foot in the gap as Carl Brunnerman went to shut his shop door behind him.

He ushered Brunnerman back inside the shop and shut the door behind them. He didn't think a gun was necessary at this stage—the sight of an SS officer in full uniform was usually enough intimidation—but he had one hand on the Mauser in his right-hip holster just in case Brunnerman decided to resist.

It was in fact quite late, 9:14 p.m., darkness having fallen forty minutes ago. Schnabel had been sure that Kraemer wouldn't be Brunnerman's only late-night visitor, so he'd returned and started staking out the shop front on his own a week later, taking a tram to nearby Operngasse, then walking the rest. He'd seen three late-night visitors in the past month: one had been innocent, but the other two had gone into the same back-panel safe room. And as Schnabel had watched again through that high side window, he'd made a note of the specific time on the ormolu clock. The last visitor had left just eight minutes before Brunnerman switched off all the lights and Schnabel's foot was in his doorway.

"Leave them off," Schnabel instructed as Brunnerman went to switch them on again. "There's sufficient streetlight filtering in from outside for us to see what we're doing."

Schnabel was wearing black gloves and carrying a large black leather bag, which he put down at his side as they came up to the counter. He pointed to the clocks behind. "Please do the honors with the ormolu clock, if you will."

"I… I don't know what you're talking about," Brunnerman said uncertainly.

Schnabel took out his Mauser and pointed it at Brunnerman. Some encouragement was obviously needed. "Now, I already know the time required—11:27. But I'd rather you do it for me." Schnabel smiled tautly. "After all, it's your shop."

Brunnerman went behind the counter with visibly shaking hands and turned the ormolu clock dial to 11:27.

"Now the cherub's arm," Schnabel instructed.

As a click sounded on the back wall, Schnabel took control, hustling Brunnerman through to the small back section at gunpoint. He closed the panel behind them.

"Now the safe!"

Brunnerman looked at Schnabel defiantly. He shook his head after a moment. "I can't."

"Ah, but I think you can." Schnabel aimed his gun at Brunnerman's face. "Now if I was an everyday robber, you might risk your life for whatever's in that safe. But it goes beyond that. I've been doing my research, you see."

As Schnabel mentioned his wife and two teen daughters he'd found on file, Brunnerman closed his eyes for a moment. "A conspiracy like this, they'd be joining you in a death camp."

"You're despicable," Brunnerman hissed. "A monster!"

"A bit late in the evening for dramatic insults, don't you

think?" Schnabel stared back coldly, becoming quizzical after a second. "And what I don't understand with all of this—you're not even Jewish."

"It's not only Jews who have a conscience with what's happening now," Brunnerman said flatly.

"As may be." Schnabel took a fresh breath, as if clearing the air of Brunnerman's comment. "But at what price such misplaced chivalry? Because we have not only your own family at risk, but your brother's too. Now, he's been really busy with a family—four children already and his wife pregnant again."

"He—he's nothing to do with this," Brunnerman stuttered.

"Perhaps not. But he's a servant of the Reich, serves in a local Vienna government office—so a far dimmer view would be taken of such betrayal, even if only by association."

"He's only a minor functionary, responsible for little more than parks and public places." Brunnerman held out a shaky hand in plea. "Leave him and his family be."

"And it wouldn't take much, the mere slip of the pen on an official denouncement," Schnabel continued, as if Brunnerman hadn't spoken, "to make it appear as if he was involved in all of this." Schnabel waggled his gun toward the safe.

Schnabel sensed that Brunnerman was on the edge of a precipice—on one side condemning his own and his brother's family, on the other betraying whatever secrets were held in his safe. One last shove.

"And what point?" Schnabel held a hand out. "Within an hour, I could have a squad here with oxyacetylene torches and explosives to break open your safe—so you'd have condemned your family and your brother's for nothing."

Brunnerman nodded solemnly, his bottom lip trembling. "I don't seem to have much choice."

"You didn't from the outset."

Schnabel watched expectantly as Brunnerman turned to the

safe like a condemned man, turned its dial back and forth, and opened it.

Inside was the largest collection of cash and diamonds Schnabel had seen outside of a Reich or bank vault: two or three hundred thousand Reichsmarks, half as much again in US dollars, and two trays of assorted diamonds. Schnabel was no expert, but it looked like they could equal or exceed the amount of cash.

Schnabel waved Brunnerman aside with his Mauser, counted one bundle of notes to affirm his initial estimate, then piled all the cash in his black bag and started tipping the diamond trays on top. As he lifted the second tray, he noticed a small black notebook and a large envelope wedged at the back behind it.

Schnabel reached in and lifted them out. Brunnerman looked even more downcast in that moment, as if discovery of the notebook and envelope represented a particularly shameful moment for him. And as Schnabel leafed through the notebook and started to make sense of the columns of names and figures, he could see why Brunnerman had initially been so reluctant to open the safe; the toss-up between his own family and the names on that list a close call.

Lendt's was one of the first names he spotted, with dates and figures alongside mostly in Reichsmarks with a few US dollars. Then followed over thirty other names, dates and amounts. They hadn't needed to find Deya's cousin to pull apart this ID-change network. They could pick them off one by one from this list! In terms of purely internal SS kudos, a far more valuable find than the cash and diamonds.

But as he opened the envelope, his elation hit new heights. A bundle of photos inside, at first he wasn't sure of their significance, until he noticed Sigmund Freud present in every one, among various other people, mostly men—ranging from small groups of four or five to as many as forty all together.

The elusive "Freud Circle" photos. They'd all but given up

on them, but now his last comments to Piehler about the photos would in fact ring true!

"Who gave these to you?" Schnabel asked.

"I... I don't recall."

Schnabel looked at Brunnerman disdainfully. Probably Martha or Anna Freud, or someone acting on their behalf. Now that he had the notebook and photos in his possession, it hardly mattered.

"What happens to me now?" Brunnerman asked hesitantly. "I'm executed or sent to a camp?" He shrugged. "Which I suppose means more or less the same these days."

"No. I have something far more imaginative for you in mind. I plan to stage this as a robbery gone wrong. If you play along with me, you'll only be wounded."

Schnabel guided a perplexed Brunnerman to stand in the middle of his shop, facing one wall by his front window. He took a Sauer 38 from his bag and, keeping his own Mauser trained keenly on Brunnerman, slipped the Sauer from behind into Brunnerman's right hand.

"Now, don't for a minute think of turning with that gun, or I'll shoot you in the back of the head, and your family and your brother's will end up in a death camp." Schnabel pointed. "Now take careful aim with that gun and fire two shots into the wall there two feet from the window—as if you've fired at a robber and missed. Then very carefully hand the gun back to me."

Brunnerman nodded slowly, as if he was still struggling to make sense of all this, then dutifully fired the two shots.

As he handed the gun back: "Where's the robber?"

"He's yet to arrive. But when he does, he'll be carrying this gun." Schnabel pulled another gun from his bag, a Radom 9mm. He moved so that his back was toward the shop window and pointed it at Brunnerman. He fired and hit Brunnerman in the right shoulder, saw him reel back a couple of feet. He waited for Brunnerman to straighten, then took aim again.

Brunnerman's brow creased, his breath sucking in with the pain, voice raspy. "I thought you said I'd just be wounded?"

"Yes, I did, didn't I." Schnabel fired two more shots, both to Brunnerman's stomach, watched him crumple to the floor.

Schnabel moved in close to Brunnerman then, put the Radom 9mm back in his bag and sprinkled some notes and a couple of diamonds by his body prone on the floor. Brunnerman's breath gasped through flecks of blood like a landed fish. Schnabel guessed that he'd last no more than four or five minutes. "Only I didn't say how badly," he muttered.

Schnabel took the shop keys from Brunnerman's pocket, then bag in hand left the shop, locking the door behind him as he glanced back toward Brunnerman's body: it couldn't be seen from the street.

36

Jews are forbidden to fly the Reich or national flag or display Reich colors. Jews may not employ in their household female citizens of German or related blood who are under forty-five years old.

Andreas

Helmut Vogt's gaze fixed keenly on me as he crossed the compound, but as he came close he turned and talked to Jan Renner as if I wasn't there.

"Almost finished I see." Vogt briefly surveyed the four high walls open to the sky above.

"Only three more rows to go," Jan said, placing another block in the cement I'd just laid down. "Then the roof can go on."

"So how long to go?"

Jan wiggled one hand. "Two or three weeks more. The ceiling and roof is more complicated because it holds the pipes going to the shower nozzles."

"We can't have prisoners not getting their right quota of gas." Vogt smiled crookedly. "Haas says in fact we might need a larger motor to deal with the extra chambers, or even an additional motor."

Jan shrugged. "I wouldn't know about that." He looked uncomfortable at hearing such details.

"Of course." Vogt tapped his black cane with its bulbous silver head on his left palm. "They might take too long to die otherwise. No need for unnecessary suffering."

Jan looked curiously at Vogt. Surely he was being sarcastic? Jan as quickly brought his attention back to spirit-leveling the block he'd just laid.

Stories abounded about Vogt's brutality, seeming to take delight in the suffering of others; it hadn't just been trying to dispatch me to a "shower" in search of water. Vogt reached out with his cane and rapped its silver end against a lower part of the wall. It thudded heavily.

"Sounds solid enough."

Some of those stories were in fact regarding his cane. Its bulbous silver end covered solid lead, and Vogt had been known to strike out suddenly and viciously, cracking ribs and skulls. And on a few occasions he'd carried on and methodically beaten prisoners to death.

Vogt turned to me finally then. "I've been talking to Vice-Commandant Meisel about you."

And as he reached into his inside jacket pocket, my heart sank. No doubt a signed denouncement or death warrant. Vogt handed it to me.

"I understand from him that you're quite a skilled calligrapher." Vogt pointed to the sheet of paper I'd started reading. "And I need twenty-four of these, one for each dormitory, prepared in large lettering. Perhaps a classic style like Luthersche."

"Yes, of course." My eagerness more because of the reprieve than the task itself.

"No later than the day after tomorrow."

"Yes…"

But Vogt had already nodded curtly and started walking away.

"What does it say?" Jan inquired.

"It's about summer hours in the camp. Work rosters to start half an hour earlier and finish half an hour later." I turned it toward Jan, but he looked at it blankly.

"I… I can't read."

The next few months were among my best and most formative in the camp.

After Jan had admitted he couldn't read, he looked perturbed for a moment before walking off, leaving me to clean and pack up our tools. When I caught up with him back at the dormitory, he didn't look in the mood to discuss it, so I avoided the subject too.

The next morning I was back in Meisel's office for the first time in five days, and worked steadily on the twenty-four posters, which I completed by late afternoon the next day—so Jan and I spent the rest of that day pinning the posters on each dormitory.

And it wasn't until we were finished and sitting in our favorite position in front of our own dormitory on two upturned crates—Jan having just lit a roll-up—that he started to talk about why he wasn't able to read.

"I was a terrible truant at school, hardly ever there. And as I got older, there hardly seemed any point. I was headed down the mines, like my father and everyone else in my town—what would reading help?" Jan shrugged. "But as I reached my twenties, I started to question, what would my future wife think of me not being able to read? Or what would I tell our son or daughter when they asked me to read them a bedtime story? I started to have second thoughts." Jan took a heavy draw on his cigarette, an uneasy smile curling his mouth. "Then I ended up here, and again I was hit with—what's the point?"

I nodded slowly, matching his solemnity. But the mood felt wrong without some uplift. "If and when you're handed your death warrant, you'd at least be able to understand what it said."

Jan looked aslant at me for a second, then his swiftly rising smile lapsed into a hearty chuckle. "I could at that."

"It's never too late to learn...and you've got one of the best teachers right here." I spent the next half hour cajoling Jan just how and when I'd be able to teach him to read before he finally relented.

Meisel had a stack of books half-forgotten on the floor each side of his main bookshelf, so I'd borrow one or two of those. We started with Schiller's *Don Carlos* and Jünger's *Sturm* and put in an hour or so each night after dinner in our dormitory going painstakingly over spelling, vocabulary and pronunciation. And after almost a month, Jan was able to read some short passages by himself.

But one night we almost got caught as Vogt walked into our dormitory without warning. Jan quickly slipped the books back under his mattress and pulled out the cards we used as our cover, laying them out.

Vogt had another poster he wanted done. "But just four this time for the officers' quarters."

I studied the A4 sheet he handed me. "I'll have it ready late tomorrow."

"Good." Vogt looked back just before going out of the door. "Must say, you two do seem to spend a lot of time together playing cards each night. Very cozy." He smiled slyly, his gaze shifting more to me. "But not as cozy as the little arrangement you no doubt have with Vice-Commandant Meisel."

As Vogt left, I turned to Jan, my brow furrowing. "What does he mean?"

Jan shook his head. "It doesn't matter."

But it clearly did. Jan looked troubled, awkward. I pressed again and Jan finally told me what it was.

"Because of all the time you spend in Meisel's office," he said with a sigh. "There's a rumor going around that you...you like men more than women." He held a hand up helplessly, as if to stress: *not my rumor*. "And that obviously Meisel leans the same way."

"That's ridiculous, we're..." But I stopped myself short again, remembering Meisel's insistence about secrecy. I shook my head. "But I'm married with two children, and he's got a family too."

Jan shrugged, further distancing himself from the rumor. "I don't for a minute believe it, but obviously some like Vogt have been taken in." Jan grimaced. "I don't think what happened with Meisel his first month here helped."

"What was that?"

As quickly Jan seemed to retreat, his face clouding. "It doesn't matter," he muttered again. Clearly regretting he'd said anything.

Another of Meisel's buried secrets. But from Jan's stonewall expression, I doubted I'd get anything more, even if I pushed. Two buried secrets revealed in one night was expecting too much.

The first buried secret revealed by Meisel had in fact been the main thing leading to my most settled period at Sobibór, particularly our collaboration on his manuscript.

While I was working on the first set of posters in Meisel's office, he commented just before I was finishing up, "You should come here tomorrow as well, so that we can start work on the manuscript again. I have something to tell you."

Although it wasn't until midway through the next day, as we were working steadily on general scenes, that Meisel finally got around to what was on his mind, as if he was building himself up to it and some preamble was required.

"I owe you an apology for the other week." He lit up his pipe and took the first puffs. "It took me a little while to accept that you were right. You see, I found it hard to fully express what Karina was feeling, because…" He looked fleetingly to one side, as if still searching for the right words. "Because I never knew what my wife, Luisa, was feeling after the death of our son. She never told me."

It hit me with a jolt then: Eine Flackernde Kerze was partly autobiographical! I should have guessed from the raw emotions peppered throughout.

"I'm sorry. I… I didn't realize." *Sorry that your son died, or sorry that I didn't pick up the connection with your manuscript?* I felt suddenly numb, adrift. Trite consolation was all I could manage.

"I was in the military, so it made sense that my son Lukas joined too. My wife, Luisa, was against it, but conscription was coming later anyway—so maybe I shouldn't blame myself." Meisel shrugged, took another pipe puff. "But the thing is, I did. I pushed for Lukas to join a regiment only months after Anschluss and Austria's full integration into the Reich. He joined the 4th Army division, who at the outset of war were on the front line of infantry assaults in Poland. Lukas was killed in the battle of Gdynia, barely a month into the war." Meisel's eyes misted with the memory.

I nodded sullenly, my eyes shifting for a second to the framed family photos on Meisel's cabinet. No doubt the eldest boy in the photos.

Meisel sighed. "Luisa never forgave me. A rift developed between us. But the thing is, she never told me how she felt. It was all just in those silent, accusing stares." Meisel held a hand to one side. "Two months later, possibly to escape those haunting stares, I applied and was accepted as vice-commandant of Chelmno. But maybe I was partly punishing myself too." He smiled crookedly. "After all, why else would someone consign themselves to hellholes like here or Chelmno?"

Meisel got up and went over to a side cabinet, lifted out a bottle of aged brandy. "A bit early in the day to be drinking, but I feel I need it right now." He poured a double-shot into a small balloon glass. He raised the bottle. "Would you join me?"

"Yes…thank you." Not only might it seem impolite to leave Meisel drinking alone, it would probably be my only chance to drink fine brandy while in Sobibór.

Meisel poured my glass and handed it across. Pained grimace as he sat back down and took his first slug. "Though maybe there were other reasons for my choosing places such as this. Perhaps I feared active front-line duty because it would have been too painful a reminder of how my son was killed. And also in places like this—" Meisel waved his balloon glass "—you need to be partly desensitized to death, which losing Lukas had already achieved for me. My own son's death made little sense to me—so how could I be expected to make sense of all these other deaths?"

Meisel could have looked at it the other way: seen all these other deaths as multiplications of his son's death, so found them painful rather than numbing. But I kept to safe, consoling ground. "It must have been very difficult for you." I took my own sip of brandy.

Meisel took a fresh breath. "Four months after arriving at Chelmno, I started writing Eine Flackernde Kerze—perhaps as a sort of exorcism of Lukas's death and the guilt I felt. I thought if I can write about it, it might help. But of course, I could never write fully about Karina's emotions…because Luisa had never told me what she felt about Lukas dying. All I got were those brooding, accusing stares."

Silence for a second. Meisel took a heavier slug of brandy.

"It's often difficult dealing with the thoughts and feelings of others," I said. "Especially when those emotions are close and personal to you." But now wasn't the time for a full-blown discussion on character development.

Meisel held a palm out. "That 'closeness' you mention was indeed one of the main reasons I set Eine Flackernde Kerze in World War I—so that it wasn't too close to what had happened with Lukas." Meisel glanced to one side, as if in deference to an unseen spectator. "And of course the fact that any criticism of the Nazis in the current war wouldn't be acceptable. But perhaps something else with World War I, some sense and final resolution could be found with it—whereas with this war, I have no idea how it will end."

I nodded in understanding. I could see that Meisel's heart-rending account had drained him, even propped up by the brandy. I doubted he'd ever shared this with anyone else, so in that sense I should feel privileged. And strangely, although we were miles apart in every other regard, he'd adopted the same common ground as myself and Mathias-Daniel in avoiding the current era for his book. *Was every book currently produced dishonest, blatant propaganda, or simply avoided the era completely?*

Meisel looked across poignantly as he arrived at what he'd been building up to. "So do you think you might be able to help me write Karina's views and emotions…since they're not quite so close and personal to you?"

"Yes, I…" I paused then, suddenly uncertain whether I'd be able to capture that depth of emotion. But then I thought about what Stefanie would be feeling at this moment, not knowing if I was alive or dead. How distraught she'd be. *Maybe I could transpose some of that?* "…I think I would be able to."

After that meeting our work together on Eine Flackernde Kerze was far more positive and harmonious, and three weeks later Meisel's eyes misted over again when he read the key scene we'd initially argued about, now rewritten with far more of Karina's emotions.

"Yes, it's very good, very moving," he said. "It works well now."

Though I could almost hear a silent rebuke in his head: *Goodness, is that what my wife was feeling at the time? I shouldn't have deserted her.*

With that more settled period over those months in Sobibór—not only the stronger working accord with Meisel, but Jan's reading lessons progressing well—I should have realized it couldn't last. Even before the incidents which brought that period to an end, I'd started to feel uneasy—but shrugged it off as simply guilt that I should be feeling so settled when all around me was such suffering and death.

But then that guilt hit me harder with the first storm cloud to arrive when one afternoon I saw Jan, head in hands, having just returned from speaking to one of the Sonderkommandos by the wire fence.

"What's wrong?" I asked.

"Lara, one of Rina's friends—he just confirmed he's buried her body." Jan hooked a thumb in the direction of the fence and the pits beyond, lit a roll-up. "I took her up to the fence in a cart just this morning."

I nodded solemnly. I knew now how the system worked. Jan would only take carts through the wire fence with those who'd already died in the camp from typhus or other ailments to bury in the pits beyond—which was where he'd been that first day when I arrived. Those killed in the chambers were removed and buried by the Sonderkommandos beyond the fence, who never came our side. They generally lasted only eight to ten months before being killed themselves, *to maintain secrecy.* That's why Jan had been anxious when Vogt had gone into detail about the fourth death chamber. Knowing too much might mean our days were numbered. Jan and the others in our hut were the only crossover, *Überleitung*, Sonderkommandos. All other camp laborers stayed on their respective sides—until time for them to be buried.

Jan closed his eyes for a second as he exhaled the first smoke. "She used to do the typing in Meisel's office before you arrived, then they put her working in the laundry. But Vogt kept complaining she was no good, a poor worker." He took a longer draw. "She fell ill last week, and Vogt finally got his way with her—condemned her to a chamber. Made sure, too, I was the one to take her to the fence."

My stomach sank. I felt physically sick. My guilt because of the contrast with my work situation to everything else around me was one thing—but in this case I'd been almost directly responsible for this young girl's death. *If I hadn't arrived, no doubt she'd have kept her job in Meisel's office.*

And perhaps both Jan and I were still partly in a daze from that, so weren't as vigilant hiding the books from Meisel's office as we should have been—because it was only six days later when the second storm cloud hit.

I returned to the dormitory to see Jan being yanked out by his shirt collar by Vogt, two books thrown down on the ground at his side.

"How did you get hold of these books?" Vogt snapped.

No answer from Jan. He looked blankly ahead.

"They're from Vice-Commandant Meisel's office." Vogt stared intently at Jan. "You've stolen them, haven't you?"

Jan gently shook his head, but kept his stare resolutely ahead. Didn't give even a hint by glancing my way.

Vogt moved close, staring into Jan's face from only inches away. "You'll look me in the eye and tell me or I'll—"

"No...*no!* It was *me*," I cut in as Vogt raised the bulbous silver end of his cane above Jan's head. "I borrowed them from Vice-Commandant Meisel's office."

"Borrowed?" Vogt looked at me incredulously. "Did you get Vice-Commandant Meisel's permission for this?"

I didn't want to compound the problem with a direct lie, so simply cast my eyes down.

"I see." Vogt moved toward me then. "As you know, *without permission* is the same as theft." Again, as he had with Jan, he stood only inches from my face, speaking softly, menacingly. "I'll see you in a chamber for this."

37

The state forbids an individual to do wrong not because it
wishes to do away with wrongdoing, but because it wishes
to monopolize it, like salt and tobacco.

—*Sigmund Freud, Reflections on War and Death*

Daniel

The blood raged through my body, a pounding and faint buzz
in my head from its pressure. Heinrich Schnabel sat opposite
in a chair, a Mauser held loosely pointed at me, as he talked
calmly and methodically about what he'd discovered and what
my options were.

Alex had only been in bed forty minutes when I'd heard a
light scratching on the front door. But when I looked through
the peephole, nobody appeared to be there. When the same
sound came a minute later and still nobody could be seen the
other side, I opened the door. Schnabel came in swiftly from

one side before I could shut the door, pulling out his Mauser and directing me to a chair. He took a chair opposite, put a large black leather bag at his side and started to lay out my fate.

"Now, I know that you're a Jew and your original name was Mathias Kraemer," Schnabel said. "That fact is not up for discussion." But then he went through an explanation of how he'd arrived at that conclusion, some of it mentioned before in our bookshop meeting—the similarity in writing styles between Kraemer and Lendt, seeing someone similar to me previously in Café Mozart, discovering that in fact my identity change was part of a larger organized network—as if concerned I might try and contest it. Or perhaps simply demonstrating how thorough he'd been.

"But you're just small-fry in all of this," Schnabel concluded. "It's this wider network I'm interested in. So if you're willing to give up the names in the rest of this network and tell me how it's all been executed, I could let you live."

I looked at Schnabel levelly. There seemed little way out. But I doubted he'd keep to his promise in any case—which was why he'd used the indefinite *could* rather than *will*—even if I might have been tempted to sacrifice the lives of scores of other families to save my own neck. I shook my head resolutely.

"I'm sorry. I couldn't do that."

Schnabel met my stare for a moment. "Of no matter. The little booklet I just found in Brunnerman's safe full of dates, payments and a list of thirty-four names, including your own, I'm sure will bear fruit." Schnabel smiled wanly. "Not to mention the photos of Freud Circle associates I also found there."

I tried not to let the shock show on my face. *He'd been to Brunnerman's!* I'd seen Brunnerman make a note in that booklet from his safe after our own transactions, but hadn't realized he'd noted all the others too. No doubt why he kept it at the back of his safe. But the Freud Circle photos? I know we'd all been asked to destroy any photos, but maybe someone in the group had left theirs with Brunnerman for safekeeping. All I could think of.

Schnabel shook his head gently. "You're as bad as Deya, Weber's girlfriend. She refused to say anything too. That's why I had her sent to Dachau."

The buzz in my head grew stronger. *Deya!* Surely this part was a bluff. "But she simply left Vienna, possibly the country. She wrote Josef a letter—I saw it."

"That was purely to throw Josef off the trail," Schnabel said with some self-satisfaction, pleased his ploy had worked. "The last thing I wanted was him sniffing around, trying to make a plea for her. Not that it would have helped in this case."

Still one thing didn't add up to me. "But why would Deya agree to write such a letter?"

"Because I said if she did, I'd let her daughter live. She could have her spirited away somewhere with other relatives, and I'd turn a blind eye. Mind you, not everyone was so reluctant to give others up."

"What do you mean?"

"You don't know?" Schnabel looked at me keenly. "My, my, doesn't anyone tell you anything?" He leered, his self-satisfaction reaching new heights. "Your agent, Julian Reisner, gave up your good friend Johannes Namal—later known as Andreas Siebert—quickly enough. Although in that case it was mainly to save *your* neck."

The buzzing became more insistent. *Friend?* So at least Schnabel didn't know we were related. I shook my head incredulously. "But Julian told us they'd caught up with Johannes... *Andreas* simply through a loose link in the network. Someone else informing or some paperwork uncovered where it shouldn't have been."

"I can easily see why Reisner would be reluctant to admit he gave up your friend Namal because of you." Schnabel smiled ingratiatingly; he was clearly enjoying this, stripping apart all

I'd held true bit by bit, layer by layer. "You see, I was far surer of you having a false identity than Namal. The similarity of writing styles between Daniel Lendt and Mathias Kraemer for one thing. So I confronted Reisner—it was either *you* or someone else—and he gave Namal... *Siebert* up quite easily." Schnabel shrugged. "I must admit, I'd have preferred it had been you rather than Namal. You're a full-blown Jew, whereas he's just a Mischling. And it was Reisner who insisted that he be sent to Sobibór—far from the easiest of camps."

I closed my eyes for a second and shuddered, the thought that Andreas had ended up in such a dire camp—the chances of survival so low—because of me, weighing heavy on my shoulders, almost unbearable. Especially with the promise I'd made to Uncle Samuel. *Not only have I let him down, I'd been the cause of his son's demise.* And Julian's betrayal of Johannes was even harder to fathom. The buzzing in my head made me feel suddenly unsteady, the room starting to sway. It felt as if half my world had been ripped apart, the remainder turned upside down. *Nothing is what it seems anymore.*

"What now?" I asked, my voice shaky, barely a whisper.

"The offer I made to Deya with her daughter—I'm making the same offer now with your son."

I thought my spirits had hit rock bottom, but now it felt as if I'd been dropped into an icy well with those words. I stared coldly at Schnabel as he related equally as coldly that having just come from Brunnerman's and viewed my last visits there, he knew I had a stash of diamonds at home. "The only question remaining is *where*. Now, if you give up those diamonds without me having to rip half your home apart searching, then I'll let your son live."

I closed my eyes for a second as that shudder ran deeper, a sharp spasm now in my left thigh. Ivor-Alex was still asleep in his bedroom. I thought I'd heard him stir a short while ago, but nothing since. An innocent in all this, and now Schnabel was using him like a pawn in the decision I might make. I nodded numbly, imperceptibly. *What other choice do I have?*

"And if you go along with the other part of my plan," Schnabel continued fluidly, "I'll let your mother and sister live too."

The shuddering ran fully through me, my whole body starting to tremble. I stared back coldly, impassively, as Schnabel explained in equally impassive tones—as if I was simply going with him to the local shops or park—the part he had planned for me in Brunnerman's demise: "Right now, he's lying on the floor of his shop, dead from three bullet wounds from *this* gun." Schnabel lifted a gun from his black leather bag with a gloved hand. "If you're then found opposite him with this in your hand and shot with the gun found in Brunnerman's hand—it will look like you've killed each other during some negotiation gone wrong. Some diamonds and money left by Brunnerman's body will support that."

I nodded blankly through my haze of thoughts and the buzzing in my head. "So, in this little plan of yours—the idea is that I'll be killed as well?"

Schnabel looked at me incredulously, as if I was missing something. "You'd be executed or perish in a concentration camp in any case with your background uncovered and all this falsifying of documents and hiding assets from the Reich. The only question remaining is whether your son, sister or mother join you in a death camp. The choice is yours, Mr. Kraemer."

My eyes darted for a moment, as if searching for options. But I realized—even if I was able to forge some clarity through the haze and heavy buzz in my skull—that Schnabel had planned all of this too carefully. Left *no* options. *No choice!* My voice felt trapped in my throat, barely a whisper. "But why should I trust you?"

"You have no good reason to, I accept. But you're the crime and thriller writer—think about it for a moment. With me walking away with this stash from Brunnerman and what you'll now add to it—" Schnabel gestured toward his bag "—the last thing I'd want is any connection to Brunnerman or your background being uncovered. Or even that I've been here now."

I nodded slowly; one chink of clarity starting to emerge. "So, nobody else knows you've come here now or been to Brunnerman's?"

"No, of course not." Schnabel leered back crookedly, as if I was stupid. Then, as I sank into thought again, he added, "I'm sure in the end you'll do the noble, right thing and choose to save your own family. Sometimes it's necessary to give something up—even if it's your own life—to save others."

Noble, right thing? Yet Ivor-Alex, my mother and sister would probably never even get to know or appreciate my sacrifice. It would just appear as it was in that final crime-scene setup: my life lost because of some strange confrontation with Brunnerman over diamonds and money. *But what other choice was there?*

Though as that chink of clarity finally worked through the haze, I hit a flaw in Schnabel's plan. "If you're not meant to have been here or at Brunnerman's, what about the booklet and photos from Brunnerman's safe?"

"I'll have them sent to me anonymously. Could have indeed come from anyone in the network—any loose link. So I'll still get the kudos and praise for that internally, too, as I track down the rest of the network and Freud Circle associates."

I sighed resignedly, the last option gone from my grasp. "You seem to have thought of everything."

"Yes, Mr. Kraemer. I'm not one to leave anything to chance." He raised a brow curiously. "Why do you think I read all those crime novels like yours? This is the perfect crime—no possible trace back to me."

I stared back defiantly. "Not exactly the behavior of a model Nazi, is it?" I sneered: *a last taunt to hopefully throw Schnabel off-kilter.*

"You get me wrong. I'm the very best of Nazis when it suits

me. But putting the party's ambitions before my own would be foolish in some cases. You see, while I don't particularly have time for Jews, I nevertheless don't hate them." A reluctant shrug. "At least, not enough to see them exterminated to the last one. But I'm wise enough to know that to be a good Nazi, that is how I should act. That I should relish it, as if it pleases me no end. Because *that* is the behavior that will get me the promotions—help me rise to the top." Schnabel patted his bag to one side. "But when the opportunity arises to leap to the top without all of that saluting and kowtowing in the hope of the next promotion—then I'd be foolish not to take it, wouldn't I?"

I nodded, still struggling for clear thought beyond that buzzing. "A time to put self before party."

"Yes, *exactly*." Schnabel smiled crookedly. "A true writer, I see. Still quoting to the end."

We stared at each other a moment longer before, gritting my teeth against the spasms in my thigh, I eased out a final defeated sigh and got up.

"Okay. I'll get that diamond stash for you." *No choice!* The buzzing heavier, drowning out all else, my legs felt unsteady as I headed to the next room. "I just need to get the keys to where they're hidden."

Of course, no keys were needed for under the floorboards where the diamonds were tucked away. But in that drawer, alongside my car keys, was the Browning 640 from Lorenzo and Alois. ...*if you hear the Gestapo coming up the stairs for you, I suggest you take out as many as you can before turning the gun on yourself.* The problem was with my legs unsteady and the room swaying, the pain in my thigh biting stronger, I wasn't even sure I'd be able to make it to the drawer with the gun. But it was the only remaining slim option.

I couldn't trust Schnabel. He'd take this stash now and then later think of a way of sending my son, sister and mother to the death camps. And aside from my own family, there were the other thirty-three names on that list and all the Freud associates in those photos. The heartache, death and destruction that Schnabel would bring to bear on those families also. *However slim the chance, I had to do whatever I could to prevent that.*

As Schnabel had said, *"You're the crime and thriller writer."* If anyone knew how to dispose of and cover up for a dead body, it was me.

Only one possible way out!

But my step felt increasingly unsteady as I approached the drawer with the gun. And now Schnabel's voice was behind me.

"And don't think of attempting anything brave or foolish." The sound of him getting up, his step now not far behind me, no doubt his gun trained on my back.

The chances now would be even slimmer. The only hope would be to turn swiftly and fire. *Surely that element of surprise would help?*

My hands were shaking uncontrollably as I reached for the drawer, the buzzing in my head reaching a crescendo.

I opened the drawer. The gun wasn't there.

38

Andreas

The first lash of the leather whip took my breath away. Jan had warned me it would be painful. "Brace yourself and try and think of things beyond it, beyond the pain." But that forewarning had hardly helped. In that instant, the searing pain was so excruciating that it was impossible to think beyond it.

With the second and third whip-strikes, I could feel my flesh tearing and ripping from my back. I hissed and clenched my teeth against the pain. Already I could see some among the on-looking crowd making hand signals to each other, confirming or changing their bets on whether I'd make it.

The hearing in Commandant Walter Toepfer's office had been a farce. A bigger version of Meisel's office, but with a lot of hunting trophies on the wall and a large Persian rug at its center.

Toepfer ran the questioning, with Vogt giving evidence and

Meisel there to offer supporting confirmations. Toepfer started with Vogt verifying where he found the two books.

"In the dormitory shared by Prisoners Renner and Siebert, but under Renner's mattress."

"And did Prisoner Renner offer any explanation of how they got there?"

"No. He remained silent under questioning, refused to say anything."

The fourth whip-strike came, raising a muted groan from me. More hand signals and bets taking place, some muttering now among the crowd.

"Then how did you in fact reach the conclusion that Prisoner Siebert had removed those books from Vice-Commandant Meisel's office?"

"Because Siebert admitted as much while I was pressing Renner further on the matter."

"And what explanation, if any, did Siebert offer for removing those books from Vice-Commandant Meisel's office?"

"He said he *borrowed* them." A sneer heavy with doubt from Vogt.

By the time of the fifth and sixth whip-strikes, the searing pain had a numbing edge to it. Jan had warned me that Vogt had sewn shards of lead into the leather, and I could feel the effect of those. My flesh already raw and bleeding and the nerve endings ripped out.

Toepfer turned for the first time to me then. "And is that true? Was that your explanation—that you'd borrowed those books?"

"Yes, it was, sir."

"And did you at any time ask Vice-Commandant Meisel's permission to borrow those books?"

I glanced down in submission. "No, I didn't, sir."

The whip-strikes kept coming, raising a guttural groan from me, and I noticed mixed emotions from the crowd watching: some wincing with each strike, some gloating, others simply blank with horror. Jan looked on with eyes heavy with concern, and next to him Rina had one hand over her mouth.

Toepfer turned to Meisel. "And can you confirm that the two books in question are from your office?"

"Yes, they are." But then with a fresh breath, Meisel added, "If Prisoner Siebert says that he only borrowed these books, I have no reason to disbelieve him. I have found him honest in every other regard while he's been working in my office."

After the fifteenth or sixteenth whip-strike, I lost count, my eyes started to flicker shut at points, as I slipped in and out of consciousness. More furious hand signals and betting taking place among the crowd in the glimpses in between.

Toepfer turned to me again. "What were you doing borrowing these books? And why were they under Renner's mattress?"

"Because I was teaching him to read, sir."

Five more whip-strikes later, I finally blacked out, my last view of Jan in the crowd with his eyes cast down, hardly able to look anymore, and Rina, her eyes moist with tears, patting his shoulder in consolation. Both of them clearly worried whether I'd survive.

"While your intentions may be admirable," Toepfer concluded, "it cannot be overlooked that you did not ask Vice-Commandant Meisel's permission to borrow these books, which is tantamount to theft." Toepfer wrote briefly in a register open before him. "Thirty lashes in the Forward Camp Yard, to take place at eleven tomorrow morning." Toepfer looked at Meisel before looking back sharply at me again. "And you have Vice-Commandant Meisel to thank for speaking on your behalf. Without his intervention, I'd be sending you to a death chamber right now."

Afterward, as I shared the news of my reprieve with Jan, I should have read the signals when he didn't share my relief, simply nodded blandly with a subdued, "That's good."

"What's wrong?"

"It's okay." Jan turned his attention back to positioning a beam on the fourth chamber roof.

I didn't in fact find out what was concerning Jan until later that night when he got into an argument with Tibor, a Ukrainian Jewish Sonderkommando, at that moment involved with excitably organizing some betting with five or six others at the back of the dormitory.

"Keep your voices down," Jan snapped at them. "Show some respect."

"Aren't you going to place a bet too, Jan?" Tibor taunted.

Jan just glared at him, and Tibor's gaze shifted to me.

"He hasn't told you, has he? Almost half of those who get twenty-five lashes or more don't actually survive. The whipping's bad enough, but it's the infection afterward that usually gets them."

Betting took place on all sorts in the camp. From rats and beetles racing to whether a prisoner edging too close to a perimeter fence might get shot by a guard. The currency used either tobacco, tinned food sneaked from provisions or gold fillings pocketed from death-chamber victims while the guards weren't looking. But I realized then with a sinking sensation that these bets were taking place on my life.

Tibor smiled slyly. "And your chances of survival will probably be even less, because Vogt will lay into you harder for being Meisel's pet."

"You no-good shit!" Jan stood up, bristling for a fight with Tibor, but I put a calming hand on his shoulder.

"It's okay. The chances are far more than I'd have got in a death chamber," I commented ruefully. "I'll survive."

The Forward Camp Yard was where new prisoners were greeted and floggings took place. Prisoners were ordered to watch, as it served as a warning to any other possible miscreants. So that morning a crowd of over eighty—whether keen or reluctant—had gathered to watch as I was strapped to a post at its center and flogged by Helmut Vogt, the odds on my survival visible from the winces and downcast looks or the hand-signal betting taking place.

But as I looked across just before blacking out and saw Jan cast his eyes down, all but giving up on me, I knew my chances of survival were slim.

39

Jewish and Mischling students are henceforth excluded from taking exams in medicine, dentistry, pharmacy and law.

Josef

"I've written to the camp directly twice now, but nothing in response." Stefanie looked across at Josef. "The only answer I've received is from some separate Wehrmacht office in Lublin, saying that information on prisoners cannot be given except through the Red Cross."

"And have you written to them yet?"

"Yes. They took over a month to answer. Got their answer just a few days ago. They had a scheduled visit to the camp a few weeks back, but it was canceled. They're waiting for a new date to be set for their visit there."

Sitting behind his steering wheel, Josef looked back at Stefanie—her eyes red rimmed and haunted from worry—then past her to the apartment-block entrance her children had run into minutes ago. They wouldn't have long. Stefanie hadn't wanted to talk openly in front of the kids, so this was just a few grabbed moments before she joined them seeing their grandmother, Franciska, Andreas's mother.

These journeys to the grandparents that Andreas would normally undertake, Josef and Daniel now shared between them. Daniel had invested in a Stopel 100 to see his mum and sister, and while Andreas had done the same with an old runabout, Stefanie hadn't yet learned to drive. Josef was quite happy to help out; besides, he reflected wistfully, he had far more time on his hands now with the nights free that he used to see Deya.

"Will the Red Cross pass a letter from you to Andreas?"

"Yes, they said they would. Plus also pass any letter from Andreas to me." Pained grimace, as if concerned what such a letter might say, or if one would return. Whether Andreas was even still alive. "But I have to wait for their visit to the camp."

"Then there's still hope," Josef said reassuringly. "Keep your chin up."

Another taut smile and Stefanie got out to join her children and Andreas's mother. Josef said he'd pick them up again in two hours.

He could have headed to the Kärntnerstrasse station only two miles away to catch up on paperwork, but he didn't feel in the mood. So he'd brought a few files with him to work on and found a local bar.

It had been a busy few weeks. Since a Soviet aircraft raid early in the month, there had been intermittent blackouts in the city. All of them false alarms, but on those nights burglary had increased threefold. Robbers taking advantage of the extra cover of darkness or people out of their homes in air-raid shelters.

Josef sipped at a beer and made notes as he went through the files on the different robberies. He realized he'd been drinking more since Deya had left and should cut back; maybe next week. But he was better in those two hours than he was many nights, managed to keep it just to two beers and a kirsch chaser. He popped a couple of mints in his mouth and went to pick up Stefanie and her kids.

"*Hell!* All we need," Josef exclaimed as halfway running them home all the streetlights went out.

Even with his headlamps on full beam, shadows were heavy, shapes difficult to make out. Josef found it remarkable how impenetrably black everything became when all the lights in a city went out. But keeping to little more than 20 mph, they managed to limp back to Stefanie's apartment safely.

"Thanks, Josef. I don't know what we'd do without you."

"That's okay. Next run's on Daniel, I think—so see you in a couple of months." A taut, reassuring look in parting. "And like I said, keep your chin up."

The streetlights went back on when he was just over a mile away, and the police radio dispatch call came through only minutes after about a burglary in Karlsplatz.

Josef pulled over to the side and picked up, asking the operator, "Where exactly?"

"A jeweler's on Mahlerstrasse… Brunnerman's."

"Okay. I'll head straight there." *Brunnerman's!* Josef hoped his voice hadn't betrayed any qualms.

"Two males found on the premises, both dead from gunshot wounds. So forensics will be there shortly too."

"I'm on my way." Unease curdling in Josef's stomach, he popped two more mints in his mouth and turned his car around.

40

Andreas

"You're a good man, Andreas…don't die on Jan and me. Stay alive for us!"

I opened my eyes. Rina was even more beautiful close-up, her dark brown eyes like giant orbs. I could practically see my reflection in them. Easy to see why Jan was so attracted to her.

She soothed my brow with a damp cloth, and I attempted a smile at her, but her face blurred in front of me and I slipped back into darkness.

Jan and Rina had taken turns in caring for me the past few days.

I'd been unstrapped from the post and carried back to the dormitory by Jan and Mikel, another Sonderkommando. I'd regained consciousness to see my feet dragging up its two wooden steps. Then I was laid facedown on my bed and Jan told me what he was going to do next would hurt.

"It's vital I clean the wound, keep away any infection."

Opening a bottle of vodka, he started dabbing some on my back with a cloth. Burning cold quickly became intense stinging. My hissed-breath shriek from the pain lapsed into a guttural groan. Halfway through the dabbing, I blacked out again.

At some stage, I wasn't sure if it was half an hour later or several hours, Jan was shaking my shoulder again, waking me.

"You're going to be okay, Andreas. Rina and I and some others are going to take care of you. Infection's the main thing. If we can avoid that, you'll be fine."

I nodded numbly.

Rina was at his side, and he looked past her to the eight or nine others in the dormitory—some also looking on with concern, others nonplussed or busy with their own activities. "Let me try and pick the best from this sorry bunch."

Jan called out who, among those who had actually placed bets, had bet that I would live? Three hands raised, including Mikel. Jan chose him and another young Sonderkommando, seventeen-year-old Nahum.

"You two take care of him whenever Rina and I can't be here—see if you can make good on your bets. So water when he needs it, and keep his brow cool with a damp cloth to keep his temperature down."

That routine kept up for the next twenty-four hours, the faces changing periodically as I slipped in and out of consciousness, mopping my brow as they looked on with concern, or taking my temperature or leaning me forward for sips of water when I was awake. But I could almost gauge how I was faring by the depth of concern in those looks.

Midway through the third day, I knew I was slipping—if I hadn't already half guessed from the fever gripping me, my body shaking uncontrollably, cold one minute, boiling hot the next—from the look of alarm on Nahum's face just after he'd taken my temperature.

The same look of alarm when an hour later he handed over to Rina, though with him muttering I didn't hear the temperature he related to her. I faded back into darkness soon after.

I was on that Ferris wheel, the whole of Vienna spread before me as Nadia clutched at my hand. "We're up high now, Papa." Then her grip on my hand became tighter. "Don't leave us, Papa…"

My eyes flickered open and it was Rina clutching my hand as she dabbed my forehead with a damp cloth. "…don't die on Jan and me. Stay alive for us."

I attempted to smile back at Rina, but she slipped and faded along with everything else back into blackness.

Helmut Vogt had insisted that Jan work until nightfall finishing setting the roof beams on the fourth death chamber—perhaps on purpose to restrict his time taking care of Andreas—and came into the dormitory only a minute after Jan had entered to take over from Rina.

Jan was sure that Vogt had seen him crossing the yard and followed him. He was only halfway through getting brought up to date by Rina when Vogt marched in. Vogt looked sharply toward Andreas, eyes closed, pale and gaunt with a sheen of sweat on his skin.

"He looks ready for a death cart."

"He's just had a couple of rough hours," Jan defended. "I'm sure his fever will break soon." Far from the truth, but anything to buy time.

Vogt looked back doubtfully at Andreas's prone body. "Okay. You've got until nine tomorrow morning. If he's still like this, he goes on a death cart." Taut grin fired at Jan and Rina. "You know how the camp works. Can't have other people's time taken up unnecessarily with dead wood."

Uneasy silence for a moment after Vogt left. Rina looked back at Andreas.

"He's not going to make it by tomorrow morning, unless

overnight there's a miracle. He'll probably be hardly different from this."

"I know." Jan nodded forlornly.

Dead wood. Jan hardly needed reminding of the harsh realities of Sobibór, since he spent half his time disposing of that *dead wood* with the bodies he regularly dumped in pits. And if, along with his laboring duties, he didn't have those to regularly dump, he might be considered the same, too, of no functional value.

Jan knew that the survival statistics from floggings quoted by Tibor would have been far higher if it wasn't for the stringent camp regime of consigning anyone to death chambers as soon as they became seriously ill, a potential burden on others having to take care of them. A liability to the camp.

Jan shook his head. "Vogt planned all of this. He knew that all he had to do was whip Andreas severely enough that he'd be ill for a few days, and he'd be able to get him on a cart to the chambers—or maybe even straight to a pit, buried alive."

Rina closed her eyes for a moment, sighing. "You and I might both know and agree that—but how will that help Andreas now? He's still not going to be well enough by tomorrow morning."

"I need to gain more time."

"But *how*? You heard Vogt—tomorrow morning and that's it."

Jan's eyes searched the air emptily for a moment before hitting the thought. "*Meisel!* Andreas appears to mean something special to Vice-Commandant Meisel—don't ask me why." Jan clutched at Rina's hand. "I'll go and see him, beg for more time for Andreas."

Rina glanced toward the clock on the far wall. "But Meisel will be in the officers' mess room having dinner now—you can't just burst in on him while he's there."

"I'll go afterward."

Darker shadows fell in Rina's eyes. Now she was getting frightened. "But it will be after ten by then—it will be too dangerous."

They both knew the camp rules: guards in the watchtowers had strict instructions to shoot any prisoners seen crossing the compound after ten at night.

Jan clutched her hand tighter. "I can't just let him die, Rina. This has all happened because he was helping me to read. Who, apart from you in this miserable place, has ever cared anything for me—whether I live or die? Let alone be able to read."

Rina met his gaze solemnly. She knew that however much she tried to dissuade him, it would do no good. He'd made up his mind. "Be careful, is all I ask," she said.

"I will." He smiled gently after a second, sensing he should lighten the mood and try and put Rina more at ease. "Besides, it's quite a bright moon tonight and the guards know me. I wave up at them, they'll see me."

Rina returned his smile unevenly. "Full moon. Just about right for something madcap like this."

Rina left for her own women's dormitory five minutes later, and when it got to ten o'clock, she looked out the window, working between her fingers the Chai pendant from her father she'd had with her since the Warsaw Ghetto as she said a silent prayer.

She noticed that a light rain had begun to fall, the moon heavily obscured, shadows heavy in what little of the main compound yard she could see from where she was. And as minutes later she heard two shots ring out and a searchlight beam come on, she began to fear the worst.

41

Public officials and civil servants who are not of Aryan descent, whether Jewish, Gypsy or Mischling, are to be retired; if they are honorary officials, they are to be dismissed from their official status.

Josef

Forensic Examiner Otto Lanz was the first person that Josef saw as he walked into the crime scene, busy inspecting a couple of bullet holes in the wall to the left of the front door.

Two policemen in uniform who Josef didn't know, presumably from the nearest station, an SD and two SS. Finally, he spotted someone else he knew over the far side, Niklas Krenn, one of the young assistants from his team at Kärntnerstrasse. A photographer's flash was going off, and another plain-clothes man to his side, possibly Gestapo, took notes.

A busy scene, so at first Josef couldn't get clear sight of the two bodies on the floor. The first to become visible was Carl Brunnerman, but as the second body came into view, Josef found it hard to hide the shock on his face.

"Are you okay, sir?" Krenn remarked as he approached.

"Yes...*yes*." Josef looked up at Krenn, forced a smile. "Just not used to seeing SS as victims at murder scenes, that's all. Anything unusual—outside of finding both victims armed?"

As Krenn ran through the main details—"Three gunshot wounds to the jewelry shop owner, two to the SS officer. All appear to have been fired more or less at the same time..."—Josef took in Heinrich Schnabel's body in more detail: his head turned sharply to one side in a rictus, as if he'd been surprised, his SS jacket dark from coagulated blood. One shot appeared to be to his lower side, almost by his kidneys, the other directly to his chest. Brunnerman had two wounds to his stomach, the third to his right shoulder.

The sprinkling of diamonds and banknotes on the floor, mostly Reichsmarks, Josef found odd. He knew that those would only come from Brunnerman's hidden safe at the back, but as he glanced toward the back panel, he could see that it was closed and in place. Only a flat wall with an array of clocks.

"Schnabel, you say?" Josef confirmed as Krenn finished, as if making out he didn't know him.

"Yes. Found papers on him, which also gave his unit. When we contacted them, that officer over there, Unterscharführer Lindner—" Krenn pointed "—came and confirmed his identity."

Josef looked briefly toward the young officer. "Did Lindner have any idea why his fellow officer might have visited Brunnerman's?"

"Schnabel was actually his boss, a Scharführer, and Lindner said they'd been observing Brunnerman's as part of a lookout—but he had no idea why Schnabel might return here."

Josef nodded. Those two pieces of information didn't seem

to fit together. "Did Lindner tell you why they were staking out Brunnerman's?"

"No. We didn't get to that. The photographer and a Gestapo man arrived then, started asking questions, and you arrived soon after. So it's on my list of queries, among many other things."

"It's okay. I can pick up from there with him."

Josef ambled over to Lindner and showed his badge. "You were talking with one of my colleagues a moment ago…" As Josef probed about the reasons for the stakeout of Brunnerman's, he felt an uneasy twinge when Daniel Lendt's name was mentioned and those reasons became clear.

"We'd observed Lendt visiting Brunnerman's on two previous occasions, and Scharführer Schnabel thought his visits were connected to an identity-change network he was trying to track."

"I see." Josef kept his expression as bland as possible. But that made Lindner's earlier comment stand out even more as a non sequitur. "That sounds quite serious. Yet you told my colleague that Scharführer Schnabel had no reason to return here?"

"Yes. Because on our last visit three weeks ago, while I remained in our car observing the front of the shop, Schnabel went to the high window there—" Lindner pointed to his side "—and looked in shortly after Lendt's arrival. When he returned to the car, he said he'd seen nothing untoward. Just Lendt getting a watch fixed. Obviously, after that, we didn't return."

"I understand. Thank you."

Josef felt unsteady as he turned away from Lindner. Perhaps he shouldn't have had those two beers and a kirsch earlier. It had hit him in a rush in that moment: *Schnabel had seen something!* Something that he'd decided not to share with his colleague. Josef glanced again at that high side window, checking its line of view toward the back wall. Schnabel would have clearly seen that back-panel opening; he doubted Daniel and Brunnerman would have hung around long with small talk before getting down to business.

Josef also knew that Brunnerman held far more in cash and diamonds in his safe than the sprinkling now on the floor. Which meant that was all still in the safe, or a third party had been involved and gone off with them. Josef's eyes fixed on the back wall with its clocks, boring through for a moment to that small back room. Many of the answers lay there, but the last thing he could do was reveal its existence in this room full of SS and Gestapo.

He'd need to return alone to the crime scene in the dead of night to check the safe.

42

Because every man has a right over his own life and war destroys lives that were full of promise; it forces the individual into situations that shame his manhood, obliging him to murder fellow men, against his will; it ravages material amenities, the fruits of human toil, and much besides.

—*Sigmund Freud (letter exchange with Albert Einstein)*

Andreas

"You shouldn't have taken the risk," I said.

"This is an argument I've already had with Rina, so I'm not going to have it again with you, Andreas." Jan took a hard draw of his cigarette, looked away.

"But Rina said you almost got shot."

"If you're going to listen to the worries and hysterics of women, you're not going to last long in here." Jan waved one hand dismissively. "The first shot was just a warning, the second went at least a yard wide. The moment I looked up at the watchtower, said I had an urgent message for Meisel, the shooting stopped." He smiled crookedly. "You should know by now they're rotten shots—why do you think half of them have machine guns?"

I returned his smile uncertainly. "It's not that I don't appreciate what you did."

"I should hope not," Jan said with mock indignation. "If I hadn't gone to Meisel, we wouldn't even be having this conversation right now."

I nodded soberly. Meisel had granted an extra two days, but I hadn't fought off my fever and rallied until the night before that fresh deadline was due to expire; at nine sharp the following morning Vogt would have turned up and ordered Jan to load me onto a death cart.

"Besides, it was a calculated risk," Jan said, stubbing out his cigarette and picking up a fresh block to lay. "I knew that Meisel was appreciative of the work you did in his office. Perhaps more than I could understand." A brief knowing look toward me before spirit-leveling the block, as if Jan sensed something else was going on between Meisel and I, but he wasn't going to delve. "But also Meisel had his own past run-in with Vogt. So I knew that something like this involving Vogt, Meisel would be keen to make a stand on your behalf."

I looked up at the sky. Some clouds had come over, the dusk light fading fast. The edge of autumn, already the air was crisp. I'd only been fit for office work the first week, so by the time I was back helping Jan and half a dozen other Sonderkommandos with two hours laboring at the end of the day, they were laying the first rows of blocks on the fifth death chamber.

"What was that past conflict between Meisel and Vogt about?" I asked, laying a fresh trowel load of cement on the next block.

Jan laid a block on top, tapped it in and leveled it. He was slow in responding, as if applying some thought as to whether to say anything or not.

"It goes back to the first two months they were all at the camp," he said with a resigned sigh. "At first, everything was fine between Meisel, Commandant Toepfer and Vogt. All comrades together. Vogt used to arrange these little parties for his two superiors and other camp officers. Some girls were chosen from the camp to join them, and whatever happened was in back bedrooms or the officers' private rooms. But then the third party, Vogt invited twelve girls along, four more than the number of officers present, and it quickly turned into a full-scale orgy. Meisel was present and apparently went with a couple of girls there, but that was the last one he attended."

Jan's tapping of the next block seemed to be heavier, more insistent, his jaw set tight as he continued. "The next morning, nine of those girls were stripped naked and shoved into the first death chamber. It was newly built, so they had no idea what was about to happen to them. Vogt had set it up, said they needed some kind of 'test' for the new chamber—so the girls from last night were 'ideal.'"

Jan's eyes smoldered with a mixture of anger and loathing. "So there they were, half the camp officers, looking through that small glass pane into the chamber, praising its efficiency and gloating as the girls they'd been with the night before writhed in agony and died." Jan sighed heavily. "Meisel left early on, and while he didn't openly voice his disgust at his fellow officers— it was pretty clear how he felt. Vogt arranged the same orgies practically every month, but Meisel didn't go to any more of them. And that's when the rumors started."

It hit me then that this was the story Jan had been reluctant to tell me before. "Oh, you mean the one now that's come back with me spending so much time in Meisel's company? That we prefer men to women?"

Jan nodded, reached for another block. "Don't be bothered

by it. These rumors happen to the best of us." Jan went on to tell the story about stripping off his shirt a few hot summer afternoons while he was digging trenches and one of the guards staring at him for a while. "When later that guard commented to a colleague that 'I looked like a Nordic god,' a rumor started that there was something going on between us."

I joined Jan in a smile before he became more contemplative again.

"The first story to go around was that Meisel had become attached to one of the girls, so was upset when she was put to death the next day. But later most of the girls weren't put to death afterward—or at least not the very next day, it might be weeks or months after and for other reasons. So when Meisel was still shying away from these get-togethers, that's when the other rumor took root that he wasn't that keen on girls."

"Then I showed up," I said, the pieces falling into place. "And I'm spending half my time in his office."

"Exactly." Again that look from Jan, as if he was hoping I might finally fill that gap with an explanation—but having made that solemn promise to Meisel, I was keen not to betray it. Jan shrugged it off after a moment as he laid another block. "As I say, nothing to worry about. I'd get the same if I spent so much time in Meisel's office. Especially looking like a Nordic god."

Our laughter rang out in the dusk light, until we noticed Helmut Vogt staring at us sharply from across the yard. At most, twenty more minutes of light. We put our heads down and worked silently through the remainder.

The fifth death chamber was finished two months later, but by then winter had set in with a fury and the ground was so hard that new burial trenches couldn't be dug.

Bodies in the trenches were sometimes doused in benzine and set alight, a sort of makeshift cremation. But now, the bodies arranged in piles, this had to take place above ground. The rising flames often drew attention from the rest of the camp, and the saddest thing was watching prisoners, particularly children, looking longingly toward the fires through the wire-mesh beyond the tunnel. As if, as the sole beacons of warmth in the camp, they'd do anything to be within that glow and get warm—even if it meant doing so on flames rising from dead bodies.

I was saved from that with the time I spent in Meisel's office, where his woodburning stove kept it snug and warm; another notch of guilt on my shoulders. There was also a single paraffin heater in the Sonderkommandos' quarters—insufficient for the room's size, but enough if you huddled close to it before bedtime then immediately dived under the ice-cold blanket.

But in the rest of the prisoners' quarters, there was no heating at all. We lost almost 20 percent of the camp to flu and pneumonia that winter, including Rina's young sister, Elsa. Frail at the best of times, that winter was simply too harsh for her.

Jan managed to sneak Rina, myself and a couple of Elsa's friends through the tunnel so that we could hold a small ceremony in respect, laying a small stone each on the ground where she was buried. No doubt an SS jackboot would kick aside and disperse those stones in no time, but it was something. The best that could be done under the circumstances.

The only light in the gloom of that winter was Christmas, in particular because we heard that the Red Cross would finally be visiting the camp then or soon after. *A letter finally from Stefanie and my family, and a chance for me to get a letter to them.*

Although Jan was doubtful they'd show up. "Their visits have already been delayed twice, and the same will happen again now. You watch."

"I hope you're wrong, for my sake and the rest of the camp. My wife and family have no idea if I'm even still alive—and I'm sure it's the same for many here." I held a palm out. "What's the point in them forever delaying?"

"Because this is simply an overflow for other camps, not

meant to exist. Its only purpose is for extermination—no forced or factory labor. So they don't even have those other things to cover up with."

"I'm sure they'll show up this time, won't delay again," I said. I needed desperately to cling to that hope—*contact at last with my family*—however much what Jan said rang uncomfortably true.

The only Christmas tree outside of the officers' quarters was in the Forward Camp Yard, strapped to the same central post I was whipped against months ago. Many of the Jews in the camp didn't celebrate Christmas, but used the opportunity to quietly celebrate Hanukkah and say a few prayers. It was at least a holiday, a day off from work, so any relief from the daily grind at Sobibór was gratefully received. Used to celebrating both at home, I did the same in the camp, and Jan and Rina enjoyed each other's traditional celebrations too.

But dark clouds quickly loomed again when it was announced that the Red Cross wouldn't be visiting after all, the winter weather was too severe. It looked like Jan's prediction had been right in the end.

There had been a flurry of Christmas and New Year posters for me to ink-sketch in seasonal typestyles, and straight after I buried myself back into Meisel's manuscript—so often my escape and refuge from all around me.

There were occasional differences of opinion and edgy debates as we went through, but I'd learned my lesson from that early confrontation to ease back if Meisel became defensive—just plant the suggestion, then let Meisel come around to it in his own time.

We received news that the Red Cross would now arrive in the spring, but Jan was convinced it was just another ruse.

"They'll delay again to the summer, then autumn...then never!"

Although as spring approached and Vogt and the head guards had Jan and the other Sonderkommandos—myself included when I'd finished each day in Meisel's office—furiously getting the camp cleaned up, we began to believe that this time the visit would actually take place.

The main problem was many of the unburied corpses hadn't burned thoroughly, and as the remains thawed, a heavy stench of rotting flesh drifted over the camp.

With the ground now softer, rows of new trenches were hurriedly dug and the bones and remains shoveled in. Fresh fires were then lit, and as a final measure two truckloads of lye brought in and laid in the trenches to dissolve any residual flesh and bones. With many of the Sonderkommandos beyond the fence also lost to pneumonia that winter, Jan and I were commandeered to help with the trenches.

It was laborious, filthy and dangerous work, though as Jan had said halfway through, shrugging, "Far better to be on top shoveling the lye than underneath it." A couple of times he'd warned me not to get any on my shoes. "It will burn straight through, then start dissolving your flesh."

The aim was that by the time the Red Cross arrived, no trace of those burial grounds and their dark secrets would remain.

Although as much as I was enlivened by the prospect of a Red Cross visit and finally having contact with my family, something else had begun to worry me.

I was in the closing stages of the manuscript with Meisel, planned to finish five or six weeks after Easter. Would I then outlive my usefulness?

43

Josef

A lone SD Junker stood on guard in front of Brunnerman's when Josef approached with the gray-haired man at his side.

"I daresay you haven't had a tea or coffee break yet?" Josef said to the young SD as he showed his inspector's badge. He pointed along the street. "There's a good café just around the corner. My colleague here's just assisting me studying some ballistics here at the scene—so we'll be okay alone for the next half an hour."

Josef had voiced it almost as an instruction, and the young SD was a second slow in nodding his affirmation. "I see, yes. Thank you."

Josef watched him walk away, then turned to the man with him. "Are you sure half an hour will be sufficient?"

"I'll probably have it cracked in only fifteen minutes."

Josef nodded and they walked to the back of the shop. He

doubted that the young SD would have any inkling that the man with him, Felix Klein, was a master thief and safecracker rather than a ballistics expert; now in his sixties and long retired, it was almost twenty years since his photo had appeared in any police files. But Felix had assured Josef his touch was as good as ever.

Josef looked anxiously back to check that nobody was looking, then turned the hands on the ormolu clock to 11:27 and pushed down the cherub arm. As the click in the panel sounded, he pushed it open and Felix went behind.

"The lever on the inside opens it again. But edge it just an inch and peek out before opening it fully—just in case someone else is around."

Felix nodded his accord and Josef quickly shut the panel back behind him.

Josef went to the front of the shop and looked at the two bullet marks in the wall that forensics expert Otto Lanz had mentioned. As they'd been leaving the crime scene, Lanz had commented that he didn't think the bullets matched the gun in Brunnerman's hand, a Browning 640. "But I'll know more once I've got the bodies back to the lab and examined everything."

Early the following afternoon, Lanz had finished the two autopsies and confirmed his initial suspicions. "The bullets found in Officer Schnabel's body are 9mm and do in fact match the Browning, but the two in the wall are smaller caliber—7.65mm, from a Sauer or similar would be my guess. The line of fire to where Schnabel's body was found also doesn't marry up—unless Brunnerman was a particularly bad shot."

Josef studied that line of fire now, beading a line from where the two bodies were found—indicated only by faint residual bloodstains still on the parquet-wood shop floor—to the bullet marks in the wall. At least a yard adrift. The other issue Lanz had raised was that blood lividity in the bodies indicated that Schnabel had died sometime after, as much as an hour, and he might have been moved meanwhile.

The only hypothesis Josef could think of was that Schnabel, in taking longer to die, had moved in that period—which would then answer the two wall shots being a yard or so off.

"Possibly," Lanz conceded. "But we might then have expected a larger and wider-spread bloodstain area below Schnabel."

It was certainly an odd crime scene. Sometimes, Josef might find one or two things that didn't add up, but here practically nothing did.

He studied that line of fire again from the bodies to the wall, adjusting for where Schnabel's body would have had to move to—no bloodstain patches there—then went over to the wall and studied the line back.

A sudden noise made him jolt, thinking the SD guard might have come back early—but it was just a middle-aged couple walking by on the street. He watched them go out of sight, then turned his attention to a closer inspection of the two bullet marks in the wall. *Even if the body positioning could be answered, why a different caliber?*

The hand touching his shoulder jolted him for a second time...

The hand shook gently. Josef opened his eyes.

"You asked to be told when we got to Salzburg," the train guard said, looking down at Josef with a gentle smile. "You appear to have fallen asleep meanwhile."

"Yes. Thank you." Josef rubbed at his eyes and sat up.

He'd fallen asleep on the train reflecting back on that night visiting the crime scene with Felix Klein. Felix had finished early with the safe, touching Josef's shoulder to lift his absorption with the bullet marks.

The safe had been empty! But the events following had been even odder than the crime scene.

Josef knew that he should contact Mathias-Daniel straightaway about the two deaths. Not only the tragic news of Brunnerman's death, who Daniel had got to know during his visits, but lifting the specter of Schnabel from Daniel's life; particularly because it appeared Schnabel and his colleague had been observing Daniel visit Brunnerman's. Daniel might not have been aware of that.

He'd phoned Daniel early the next morning. "I've got something to tell you." But Daniel's response, "I've got something to share with you also," intrigued him. As always, no names or details given away over their phone lines, they met an hour later at a small café close to Daniel's apartment.

"You first," Daniel suggested, and Josef related the dramatic events of the past thirty-six hours. But as Josef finished by mentioning that it appeared Schnabel and a colleague had been observing his visits to Brunnerman's, he asked, "Has Schnabel approached you at any time over the matter?" and Daniel admitted that he had.

"He came to see me earlier that night before going to Brunnerman's. And that's when he told me what I have to tell you now, Josef."

Josef realized that something poignant was coming as Daniel looked across meaningfully and clasped his forearm across the table. But that still hardly prepared him for Daniel sharing the alarming news that Schnabel had consigned Deya to Dachau the night she'd disappeared.

Josef had shaken his head—mentioning the letter she'd written, the comment from Lorenzo that he thought "she'd left the country"—refusing to believe. But Daniel had been firm and insistent. "I raised the same with Schnabel when he told me, but he seemed sure of his ground. Said he got Deya to write the letter under threat of her daughter Luciana's life, because he didn't want you sniffing around interfering, trying to make pleas on her behalf."

Josef had been too shell-shocked with the news to probe too deeply about Schnabel's visit. Daniel said that Schnabel had visited him with the warning that he knew something was going on between Daniel and Brunnerman, and planned to visit Brunnerman's and discover exactly what. That seemed to tie in more or less with what Josef knew from the crime scene, only one oddity striking him: "Why didn't you phone Brunnerman straightaway and warn him?"

"I did, but there was no answer. Also, I didn't know that Schnabel intended to go there straight after leaving me. It was getting late by then, his shop might well have been closed."

With the mention of time, Josef had looked sharply at his watch. "I've got to go and see her."

As soon as he got back to Kärntnerstrasse police station, he put a call through to Dachau.

"From the details you've given me, it appears she was transported as 'Charani the gypsy,'" Commandant Keppler confirmed. "And, yes, she is still alive."

A slight hesitance as Keppler had said it; he might as easily have added "just." Or perhaps he was simply ruffled by the intimation that prisoners were so readily and quickly killed there.

Within the hour, Josef had boarded a train at Vienna's Westbahnhof station bound for Dachau. A nine-hour-twenty-minute journey, he was scheduled to arrive at about 9:40 p.m. *Neulengbach, St. Pölten, Loosdorf, Melk, Amstetten, Hochhof, Linz... Vöcklabruck...*

Each station seemed grayer than the last—artillery, munitions and tanks in every other rail siding—a reminder not only that they were in the grip of war, but of the dire, soul-destroying journey Deya would have endured, especially knowing what awaited at its end. Cut off from Luciana, himself and Lorenzo, possibly not seeing any of her loved ones ever again.

The carriage he was in was quite comfortable, but Deya would have been transported in a bare carriage with hard wooden bench seats or a cattle truck, her journey four hours longer. The hell on earth would have started with that journey, not just what awaited her.

Josef took the ring box from his pocket, looked inside. *How pathetic was that?* He'd grabbed it from his bedroom drawer along with a few essentials before leaving home—but what was he hoping to do? Show Deya the ring and tell her all the plans he had for them, without having the first clue how he might get her out of Dachau with the charges against her?

That might just come across as an added cruelty. Dangling such a golden prospect before her that she'd never be able to reach. And telling Deya that he'd bought the ring before their last arranged date, that his plans went back to then, would be just as bad. *Look, I really did love you…but I was unable to fully show it before you were condemned.*

Tears welling in his eyes, Josef put the ring back in his pocket, suddenly uncertain he'd even show it to Deya.

As Josef had started to drift toward sleep with the gray monotony of the passing stations, he'd asked the ticket guard to tell him when they were approaching Salzburg. Not only because then only two hours would remain of the journey, but also hopefully there'd be greener and more dramatic scenery.

That dramatic relief was short-lived, though, and within the hour it was back to the flat monotony of passing stations, grayer and darker still with the fading light as the train approached Munich, then finally Dachau.

Walking through its dank, oppressive confines, words revolved in Josef's head of what he was going to say to Deya, but all of them seemed to trap in his chest; they sounded feeble or trite, empty consolation.

And then finally when he'd seen Commandant Keppler and been led by a guard down a long corridor to a waiting area, his chest tightened more intensely when he saw Deya approaching along the same corridor: already frail and gaunt, a large bruise on her left cheek, her eye above half-closed with it. But as she got closer, there was something else about her face beyond the

frailty and her injuries; small, subtle differences that only someone who'd known Deya a while might discern.

Although Josef waited until they were sequestered in a private room and the guard had shut the door behind them before
he asked, "Who are you?"

44

Jewish, Mischling and Gypsy students shall be excluded from all Reich schools, universities and learning institutions.

Daniel

"Please tell me it's not true, Julian?"

"Tell you *what's* not true?"

"What Schnabel told me before he went to Brunnerman's two nights ago. That you gave up Johannes... *Andreas*, had him sent to Sobibór?"

Julian looked intently at me for a moment, as if trying to gauge what I might already know, deciding whether to confirm or deny it.

"Schnabel actually came to see you?" An incredulous edge to Julian's voice. "Why on earth would he do that?"

"He said he suspected something was going on between Brunnerman and me..." I related what Josef had told me about

Schnabel and his partner, Lindner, observing as I'd visited Brunnerman's, then kept the rest to what I'd in turn shared with Josef. It was important I kept my account consistent. *And perhaps if I repeat it enough, I'll be able to blot from my mind what really happened that night.*

Knowing what I'd come to discuss, I'd arrived at Julian's office just before lunch. And, as expected, his secretary, Krisztina, peeked her head around his door minutes afterward, saying she'd be back later. We were left alone.

But three streets before Julian's office, I'd been asked for my papers by an SD officer, and for a moment I'd forgotten my ID had changed. *Or perhaps there was an alert already out for me because of Schnabel.* It took me a second to respond when he said, "That's fine," and handed my papers back. But my nerves were still racing as I pressed Julian's buzzer, almost imagining I could still hear those Hitler-rally crowds in Heldenplatz a block away, chanting Jew, Jew... *Jew!* As if I was back again in those nerve-wracking weeks after Anschluss.

Julian's eyes darted. "And you say Schnabel is dead?"

"Yes. It appears he was shot when he went to confront Brunnerman, both of them firing at more or less the same time."

Julian shook his head. "I read about the break-in at Brunnerman's and his death, but I had no idea the person referred to simply as 'another man' in the newspapers was Schnabel." He sighed after a second, as if a weight was easing from his shoulders with the news.

"I daresay the SS are sensitive about the death being announced of one of their own, especially if he was somewhere he shouldn't have been." But it hit me then that Josef hadn't shared anything with Julian. Perhaps with him rushing off to see Deya in Dachau, there simply hadn't been the time. I wondered whether to tell Julian about that, but decided against it. That was a personal story for Josef to share, if and when he wanted to. I looked at Julian levelly.

"You haven't answered my initial question."

Julian appeared to collapse in on himself in that moment, starting to shake his head again.

"You don't understand—I had *no choice*."

I kept staring steadily.

Julian glanced to one side for a moment, as if searching for inspiration, before looking back at me. "Schnabel wanted to send *you* initially, Mathias." Again, when we were alone, nobody listening in, Julian referred to me by my old name. *So many years now between us*. "He'd deduced that Daniel Lendt and Mathias Kraemer were one and the same, spent a while here in my office going painstakingly through the similarities in writing styles." Julian grimaced crookedly at the memory. "And when he'd finished, he gave me a stark choice—either I gave you up, or he'd return with a squad to raid my office. They'd uncover every other false identity in my files—yours and Andreas's included. So nothing would have been gained." Julian sighed heavily. "I was still reluctant to give you up, though…said we went back too long. And when Schnabel pressed, if not you, then I had to give him *someone*—otherwise he'd call his men in to raid my office… I… I gave him Andreas."

Julian closed his eyes for a second as he uttered it, as if he never dreamed those words, that admittance, would leave his lips.

I stared at him incredulously. "You think that knowing I was partly responsible for Andreas being sent to a camp would make me feel *better*?" I could hear my own voice cracking.

Julian shook his head, looked down lamentably. Then, his hands visibly trembling, he reached for the silver holder to one side with a lime-green Sobranie and lit it. I hadn't seen Julian smoking in years, but my mind was too burdened with everything else in that moment to question it.

Since that night with Schnabel, my nerves had been constantly on edge, hardly able to think straight. As if my life was teetering on the edge of a precipice. *Knowing that if the SS uncover what happened that night, there'll be nothing to save me from execution or a death camp.* My only clear, rational thoughts had been getting a message to Josef about Deya and confronting Julian to find out why…*why?* But now hearing that I'd been partly responsible for Andreas's fate was soul wrenching, unbearable.

"But if Schnabel wanted me…you should have sent *me*, not Andreas." *Then the confrontation that night with Schnabel wouldn't have happened, and Andreas would have been saved.* "You know how close we are. What he meant to me."

"I know you're close. But, like I said—there was little other choice."

"Not only that, but the promise I made to my uncle Samuel, his father," I rode on, ignoring Julian's protests. And as Julian arched one eyebrow curiously, I explained about my deathbed promise to Samuel that I'd take care of Johannes-Andreas, keep an eye out for him. "Now not only have I let him down, but I've been responsible for his son being sent to a death camp."

"I'm sorry, I didn't know," Julian said, seeming to sink further within himself. "Why didn't you tell me?"

"Because it might have seemed I was only introducing Johannes to you as part of that deathbed promise to his father. I wanted him to be able to make it on his own merits as a writer."

Julian nodded forlornly. "Believe me, if there'd been any other choice. But can you see the dilemma I faced?" He held out a hand in plea. "You're fifteen years older, Mathias, and there's your leg deformity too. You'd have been singled out straightaway and sent to a gas chamber." Julian drew heavier on his cigarette, looked across steadily. "Also there were certain attributes Andreas has that I felt might help him, such as his calligraphy."

It seemed that Julian already had all of this worked out,

whereas I was still desperately grasping for reasons, for some sense. "But why Sobibór—such a harsh camp?"

"Because that was the only camp where I knew someone who might be able to help Andreas, keep him safe. He wrote to me a while ago."

My brow knitted as I struggled to comprehend.

Julian reached into a side drawer and pulled a carbon-copy letter from a file, passed it across. "This is the letter I gave Andreas to pass to Vice-Commandant Meisel upon his arrival at Sobibór."

I started reading.

My eyes began to well up halfway through, a turmoil of emotions running through me. Abject anger still that Julian had given up Andreas instead of me, but an overriding wave of relief that Andreas might actually be safe, combined with Julian's ingenuity in arranging this scenario and writing the letter. *Another one to have duped Schnabel.*

"I... I'm sorry," was all I could manage, lighting my own cigarette as I finished. "I had no idea." Normally I refrained in Julian's office, but with him already smoking, I couldn't be blamed for tempting him. "And you didn't tell Schnabel that we were cousins?"

"No, I didn't. He didn't appear to know, so no point in complicating matters." Julian grimaced. "Following that same ethos of Andreas making it on his own steam, there's little or nothing in book blurbs or press releases linking the two of you."

I nodded. This tied in with Schnabel's reaction and comments. "And does Hannah... *Stefanie* know about this letter you gave Andreas to take?"

"No. Because I had no idea whether Meisel had taken the bait. I thought it would be cruel to build up her hopes that I'd saved Andreas—only to find out later that my ploy had failed. All I've received from Meisel is this, just a few weeks ago."

Julian passed across a second letter. I read.

Dear Mr. Reisner,

The prisoner you mention arrived on the due date and passed me your letter.

All correspondence to Sobibór is monitored through an SS office in Lublin. In any case, any correspondence should make no reference to the manuscript in question. When it's finished, I will give you a PO box number in Chelm for any replies.

Kind Regards,
VCC Dieter Meisel

I looked up. "Hints that they might be working together on the manuscript, but by no means certain."

"Exactly. Appears also that Meisel is keen to keep it secretive, making correspondence on the subject difficult. Which is why I thought I'd be overstepping the mark to say anything to Stefanie, falsely build up her hopes." Julian took a fresh breath. "Besides, I hear she's written to Andreas through the Red Cross. So hopefully she'll get a letter back or hear something through them."

"Hopefully." I nodded solemnly, glancing at Julian's lit cigarette in its holder. "When did you start smoking again?"

"About five minutes after I said goodbye to Andreas and his train left for Sobibór."

45

Thus we may define "right" (i.e. law) as the might of a community. Yet it, too, is nothing other than violence, quick to attack whatever individual stands in its path, and it employs the self-same methods, follows like ends, with but one difference: it is the communal, not individual, violence that has its way.
—*Sigmund Freud (letter exchange with Albert Einstein)*

Andreas

The Red Cross visit was strictly controlled. Only two delegates were granted entry to the camp, one from their Geneva HQ and the other from the Polish ICRC office in Krakow. They would only be allowed into the Forward Camp Yard, where Commandant Toepfer would initially greet them and receive mail to give prisoners from their families. They would be assigned an office there for an hour to interview six prisoners, ten minutes for each, at the end of which they would in turn be given letters from various prisoners in the camp to pass to their families.

"But a word of warning," Vogt concluded, who'd come to tell us how the visit would proceed. "Those letters, only one per prisoner, should not mention or hint at any extreme or harmful conditions at the camp, let alone any deaths. If they do mention anything untoward, they will not be passed on to the Red Cross delegates to hand to your family. Is that clear?"

Then we heard on the camp grapevine that those six had been carefully selected and briefed beforehand. Three men, three women, and all with fairly mundane, day-to-day responsibilities such as working in the kitchens, tailors or laundry. Nobody who'd had a relative die in the camp, but all with relatives outside or in other camps, which became the final threat for them to say the "right thing" to the Red Cross representatives. "You'll be given a basic script and some guideline notes to work from. Step outside of that and say anything detrimental about the camp, and you or your family won't last long after their visit."

Jan shook his head when he heard. "They're making sure nobody outside hears anything bad about the camp. That we're all being treated well, as if it's some sort of holiday camp."

"*Sanitizing* is the expression from my journalism days." It reminded me of that declaration the Nazis insisted Freud sign before they agreed to let him leave, painting the picture that he'd been treated well and fairly. I scowled. "Worse still, looks like they're using it as a Nazi propaganda exercise for these camps."

Jan nodded slowly after a second. "Now I know why they finally allowed a visit to the camp. They found a way of turning it to their advantage."

The Red Cross visit in fact led to more lives lost rather than saved. The day before the visit, Toepfer and Vogt had everyone assemble in the Camp Two Yard, and went along the rows of prisoners with three guards, picking out people at random.

Jan and I noticed that they were selecting anyone who looked too thin, ill or infirm. We'd noticed in fact that food rations had been more plentiful the past week, and now we understood why. They wanted to have everyone looking as healthy and well-fed as possible, and this was the final culling process. Anyone who hadn't finally made the grade.

Nineteen people were picked out in total, and an hour later they were herded at rifle point into a death chamber and the motor started.

After forty minutes, the usual time-gap to ensure everyone was dead and the fumes had cleared, four Sonderkommandos started wheeling their carts toward the tunnel, but Vogt stopped them.

"You can do that later, in an hour or so. I want to inspect these bodies first."

Helmut Vogt walked among the bodies strewn on the floor in the death chamber.

He paid attention only to the male prisoners, and by the time he'd narrowed down yet again to those between twenty-five and forty, he was left with five choices.

His eyes darted from one to the other, assessing. Three were far too thin and emaciated, which had been the whole point of this particular exercise. He concentrated on the remaining two.

On one, the body weight was reasonable, at least not over-thin or emaciated. The man had been picked out mainly because of terrible blotches and patches of dry, scaly skin, which could be scurvy. Vogt knelt down and lifted the man's right hand. A dry scaly patch was on the back of the wrist, part of it extending onto the hand.

Vogt focused on the fingers. None of it appeared to have reached the fingers.

Taking the knife from his belt and a piece of cloth from his pocket, Vogt lifted up the man's index finger and cut it off as close to the hand joint as possible. Then, letting it bleed out for a moment, he wrapped it tightly in the cloth and put the severed finger in his pocket.

I looked on with the eagerness of a child at Christmastime as Vogt and another guard came and started going around our dormitory handing out the letters brought by the Red Cross.

Jan announced he had a letter from his uncle in Legnica, beaming excitedly as he opened it—a small nod in thanks to me as he started reading. Something he'd have been unable to do six months ago. Nahum, Tibor and others had letters too.

But as the last letters were handed out and I hadn't been given one, my face fell.

"What, *none* for me?"

Vogt turned to me. "There are two others without letters, so don't be so surprised."

"But my Hann… *Stefanie*, would have written," I said, a mixture of exasperation and disbelief.

"Maybe she put something in her letter which our censors didn't approve of." Vogt shrugged. "Or perhaps she doesn't love you as much as you thought…or has a new boyfriend who isn't a stinking Jew or dissident."

A sly gloat on Vogt's face as he said it. I glared back for a moment before looking away, didn't rise to the bait.

"Still, you have the satisfaction at least of being able to get a letter to your wife." Vogt held a hand out and I handed him the letter I'd painstakingly written over the last two days, the last part in stylized italics.

Only one per prisoner. I had hoped to send a letter also to Mathias-Daniel, but had to make do with a brief mention in my letter to Stefanie. *Give Daniel my regards. Tell him I'm safe and well. Hope all is well, too, with him and his family.*

Vogt and the other guard started collecting from the others. "Remember, as I mentioned before, leave the envelopes open so that we may check them before sending off. Any that are already sealed will be immediately destroyed."

When Vogt came into the room where the interviews were taking place with the six prisoners, they'd already been underway for twenty minutes. He sidled up to Haas looking on from the back of the room, muttering, "Everything fine so far?"

"Yes. No problems."

He stayed observing for a while with Haas, watching the two ICRC men—Tomas Wabersky from Krakow in his late thirties, and Gabriel Rosch from Geneva, five or six years older—take turns in interviewing each prisoner. The six appeared to have taken their instruction well, saying they were generally well-fed and cared for.

Vogt tapped one finger on the silver head of his cane, as if warning, *Say the wrong thing and you'll be beaten with this when they're gone and dragged off to a death chamber.*

The only small gripes from some prisoners—which Vogt had said was okay to mention to give a touch of realism—was that the accommodation was spartan but comfortable and the work at times monotonous and tiring. Though when pressed on that issue, they said that they worked normal hours, nine till five, and had lunch breaks and weekends free.

Vogt checked his watch and was about to leave the room when Gabriel Rosch got up and approached him.

"I noticed a heavy smell of diesel fumes over the camp when we approached, Sergeant. I wondered what that might be from?"

"Probably from the generator, or could be from the boiler for the heating and hot water." Vogt smiled tightly. "Have to make sure everyone's comfortable and warm."

"Yes, of course."

"Now, if you'll excuse me for a moment. I have to make sure those letters from the prisoners for their families are ready for you when you leave."

With a polite nod, Vogt left the room and went into the adjoining office. On the desk were piles of envelopes from the prisoners, with two guards sitting to one side.

"Have these all now been checked?" Vogt asked.

One of them answered that they had, pointing. "Only five seem unacceptable, which we've put to one side here."

"Thank you. I'll check those myself, plus also look quickly through the others. Should be no more than ten minutes—I'll call you again when I'm finished and they're ready to pass to the Red Cross delegates."

It took a second for the two guards to realize they were being dismissed. They got up and left.

As the door shut behind them, Vogt took the two letters from Stefanie Siebert to her husband, Andreas, from his second drawer down, briefly scanning the letters and the photos of their two children inside. *Very touching*, talking about how the children had grown and they all missed him terribly. Vogt ripped the photos and letters in half and dropped them into the wastepaper bin at his side.

Then from the bottom drawer, he took out a small package wrapped in brown waxed paper. The night before, he'd taken the severed finger from its cloth, slid Andreas Siebert's wedding ring from his pocket onto it, then carefully wrapped the finger in the waxed paper.

He took the envelope from his pocket that Andreas had just handed him, removed the letter inside, tearing it in half and dropping it in the wastepaper bin on top of the letters and photos from his wife. Then he slipped the small wax-paper package inside the same envelope and sealed it.

46

Josef

The click–clack of the train returning from Dachau seemed to merge for a moment with the tabletop tapping in Josef's thoughts.

"Who are you?"

Straight after saying it, Josef had held one hand up, suddenly worried about listening devices. He checked and couldn't see any visible on the walls or the small wooden table they sat on either side of, so he leaned forward, muttering, "Stay close together and keep your voice low as we speak. Meanwhile, I'll tap one finger on the table to further obscure any possible listening devices."

The woman, who gave her name as Rosella, spoke in soft tones only inches from Josef as she related her story. Josef was sure that to the guard looking intermittently through the six-inch-square glass in the door would assume they were lovers, whispering sweet nothings to each other.

Rosella was also from a Romani family and had initially gone with her husband to see Lorenzo about having his identity changed.

"I saw that Lorenzo was taken aback when he met me. When I asked him what it was, he said that I looked almost identical to a cousin of his. 'You could be twins.'"

"Did Deya also meet you, see the likeness for herself?"

"Not immediately. But while Lorenzo was arranging everything for my husband, he asked why I wasn't having my identity changed as well? After all, I was Romani, too, so faced the same risks. That's when I told him I had terminal cancer, with only a year or so to live."

Josef had offered his sympathies at that moment, Rosella smiling tautly, as if she'd heard similar a hundred times before. Lorenzo had requested she return when her husband's new identity was ready for a personal meeting with Deya.

"I saw then myself the tremendous likeness. I didn't know whether Lorenzo had something in mind at that moment or not, but then I got a call from him."

Rosella's voice quavering inches from Josef's ear, she related the proposition Lorenzo had made to her: she was to go to an apartment building in Herminengasse, where Deya was being held to be shipped to Dachau.

"I was to pose as her sister and turn up in traditional Romani gypsy garb. Deya would request a private moment alone, and we'd then switch clothes and I'd carry Deya's ID. If I agreed to do this, a handsome payment of twenty thousand Reichsmarks would go to my family."

Handsome indeed, Josef reflected: enough to buy an apartment or small house. Her husband had been against it, but she'd pressed hard, keen to go ahead.

"All that money—enough for my family to live well and help

them survive—against only a few months of remaining life. And in turn, I'd be saving the life of a woman who was healthy and had her whole life ahead. For me there was only one choice…"

As soon as Josef left the train at Westbahnhof station, he took a taxi to Johannesgasse, noted the phone number of the kiosk at the beginning of the street, then walked three hundred yards to another kiosk and phoned Lorenzo's contact number in Switzerland.

Josef left the number of the first phone kiosk, and the next day he was back at that kiosk to take Lorenzo's call.

Josef cut straight through the preambles and niceties.

"Why didn't you tell me what happened with Deya? I just came from seeing this other woman at Dachau."

Labored exhalation from Lorenzo. "Because she was afraid you were being followed. And if you could find her, so could the Nazis."

Josef's stomach dipped with that news. He knew that Daniel and Brunnerman had been watched, but hadn't realized he might have been tailed as well.

"Also, she worried that as soon as you found out," Lorenzo commented, "you'd go to the camp—as you've done now—and the truth would come out. Schnabel or other SS would keep hunting her, and eventually find her."

"I was careful when I visited the camp. Her secret's safe." A moment's poignant reflection hugging Rosella as they'd parted, thanking the woman who'd given her life to save Deya's. "In any case, Schnabel is dead."

Pregnant silence the other end, as if Lorenzo didn't quite believe it, and Josef went on to explain the events at Brunnerman's four nights ago.

"Strange to say the least," Lorenzo said wistfully. "But at least one less thing to worry about."

"I suppose." Tame acceptance. With the news about Deya,

all his other thoughts seemed to have become trapped. He'd applied scant focus on the oddities of the crime scene or how Schnabel's death changed things. That portent suddenly lifted.

"That last night when I planned to see Deya—the night she disappeared—I had a ring in my pocket, planned to propose to her. Finally do the right thing." A strangled, uncomfortable laugh escaped. "How stupid was I?"

"I'm so sorry, Josef. I wish things could have worked out different."

Josef felt the same as Rosella had no doubt felt when he'd offered his condolence about her terminal cancer. Josef as quickly shook off his maudlin mood, took a fresh breath. *Fresh hope.*

"So where is Deya? Where did she go in the end?"

"She kept the exact location secret even from me—possibly concerned about that past network breach. All I know is that she went to Portugal—the last letter she sent was postmarked Lisbon a month ago. But there was no return address. So I have no idea exactly where she is."

47

Jews, Mischlinge and Gypsies are forbidden to own or use electrical or optical equipment, bicycles, typewriters and records, or have access to libraries.

Andreas

As I got into the final stages of the manuscript with Meisel, things became tenser.

There was an element in the book that I still wasn't entirely satisfied with, the death of main character Tobias's first love, Isabella, in her late teens. But having tamely broached the subject two months ago, I'd quickly backed off when Meisel remarked, *I think it's fine as it is.*

Reminded of the heated confrontation when I'd tackled the issue of Tobias and Karina over the death of their son, Jakob, in the first year of World War I, I wanted to avoid a repetition. Nevertheless, I thought the manuscript was weaker without the issue being addressed, as if there was a key element missing. I approached cautiously.

"You recall I mentioned before Tobias's reaction to young Isabella's death?"

"Yes." Meisel looked at me steadily, puffed at his pipe. "But I thought we'd decided that was okay as it was."

I nodded. My backing off earlier might have made the subject more difficult to raise again now. *Walking on eggshells.* "It's 80 or 90 percent fine, almost perfect. As with so much else, you've dealt with Tobias's direct emotions over Isabella's death tremendously well. Those ring true and are very heartfelt." I needed to sweeten this pill as much as possible to make it acceptable. "But it's how Tobias deals with Karina later in relation to Isabella's past death."

"In what way?" Meisel's stare intensified.

I swallowed imperceptibly. "Well, it seems that at times Tobias makes some comparisons between the two—small things that Karina does that remind him of Isabella. But we never get that too openly from Tobias, it's never expanded upon."

"I… I don't follow you." Clouds in Meisel's eyes, his expression darkening.

My mouth felt suddenly dry. I wished now I'd never said anything. "It's almost as if Tobias in some ways sees Karina as a copy, a replacement of Isabella. But ultimately one that can't live up to Isabella. I think that needs explaining and rationalizing more in Tobias's thoughts."

Meisel continued to stare for a moment, his expression lost. Then he got up abruptly and went to the window, looking out.

Stone silence. I felt sure then I'd overstepped the mark again. Meisel would turn around and berate me, and I'd be in the doldrums for another three or four days. Or perhaps this was the last straw; he'd decide to end our association and cast me aside to whatever fate Vogt had in store for me.

Meisel's tone was soft, almost defeated, as he finally spoke. "I think that was the other thing I found hard to face. Because I never fully got over Helena's death… *Isabella* in the book." He turned slowly from the window, came to sit down again. "And it was wrong of me to expect Luisa to live up to that. She was always going to come off second-best."

I should have realized: if Tobias's relationship with Karina was based on real events in Meisel's life, then Isabella's early death might have been too.

Meisel relit his pipe and talked about when he'd first met Helena at Heidelberg University. He'd been in his second year there, she'd only just arrived.

"She was probably the first real love of my life. We were inseparable. Then within eighteen months, I was standing at her graveside. Dead from meningitis, two months short of her twentieth birthday."

I gave Meisel a solemn, understanding look, stayed silent. No words would have been adequate. In Eine Flackernde Kerze, Isabella had died from pneumonia. Obviously, Meisel felt it would be too close if her death had been from meningitis as well.

Meisel took a fresh, burdened breath. "I never got over it, and perhaps married Luisa too soon afterward. Saw something of Helena in her, but as you rightly say—and as becomes clear as Eine Flackernde Kerze progresses—in the end, not enough. Not nearly enough."

Meisel puffed at his pipe, eyes distant again as he reached for the memories. "It was unfair on Luisa, and I shouldn't have done it. But needs must, and I was lonely. Then when Lukas was born, in a way he became a bond between us—filled something which until then had been missing from our marriage."

Meisel grimaced ironically, waved a hand to one side. "Of course, when Lukas died, that made it all the worse. As I told you, Luisa blamed me for his death, and for me that void was back again between us. But even greater than before—because this time we were *both* guilty of keeping each other at arm's length, albeit for different reasons."

I glanced down for a second, nodded gently. "The pain you felt, what I sense coming from you now. If that could come through in the manuscript—especially how you felt as a result you'd been unfair with Luisa—*Karina*—it would make the book stronger. Give readers a better understanding of Tobias's thoughts and actions."

Meisel looked across, his eyes still slightly lost, bleary. "What makes you think I'd be able to handle that well? It might be too close, too painful."

"I think you're braver than you realize. Going through all of that, then consigning yourself to places like Chelmno and here. Writing the manuscript in the first place." I shrugged. "Besides, that's what I'm here to help you with."

Meisel looked across hopefully for a moment, but it was as quickly lost again. *"Brave?"* he snorted. "I consigned myself here to escape—not only from Luisa's accusing stares, but because if Helena's and Lukas's deaths taught me anything, it was that life was cruel. Death often random and pointless. What's the point in becoming attached to people, when all that means is that you become more heartbroken when they die?"

Vogt was convinced something was going on with Andreas Siebert and Meisel. All those late nights with them working together in the study.

Surely there wasn't that much correspondence to send to Wehrmacht or SS offices in Berlin or Vienna, or even the local outpost in Lublin? He'd used Siebert only a handful of times for calligraphy on posters, and was aware of at most a dozen other instances for camp notices. So what were they doing the rest of the time?

Of course, there were those camp rumors that they were having a raging homosexual affair together. He'd probably been one of the first to instigate those rumors, and had taken a delight in spreading them. Part payback for Meisel reprimanding him when Siebert had first arrived at the camp, plus also tied in nicely with the existing rumors after Meisel turned his back on coming to any more of the little parties he organized with camp girls.

But even if something was going on between Andreas Siebert and Meisel, at most that would involve twenty minutes or half an hour of passion here and there; yet they were inside together for hours, and increasingly so over the past few weeks. Meisel had even put a stop to Siebert's two hours' end-of-day laboring for those weeks, so that he could spend that extra time in Meisel's office. What was going on?

And what about the times that Siebert was left alone in Meisel's office? Very often those would occur late in the day as well, as if the two of them had discussed something, with Siebert then left on his own to get on with it while Meisel went out to busy himself with other camp duties: tailors, laundry, provisions store or officers' hall, or meetings in Commandant Toepfer's office.

Vogt didn't think it would be a good idea to barge in unannounced when the two of them were together; that would simply earn him another sharp reprimand from Meisel. But if he chose a time when Andreas Siebert was alone in Meisel's office, then he could cover by saying he thought the vice-commandant would be there; he'd return later.

Vogt kept an eye out for when Meisel might next leave his office.

Once we'd identified and agreed upon that final missing element of the past tragedy with Isabella affecting Tobias's later relationship with Karina, and *why*—a far more intensive work schedule with the manuscript ensued.

After dealing with the camp correspondence first thing in the morning, I'd get Meisel's thoughts on the next planned scene, make notes and raise a few suggestions, then in the afternoon I'd set about writing or reshaping what we'd agreed upon.

Either last thing in the day or the next morning, Meisel would read what I'd worked on and any final changes would be made. With that more intensive work schedule, we planned to finish within the month and send the revised manuscript to Julian.

Part of the tension in those closing stages was therefore not only anxiety that we got everything finally right, but mounting anticipation as to what Julian's reaction might be.

"Just going to the provisions store to sort something out," Meisel announced midafternoon on day twenty-two of our more intensive routine. "I won't be long."

I'd been working on my own for the past hour while Meisel went through some work files and made some notes. I looked up. "I've got an hour or so more on a couple of scenes."

With a curt nod, Meisel left the office.

I put my head down again, concentrating on an awkward couple of paragraphs.

The office door swung open only two minutes later. I thought at first Meisel must have forgotten something, but Vogt stood there, eyes darting between me and the manuscript spread out on my desk.

If there had been some warning, a knock on the door or a voice on the other side, I'd have swiftly shifted everything into the drawer to one side—the arrangement with Meisel if anyone came by unexpectedly. *Under no circumstances mention either that you're working on my manuscript, or indeed that I've written one. It's just between the two of us.*

But Vogt had just burst in, and had obviously approached silently; I hadn't even heard his footsteps beyond the door.

"My, my...what's this?" Vogt gloated. "Writing something privately while Vice-Commandant Meisel's not around. While the cat's away..."

I stared back blankly. I'd gone into a half-defensive position, one arm over the pages in front of me, as if guarding.

Vogt reached over to the larger stack of papers to my left and flicked through the top pages.

"Working on a manuscript that nobody knows about. You wait until Toepfer hears about this."

"No, no…it's not that at all," I said desperately. But then suddenly stopped, said no more. *I promised. I can't betray Meisel's secret.*

"No doubt telling the world about the camp's dark secrets," Vogt said cuttingly, a crooked leer rising. "You'll burn for this for sure this time."

I shook my head, a shudder running through me.

"And your manuscript will burn too—so it will all have been for nothing."

"No, you…you don't understand! It's not what you think." But still I couldn't bring myself to betray Meisel.

My rising panic only seemed to fuel Vogt. His leer widened. "Maybe I should burn it right in front of you."

Vogt grabbed a heavy sheaf of papers from the top, fifty pages or more, holding them up high as he took a Zippo lighter from his pocket.

"No…*no!*"

But my shrill protest seemed to be lost on Vogt. He flicked the lighter six inches below the pages, moved the flame closer.

"*No*…it's *not* mine!" I shrieked.

A frozen moment. Vogt stared at me, doubting, disbelieving.

The office door had opened behind us; Meisel stood there, taking in the scene with equal disbelief.

"What's going on?"

48

No one who, like me, conjures up the most evil of those half-tamed demons that inhabit the human beast, and seeks to wrestle with them, can expect to come through the struggle unscathed.

—*Sigmund Freud*

Stefanie opened the envelope with eager excitement. Postmarked from Krakow, she'd recognized the handwriting on its front straightaway. *A letter from Johannes at last!* The sender's address on the back had his new name, Andreas Siebert, then simply, Lublin. No full address for Sobibór—or maybe he'd been moved somewhere else nearby.

Her hands were trembling in anticipation. But as she looked inside and saw only a small brown waxed-paper package, she paused for a second. *No letter?* It seemed odd that Johannes would send her something, even if it was a nice gift or memento, without including a letter. Perhaps a letter was inside the package?

She continued eagerly, then suddenly froze as she got the package fully open and saw what was inside. At first, when the letter had landed on the doormat, she'd wished the children had been there so that she could share the excitement of a letter from their father.

But now she was thankful that they were both at school. Wouldn't be there to witness the shock on her face, the horror of what was inside the envelope.

Her stomach churned, the bile rising swiftly. She put one hand to her mouth and rushed to the bathroom, the surge of vomit hitting when she was halfway there, trickling between her fingers.

Daniel

I'd put the phone down from speaking to Stefanie and Julian only an hour before the knock came on my door.

Stefanie had been distraught and tearful as she told me about the package arriving and what she'd found inside. I'd tried to placate her, saying I was sure it was a mistake, "Somebody playing a cruel joke. I'm sure he's okay." But I held back on why I was clinging to that belief; that was something for Julian to share, if and when he was more certain. Though Stefanie was practically beyond consolation—my own guilt with my promise to Uncle Samuel and my part responsibility weighing heavier—and I called Julian straight after putting the phone down on her.

Julian had been equally distraught at the news, muttering, "Oh, God. Maybe my ploy wasn't successful after all." Then, as if desperately seeking an explanation: "And was Stefanie sure that it was Andreas's wedding band?"

"Yes, she was sure." A measured sigh. "I asked her the same."

Brief silence, then a more defeated sigh from Julian. "I thought that Meisel would have kept Andreas alive to work on his manuscript—especially after that letter I got last month."

"You'd have thought so." An afterthought struck me. "Unless something has happened to Meisel since he wrote to you."

"A possibility, I suppose."

All we could think of as an explanation.

The two calls were still on my mind when the knock came on my door.

I looked through the spyhole: an SS officer stood there, an older man with glasses in a dark gray suit to his side. I thought for a moment of not opening the door, but I was sure they'd probably heard my footsteps approaching. As a more insistent second knock came on the door, I hastily opened it.

The SS officer introduced himself as Scharführer Lindner, the older man cutting in abruptly, "And I am Heinz Piehler, Kriminaldirektor of the Geheime Staatspolizei."

They walked past me halfway through me inviting them in and remained standing in the main front room, didn't take seats.

"We have come about the matter of the death of Carl Brunnerman, watchmaker and jeweler," Lindner announced. "Who I understand you knew?"

"Yes, I... I read about his death. Very sad," I said forlornly. It had been in the newspapers, so showing surprise would have struck an odd chord, started on the wrong foot. "And, yes, I did know him."

"You visited him on a number of occasions."

A statement rather than a question. I nodded. "Yes, I did."

"What was that for, may I ask?"

"To get a watch fixed." The stock response advised by Lorenzo; Brunnerman dealt with clocks and watches more than jewelry and diamonds.

Piehler looked at me doubtingly. "You went *three* times just to get a watch fixed?"

I shrugged nonchalantly. "Well, the first time I went to buy a clock. But then I found out he mended watches. I returned another time to get an old watch fixed, then came back when it was mended to pick it up."

Piehler continued to look at me doubtingly. Though he had one of those dour, scowling countenances, his dark eyes oddly magnified through thick-lensed glasses suggested he doubted practically everything he heard.

I hoped I'd appeared outwardly calm—*as calm as anyone could hope for with a Gestapo and SS officer in their front rooms*—but inside my stomach was writhing. So many times I'd written scenes like this, convinced I'd know how to give the right, balanced impression in such a situation; but the reality was something else. I could hardly think straight. Constructing these scenes, I was calm, looking at them objectively, detached. Here, I was far from detached.

"And have you visited Brunnerman's on other occasions?" Lindner asked.

I wondered whether they might know I'd visited other times, and this was where they'd catch me out. "I'm not sure. I might have visited another time to look at his collection of new watches," I answered ambiguously. "I can't remember now."

Lindner and Piehler exchanged a glance. *They knew something.*

"And is your son here now?"

My heart skipped a beat. What on earth would they want with Ivor... *Alex*? "No, he's still at school. Why do you ask?"

Piehler answered curtly. "Because some things might be difficult to handle while your son is around."

That was the first moment I realized they'd probably come to arrest me. Any answers I gave that didn't match what they already knew would later be used against me, further putting my head in the noose.

Piehler looked down. "New rug, I see?"

"Yes, it is," I said as plainly and calmly as I could. *Quick flash image of the old rug with Schnabel's body, too bloodstained to be cleaned.* His body had been rolled up in it before being bound in double plastic, taken out and dumped in the boot of my car. "Yes, changed not too long ago."

"I see." That doubting stare again, then Piehler's eyes shifted to look around the room.

I'd scrubbed the wooden floor beneath as thoroughly as I could with bleach, but I daresay Piehler might still discern a faint bloodstain if he lifted up the new rug and looked. He didn't. He moved to the far side of the room, focusing on a large mountain-scenery painting on my wall.

"And you visited Brunnerman's quite late at night?" Lindner asked, pulling my attention away from Piehler on the far side. "Why was that?"

"Brunnerman said that he handled many repairs after his shop had closed." Again, the stock answer recommended by Lorenzo. "He preferred that, leaving the day free for handling sales."

My nerves tensed, noticing that Piehler was lifting up the painting, peering underneath. *He's looking for a safe!* They'd already discovered Brunnerman's empty safe at the back, were looking for the diamonds and cash.

"And you wish to keep to that account?" Lindner asked, staring at me intently.

My chest tightened. *What is it they might already know that I haven't answered satisfactorily?* Of course, there were a myriad.

"Yes…because that's what happened," I said, hoping I didn't sound as uncertain as I felt.

I didn't have a wall safe, so Piehler searching for one didn't worry me—but I suddenly realized with panic what was behind the third painting along, which I'd hung up only two days ago. *The hole made by Schnabel's stray bullet.* Hopefully the plaster would have dried by now.

Piehler lifted the bottom of the painting, and was halfway through putting it back down again when he appeared to notice something. He put one hand underneath, feeling for a moment. He looked toward me.

"You appear to have an area of freshly laid plaster beneath this painting. Would you care to tell me what that is from?"

I looked at Piehler evenly as I considered my answer, knowing that if I answered wrong, the handcuffs would come out and I'd be marched off.

Being a crime-thriller writer had the benefit of knowing various ways to cover up a crime. But it also meant I knew the countless ways the police could catch me out.

49

Andreas

"What were you writing about in this manuscript?" Commandant Toepfer demanded.

I didn't answer.

"Was it anything to do with what goes on in this camp?"

I shook my head. "No, it wasn't." At least that part I could answer openly.

We were in Commandant Toepfer's office. He ran the questioning while Vogt and Meisel sat to one side. Vogt had started with a statement of what he'd discovered upon walking into Meisel's office, then Toepfer took over with his questioning, referring to the two of them only briefly for confirmations and clarifications.

"And you announced that this manuscript wasn't yours. Who might it have belonged to, if not you?"

I stayed silent, looked down, didn't even glance Meisel's way.

"As I thought," Toepfer said with some satisfaction. "You obviously said that simply to try and save your own neck. And you wrote this without Vice-Commandant Meisel's knowledge? Or without at any time asking his permission to do so?"

I kept my gaze stoically down, said nothing. *If Meisel was to intervene on my behalf, it would be now.* But he remained silent also.

"Your refusal to say anything on the matter speaks for itself. And could be seen as tantamount to insubordination and disrespect." Toepfer took a tired, fresh breath. "Which at least makes my decision now simpler. We have a fresh consignment of prisoners arriving tomorrow afternoon. You will be put in a chamber along with—"

"It's *mine*," Meisel cut in with a heavy sigh. "Prisoner Siebert has been helping me with it over the past months."

Toepfer and Vogt exchanged a look, as if that answered a number of things in their minds.

Toepfer looked at Meisel sharply. "I therefore ask you the same question I asked the prisoner. Does it involve any activities here at the camp?"

"No, it doesn't," Meisel said resignedly. "It's set in the lead-up to World War I and its first years."

"I see." Toepfer considered the information for a moment, then looked at me. "You are dismissed. I wish to talk for a few moments in private with Vice-Commandant Meisel about this matter."

Meisel left Toepfer's office about forty minutes later without looking my way—I was sitting in front of the Sonderkommando dormitory looking across the yard—or toward anyone else for that matter. Head down, as if he didn't wish to see or acknowledge anyone at that moment.

No message the next day from Dalit, Meisel's new coffee and cleaning maid, to go to his office. I was back laboring with

Jan. And when it got to the second day with the same, I began to worry.

I understood that Meisel would be angry at his secret being revealed, and would hold me partly responsible—but surely we were so close to finishing now that he wouldn't give up at this stage?

Then it struck me: perhaps with only thirty pages to go, Meisel thought he could handle those on his own from my notes and the discussions we'd had. I was suddenly surplus to requirements.

An outbreak of typhus had hit the Sonderkommandos beyond the fence harder than our side, so after some tilling and planting in the vegetable patch, once again Jan and I were commandeered to help out. Halfway through helping Jan level the ground over the last batch of bodies in a burial ditch, I voiced my concerns. After all, now that Vogt knew, it was no longer a secret, would be around the camp in no time.

"Explains those long hours you've been spending in Meisel's office," Jan commented as I finished. A faint smile teased his lips after a moment. "At least you won't have to put up with any more camp rumors about the two of you having a raging affair."

"Every cloud, eh?" I joined Jan in a smile and light chuckle. Jokes and laughter were a welcome release in the camp, even if they were often gallows humor or at your own expense. Though at that moment, with the line of bodies only a foot beneath the fresh soil we'd laid, I felt a stab of guilt.

When we'd first approached, I'd noticed a couple of young children in the ditch, hardly older than Nadia. I couldn't look, had to let Jan lay down the first few shovel-loads—until those frozen, gaunt eyes were covered and not staring up at me— before I joined in.

"I know what you mean, though." Jan's expression as quickly became more serious. "I've got pretty much the same worry now."

"In what way?"

Jan waved one hand toward the ditches. "Last night's consignment was only about eighty people—whereas six months ago we'd be getting a hundred-and-fifty or more. Sometimes two or three hundred. They're getting less each time, and rumor has it that the next one might be only fifty or sixty."

"Why is that?"

Jan looked around, took a quick bead on where he thought was east. "The Red Army's making strong advances on the eastern front, and word has it that the SS are winding down the camp operations, getting ready to pack up if and when the Red Army gets too close."

"What will they do?" I held one hand out from my shovel. "Move us all to another camp?"

"No, I don't think so. The people remaining here will be put in death chambers by myself and the other Sonderkommandos. Then, as happened when the camp was first built, we'll have to dismantle and knock it down at rifle point before being shot by the guards. The guards will then raze the rest to the ground. No trace will remain."

I looked emptily across the field of body trenches toward a gray mist beyond. Even if I survived a short while longer with Meisel's manuscript, there was no long-term hope.

50

The children of Jews, Mischlinge and Gypsies shall not be allowed to attend Reich schools, and any currently attending will be expelled.

Josef

"So who was it that came to see you, Daniel?" Aware that they were in a public place, Josef kept to his new name rather than Mathias.

"Scharführer Lindner from the SS and a Gestapo Kriminaldirektor, Heinz Piehler..."

As Mathias-Daniel related their visit, Josef noticed his hands shaking on the table. They'd gone to the University of Vienna coffee shop again. One of the few places they'd never seen an SS or SD officer, possibly due to its proximity to the library.

Josef had taken a tram and walked the rest, mindful of the fact he might have been tailed. His car was too distinctive.

"Piehler's as heavyweight as you can get," Josef remarked. "He introduced himself to me briefly after I spoke to Lindner at the crime scene. Then he phoned me at Kärntnerstrasse two days later to confirm how he saw the investigation running. He'd primarily investigate Schnabel's death, I'd be investigating Brunnerman's death. In his own words—'Though obviously there will be areas where the two will cross over and we should share information.'" Josef noted that Lindner had been promoted to a Scharführer—possibly to take more of a lead in the investigation, or with Schnabel's death there was a gap to fill in that SS unit. "Do you think they accepted your explanation of why you went to Brunnerman's three times—first buying a clock, then dropping off and picking up a watch to be fixed?"

"I think so. Perhaps a moment's doubt at first, but then they moved on to other things."

"They didn't suspect you might have visited other times, perhaps even seen you directly?"

"I don't know." Daniel looked aslant for a moment. "I answered vaguely, just in case. Said I might have visited one more time, I wasn't sure."

Josef nodded slowly, slotting the pieces into place. He was sure Mathias-Daniel was holding something back. Not just because of what he'd uncovered the past twenty-four hours, but also Daniel's shaky, distressed disposition. There didn't appear to be sufficient threat in this recent visit to make Daniel so nervous. And it also seemed like a curtailed account, as if Daniel was only sharing half the story.

Josef had been the one to call for this meeting—the elements he'd struck upon burning too strongly through his mind—saying simply there were a couple of things he wanted to clarify, with Daniel adding with a resigned sigh, *Good idea. I in fact had a visit just yesterday over this that I wanted to discuss with you.*

Josef took a sip of his coffee. "And Lindner's and Piehler's questioning just revolved around Brunnerman? They didn't ask you whether Schnabel might have paid you a visit?"

"No, they didn't."

Josef looked at Daniel steadily. This at least struck Josef as the truth. For various reasons, it appeared the SS and Gestapo were keen to keep the identity of that other body under wraps. Until they'd ascertained how and why Schnabel might be implicated.

Daniel lit a cigarette, took a heavy draw. "I… I worried that they might know about Brunnerman's diamonds and cash in his hidden safe. Because Piehler started peering under some of my paintings at home—as if he was looking for a wall safe I might have."

One possible reason for Daniel's hands trembling.

"They still don't know about Brunnerman's safe—the panel at the back is still in place and hasn't been disturbed." Josef exhaled tiredly. "Though I daresay if and when they do discover it and also find it's empty, as I did, it will be a different matter."

"I know." Daniel closed his eyes for a second, shook his head.

Something about the empty safe seemed to particularly disturb Daniel. And while Josef could understand Daniel's nervousness at telling him everything—concerned perhaps that he might be forced to share some of it with the Gestapo, or that with something so serious, his hands might be tied—at the same time, Josef felt slighted. He thought their long association and friendship went beyond that. *I nailed a cross above his mother's door to mislead the SS, introduced him to Lorenzo's network in the first place. What was so terrible that Daniel didn't think he could share it with me?*

Josef spat it out. "Why are you holding things back from me, Daniel?"

"I—I'm not."

But Daniel's hand trembling on his cigarette belied his words.

Josef shrugged, held out a palm. "Put it this way. If Lindner and Piehler *had* asked if Schnabel had visited you, what would you have told them?"

Daniel considered for a moment. "I'd have told them the same as I told you. That he visited earlier in the evening before going to Brunnerman's."

"Except that's not true, is it?" Josef looked at Daniel searchingly, watched his trembling bite deeper. "Schnabel called later that evening—and that's when you shot him with the gun you got from Lorenzo."

At first, Josef's thoughts had been too burdened with Deya and Dachau to think clearly. And when they did finally clear, the first thing to strike him was in fact that imparted tale about Deya.

Schnabel had specifically tried to keep that secret, so that Josef wouldn't track her to Dachau and appeal on her behalf: Why on earth would Schnabel tell Daniel, fully knowing that Daniel would share that news with him?

The only possible reason is that Schnabel didn't expect Daniel to live to tell the tale.

The other factor was the mismatched calibers—the two shots in Brunnerman's wall not matching the gun found in Brunnerman's hand, a Browning 640.

Josef didn't think Brunnerman carried a gun, and if it had been Schnabel's as part of a setup, then no doubt the bullets in the wall would have matched the gun in Brunnerman's hand. But what if the gun had been Daniel's?

Josef had made another phone-kiosk call to Lorenzo's number in Switzerland, returning to that kiosk eight hours later to get Lorenzo's callback.

"The gun that was given to MK in the batch you had in mid-November—what type was that?" Josef had masked the original Mathias Kraemer name as much as possible and had said batch rather than *people*.

"One moment." Another voice in the background, Lorenzo no doubt checking with Alois. "It was a Browning Hi-Power 640."

Josef watched Daniel crumple in front of him as he laid out how he'd arrived at his conclusions.

"That gun is no longer with you, is it?"

"No…it isn't." Barely a whisper, Daniel's body shuddering.

"It's the gun we found in Brunnerman's hand at the crime scene, isn't it?"

"Yes, it is." Daniel's hand trembled on his cup as he finished the last of his coffee. He shook his head. "I'm sorry. I should have told you before. But I was *afraid*…and maybe thought, too, that if I didn't admit it to anyone, I… I'd start to believe myself that it hadn't happened. Blot it from my mind."

"I understand." Josef took a fresh breath. "But if I can work out what happened, it won't take long for the SS and Gestapo to do the same. So you're far better off going through a dry run with me first—then we can start to lay plans, see if there's some way out of this mess."

Josef lit his own cigarette as Daniel—starting uncertainly at first, tremulously—related the events of that night: Schnabel threatening him, having just come from Brunnerman's. Schnabel's plans to leave Daniel's body at the scene and make it look as if they'd shot each other in a robbery gone wrong.

"He already had Brunnerman's stash of diamonds and cash from his safe, and wanted to add mine to that haul. If I didn't go along with it, he'd kill Ivor… *Alex* as well, asleep in his room."

"And that's when he told you what had happened with Deya?"

"Yes. He was gloating about it, reveling in how ingenious he'd been. He'd also found a little black book in Brunnerman's safe with a list of others in Lorenzo's network who'd exchanged diamonds for cash, plus a collection of photos of Freud associates. He planned to work through that list and the photos, pick them off one by one." Daniel shook his head grimly. "And I thought to myself, *I can't let this man live.* I told Schnabel I was going to get the keys to where I had my diamond stash—but I was headed for the drawer with the gun Alois had given me. I could hear Schnabel not far behind me, warning me not to try anything. But I thought—if I turned quickly enough, I might catch him by surprise." Daniel sighed heavily. "But when I opened the drawer, the gun wasn't there!"

Josef looked across intently. Daniel's mouth was slightly open, as if aghast again as he relived that moment.

"What happened then?"

Josef shook his head in disbelief as Daniel related the remaining events, ending with Piehler the other day peering under one of his paintings at home and asking about the fresh plaster patch where he'd covered up Schnabel's stray bullet.

"I told him it was from where I'd initially put in the picture hook too low." Daniel smiled uncertainly. "Something I'd used in a past book."

"Did Piehler appear to accept that account?"

"I daresay I won't know unless or until they return." Daniel exhaled tiredly. Relating the events seemed to have drained him.

"But return, they will—of that you can be sure." Josef stared the message home. "And the diamonds, money, this little black book and the photos?"

"I've got those safe."

Josef nodded. He'd anticipated it would be bad, but it was far worse than he'd thought. And having said he might be able to find a way out of this mess, he didn't have the first clue how to start. *The weight of circumstances against Daniel was too damning, too conclusive. No possible escape route!*

But at least he now understood why Daniel had been so reluctant to share those final details with him.

51

Dark, unfeeling and unloving powers determine human destiny.

—*Sigmund Freud, Introductory Lectures on Psychoanalysis*

Andreas

The mood in the camp was tense, on a knife edge.

The rumors that the camp might be closing had spread, and the Sonderkommandos were particularly agitated, knowing that fairly soon they wouldn't be needed and would also be killed.

On the third day after Toepfer's informal hearing about Meisel's manuscript, Dalit visited me at the end of a day's laboring, told me that I should come to Meisel's office first thing in the morning.

The grapevine whispers among Jan and some of the other Sonderkommandos were that a camp rebellion was brewing, which I viewed firsthand when I was in the tailor's one day with Jan and saw a meat cleaver being sewn into a coat lining.

Picking up that I'd noticed, Jan commented, "You'd better hurry finishing Meisel's manuscript. There might not be much more time left."

Three or four weeks, Jan reckoned. Long knives and meat cleavers had to be sneaked from the kitchen gradually, so that their removal wasn't noticed.

Under normal circumstances, that would have been more than enough time. But part of Toepfer's conditions had been that work on the manuscript shouldn't take place in normal camp working hours. So my mornings were taken up solely with handling official correspondence in Meisel's office, then I'd put in a full afternoon's laboring with Jan and the other Sonderkommandos before returning to Meisel's office in the early evening to work on his manuscript.

To aid my workflow, not have it interrupted, Meisel would get Dalit to bring me stew and bread from the canteen at dinnertime; and often I'd work through solidly until almost midnight, Meisel getting a guard to come and escort me back across the compound so that I didn't get shot by one of the watchtower guards.

"I'm sorry. I should have said something sooner," Meisel remarked on my second night's work on the manuscript. "But I had little choice after Toepfer's little hearing."

He'd just returned from the officers' dining hall, and I got the impression he'd had a few glasses of wine, which perhaps had made him feel mellow and inclined to open up more. I realized then that the three-day break had been imposed by Toepfer, it hadn't been Meisel's choice.

"I'm sorry too. I shouldn't have said anything."

"Well, you were left with little other choice, with Vogt about to burn it. And you didn't directly say it was mine." Meisel shrugged, smiled awkwardly. "Though I suppose once you'd said it wasn't *yours*, by natural elimination they could have worked out it was mine. If they'd been a little smarter."

I joined Meisel nervously with a smile. While Meisel no doubt had the privilege of taking verbal swipes at his fellow officers, I wasn't sure it was one prisoners could partake in.

Meisel lit up his clay pipe, became more contemplative. "Of course, I'll now have to put up with all the sly looks and whispers behind my back—Vice-Commandant Meisel is writing a book. And partly a love story too—isn't that usually what women write?"

I grimaced sympathetically. While that trait, showing a softer, more emotional side, might be seen as admirable in some circles, that certainly wasn't the case in a hard-edged death camp like Sobibór. "Is that why you were keen to keep your manuscript secret?"

"Partly that. But also a bit of history between me and Vogt." He looked at me inquiringly. "You've probably heard some of the rumors about me yourself."

"I'm not sure." I chose safe, noncommittal ground.

Meisel waved his pipe hand. "Of no matter. I'm not blind to them, and the last thing I needed was something else to feed that—not only am I not attracted to women, but now I am acting like one too."

"I understand. Not an easy situation." I bit my tongue on commenting how my long hours in his office might have also added fuel to those rumors.

"Not that it bothers me much what Vogt thinks anymore." Meisel puffed harder at his pipe, eased out a cloud of smoke. "Nor Toepfer for that matter. If you gave two Pfennigs for their worthwhile thoughts, you'd still be overpaying."

This time I allowed myself a more open smile; it might have come across as obdurate or disapproving if I hadn't joined in.

Meisel became more serious, reflective. "Although it wasn't always that way between us…"

As Meisel started talking about the parties with camp girls that Vogt would organize, I realized this was the same story I'd heard from Jan, but from a different perspective.

"...I felt uncomfortable at first, but then I found a girl that I warmed to, felt a connection with. I think perhaps because some things about her reminded me of Helena. A warmth in her eyes, an endearing tease in her smile."

No prompts about Helena were necessary between us. We'd spent the last weeks getting Tobias's emotions right over Isabella in Eine Flackernde Kerze, who'd been based on Helena.

"Then the next day she was put in a death chamber with eight other girls from the party, while Vogt, Toepfer and some other officers looked on as they died. Smiling and self-congratulating over the efficiency of the motor pouring in the fumes."

I nodded desolately, as if I hadn't heard the story before, though my stomach churned and my hands clenched tight in anger and horror just the same this second time.

"I didn't go to any more of the parties...and that's when the rumors started."

"Is that because you couldn't face the thought of the girls being killed afterward?"

"Not only that. But because there was little point. If they'd been just any girls, I could have switched myself off, become impassive—the same way I've dealt with much of the death around here." Meisel's expression was bleak, lost for a moment. "But I knew at heart I'd only feel comfortable with these girls if I felt some connection with them. And part of that, as with the girl at that first party, might be due to seeing something in them that reminded me of Helena." Meisel sighed dejectedly. "So them dying afterward would have felt like going through Helena's death all over again. That's what I felt I couldn't face."

We finished Eine Flackernde Kerze twenty days later and it was packed off to Julian with silent prayers and hopes.

Meisel wrote a covering letter, and with his approval I put a short, handwritten note on the third page under Meisel's dedication—"Happy reading, Julian—hope this hits the mark! It's been a joy working on it—Best Wishes, Andreas."

But having finished, again I was hit with that concern I'd had earlier, though this time reinforced by Vogt's hawkish stare at me as I crossed the Camp Two Yard, as if to say: *Now you're finished with Meisel's manuscript, what earthly use are you?*

52

Scharführer Kurt Lindner stood just beyond where Brunner-man's body had been found and beaded a line to the position of Schnabel's body and the two bullet holes in the shop wall behind. He voiced his thoughts out loud.

"So, not only do we have a different caliber of bullet from the gun found in Brunnerman's hand, but those shots on the wall are a couple of yards wide." He turned to the assistant he'd brought with him, SS Junker Helmut Siegl. "What are your thoughts on this conundrum?"

"Perhaps those bullet marks came from another time?"

"Perhaps. But Lanz from forensics said they are recent, at most a day before." Lindner smiled lightly. "Mr. Brunnerman would have been very unlucky indeed to have *two* confrontations or robberies at his shop only a day apart."

Siegl nodded a tame agreement. He hadn't realized that Josef Weber was involved in the investigation until a couple of days

ago and had started to comment, "That's the inspector who…"
Then broke off, thinking better of it. It had struck him as odd
at the outset that Schnabel had instructed him to tail Weber
and also keep it secret. Rumors were starting to circulate internally that Schnabel had been involved in something clandestine, was perhaps where he shouldn't have been at Brunnerman's
that night.

Perhaps Schnabel had been hoping to get some dirt on Weber
to blackmail him or ensure his investigation of whatever Schnabel was up to at Brunnerman's was curtailed. Either way, investigating a police inspector without notifying superiors was
decidedly against regulations, so the less Siegl said about being
part of that, the better—if he hoped for a continued career with
the SS.

"The inspector who *what*?" Lindner had looked at him sharply.

"Who…investigated the Holzer jewelry robbery a few years
back," Siegl had said, quickly pulling from his memory a high-
society robbery that had been in the newspapers. Comparisons
made to "Raffles" and "Lupin," with Josef Weber named as
leading the investigation.

Now Lindner considered again the position of the two bodies, then turned to look at the back wall with its array of clocks.

"If you can stay by the counter here," he said to Siegl. "I'm
just going outside to check something."

Lindner went into the side alley, taking a step up on the
storm-drain cover and looking through the high side window,
just as he'd seen Schnabel doing that last observation night.
Lindner could clearly see Siegl at the counter, as well as the
back wall with its array of clocks. The only blind spot was the
far left-hand corner.

Lindner pulled back from the window. But as he did so, looking along the length of the alleyway, he thought he noticed
something odd. He looked back through to the shop again,
then to the alley. Where the brickwork of Brunnerman's shop

ended and the one behind started didn't seem to correlate with the space inside.

Lindner stepped down and paced the outside, then went inside and did the same.

"What is it?" Siegl inquired.

"The shop inside appears to be a pace or so short of where it should be." Lindner went to the back wall and started knocking, coming to a hollow-sounding patch halfway along. He barged against it. It wouldn't budge. He held his keys out to Siegl. "If you could get the tire lever and wrench from my car."

It took only four minutes to break through, lift the lever to open the panel and see what was behind. Lindner went to his car to radio in for a safecracking team with oxyacetylene torches.

Josef

If the woman from Daniel's apartment building had known the difference between the SS, Gestapo and standard police inspectorate, Josef might not have heard her crucial witness account; or, at least, he'd have been the last to hear it after the SS and Gestapo, if at all.

Although Piehler had clearly stated they should share information on the case, Josef knew the SS and Gestapo's idea of "sharing." Invariably, it meant you were expected to share all your information about a case, but little or nothing returned from their end. Usually excused under Reich or state secrecy rules. Their cards played close to their chest.

Neither Piehler nor Lindner had announced their visit to Daniel either before or after, and no doubt that pattern would continue.

For that reason, Josef had contacted Assistant Prosecutor Martin Engel to lead the case. Possibly jumping the gun, since normally Engel wouldn't get involved until a prosecutable case had been prepared. The exceptions being notable or complex investigations with more than one party involved, which Josef felt was warranted here. And in those cases, Engel would act like an examining magistrate, pulling the disparate threads of the investigation together.

Most importantly, because Engel outranked Piehler, he wouldn't dare sideline him or withhold information, which Josef felt he had been subject to. Finally, having worked with Engel before, Josef had found him to be thorough but fair. Josef trusted him, whereas he didn't trust Piehler or Lindner one inch; nor practically anyone in the SS or Gestapo, for that matter.

Josef turned his attention to Mrs. Sommer, the woman he'd come to see at her local police station.

"Can you please describe again this uniformed officer you saw visit Mr. Lendt's apartment on the night in question?"

In her late fifties and wearing a distinctive burgundy hat—perhaps she thought it was important to dress up to see the police—her account was at first faltering, but became steadier and clearer as she progressed.

Midthirties. Sandy-blond hair. Quite tall. Senior SS from her description of his uniform. Certainly it sounded like Schnabel.

"And you're sure of the time? It was after nine in the evening?"

"Yes. Possibly even closer to ten o'clock. I'd cleared up after dinner at least an hour or so beforehand."

Josef looked back over his notes after she left. Upon returning from some shopping, she'd heard from some neighbors that uniformed officers had been making inquiries in the building about "anyone suspicious or noteworthy visiting Mr. Lendt at number 14, especially on the twenty-first?" Something else Piehler hadn't shared with him.

So she'd gone to her nearest police station. They'd in turn contacted Josef, who came over immediately to interview her about what she'd seen: "I noticed him in particular because he seemed to be waiting a moment anxiously outside Mr. Lendt's door, as if uncertain whether he'd open it."

Josef knew that he'd have to share this immediately with Martin Engel, but he'd at least wait until he got back to Kärntnerstrasse. Although as he walked into the station, Niklas Krenn hit him with the news that Engel had just phoned.

"Lindner's apparently found a small secret room with a safe at the back of Brunnerman's. Piehler and a safecracking team are there now."

"Thanks."

Josef cradled his head in his hands as he sat in his private office. Combined with the information he had now, Piehler and Lindner would be at Daniel's door in no time. Josef picked up the phone and dialed Daniel's number. It answered after two rings.

"Mr. Lendt. Josef Weber at Kärntnerstrasse. I need to see you regarding the Brunnerman investigation."

"I... I have to go out right now. But I will be back in a couple of hours."

Josef checked his watch. "Okay. I will be there at seven o'clock sharp."

To anyone listening in, a totally innocuous call that tied in to the investigation. Already Josef feared the Gestapo might be tapping Daniel's line.

But the call was in fact the signal he'd agreed with Daniel at the end of their last meeting: the SS or Gestapo are on their way. Get out of there now!

53

All Jewish citizens, regardless of age, are to wear a yellow-star armband. The stamped letter J should also be denoted in the identity cards of all Jews. All male Jews shall add "Israel" to their names and all female Jews "Sarah."

Julian Reisner's hands trembled on the large package as he opened it. Having seen the Lublin postmark, he'd quickly picked it out from the pile of seventeen packages Krisztina had handed him that morning.

Some mornings he'd get as many as thirty manuscripts to read. Always the same routine: he'd put manuscripts from his regular authors and recommendations to one side to personally read, then skim the first few pages of the remaining manuscripts. If they showed merit, he'd pass to Krisztina or one of two regular outside readers for a full read and report.

Still, even with that system, there was a mountainous pile of reading that he never felt he was fully catching up with.

Smiling with appreciation at Andreas's opening comment, he started eagerly reading while he sipped at his morning coffee. It certainly did hit the mark. Andreas had done a marvelous job. In no time it seemed he'd read the first few chapters.

Julian turned back to the opening pages with Meisel's dedication and Andreas's note, giving it a confirming pat as he made his decision.

He called out, "Krisztina. I'm going out for a while—should be back in an hour or two."

Bundling the manuscript under his arm, he went to his car and drove southwest across Vienna, until he came to Andreas and Stefanie's apartment in Neubau.

Stefanie looked surprised to see him. His meetings with Andreas were usually at his office or cafés like the Mozart, and apart from that strained, emotional night he'd collected some essentials before Andreas was shipped to Sobibór, he'd only met Hannah-Stefanie a handful of times at book launches or publisher's parties.

He cut through the greetings, pleasantries and her offer of coffee—which he accepted—as quickly as he could, lightly grasped her hand.

"I have marvelous, exciting news, Stefanie. Andreas is alive!"

She looked at him uncertainly for a moment, wanting desperately to believe it was true, but heavy doubt still there. "But I… I received this package a month or so ago."

Julian nodded solemnly. "Yes, Daniel told me. But I think it was some sort of cruel prank." Julian knew that any amount of words wouldn't dispel her doubt. He'd seen her eyes shifting at points to the manuscript bundle, wondering what it was or why it was with him.

He passed across Meisel's covering letter and the page with Andreas's handwritten note. "I received this just this morning, postmarked Lublin, only a stone's throw from Sobibór."

Stefanie's eyes started filling as she read them. Belief finally that Andreas was alive, but still some lingering question marks. "But how did this all come about... I don't understand?"

As Julian explained, Stefanie's eyes filled completely, tears streaming down her cheeks. He mentioned only that Meisel had been a camp vice-commandant who'd written to him a while ago with his manuscript, and that's what had given him the idea. He avoided any reference to Schnabel and being forced to give someone up. That guilt still weighed heavily on his shoulders; he had trouble coming to terms with it himself, let alone telling Stefanie.

"So, Andreas has been helping this Meisel with his manuscript," Stefanie confirmed, dabbing at her tears with a handkerchief. "That's the main thing that's been keeping him alive?"

"Yes, more or less." Julian waved a hand. "I would have said something earlier, but I wasn't at all sure my ploy with Meisel and Andreas had worked."

Stefanie leaned forward and hugged him. "Thank you, Julian...*thank you*. What you've done has been marvelous, a godsend! Wait until the children hear about this." She glanced at her watch. Five more hours before they returned from school and she could tell them.

"That's okay. It's the least I could do." Julian smiled reassuringly, but his guilt had simply wormed deeper as Stefanie had hugged and thanked him.

"But what happens now?" she asked, struck with a new concern. "Now that Andreas has finished working on this manuscript?"

Julian had pondered the same over the past months, but with no firm answers. Though having just dispelled Stefanie's main fear, the last thing he wanted to do was plant any fresh ones. He patted her hand. "I'm sure he'll be fine."

Soon after Julian left, Stefanie picked up the phone and dialed Mathias-Daniel's number.

Julian had commented that Daniel should also be told about

the manuscript and letter arriving, "Because I know he'll be anxious too," and she'd offered to make the call. Julian had pressed whether she was sure, but she'd sensed some underlying relief and gratitude at her offer.

The number started ringing.

She knew that Daniel would be anxious about Andreas not only because of how close they were, the two of them like brothers rather than cousins—but the added responsibility he might feel because of the deathbed promise he'd made to Andreas's father, Samuel.

Andreas had never told her directly, and it was something she was sure that Samuel had never shared directly with his son, perhaps feeling it might embarrass Andreas that his father thought he needed support. Samuel had come around one day to see them, but it had been Andreas's usual time to visit the library for research. "Oh, I should have realized," Samuel had commented. But with the conversation that followed after accepting her offer of coffee, she realized he'd purposely chosen a time when Johannes-Andreas wouldn't be there.

Samuel at that point had no more than eight months to live and commented he was concerned how hard Johannes-Andreas would take his death. "He'll need both solace and support—so I'm so glad he has you now for that. I've also told Mathias to keep a special eye out for Johannes. So if you ever feel you need extra support—don't hesitate to call Mathias. He'll be there to help too."

But the number kept ringing, and on the seventh ring Stefanie gave up. Mathias-Daniel obviously wasn't there. She'd try again later.

Josef

Josef's eyes shifted every few miles to his rearview mirror to check if anyone was following him.

That had been more difficult to do in Vienna with the number of cars, but as he got out on the open road outside, it was easier to check. Few cars on the road, and any that appeared to be following him for a while were easy to spot. One he'd been suspicious of, a black Volvo PV53 staying a steady hundred yards behind for an eight-mile stretch—so he'd finally pulled over to refill his tank and let it pass. He hadn't seen the Volvo since.

But even those cars that stayed with him for short distances, he'd find himself looking anxiously in the mirror again, beads of sweat breaking on his forehead.

He'd arranged to meet Alois in Kitzbühel, a picture-postcard Tyrolean town a hundred miles from the Swiss border. En route, Josef had passed convoys of Wehrmacht army trucks, tanks and artillery—but in Kitzbühel itself, it was hard to imagine there was a war going on. He'd heard that comment, too, about Vienna due to the lack of air raids, but at least in Vienna there was a heavy contingent of men in uniform and patrols and sentries on every other corner. Here in Kitzbühel tourists predominated, a number of them in skiing apparel, and the few in uniform also appeared to be taking a break from the war, sipping coffee or Glühwein on café terraces while admiring the brightly colored buildings and profusion of window boxes.

Josef sat on one such terrace with Alois, though they'd taken a table at the end with a view over the hotel's car park. They were both keen to keep an eye on their respective cars, especially given what Josef had transferred from his car boot to Alois's before they sat down and ordered coffee.

"And everything's in that bag?" Alois confirmed. "The money, diamonds, Freud Circle photos and the black book from Brunnerman's safe?"

"Yes. Everything's there." The main reason for Josef's anxiety on the journey. *If he'd been stopped by the SS and they'd found the bag, he'd have found himself on a gallows or guillotine alongside Daniel.*

As Josef had seen the sign announcing the town, he recalled that he'd gone with Deya to a Tyrolean restaurant in Vienna by that name, Kitzbühel. Smiles and laughter, clinking glasses. *Happier times.* Lorenzo had repeated that he still didn't know Deya's exact whereabouts. All he had was her last letter postmarked Lisbon. *Hopefully, with her next letter we'll get an address.*

One advantage of this fresh drama with Daniel—he'd laid off the bottle the last couple of days. He needed his thoughts crystal clear.

"As I mentioned, it's easier for me to get in and out of Switzerland than Lorenzo," Alois said. He went on to explain that the past ten months under a new identity he'd set up a good side business bringing goods out of Switzerland for Wehrmacht soldiers. "Nylons, chocolates, cigarettes. Helps both sides financially, so I generally cross the border with no questions asked."

"What time will you be back in Geneva?"

"Not long after you're back in Vienna. That's why I suggested here. It's almost equidistant."

Josef nodded, lit a cigarette. He hadn't hit the bones of a plan until the morning after hearing Daniel's nightmare account. He'd called on Daniel shortly after he'd packed Alex off to school and ran through the details: the bag transported to Switzerland, warning calls and final arrangements.

"Do you think it will work?" Alois asked.

"I don't know." Josef took a heavy draw. Sat here, looking at snowcapped mountains and flower-filled window boxes, it was easy to believe it might. But Josef was reminded that at this moment, Daniel would be running the gauntlet with the SS and Gestapo back in Vienna. "There are five vital components, of which this is only one." Josef gestured toward their cars. "If any one of those fails, then the whole plan collapses. So, on the face of it, the odds are against it."

54

The virtuous man contents himself with dreaming that which the wicked man does in actual life.

—*Sigmund Freud, The Interpretation of Dreams*

Daniel

With the gentle rocking motion of the tram, I almost fell asleep at one point.

I hadn't got much sleep the last two nights. The first night, after sharing everything with Josef, my sleep had been fitful, images of those final shots and Schnabel's blood-soaked body on the floor, lifting his body into the boot of my car, driving out with tightrope-tense nerves in case I was stopped…even more tense and fearful that I might be seen as I took the body into Brunnerman's shop and laid it opposite the jeweler's body on the floor, dumping the bloodied rug and plastic at a waste-site two miles away. Piehler commenting, *New rug, I see…* Though in the dream, he was lifting it, looking at the faded blood patches beneath.

I woke up sharply. The Gestapo and SS were probably already at my apartment, searching and probing every corner, tearing it apart. Josef had my own stash of diamonds and cash safe at his own place, the bag Schnabel had taken from Brunnerman's now on its way to Switzerland. *But will he make it okay?* So many elements still to worry about.

My own focus was to get Alex to safety with Emilia for a couple of days. So I'd called her from a phone kiosk the day before and told her that something urgent had come up, could she pull forward her planned visit next month to see Alex? *And Alex will need to stay with you a couple of days this time, if possible?* She was hesitant at first, but when I stressed its importance and reminded her that she'd often commented before how she'd like Alex to stay with her longer on occasions, she relented. With the travel time from Stuttgart, we arranged to meet the next day at the Tiergarten zoo café, as we had last time.

"Not much longer now." I smiled reassuringly at Alex beside me on the tram. "About twenty minutes."

"Okay."

A hesitant return smile, mirroring his mixed emotions. Looking forward to seeing his mother, but still getting to grips with having to leave our apartment in such a rush. Alex's prized stamp collection and a few things stuffed in a carryall, my essentials, change of clothes and a washbag in a small suitcase.

Will we ever see our apartment again?

But Alex hadn't asked me that unspoken question. Our stopover last night at a nondescript hotel in the Meidling district recommended by Josef, *They don't ask too many questions there*, had led to my second fitful night's sleep. Not only the strange bed, but so many things revolving in my mind about Josef's plan. *All the things that could go wrong!*

The first thing I feared had gone wrong had been coming

down in the morning to check out—only to find two uniformed SDs at the reception desk! I pulled back sharply on the stairway out of view again, my mind spinning. Apart from the scant registration, Josef had assured me that my photo and story wouldn't hit the newspapers until later. Josef had dragged things out from his planned seven o'clock appointment to ten and finally eleven o'clock, only putting out an official "no-show" announcement at Kärntnerstrasse after midnight, by which time he knew the local presses would already be rolling.

But as I'd listened in from the stairway, I realized it was just a general notification about some local Meidling robberies. A moment later the two SDs had gone.

As the tram passed the Elysium cinema where four years ago I'd taken Ivor-Alex to see *King Kong*—*Between Heaven and Earth* was showing this week—I closed my eyes again. Shutting out the memories. Machine guns rattling as King Kong toppled… *flashlights darting at the back of the cinema.*

Suddenly it felt as if I was back again in those nightmare weeks after Anschluss. Except now it was ten-times worse. Then, the attention of the SS and Gestapo had been spread among half the Jews in the city. Now they were searching only for *me*! *Hunting down the man who'd been bold and stupid enough to kill an SS officer.*

I opened my eyes again. The sense of someone looking at me. The middle-aged woman opposite looked as quickly away, back to the newspaper in her lap. Perhaps it had been the way I'd looked sharply across as I'd opened my eyes?

But then as I looked to the side, taking in the rest of the tram carriage, I noticed in my side vision her eyes drift toward me again, then as quickly back to her open newspaper, as if she was making some comparison between me and something there.

Surely not? Josef had told me! Any photo and linked story wouldn't be in the newspapers until the late editions, midafternoon at the earliest—now it was only ten forty in the morning.

I tried to reassure myself that it was nothing, settle back into the gentle rocking motion of the tram; and she, too, appeared to distract herself for a moment with other articles in her newspaper.

But as the ticket guard moved closer down the aisle toward us, I noticed her eyes drift to him then briefly back to me again.

A final spark of recognition ran between us.

The tram started slowing.

I nudged Alex. "Come on. This next stop is ours."

Alex looked momentarily surprised. He knew that we were meant to stay on for several more stops.

The tram brakes came on harder, the stop only fifty yards away.

Any remaining pretense from the woman was lost then. As we edged past the ticket guard on our way to the doors, she pointed, calling out, "That man. *Stop him!*"

The guard, distracted from handling the tickets of two passengers to his side, was momentarily confused. "What's going on? Has he robbed you?"

"No, *no*…it's not that…"

The tram braked to a halt the last few yards.

She pointed frantically to the newspaper in her grasp. "It's this *here*!"

The ticket guard's brow knitted. He moved closer for a better look.

The tram doors opened.

Heart galloping, I made my way swiftly out with Alex, a rapid walk quickly becoming a run—the shout from the ticket guard of *"Du halt!"* and the blowing of a whistle coming when we were almost forty yards away.

Some people in the street looked around, including a couple of Wehrmacht soldiers, but nobody pursued or apprehended us. Perhaps not immediately associating the shout and whistle blowing with us. *After all, few robbers attacked their targets with young sons in tow and carrying baggage.*

Already from the short-burst run, I was breathless. As we

turned the next corner, we cut back to a fast walk, the first twinges of a cramp biting my left leg. I didn't think anyone was following us. But just in case, I led us into the next sharp turn, then another soon after—all the while listening out for any rapid footfall behind us. *Nothing.*

Josef's final warning words resurged: *Be especially careful running the gauntlet with the SS and Gestapo on the way to the zoo. If you get apprehended by them before you can get Alex to Emilia, the game is over before it's even started!*

But how on earth was I going to successfully run that gauntlet with my photo in every newspaper?

I stopped halfway along the next street as I spotted a news kiosk thirty yards ahead, struck with an afterthought. *But I couldn't risk standing in front of the newsstand myself.* I took a two-Reichsmarks coin from my pocket, passed it to Alex.

"Could you please go up to that news kiosk and get all of today's newspapers?"

"Won't they think that strange?"

"They'll just think you're studious, or perhaps doing a school project." I smiled tightly, resisting the harsher words my thundering nerves were screaming at that moment: *Just do it! Don't ask questions!* Alex had enough burden on his young shoulders as it was with this sudden flight.

I sat down on a nearby bench shielded from the kiosk by a tree and started frantically leafing through the newspapers Alex returned with. *Wiener Zeitung*: nothing. *Kleine Zeitung*: nothing. *Kronen Zeitung*: nothing. *Das Kleine Volksblatt*: a photo of me with a few lines beneath on page five. *Arbeiter-Zeitung*: nothing.

Hands trembling, I went back to the photo and brief article in *Das Kleine Volksblatt*. Only my name, brief description, and that I was a suspect in a robbery and murder case. No mention of Brunnerman or any other names. "Approach with caution. Very likely armed and dangerous."

I sighed dejectedly. The photo and description were damn-

ing, but at least it was only *one* newspaper. Perhaps for some reason their presses had run later than the other newspapers, or the
Gestapo had got an alert through to them earlier.

The question remaining was how on earth could I get to the
Tiergarten zoo with Alex without any SS guards or readers of
Das Kleine Volksblatt seeing me? The zoo was still over three
miles away.

55

Andreas

I was back laboring in the afternoons with Jan while Meisel waited on a full response from Julian. Meisel had received an early reply from Julian saying that he was reading and enjoying Eine Flackernde Kerze thoroughly and hoped to finish in no more than ten days. So, encouraging news, but still a tense wait for Julian's final thoughts.

Most of our work had been in the farm patch, but one day we'd had to again assist the Sonderkommandos beyond the fence—their numbers still heavily depleted from typhus—scrubbing out the death chambers with chlorine. They quickly became fetid, many victims soiling themselves from panic and fear in the final moments of death.

Joining Jan that afternoon, I noticed he was sullen and thoughtful. I asked him what was wrong.

He looked down for a moment, as if weighing up a few final things, before answering. "Vogt came to see me earlier. Said he wanted Rina to be at the officers' party this Saturday."

"Why did he ask *you*?"

"Vogt said that he'd already asked Rina, but she didn't want to say anything—except that he should ask me." Jan shrugged. "I said it was *her* decision, not mine. That I couldn't agree to something like that on her behalf. And so he starts taunting— you know what Vogt is like—saying I should be a man for once, take control of my woman. So in the end, I told him I wasn't happy with the idea—so if he was asking me, the answer was *no*."

"What was his reaction?"

"I think Vogt half expected it, because his answer came quick. He said that in case I hadn't noticed, there were less prisoners now in the camp, so a dozen guards had been transferred last week to support troops on the eastern front. So, less laundry, less work for the tailors and seamstresses." Jan looked at me dolefully, eyes stinging from the chlorine or perhaps the emotions of this dilemma. "He said that with those lesser requirements now, how would I feel if I was responsible for condemning my girlfriend to a death chamber because she was no longer seen as *useful*?"

"*Bastard!*" I hissed. "I'm sorry."

Jan shrugged again, as if he'd heard Vogt called far worse. In fact, one of his favorite nicknames for Vogt was "the stiff-assed cunt," *der steife-arsche Fotze*. Very often with other Sonderkommandos, Jan wouldn't even use Vogt's name directly, as if it might sully his lips; "the stiff-assed cunt" was enough for everyone to know who he meant. And sometimes to smiles of encouragement, he'd elaborate on how he'd arrived at that nickname. *He walks around the camp as if he's got that silver-knobbed cane of his shoved up his ass.*

"But at least it's led me to make a decision," Jan said with a resigned breath. "The overthrow's going to come earlier than planned."

"The overthrow" I knew was the term for the camp uprising brewing these past weeks. It carried more positive overtones; "uprisings" and "rebellions" could be quashed.

"But surely it's too early? You're not fully prepared."

"We're prepared enough." Jan held a hand out. "As Vogt said—some guards have left in any case. And each day we sneak weapons away and hide them, we risk getting caught. So maybe this was the push we needed."

I nodded. I'd seen knives, cleavers and hatchets hidden in coats, blankets, under and even inside mattresses while the guards weren't looking. I saw that Tibor in fact had taken a broken spade and sharpened its end with a file, so that now it was a deadly stave tucked under his mattress.

But half of my reluctance, I realized, was because I wanted to see how things turned out with Meisel's manuscript. It would be like reading a book and not finding out how the final chapter ended. Now Tuesday, the "overthrow" would be going ahead in only a few days to save Rina going to Vogt's next party.

"I understand why you have to go ahead with this now, Jan. And I wish you well with it." I shook my head. "But I don't think I'll be able to join you and the others."

Jan looked at me questioningly. "What are you waiting for? Now that you've finished working on Meisel's manuscript, you know your days are numbered. Vogt and Toepfer are already making noises about it, and if Meisel tries to hang on to you much longer, Toepfer will just take the decision out of his hands." Jan gestured helplessly. "So why wait for that axe to fall?"

56

Jews, Mischlinge and Gypsies shall forthwith have their tele-phones and radios confiscated. Furthermore, they are banned from using public telephones.

Daniel

Running the gauntlet.

I kept the brim of my brown trilby pulled down sharply as I took a seat at the back of the bus and opened my newspaper, the *Wiener Zeitung*. I'd left the other newspapers on the bench seat, then after taking the next turnoff asked Alex to go into a men's shop to buy the trilby hat I'd seen in their window.

The only plan I could think of. It was too far to walk to the zoo and too many people passed who might have seen my photo in *Das Kleine Volksblatt*; but on a bus, all the seats were facing forward. If I kept my head tilted down as I walked toward a back seat with Alex, the chances of anyone getting a clear look at me were reduced. With a newspaper in front of me, I was shielded even more.

At one point, I noticed an elderly man who'd got on at the last stop looking my way as he walked down the aisle to get a seat, but as I glanced above I saw that his eyes were fixed on something on the newspaper's front page facing him: *an article about the 6th Army holding the Dnieper line against the Red Army.*

I kept my head tilted down as we left the bus and as much as possible on the hundred-yard walk to the Tiergarten zoo entrance.

Then I froze.

Two SD guards by the main turnstile entrance. I turned, looking around aimlessly, avoided staring at them and drawing attention—but in my side vision I noticed they were only half-heartedly monitoring those coming in and out. Only one person out of the last fifteen approaching had been asked for their ID card.

I noticed then a stand five yards from the entrance selling small pennants with Tiergarten zoo with a swastika beneath and a picture of Hitler the other side. One of the guards appeared to smile appreciatively at those buying them, with a more disapproving look toward those who didn't.

Not for the first time, I wondered about all the parks and zoos being open. As if keeping them fully functioning was part of Nazi propaganda: *There might be a war going on, but see how good life is under the Reich.*

An idea forming, I moved toward the entrance with Alex. One of the SD appeared to look my way, then he was distracted by a pretty blonde woman, smiling at her courteously and her young son waving a pennant.

As we got closer, my heart was in my mouth. *If they saw that morning's* Das Kleine Volksblatt *with my photo, or their unit had received an alert, I am sunk.*

Four yards from the entrance, I gave Alex a one-Reichsmark

coin, urging so that the SD would hear: "You grab one of those pennants while I get the tickets." I turned as quickly away to the turnstile, hoping the guards' eyes would follow Alex more than me.

Three people ahead of me in the ticket queue. I kept my view rigidly ahead, only looking round briefly with a smile as Alex rejoined me with the pennant. My ploy seemed to have worked. After one of the SD guards had fired a quick smile at Alex with his pennant, neither of them appeared to be looking my way. Two people ahead now in the queue.

One person.

The voice at my shoulder made my nerves leap:

"Papers, please?"

But as I looked around, it was directed at the two young men who'd joined the queue behind us. One had a heavy olive complexion, so perhaps they were checking if he was a Jew or Romani, or it could be with neither in uniform the SD checking for deserters. *Why weren't able young men off fighting at the front, or at least in uniform?*

The last obstacle was the ticket girl, my chest tight that she might have seen that morning's paper—but she showed no recognition.

Then we were finally through, my breath easing as we walked away the other side. Head tilted slightly down, suitcase and bag in hand, we made our way swiftly to the café, saw Emilia in quite a prominent position at a center table as we entered.

She smiled and waved at us, and I suggested a more discreet table to one side, partly shielded by a plant display. Emilia already had a coffee, so I ordered one for myself and a lemonade for Alex, who I steered to the next table over from us. Part of what we had to discuss was awkward, delicate.

"New hat, I see," she remarked. "It suits you."

"Thank you." I didn't explain that it was partly a cover, and she didn't ask if I was taking it off. Perhaps from our years together, she remembered it was a Jewish tradition: *hats and keys placed on a table signified a person's death.*

She looked as beautiful and radiant as ever in a lilac two-piece suit; the war didn't seem to have affected Emilia in the slightest. Still as flighty and carefree as ever, which I loved about her. She was clinging to her youth, whereas for me it was pleasant nostalgia: a reminder of the best of what we were, what had first attracted me to her.

"So what is it that's brought about this urgency now with Alex?" Emilia asked after another sip of coffee.

So, she hadn't seen that morning's Das Kleine Volksblatt. Perhaps not surprising with her coming straight from Stuttgart. "I'm afraid I've had a little run-in with the police and SS. I'll probably have to turn myself in."

"My goodness." Her brow knitted. "What for?"

"Nothing trivial, I'm afraid." I smiled lopsidedly. "It involves the shooting of an SS officer who came to our apartment one night. They think I'm responsible, are already searching for me."

"Oh, my." The shock hit Emilia fully then, one hand going to her mouth. "How on earth did it happen?"

I went on to explain that the SS officer who came to our apartment had threatened to kill both myself and Alex. "In the end, it was self-defense." Brief nod from Emilia, as if she'd already half guessed I wouldn't kill someone in cold blood. "Not that a such a defense will help one scrap with SS or Gestapo questioning. And it could end badly for Alex too."

Eyes glassy with emotion and fear, Emilia reached across the table, patted my arm reassuringly. "Don't worry, I'll take care of Alex. Take him to Stuttgart with me for a few days…" Her eyes flickered, taking in the full implications. "Far longer, if necessary."

I looked across at her steadily. "I think you might have to take him away somewhere further and far safer than that." After a quick sip of my coffee that had arrived, I went on to explain that with a charge like this, I faced almost certain execution. "And Alex would likely be sent to a death camp as well."

Emilia shook her head, refusing to believe. "But surely not? He's my son, and my husband now is a proud and upstanding member of the Reich, supplies vital automotive components to the war effort."

I gripped Emilia's hand back across the table, willing and shaking the message home. "But Alex is a *Mischling*, Emilia. And his father is not only a Jew, but one that's shot an SS officer. Alex would go to a death camp for that alone—even if he wasn't seen as some sort of accomplice by simple virtue of him being there at the time."

Emilia looked down at my hand gripping hers. There it was, laid bare: all the problems of our past relationship now coming home to roost. She'd been guilty of taking on board rising national public prejudices against Jews, as if at the time it had been no more than popular Zeitgeist—but now it had grown into a monstrous national doctrine that was threatening the life of her son.

She sighed heavily. "Where do you propose I take Alex?"

"He'll end up in Geneva. But you don't need to take him all the way there—a man named Lorenzo will meet you just the other side of the Swiss border." I grimaced. "His people will take care of Alex, and you'll be able to see him when you like. Most importantly, he'll be *safe* there."

Emilia nodded after a second, putting the pieces together. "That's a pretty big favor to ask."

"I know. And I wouldn't ask it if it was just for me. But I'm asking it for our son."

I felt guilty as I said it. Making out it was some sort of emotional obligation to outweigh the risks. *If there was an alert out for Alex as well when they reached the Swiss border, Emilia could find herself alongside him in a death camp.*

Her eyes searched the air desperately for a moment. "Oh, God. How did it ever come to this?"

Our failed relationship? The Nazis? Mine and Alex's plight? Perhaps all three, intertwined so inextricably in her mind that she found them impossible to separate.

With raising the threat of Alex going to a death camp, I was reminded of Andreas's plight. But I avoided mentioning it now; not only the complexity of the story and bringing back my own responsibility and guilt, but it might remind Emilia that *nobody* was safe. She might balk at helping.

"Okay. I'll do it," Emilia said at length with a resigned, almost fatalistic sigh. She looked across at me, conflicted shadows in her eyes. "But what makes you think I'd do it only for our son? I have some amends to make to you as well, you know."

I looked back with equal poignancy. *As close as Emilia might ever get:* apologizing for our past after all these years…perhaps because now she feared she might never see me again. Or perhaps she was equally saying: *If you and I had been together in a different time and place, it could have worked. We'd have been good together.* I closed my eyes for a second. Whether wishful thinking or not, I'd have liked to believe that too.

With our maudlin emotions, I'd become distracted from our surroundings for a moment. Or perhaps because the two men keenly scanning the café were in plain clothes rather than uniform, I hadn't paid much attention to them. Now it hit me: *Gestapo!*

"Look. I must go." I patted Emilia's arm reassuringly, slid across a piece of paper. "This is Lorenzo's contact number, and phone this other number in Vienna as soon as Alex is safe across the border in Switzerland…"

The two men were referring to something in their hands as they looked around. Perhaps an ink press of my photo or clipped directly from the newspaper. Probably someone who'd seen my photo in *Das Kleine Volksblatt* had spotted me going through to the café and raised the alert.

"...Ask for Josef Weber," I finished telling Emilia.

One of the men's eyes fixed on me. Nodding to his colleague, they headed toward me.

With a tight parting smile at Alex, I headed away from them, pushing past the tables behind, Emilia's "Take care!" trailing after me.

The two Gestapo men were equally brusque in pushing past tables and people to get at me, but my main aim was to get far enough away that Alex wouldn't witness them actually apprehending me. Not only avoiding that extra worry on his shoulders, but also that he and Emilia would then be clear away, wouldn't be seen as part of it.

With my suitcase, I didn't get far—only thirty yards from the café exit before one of the men tumbled me roughly to the ground with a rugby tackle. He probably thought he'd apprehended some sort of madman with my rising smile.

But it was because it had been *enough*: my last view before the exit had been Emilia and Alex heading out the opposite side of the café. They'd got away clear.

57

One day, in retrospect, the years of struggle will strike you as the most beautiful.

—*Sigmund Freud*

Andreas

As Jan had suspected, the recent consignment was barely more than fifty people. The camp was winding down.

Scharführer Haas stood on a small rostrum in the Forward Camp to make his usual perfunctory welcome announcement, finishing by pointing out the sleeping dormitories, the dining hut, the building where they should initially leave their belongings, and the showers…

But as Haas came down from the rostrum, a young girl of no more than nine or ten stepped forward from the group with a piece of paper in her hand. She looked toward Haas and the officers, guards and Sonderkommandos beyond.

"My name is Anja and I've come today with my mother, father, younger brother and others from our town of Wlodawa," she announced. "My elder brother, Elias, was originally going to make this speech, because it was his Bar Mitzvah only five months ago, so he's much better at speaking in public than me. But he caught typhus while our family was in the Wlodawa Ghetto and sadly died only a week before our transport here." Anja hung her head lamentably for a moment. "So it has become my responsibility to speak to you today. Thank you first of all for your welcome. We have many good cabinetmakers, seamstresses, millers and cooks among our people. We hope we may be of use to you in the camp. Thank you."

Anja nodded politely and stepped back again into the group. I noticed she was wearing a pale blue dress, probably picked out especially by her mother for this little presentation speech, but now it had a few smudges from the journey.

Jan and I exchanged a look. This wasn't something we'd seen before. We'd in fact witnessed only a handful of brief greetings or introductions, and these had usually been from elders, group leaders or Rabbis, all men. Never a young girl before. Jan looked back at her intently.

"I'm not going to let her die," he muttered after a moment.

"*What*…but how?" I looked back at him questioningly.

Jan quickly surveyed the camp. This particular group had come in late. Now it was dusk, the last daylight fast fading, a faint mist partly shrouding the fence perimeter and the forest beyond.

"We'll go tonight instead," he said, the final threads knitting in his mind. "The conditions are ideal."

"But I thought it was all set for late tomorrow? Surely, you're not fully ready yet?"

"It's only one day difference." Jan held a hand out. "Besides, there's no guarantee that tomorrow the conditions will be as perfect as now. There might be no covering mist, or we—"

Jan broke off, his attention drawn back to the young girl as Vogt approached her.

"That's a very nice speech," Vogt said. But as he got close to her, he raised the bulbous silver end of his cane, and for a fearful moment I thought he was going to strike the young girl. But Vogt used his cane to point. "Now, if you would care to lead your good people toward the showers over there."

Jan's jaw clenched tight. I knew from his look there'd be no shifting him now from his decision. He started making furious hand signals to the other Sonderkommandos across the yard. Any guards observing probably thought they were just making bets on this latest consignment: *Who might be picked out as fit for work and spared, how long the rest might last in the chamber before dying?*

Aware of what was about to happen, I noticed Rina and Dalit moving over toward Jan. As the group started dispersing, Jan commented that he'd already alerted the other Sonderkommandos that it could happen earlier, and they'd watch out for his signal. He'd now go with Mikel into the hut where these new arrivals were leaving their belongings and advise them there was a delay with the showers. As the two guards went to check, they'd be overpowered or killed and their rifles taken. As Jan finished explaining, he turned and gripped my arm, staring at me intensely.

"Are you sure I can't convince you to join us, Andreas?"

"No...*no*. I'll stay here. Take my chances with Meisel and whatever use I might still be to him." Arriving at that decision had led to fitful sleep the last couple of nights. Although I knew I probably faced death staying, the risks with this escape were high too. "I'll be willing you on, though."

Jan gave me a quick hug in parting, "Take care, my friend," and moved with Rina, Mikel and Dalit toward the arrival hut. Rina and Dalit hovered outside while Jan and Mikel went inside.

I moved out of the central yard area to stand in front of the next hut along from them, hopefully aside from the melee that would follow. Jan looked out again after a moment, and as he saw Haas go into the engine room and Vogt return to the officers' barracks, he brought one hand down. The final signal.

I watched as a group of almost forty burst out of the arrival hut, Jan clutching on to Anja with one hand while he wielded an axe with the other, Rina and Dalit close behind shielding young boys. Gunfire started instantly, some of it from the guards, but also return fire from Sonderkommandos who'd attacked guards and grabbed their rifles in those opening seconds—one of the vital early actions stressed by Jan and Tibor in their final instructions to fellow Sonderkommandos.

It was hard to pick out everything with the mayhem that followed. That first group seemed to be making good progress across the main yard, but a number also were picked off on the way by the two guards firing down from the central watchtower—one of the guards finally brought down by a shot from a Sonderkommando who'd grabbed a rifle early. The other main instruction from Jan and Tibor: *Take out the watchtower guards as quickly as possible.*

But I suddenly realized in horror that the firing was indiscriminate. Eight of the new arrivals stood not far from me, also keeping apart from the others making a run for it, most of them elderly—possibly thinking they were too old and frail to attempt such an escape—when one of them, a man in his late sixties, was hit with two bullets in his chest.

I would have turned and run into one of the huts, but another was hit a second later in the back from a shot behind. I started running, some of the others quickly following. *We were sitting ducks standing where we were!* All prisoners suddenly appeared to be legitimate targets—the best chances seemed to be running amongst the melee, where other guards provided some sort of cover; fellow guards had to be more selective with firing for fear of hitting them.

The remaining guard on the central watchtower had a machine gun. But he'd resisted firing it for that very reason. Picking off as many as he could with single rifle shots before a shot from a Sonderkommando with a rifle finally felled him as well.

I fixed my gaze across the yard toward the perimeter fence a hundred yards away. I hadn't chosen to be part of the escape, but now there appeared little choice. *If I hold back or remain static, I'll be shot in any case.*

The fence and the misty line of pine trees beyond jolted in my vision as I ran. I saw Nahum fall to one side, Tibor taking out three or four guards with his makeshift stave before taking a shot to the leg and limping on, picking up the rifle of a fallen guard and starting to fire toward the watchtower on the perimeter. That's where most of the gunfire from Sonderkommandos was concentrated now.

Between the two watchtowers and the guards firing from behind, I could see that almost 30 percent of those running had fallen. Dalit was among them, hit just before the fence, the boy with her running on to join Jan and Rina. Halfway through the fence being broken through, the perimeter watchtower guard was finally taken out, and the first group surged through the gap.

Jan seemed to notice me for the first time then as he glanced back and saw me running feverishly sixty yards behind. He beckoned me frantically, but I saw him pause then, his eyes fixing with concern beyond me. I glanced back to see that some of the officers, including Haas and Vogt, had also run out to assist the guards. Haas's gunfire seemed to be general, but as a bullet whistled close by me, I realized with alarm that Vogt was firing directly at me.

I made it only eight more yards before a bullet hit my left shoulder, throwing me to the ground. I looked up desperately toward the fence and misty forest beyond, saw Jan start to beckon again, as if urging: *Get up! Come on, you can make it!* And for a moment among the mist, I got a vision of Stefanie, Nadia and Dominik at his side, also beckoning me on. But as gunfire started zipping through the tree branches around Jan and Rina, they turned with Anja and the two young boys and fled deeper into the mist, the image of my family fading along with them.

I turned to see Vogt standing over me, his gun pointed directly at me ready to fire again.

58

Daniel

Tick-tock…tick-tock…

I noticed that the clock in the interview room was particularly loud. Or perhaps it was just that the silences between questions and answers were heavy, only the sound of pens scratching on paper.

The walls of the room were painted a drab blend of gray and green, not unlike a jail cell—which was no doubt where I'd end up awaiting execution—and no more than twice that size. A long trestle table was at its center, with Josef Weber, Lindner and Piehler flanked across the opposite side to me and Martin Engel at one end.

The questioning and comments had so far taken place mainly between Josef and Piehler, with Engel making notes throughout and interjecting intermittently purely to clarify some points.

The ticking clock was like a metronome beat driving the

questions. *Counting down the seconds to my demise.* The small room was also hot. My throat felt dry, tight. I had trouble swallowing at times.

The questions had mostly been perfunctory so far: age, profession? How long I'd lived at my apartment? Did anyone else live there with me? *My son, Alex, just a young teenager.* Did I know Carl Brunnerman and Scharführer Schnabel? What were the circumstances under which I'd initially met them?

But now Piehler looked at me more keenly. "And did Scharführer Schnabel visit your apartment on the night of the twenty-first?"

"Yes, he did."

Josef checked his notes. "From Mrs. Sommer, whose apartment is toward the end of your corridor, we ascertain the time he visited as somewhere between nine and ten. What time exactly would it have been?"

"A few minutes to ten or just after," I said. "Alex had only gone to bed half an hour or so beforehand."

Piehler took over again. "And what exactly transpired during his visit?"

"He told me straightaway that he'd just come from Brunnerman's, made no secret of it…" I tried to remain calm, relate everything in a straightforward, methodical fashion, as Josef had advised, but it was difficult. I felt all the wire-taut tension and panic I'd felt that night resurge, tying my stomach in knots, as I ran through the events: Schnabel threatening to kill both myself and Alex, gloating about setting up a murder scene, having already killed Brunnerman and taken a bag containing diamonds and cash from Brunnerman's safe. At the end, I added something advised by Josef to avoid mentioning the little black book from Brunnerman's safe. "Schnabel had also got from Brunnerman details of some others like me, who he planned to similarly threaten and have sent to the death camps."

Josef looked at me steadily as I finished. "Not exactly commendable actions for an SS officer."

Piehler glared at him, while Martin Engel just made a note of it. Already I could see the battle lines being drawn in the interview.

I took a fresh breath. "Apart from all these others that Schnabel planned to kill or send to death camps, I didn't trust him that he'd let my son live. He'd later think of some way of sending him to a death camp too. And I thought—I can't let this man live. He's evil, a monster."

Piehler observed me coldly. "I suggest you refrain from the overblown terms, Mr. Lendt...or should I say, *Mr. Kraemer.* You're not exactly in a position to pass judgment with your own actions in this case."

"What happened then..."

Twice now Josef had asked me that same question, and each time my answer had been different.

"I told Schnabel that I was getting the keys to where I had my diamonds—but in fact I was heading to the desk drawer with my gun."

"Where did you get the gun?" Piehler asked.

"From the contact in our network."

"What's his name?"

"A Spanish name... I can't recall exactly now." Piehler didn't look satisfied, but he didn't probe there and then; perhaps something he'd return to later. "Others in the network got guns too. Mine was a Browning 640." I held a hand out. "As I approached the drawer, I heard Schnabel's voice behind me, warning me not to attempt anything foolish. So I knew he was close behind... but I thought, if I turned quickly enough, I could catch him by surprise, get in the first shot..."

"And then," Josef prompted as I paused, perhaps fearing I'd seized up, wouldn't be able to get the words out.

I sighed heavily. "And thankfully, that's more or less what

happened. I turned sharply with the gun and fired, before he'd hardly had time to think about it, his return shot going wide of me—possibly from my first shot hitting him in the side, putting his aim off. But then my second shot fired straight after hit him squarely in the chest, and that was the end of it."

Moment's silence as I finished.

Martin Engel looked up from making some notes. "And can I clarify one thing. Were you still with your back to your desk when you fired your shots and Scharführer Schnabel in turn fired back at you?"

"Yes, I was."

Josef looked at me. "And that's when you set about moving Schnabel's body to Brunnerman's to cover up. Make it appear as a robbery gone wrong?"

"Yes, it was." I grimaced hesitantly. "Though I already had Schnabel's guide of how that should be done. I was simply placing Schnabel's body where mine should have been, then, after wiping my gun clean of my prints, putting it in Brunnerman's hand."

"How exactly was that done?" Piehler pressed. "Take us through the steps."

Although having asked, I could see Piehler almost wincing with some of the details. Equal parts gruesome and methodical, but perhaps it was the fact that the victim was an SS officer making Piehler uncomfortable; or that a Jew, a far lower creature in Piehler's eyes, might have actually outwitted Schnabel.

Piehler drew a slow, tired breath as I finished, looked toward Lindner and Engel. "I think we have sufficient evidence to proceed to the next stage." He turned his attention back to me, his voice becoming firmer. "Daniel Lendt, previously known as Mathias Kraemer—I hereby charge you with the murder of a Reich citizen, namely—"

"I'm sorry. I'm not in accord with that," Martin Engel's voice interrupted pointedly from the end of the table. "You can lay charges all you like, but I won't be prosecuting them."

"What do you mean?" Piehler looked at him sharply, face reddening.

"Because, simply put, Mr. Lendt clearly didn't commit this murder." Engel shrugged. "Or, at least, not in the way he has described."

"This is outrageous!" Piehler protested. "We…we have a clear confession from him."

"That as may be. But the facts of the case aren't prosecutable as they stand." Piehler started shaking his head, but Engel rolled on. "Think about it. The first shot Mr. Lendt says he fired from the front—yet from the autopsy we know that the first shot struck between the back and the side. Furthermore, Scharführer Schnabel's return shot would have hit somewhere on the wall behind Mr. Lendt's desk in the scenario he describes—whereas we know that this bullet struck the opposite wall at the other end of the front room." Engel stared the message home. "You know this in particular, Kriminaldirektor Piehler, because you yourself originally discovered that bullet mark covered by some fresh plaster on Mr. Lendt's wall."

Josef and I exchanged a glance. Josef's ploy had worked: he knew that Engel was a stickler for detail, wouldn't settle for a half-baked case.

But a red-faced Piehler was still balking, refusing to accept. "I would strongly suggest that in a case like this, a full confession overrides such factors."

Engel contemplated Piehler soberly. "I'm not sure what might suffice in the Gestapo, Kriminaldirektor Piehler. But in my twenty years in Vienna's Prosecutor's Office, I pride myself on upholding certain standards. And I have no intention of dropping those now." Engel eased out a tired breath. "With the question remaining, if Mr. Lendt didn't commit the murder as described, then *who*?"

I allowed myself a moment's smugness at Piehler's dressing-down, but it died quickly as Engel's intense gaze shifted to me with his last words.

"So I ask you now directly, Mr. Lendt. Who killed Scharführer Schnabel?"

I looked toward the clock on the wall, which suddenly seemed to be ticking louder than normal.

"I... I can't say."

59

Jews, Mischlinge and Gypsies should hand over forthwith all
fur or woollen items. They will also no longer receive ration cards
for clothing or any form of social security allowance.

The green pastures and snowcapped mountains they passed made
it seem more like a summer excursion than a desperate, life-
saving trip, and Emilia put the roof down on her Mercedes for
part of the journey.

Wehrmacht trucks and convoys had been more evident on
the outskirts of Vienna and Liezen, but as they approached Innsbruck, hardly any were visible.

Their conversation had been stilted after the first hour or so,
Emilia suddenly realizing that she'd never been with Alex for
more than a few hours in the past years—and this was a seven-
or eight-hour trip! Or perhaps it was what this journey signified
settling heavier on them with the passing miles.

She hit on something hopefully of interest after a bit, talking about her husband, Gerhard, making some parts for the new Porsche being developed. "To be revealed as soon as the war is finished."

"Sounds wonderful," Alex said. "Shame we have to wait that long."

"Yes." Emilia smiled ruefully. Everyone it seemed had plans, *when the war has ended.*

Alex talked animatedly for a while about his stamp collection, and the unfairness of all this struck her more poignantly then: on the face of it, like any other young teenager, talking about cars or stamp collections…except that Alex's family had been ripped apart by war, *and now he was having to escape for fear of his life, not knowing if or when he might see them again.*

"…One of my recent favorites is from the Solomon Islands. A beautiful beach sunset with palm trees. Dad got it for me from Mr. Brunnerman when he last…"

Alex's voice trailed off. The memories suddenly too close again. *Brunnerman. His father. War.* Why he was on this trip now.

And then as Emilia looked ahead, the reminder of war was strong for her as well. A heavier mass of trucks, artillery and tanks as they approached the Swiss border. As if positioned as a threat from Hitler: *Step out of line and I'll invade you too.*

An even heavier succession of Wehrmacht trucks and artillery carriers lined the last hundred yards as Emilia pulled up at the border post and barrier.

Two SS guards came out from the adjacent kiosk.

Emilia rolled her window down and held her passport and papers out so that the first border guard approaching didn't need to ask for them.

"Vielen Dank." He leaned over, looking briefly at her and her son. "And what is the purpose of your visit to Switzerland?"

"Brief sightseeing trip for my son."

"I see." He straightened up, checking her passport and ID card before nodding to his colleague, who ambled back to the border kiosk. The first guard looked again toward her and Alex. "One moment. Wait here."

Despite her nerves racing, Emilia thought she'd remained outwardly calm, put on a convincing front. *After all, isn't that what she'd done for half her life with acting?* But as she watched the second guard in the kiosk get on the phone, stared pointedly toward her and her car as he spoke to someone the other end, suddenly she wasn't so sure.

The letter landed on Stefanie's doormat just as the children were getting ready for school.

Postmarked Lublin, she realized that was the nearest town to Sobibór. She opened it with trembling hands after pouring her second coffee of the morning, recalling then where she'd seen the name of the sender before, Dieter Meisel. *The camp vice-commandant whose manuscript Andreas had been working on!*

She paused mid-sip of her coffee as she read, put her cup down. She wished now that the children had already been packed off to school so that she'd have had this moment alone, they wouldn't see her distraught. Dominik had looked over, sensing something was wrong, but Nadia was still absorbed with reading an Erich Kästner picture-book by her breakfast bowl.

Stefanie turned away from them, her eyes filling as she finished reading.

Daniel

Forty minutes later, Josef followed a guard into my cell, nodding twice. They were ready for me again.

As I'd become flustered, shaking my head repeatedly, Josef had called for a break. Piehler had initially resisted, saying that they needed to keep the pressure on "to unearth the truth." But as Engel had said he could do with a coffee and wanted in any case to look back over his notes for anything possibly missed, with Josef adding that perhaps a break would help clear my head, "Hopefully help him come to his senses," Piehler had relented.

As we sat back around the long table, Engel commented, "Before the break, we had already ascertained that you couldn't have shot Scharführer Schnabel in the manner you described. Are you now ready to tell us who that person was?"

"Yes, I am," I said with a resigned sigh. *Two* nods had been the signal: Josef had received the call that Alex was safely across the Swiss border. One nod would have meant the call hadn't yet come through. But still it felt difficult, my throat tightening, to utter the words I never thought would pass my lips.

"It was my son, Alex… *Ivor*, as he was originally."

Silence for a moment, and Josef was first to gently prompt, "And please tell us how this might have happened?"

I started slowly, *remain calm, methodical*…explaining that the early part of my account was exactly as I'd described. "Up until the point I turned for the gun in my desk drawer. Because when I opened the drawer, the gun was no longer there." I exhaled, perhaps mirroring the shock and surprise I'd felt in that moment. "Schnabel was still only a few steps behind me, having issued his warning about not trying anything, and then I heard a faint sound from further behind, beyond Schnabel." I swallowed. "Schnabel turned at practically the same time as me, and that's when the first shot was fired and I saw Alex there. Schnabel's return shot and Alex's second shot came one after the other…and for a moment I wasn't even sure whether Alex had been hit as well."

"How do you think Alex got the gun?" Josef asked.

"I… I thought he was still asleep, but obviously he'd woken up, heard us. His bedroom's just one away from my office." I shook my head. "And of course, that was confirmed a moment later as I got his full story. He was frozen on the spot after the shots, then dropped the gun and started shaking uncontrollably, saying, *Sorry…sorry*. Hardly believing what he'd done. I rushed over and hugged him, consoling, and that's when Alex told me that he'd heard us talking, heard the man saying he was going to kill me, and he couldn't let that happen." I raised my voice an octave, mimicking Alex: "*I couldn't let him kill you, Papa.* Then he burst into tears and repeated that he was sorry again." Alex had in fact kept repeating *sorry* like a mantra as he sobbed, inconsolable... *I could practically feel his body quaking against me again as I recalled the events of that fateful night—as if an echo of my own body trembling now.*

"I understand," Josef said, and at the end of the table Engel nodded empathetically as he made some notes.

But Piehler stared at me coldly. "I think we have had enough with the dramatics, Mr. Lendt. Your son has killed an SS officer. Where is your son now?"

"He's across the border in Switzerland."

"I see." Piehler held his stare on me. "I sense a degree of planning in all of this." He took a fresh breath after a moment. "No matter. We will be applying for extradition for your son. And while you appear to have planned some elements, you have certainly overlooked the fact that we have more than enough to convict you in any case—accomplice to murder and its cover-up, being part of this clandestine exchange network, not to mention a considerable amount in cash and diamonds concealed from the Reich to fund this network. Where are those now?"

"They're safe across the border in Switzerland as well."

Piehler smiled crookedly. "For someone facing a death camp or execution, you're certainly far bolder than I gave you credit for."

Piehler had no idea. I was only putting on a calm front because that's what Josef had advised. Inside, my stomach was churning. I was still far from sure any of this would work. I took a piece of paper from my pocket, handed it across to Piehler.

"You might wish to give this man a call before you make any decisions."

Piehler looked disdainfully at the name and telephone number on the paper. "Who is this?"

"He's the bank lawyer in Switzerland who currently has the diamonds and cash. He has a proposition for you."

60

"Sebastian Rochat," a dapper man in his late forties with wavy brown hair announced as his secretary put the call through. "Legal administrator here at the Geneva International Bank. And I understand you are Inspector Piehler of the Geheime Staatspolizei in Vienna?"

"Kriminaldirektor," Piehler corrected.

"Of course." Rochat took a fresh breath. "As head of that unit, this should therefore make what we have to discuss far easier. You won't have to rush off every other minute to obtain decisions from others."

"We would hope so." Flat, noncommittal tone. "I understand you have some sort of proposal for me?"

"Yes. I have in my possession Reichsmarks, US dollars and a collection of diamonds from the safe of one Carl Brunnerman in Vienna." Rochat consulted some notes to one side. "The Reichsmarks total 283,000, the US dollars 117,000, and the diamonds have been independently valued at 412,000 Reichsmarks."

At the other end of the line, Josef and Daniel watched Piehler's brow rise in surprise. Engel, who they'd agreed would listen in on a separate earpiece extension for any legal advice, exchanged a look with Piehler. Both clearly hadn't expected it to be such a large sum.

"And is the boy, Alex Lendt, also with you?" Piehler inquired.

"No, he's not. But I know of his whereabouts." Equally non-committal.

"Then you might be aware that he's wanted in Austria for the murder of an SS officer. We will be seeking his extradition."

"You can seek all you wish, Herr Piehler. The affidavit I have in front of me makes it very clear it was an act of self-defense when this SS officer was about to shoot both his father and himself. The boy is also underage. He won't be going anywhere."

"We will see about that." Piehler sighed tetchily. "So what exactly is this proposition?"

Rochat tapped his pen on his notes for a second, purposely creating a gap from Piehler's impatient urging.

"If you release the prisoner you're holding, Daniel Lendt." His tone was suddenly more formal, measured. "And allow his safe passage to Switzerland—I will release half of the funds I hold here to an account of the Reich's choosing."

At his end, Daniel watched Piehler's reaction intently. Everything hinged on which way he leaned now: *whether he'd accept the proposal, or whether he'd dig his heels in and consign Daniel to a death camp.*

"We also have some very serious charges against Mr. Lendt— conspiracy to murder and defrauding the Reich from significant funds."

"I think we've already established that the incident in question was self-defense. And last time I checked, 'conspiracy to self-defense' wasn't on the statute books." Rochat left a marked pause. "The origin and rightful owner of those funds is also open to question, split partly between Brunnerman and property owners in this network. And if the Reich now gains half of them, it becomes even more of a moot point."

Heavy silence. Piehler's expression was tight, his eyes darting. Used to being the one to corner others, he didn't look comfortable with the situation being reversed. *It didn't look like he'd go for it.*

"You have one hell of a cheek," Piehler hissed after a moment. "Offering what should have ended up as the Reich's own money as part of your proposal."

"With all due respect, Herr Piehler, you're not thinking clearly," Rochat said with a worn tone. "Because I think you've failed to see the other side entirely. Now, on that side, we *do* have a clear-cut case of murder with SS Officer Schnabel shooting Carl Brunnerman. Then on top removing all the diamonds and cash from his safe, with not the slightest intention of passing them on to the Reich. All of it to line his own pockets. Not exactly a model SS officer, is he?"

Piehler's jaw set rigid, his face reddening. He looked like he might blow a blood vessel.

Rochat rolled on. "Now imagine how all of that would look if it came out? Either through a court case, or even of its own accord with the international press—with whom I happen to have extremely good connections here in Geneva. Such a tawdry affair reflecting badly on the SS and the Reich at large."

A suspended moment, the air heavy with tension—then Piehler slapped a hand on the tabletop, the sound like a gunshot.

"Who the hell do you think you are! A trumped-up bank lawyer trying to dictate what the Reich should do? Switzerland doesn't even have an army. We could invade you tomorrow and—"

Rochat cut in sharply. "And I would give you the same answer General Guisan gave Ribbentrop when asked what Switzerland's private militia would do if two hundred thousand German troops crossed the Swiss border. 'The same number of my men would mobilize from their homes, fire one bullet each and return home for dinner.' And that was two years ago, before you were facing such a heavy commitment on the eastern front." Rochat huffed jadedly. "But this isn't a chest-puffing contest of national pride and who is the stronger military power—the German Reich has proven itself unquestionably in that regard. This is purely and simply a business proposition. Nothing more, nothing less."

"I don't know," Piehler said uncertainly after a moment, appearing to calm. "I will have to take some advice on the matter."

Sensing the change in mood, Rochat pressed the advantage. "This could be something of a feather in your cap. Not only getting these sizable funds into Reich coffers, but also avoiding this entire distasteful episode with an SS officer trying to rob the Reich from ever reaching the courts or the press. The whole matter would be buried."

"I suppose. As I said, I have a couple of calls to make."

Piehler was back to noncommittal again. *Everything on a knife edge, Daniel's life hinging on the decisions made by others on those calls.*

The ticking of the clock on the wall suddenly seemed louder, more ominous.

"Oh, and while you're on the phone to Berlin or wherever, I have one final strand to my proposition. You have a writer called Andreas Siebert, currently held at Sobibór prison camp. He was in fact sent there by this same errant SS officer, Heinrich Schnabel. If Siebert's release is also secured, I will arrange the transfer of a further 30 percent of the funds I hold here."

"And the remaining 20 percent?"

"That will be left for you to wonder how much is for Carl Brunnerman's widow and my fee in negotiating this matter."

"I'll get back to you."

Piehler's return call came just over forty minutes later.

"In regard to the matter of Daniel Lendt…previously known as Mathias Kraemer." Piehler paused. "And I must stress this was not my decision. Mine might have been very different. Of no matter…the decision made in Berlin has been to approve your request in his regard. He will be freed and get clearance to go to Switzerland."

"That's good to hear. I will arrange the 50 percent transfer as agreed. Half now, half when he's safely across the Swiss border."

"I will give you the account details shortly."

At Daniel's end, the news sank in. *Josef's plan had worked! He'd be free! Reunited with Alex, the stifling yoke of fear on his shoulders finally lifted.* But his elation had only started rising as the second bit of news from Piehler cut it short, trapped it like a heavy stone in his chest.

"But unfortunately with your second request regarding Andreas Siebert at Sobibór, we won't be able to oblige. It appears there was a prisoners' uprising at the camp. Most of the prisoners were killed, Andreas Siebert among them it seems."

61

How bold one gets when one is sure of being loved.

—*Sigmund Freud*

Josef

Josef drove south through Northern Italy and Southern France, stopping for his first night at a small hotel opposite the seaside fortress of La Calanque, only a few miles from Mandelieu.

A group of Italian soldiers were on the hotel terrace when Josef finished dinner, and as he got talking with them, he discovered that their regiment were using the fort opposite—which was little more than a large manor house with buttresses—as a temporary garrison.

"And what brings you this way?" a young sergeant named Francesco asked, who'd just ordered a bottle of Armagnac to share with his three men and Josef.

"I'm in pursuit of the love of my life." Josef raised his glass with a strained smile; at that moment he wasn't at all sure he'd find Deya.

"Good luck with that." Francesco clinked glasses with him, and the other men quickly joined in, more glasses clinked and encouragement. Then Francesco became more thoughtful. "Not an easy time for love. *War*. I left a girl I loved at home in Turin almost two years ago. I have no idea if she'll still be waiting for me now." He shrugged. "Maybe she's met someone else, I don't know. I didn't get any reply to my last letter."

"I'm sorry to hear that," Josef said. "My girl's written, only she hasn't left an address."

"She's playing hard to get," one of the soldiers teased, punching Josef's arm lightly.

Francesco's brow creased. "If you don't have her address, how will you find her?"

Josef looked at him with mock sternness, as if he was missing something. "I am a police detective, you know," and they burst out laughing, Francesco pouring more Armagnacs.

Although they were laughing about it now, it wasn't far from the truth. Deya hadn't left a return address with her last letter either, but Lorenzo had noted that it was postmarked from the same district in Lisbon. *She can't live far from that post office, perhaps posts other things from there. I'm sure it wouldn't take long for a detective like you to dig down and find out.*

Lorenzo had been surprised though when a few weeks later Josef announced that he was actually going to make the trip; Lorenzo had himself been partly jesting. But with Allied bombing raids threatened, Josef couldn't think of a better time to leave Vienna. The least conflictive routes with the war on were apparently through Northern Italy and crossing through Southern France, and so he'd planned his first night's stopover near Mandelieu.

Josef had seen a few troop convoys and movements here and there, but nothing major and no visible conflicts. Francesco reported, too, that some beach-head assaults were expected along that stretch of coast by Allied forces, but they hadn't arrived yet.

Setting off again early the next morning, the only significant troop movements Josef witnessed were near Avignon, but then they became sparser again toward the Spanish border and non-existent the other side of it. Franco had been a supporter of Hitler and Mussolini in spirit only, had stoically turned his back on any involvement in a wider war, having only just pulled Spain from the shadows of its own civil war.

Josef stopped the next night at a roadside hotel near Guadala-jara, then set off again early morning for the last leg of his journey across the Portuguese border toward Lisbon.

A nation that had remained neutral throughout the war, now there wasn't a soldier in sight apart from the local Guarda Republicana, the only road obstacles an occasional slow-moving farmer's cart being pulled by horses or donkeys.

It was just after six at night when Josef finally arrived in Lisbon. The postmarks on Deya's letters were from a post office, *correio*, in the Alfama district, a quaint colonial building set on a hillside overlooking the harbor. Josef checked out the nearby hotels, choosing one where his third-floor room had a good view of the correio entrance and also a partial view of the harbor on one side.

With regular coffees, bifanas and cozidos brought up by room service and some books Josef had brought with him—Robert Musil's *Der Mann ohne Eigenschaften* (*The Man Without Qualities*), Graham Greene's *Stamboul Train*, one of Greene's last novels translated into German before the Nazis came to power, and a local Lisbon guidebook—Josef sat on his terrace watching the post office entrance opposite. The sun was out for much of the time, the air warm, so it was one of Josef's more pleasant stakeouts, particularly given his target this time.

But despite the glorious weather and surroundings, by the

fourth day, like many stakeouts, the nonstop hourly observations had become tedious, monotonous.

A couple of times he'd seen women who looked like Deya, but as he'd observed them fully, seen their faces more directly, realization dawned it wasn't her. He'd sit back again, becoming despondent. *Having come all of this way, I'm not going to find her.*

Sometimes he'd also sit at the restaurant two doors away which directly faced the correio entrance. Not only to break up the monotony, but they served better coffee than his hotel and "Probably the best Bacalhau à Brás in Lisbon," its proprietor, Vincente, boasted—which Josef had sampled a couple of times.

Vincente also had some lively conversation to help pass the time—his English was good and Josef's passable, so that became their common language. On Josef's third visit there, seeing him keenly observing the correio entrance, he'd asked Josef whether he was looking out for a spy or someone on the run?

"No. I'm looking for a girl."

Vincente had shrugged, as if to say, *They all say that*, then had continued talking about the many colorful characters he'd had come by his restaurant. "We get them all here with the war on."

By the sixth day, Josef felt like giving up. *I'm not going to find her!* He'd been foolish even to set out on this quest, hope to…

But then looking above his book, he thought he saw someone who looked like Deya. Sitting forward, looking at her more keenly, he put his book down fully to one side.

Yet the young girl with her didn't look like Luciana at first, and this woman had her hair up in a bun, which Deya never did. Though something in her profile just before she entered the correio struck a sharper chord. *It is her! It's Deya!*

Josef left the terrace and darted across his room, leaping down the three flights of stairs, taking them two at a time, suddenly panicking that he might not get down in time, that he'd lose her in that gap.

Then across the narrow cobblestone street and up the few steps to the correio, eyes adjusting from the sharp sunlight outside, then darting frantically around. He couldn't see her. *She'd gone!*

He looked outside again for a second in case she was already walking away along the road. *Nothing in either direction!*

And he'd just turned back again to inside when he saw her. Three-deep in a queue with a heavy-set man behind her, turning from the counter with an envelope.

Deya didn't spot him until she was a few paces from the counter. She stared in a daze for a moment, disbelieving, then one hand went to her mouth as the recognition hit.

Josef moved closer. Of all the things he'd thought of saying in this moment, now he was tongue-tied. To Deya's side, Luciana smiled; her recognition and welcome were more open. She'd grown a couple of inches, that's why he hadn't recognized her.

"*Josef*...you've come all this way," Deya said, her eyes misting with emotion.

"Yes." He nodded numbly, fishing in his pocket for the ring box. Praying that all the times he'd carried it with him, this wasn't the one day he'd forgotten it. "I bought something for you in Vienna. But you left before I could give it to you."

62

*All Reich camp officers, guards and soldiers shall, with the aid
of Sonderkommandos, set about destroying any evidence of mass
executions that might be discovered either by the advancing Red
Army or Western Allied troops.*

Stefanie felt a faint shiver run through her, which was strange
because the office she now sat in was fairly warm. Perhaps it
had been the train carriage journey; she'd only been able to afford a second-class ticket, and the carriage had been quite drafty.
Or perhaps it had been her final passage along the cold, clinical
corridors of this prison camp, Mauthausen.

*To think that Andreas has spent almost two years in places like this,
and worse.*

That had been among Dieter Meisel's first words to her now
in his office. "Sobibór was a far harsher camp." Meisel had recently become vice-commandant at Mauthausen. *Had he made*

that comment because he saw his transfer as preferable, or some related benefit to Andreas?

Meisel lit a pipe, held one hand out. "I'm sorry if I alarmed you with my first letter. But your husband's condition was very serious at that point. A bullet wound had turned septic and it was touch and go when he was in the hospital at Lublin." He exhaled wearily. "Indeed, some initial records had him listed as dead, when in fact at that stage he was simply missing and un-accounted for."

Stefanie glanced down, chewing at her lip for a moment. "I… I'd like to thank you for what you did for my husband. Helping him in the way you did."

"It was the least I could do." Meisel pushed a tight smile. "Your husband's a very brave man, Mrs. Siebert. And I learned much about myself, too, while he was working with me on my manuscript."

Stefanie nodded. She knew little about the mechanics of An-dreas's working relationship with Meisel, and this probably wasn't the moment to delve. "You say that Andreas is okay now, he's recovered?"

"Yes, he's out of danger and recovering well. That's why I was able to arrange his transfer here." Meisel looked across steadily. "But he's been through a lot and is still very frail, Mrs. Siebert—I thought I should forewarn you." He held out a palm. "If you're ready to see him now?"

Stefanie nodded once more, this time more hesitantly. *Yes, I was ready to see my husband. Yet I wasn't ready to see him.* Elated and filled with joy at the thought of seeing him again. But anxious and nervous at what she might see… *What would be my first words to him?*

Again she felt that chill touch her as Meisel left the room, his step echoing hollowly on the corridor outside as he went to get Andreas.

63

Dear Mrs. Freud,

I hope this letter finds you well. Please find enclosed the photos we discussed last month. Apologies for the delay, but I had to wait for a secure courier service between Geneva and London before sending them, not trusting general postal services with the war on. So this package you will find postmarked London, having been sent on by our courier.

If there is anything further I may be of assistance with, please don't hesitate to contact me.

Sebastian Rochat,
Legal Administrator,
Geneva International Bank

Martha Freud's hands trembled faintly as she read the letter. Knowing the package would be arriving, she'd hastily leafed through the photos first to ensure they were all there before turning her attention back to the letter.

When she'd got the call from Julian Reisner almost two years ago that Brunnerman's had been broken into—one of two carefully disguised calls from Vienna phone boxes where she'd taken the calls as Matilda Johnson and Julian as her cousin Frederick—she feared that the photos might surface and the Nazis would hunt down her husband's remaining "Circle" associates. By then, almost half had already left Austria, but that still left a significant number vulnerable. And she wouldn't have been able to bear it if they'd fallen victim to the Nazis due to her simply clinging to nostalgia.

But with the passing months and nothing untoward heard from the remaining Circle members, she began to relax again. And then the call from Sebastian Rochat explaining everything. The other call from Julian had been to tell her that he'd heard through contacts that sadly Sigmund's sister Dolfi had passed away from natural causes in Theresienstadt camp. "But hopefully his other sisters will survive."

"Yes, I'm sure they will. Despite their ages, they're quite robust."

It was ironic. Her husband had spent his lifetime writing numerous papers about the tendency of humans to delude themselves and gloss over painful truths, yet that was all she seemed to be doing these days.

But now with the arrival of the photos, she did feel strangely enlivened and hopeful. As she touched the photos, the memories came flooding back, as if it was just yesterday. The sense of everything coming full circle.

Daniel

July 1945

Josef didn't return to Vienna until after the war was over. A four-day trip to see everyone, tidy up some affairs and hand out invitations to his wedding in Lisbon the following month.

Deya had found a teaching job when Josef first caught up with her. Her Spanish had been quite good to cover her false identity in Vienna, and she'd picked up Portuguese quickly. Shortly after, she joined a small primary school teaching the children English and German.

Josef meanwhile had some things sent out to Lisbon, and stayed. He'd seen little point in returning while Vienna was being bombed heavily by the Allies, and had set up a small detective agency in Lisbon not long after. He quickly gained a reputation for being adept at tracking missing people, and Lisbon was a particularly transient place during wartime. Business was good.

Deya had promised they'd get married as soon as war was finished, felt that the future was still too uncertain while it was on. *Then we'll have two things to celebrate—war finishing and our wedding.*

On Josef's four-day trip back to Vienna, he'd made a quick visit to my mother and sister. "No more crosses above my front door," my mother had waggled a warning finger at him. She was frail but hanging on. She'd probably outlive all of us.

We'd even had a get-together to commemorate old times with the four of us—myself, Andreas, Julian and Josef—back at the Café Mozart. Otto had been delighted to see us, proudly boasting: "Not a single SS or Gestapo in sight. The only danger is a gum-chewing American soldier armed with nylons and cigarettes to steal your women."

We laughed. Otto had also lost some weight in the meantime. "One advantage of the Nazis and their mean rations," he joshed, patting his stomach.

Emilia's life-saving trip with Alex across the Swiss border had also brought us closer. We could at least look back at how and why our relationship had gone wrong with more clarity, and Emilia had crossed the border every month to see Alex. Like Josef, I hadn't returned to Vienna until war was finished, and had stayed practically all that time with Alex at my mother and sister's bungalow in Penzing while I found a new place for us.

"No, *no*…over there!" Josef directed. Josef had set an hour aside before the wedding to give final instructions to the caterers. Andreas and I were both staying in the small pension above the bar-restaurant, so I exchanged a wave and smile at Josef from the balcony as I looked on.

One of the highest points in the Alfama district, a small cobbled courtyard was in front of the bar-restaurant, with the chapel holding the service just two doors away. I smiled to myself: only somewhere like Portugal would you find a bar next to a church. The outlook was idyllic: four trestle tables being arranged end-on for forty guests at the end of the courtyard with a panoramic view over Lisbon and the harbor beyond.

The church service was emotional, too, even though most of the guests like me from Vienna could hardly understand a word of the Latin and Portuguese from the priest—the main moment to transcend all languages when Josef and Deya looked into each other's eyes, exchanged vows and kissed.

As the food and wine started flowing at the courtyard reception overlooking the harbor, a small combo to one side—something Deya had insisted upon and arranged locally—played a mixture of fado and samba.

Many familiar faces with Lorenzo and Alois, and even Deya's old club owner, Max Adler, had come over from Switzerland.

The only faint shadow over the proceedings had been when I looked over and saw Julian talking with Andreas. *A reminder of what I hadn't told Andreas.* The get-together in the Mozart had been awkward for a moment for the same reason. While I could accept that Julian's action had been in part to save my own life and that of other authors and their families, I knew I could never fully forgive him for consigning Andreas to a death camp instead of me. And of course there was that marvelous letter and arrangement made to hopefully save Andreas, which partly balanced that out. *Partly.*

But another factor weighing heavily in Julian's favor had been how much he'd been instrumental in helping the old Freud Circle. From the depth of information Julian had passed on about Freud and his family leaving Austria, Andreas and I had suspected Julian was more involved than he was letting on. But we hadn't realized how deeply. Julian had helped organize identity changes for five other Circle members. He'd also put Martha Freud in touch with Lorenzo for Sigmund's four sisters, but unfortunately nothing could be done: they were too well-known and were by then already being questioned by the Gestapo. We discovered that sadly all four had died in Nazi camps: one from malnutrition, the other three killed.

Martha Freud had also been urged by her husband to destroy all the old Circle photos or any taken with other associates—but she couldn't bring herself to do so. Felt that too much of their past and history was being destroyed. Yet she felt she couldn't trust any bank vault in Austria, all of them in the grip of the Reich, and the post out of Austria was also being rigorously monitored and checked. Julian had put her in touch with Carl Brunnerman.

So I knew, with all of that taken into account, that I would never say anything to Andreas, possibly destroy that good friendship he had with Julian. All he'd ever know was that Julian had ingeniously set up an arrangement that had saved his life. Or was I holding back on saying anything because at the same time I'd also have to face my own guilt? *It should have been me.* An added sting to my deathbed promise to Uncle Samuel. Regardless, I knew that secret would go to the grave with me.

Andreas

The smiles were easier now, though they'd been uncertain the first months out of Sobibór and Mauthausen, even with my own family.

At that initial reunion with Stefanie at Mauthausen, we'd clung to each other tearfully for several moments, not wanting to let go. Then, wiping away the tears, we'd sat down and she'd shown me the latest pictures of Dominik and Nadia, with a similar tearful reunion with them following not long after.

Seven months ago, Julian informed me that Dieter Meisel's *Eine Flackernde Kerze* had found a publisher. However, storm clouds were brewing over Meisel as the end of the war approached, and when the full horror of the camps emerged, the publisher pulled out. The only way it would still be published was if Julian presented Meisel under a new name and identity; ironically, following the same path as many Jewish and dissident writers during the Nazi era.

War crimes trials were scheduled for later this year and early next. Toepfer faced the death penalty, Haas, too, or at the least a heavy sentence. But with the written testimony I'd provided in advance on Meisel's behalf, his lawyers were hopeful his sentence would be no more than five years.

It was the least I could do for the man who'd saved my life—in more ways than one.

I still had nightmares at times that would shudder me awake— Vogt standing over me, his gun aimed at my face ready to fire. Only as I sat up in bed, breathless in that waking moment, would that final sequence replay in my mind: *Vogt falling away, shot from behind.*

At first, I thought that Vogt had just been struck by a random bullet. But as I looked back, I saw Meisel twenty yards behind. He'd seen the commotion outside with some of the other officers running and firing, and had come out to join them. He thought at first Vogt had just been firing generally toward prisoners running for the perimeter fence, but as he got closer he realized that Vogt was firing specifically at me.

I'd spent no more than three weeks at Mauthausen before the letter had come from Berlin granting my release. The final element of Josef and Lorenzo's plan with Sebastian Rochat in Switzerland.

Only four months ago had I finally been able to make contact with Jan and Rina. Recalling my association with Meisel, they'd written to him care of the Lublin SS Office, who'd then passed the letter on to Meisel at Mauthausen. Apparently, the numbers killed in the Sobibór uprising had initially been inflated by the Reich—possibly to deter similar attempts at other camps. Over half had in fact survived. Jan and Rina had settled in Lviv, but had plans to return to the Oder River area once the war was over.

We also heard through Julian that Kommissar Sauerwald, appointed to oversee and value Freud's assets, had also played a double-game with the Nazis. He'd hidden many valuable relics and vital papers in secret storerooms below the University of Vienna Library, and also kept secret some of Freud's foreign bank accounts. In the impending war crimes trials, Martha and Anna Freud were due to speak on his behalf to get him cleared or his sentence lessened.

"The day couldn't be more perfect," Julian commented, looking up at the sky and then the bay spread out ahead. "Good crowd too."

"Yes, a nice mix," I agreed. Almost half had come from Vienna or Switzerland—a number of whom we knew—the rest were local friends Deya and Josef had made while in Lisbon.

I noticed Daniel looking over at us, and I raised my glass and smiled at him. *My dear Daniel, more like an older brother than a cousin to me over the years.* He smiled back, though there was something else the last couple of times in his look—*as if he was still concerned for me with the time I'd spent in Sobibór and Mauthausen, feared I hadn't fully recovered.*

I'd recovered well physically, but perhaps Daniel was thinking of the shadows in my mind, my thoughts lost for longer at moments.

I was distracted by Lorenzo tapping the side of his glass with a fork, getting everyone's attention that it was time for a toast.

But as we raised our glasses to Josef and Deya and their future—a future that so many looked forward to with hope now that war was over—were we equally raising a glass to those who had perished? I'd at times questioned my survival or felt guilty about it. *Why me? Why was I spared when so many innocents had died?* I was still haunted some nights by the faces of children I'd seen go to their deaths in the chambers at Sobibór. And Daniel, too, had told me how he'd hovered close to that precipice edge with Schnabel, still haunted by images of Brunnerman and the shot fired by his son to save his life.

Yet looking out now across Lisbon harbor with its sailboats, with Daniel, Lorenzo, Julian, myself and Stefanie, and so many other close friends and loved ones wishing Josef and Deya well, the air filled with laughter, music and above all *hope*—it was difficult to think of our survival as anything other than a triumph.

Not just for ourselves, family and friends, but because without our survival and that of many others—Jan and Rina, Anja and her younger brother, Clara Ebner, old Freud Circle members and numerous others saved by Lorenzo and Alois's network—those deaths would have seemed completely empty, pointless. No hope to balance them out, let alone *triumph*.

With my champagne glass raised along with everyone as we cheered Josef and Deya, I felt some of that burden of guilt at my survival lift from my shoulders.

I knew it might take many years for the rest of that burden to lift, but at least I'd learned one thing from today: each celebration of life and hope in the years ahead would help it on its way.

★ ★ ★ ★ ★

AUTHOR NOTE

I did not know my father was Jewish until he was on his deathbed.

I was only fourteen, and I and my two sisters had been raised in my mother's Irish Catholic religion, so I had little grasp of what it actually meant to be Jewish at the time.

Though I did learn in the years following my father's death, with the first two key questions to my mother: *Why were we raised Catholic rather than Jewish? And why did my father bury his Jewish roots?*

The answer to the first question was simple but poignant: my eldest sister was born in 1943, and that year you could toss a coin on whether Hitler would win the war. And if he did win, Britain would not be safe for Jews, as had already happened through much of Nazi-occupied Europe. Following on from that partly answered the second question, but the rest was more complex.

My father saw himself very much as British. He'd arrived on British shores when he was only six years old. Britain had provided a safe haven to his family from Lithuania and many other Jewish refugees, and Winston Churchill was his hero. Indeed, my father's contributions to the war effort and beyond were notable in their own way. Having studied at Cambridge, my father went on to become one of the country's leading statisticians, providing vital weather statistics for RAF bombing raids over Germany, then later the statistics for the Whittle project on jet propulsion.

Yet despite all these marvelous contributions, my father was unable to join his local tennis or golf club because he was Jewish. Fellow Cambridge classmate Jacob Bronowski was similarly told to forget becoming a university dean for the same reason.

So this cloud of racism and my father burying his roots in order to protect his family struck a strong chord with me, and later in researching I discovered this was quite widespread, with a number of networks established to help mask identities and provide fresh papers. The issue of mixed marriages and backgrounds partly or wholly buried therefore features strongly in *The Vienna Writers Circle*.

Indeed, I was surprised that so few current Holocaust-related novels dealt with these vital elements. As we know from the heroic exploits of Oskar Schindler, once people were consigned to death camps, the game was all but over. This doesn't make the efforts of those who survived the camps any less heroic, just that these were far fewer and ignored the more widespread efforts of those desperately trying to avoid the death camps. It didn't give the whole picture. Which is why I felt it was important to show *both* sides.

The final element that made this more personal to me was that of writing. I had little knowledge of my father's extended family in Lithuania, many of whom had perished in the Holocaust. But I thought to myself: *How would I feel if one day I was told I could no longer write, then the next my family were under threat?* This then added a more personal note that I could relate to.

My choice of Vienna, Austria, was not only because of the prominent circles of writers and intellectuals there—the most notable of which had been formed by Sigmund Freud—but because Nazi edicts came into effect there over a period of only a few months. Which makes the hard decisions the main characters have to make more immediate.

All details relating to writers' groups and agents, Freud, Anschluss (the annexation of Austria by Germany in 1938), identity-change networks and Sobibór death camp are based strongly on historical fact. But in essence, *The Vienna Writers Circle*—slow-brewed over decades of family history, then a final intense period of research—is a tribute not only to my father and his extended family who perished in the Holocaust, but to the Jewish writers of Vienna and beyond of 1938–1945.

—J. C. Maetis

He just wanted a decent book to read ...

Not too much to ask, is it? It was in 1935 when Allen Lane, Managing Director of Bodley Head Publishers, stood on a platform at Exeter railway station looking for something good to read on his journey back to London. His choice was limited to popular magazines and poor-quality paperbacks – the same choice faced every day by the vast majority of readers, few of whom could afford hardbacks. Lane's disappointment and subsequent anger at the range of books generally available led him to found a company – and change the world.

'We believed in the existence in this country of a vast reading public for intelligent books at a low price, and staked everything on it'
Sir Allen Lane, 1902–1970, founder of Penguin Books

The quality paperback had arrived – and not just in bookshops. Lane was adamant that his Penguins should appear in chain stores and tobacconists, and should cost no more than a packet of cigarettes.

Reading habits (and cigarette prices) have changed since 1935, but Penguin still believes in publishing the best books for everybody to enjoy. We still believe that good design costs no more than bad design, and we still believe that quality books published passionately and responsibly make the world a better place.

So wherever you see the little bird – whether it's on a piece of prize-winning literary fiction or a celebrity autobiography, political tour de force or historical masterpiece, a serial-killer thriller, reference book, world classic or a piece of pure escapism – you can bet that it represents the very best that the genre has to offer.

Whatever you like to read – trust Penguin.